ICE MAGE

By Julia Gray

ICE MAGE
FIRE MUSIC

ICE MAGE

JULIA GRAY

ORBIT

An *Orbit* Book

First published in Great Britain by Orbit 1998
Reprinted 1999

A CIP catalogue record for this book
is available from the British Library.

ISBN 1 85723 689 0

Typeset by Solidus (Bristol) Ltd, Bristol
Printed and bound in Great Britain by
Mackays of Chatham plc, Chatham, Kent

Orbit
A Division of
Little, Brown and Company (UK)
Brettenham House
Lancaster Place
London WC2E 7EN

*Este libro está dedicado a
Nino González Delgado, un verdadero
hombre de los volcanes, en la esperanza
de que un día el mundo no necesitará
parques nacionales.*

*This book is dedicated to
Nino Gonzales Delgado, a true man of the
volcanoes, in the hope that one day
the world won't need national parks.*

Grateful thanks are due to
the National Park of Timanfaya, Lanzarote,
and the Spanish National Tourist Office, London.

PART ONE

Teguise

CHAPTER ONE

'Move. Move. Move!' Andrin's voice rose in urgency as the moment of truth drew nearer. Although everything seemed to be going according to plan, all he could see was chaos. The last of the scavengers were running over the black sea of solidified lava, taking advantage of their knowledge of the almost imperceptible paths within the jagged and treacherous landscape. Further away, using the vantage points offered by upthrusts of rock on the lower slopes of the Red Crater, the spotters were also scrambling to their assigned positions. Among them Andrin could see the dark figure of Ico, directing her charges, and he was glad that she was relatively safe there, away from the predicted path of the fireworms. Victory over those hated creatures would mean nothing if Ico suffered because of it.

Stop daydreaming or you'll put yourself in danger. The white eagle's deep, arrogant voice sounded inside Andrin's head, and he looked up at the sky. There too all was whirling confusion, as many different kinds of birds rose or fought the strong wind. Highest of all, Ayo circled majestically, a distant speck of white against the azure blue.

I can look after myself, Andrin replied. *Concentrate on your own job. Where's the swarm now?*

Two swoops, the eagle answered huffily.

Andrin was taken aback. In the bird's somewhat inexact terminology, 'two swoops' represented no more than eight hundred paces, a distance the fireworms could cover in less than a minute. They were closer than he'd thought.

How many? he asked quickly.

Thirty-seven, Ayo replied without hesitation. *And still on course. Is it time?*

Andrin glanced around, saw only the barren, apparently empty scene and grinned with satisfaction.

It's time, he said.

He tossed the shatter-stone up into the air and watched it turn lazily at the top of its curving flight before plunging back to the rock below. The stone split on impact with an explosive crack that echoed down the valley, a signal to all the Firebrands. There was no going back now. For better or worse, the long anticipated battle was about to begin.

The signal came as a relief to Ico. From her hiding place within the branches of a fig tree, she had been watching the valley, waiting for the appearance of the swarm. Her linked sparrow-hawk, Soo, had been sending her reports from high above but they were unnecessary now. Ico could see the fireworms for herself. From this distance they were little more than a grey smudge on the dark landscape, but they were closer than she had expected and – as always – they were moving with frightening speed. Fortunately they were still tightly bunched and sticking close to the expected course, following the warm fissures that stretched along the centre of the lava-filled valley. Had they spread out or deviated significantly from the predicted route, Andrin's plan could easily have turned to catastrophe and all Ico's painstaking preparations, all the training and effort, would have gone to waste. Even now there was still scope for disaster, and she wished briefly that she was with Andrin down among the scavengers, where the danger was greatest. At the same time she acknowledged that her special talents were best utilized elsewhere. And then there was no more time for thought. Instinct took over.

Lead them in, Soo, she instructed.

The sparrowhawk responded with a brief burst of wordless chatter, her equivalent of a nod.

Not all at once, Ico cautioned. *In waves, as we practised.*

We will do our part, Soo answered confidently. *Make sure your humans do not panic. My clan have no wish for frozen toes.*

Without waiting for a response, the sparrowhawk tucked back the tips of her broad wings and dived towards the swarm. Ico watched her proudly, enviously aware of a small fraction of the exhilaration of Soo's flight, her speed, her incredibly sharp eyesight. In her talons the bird carried a translucent green crystal, one of the uniquely potent gemstones known as dragon's tears. These rare products of the volcanoes had long been regarded as valuable jewels by the people of Tiguafaya, but now Ico believed them to be the only weapon that might help defeat the menace of the fireworms. A great deal, not least the lives of several of her friends, depended on her being right.

It had always been assumed that the crystals were formed when certain types of molten rock cooled rapidly in water, and centuries earlier it had been discovered that if the stones were destroyed then the process was reversed, and the gems absorbed huge amounts of heat from the surrounding area. Such a process was not only dangerous for anyone nearby but, once started, was almost impossible to control. Not only that, but the end result was the conversion of a valuable gemstone into worthless green powder, and so such experimentation was discouraged.

As a member of a prominent family within the powerful Jewellers' Guild, Ico had been familiar with dragon's tears from childhood, and had always been fascinated by the latent power that lay within their fractured, leaf-green depths. Eventually, when the need for new means of combating the fireworms had become urgent, she began to search for ways of directing that power. She had finally succeeded, perfecting a technique that started a chain reaction within the crystalline structures by means of telepathic signals. It was then possible to destroy them – and produce their deadly cold emanations – from a safe distance. Andrin became enthusiastic when she told him about this, and together they planned how to put their new weapons to the test.

It had been noted that the fireworms were less active on cold days, and that they could only stay airborne for a limited time before having to return to the heat of their underground lairs. Ico hoped that the sudden freezing temperatures around the disintegrating crystals would immobilize or even kill any creatures in the vicinity. Even so, it had taken a long time for them to be able to put theory into practice. Several of the Firebrands, Andrin's ill-assorted group of young malcontents, had had to be trained in Ico's psychic method; the birds, with whom many of them were linked, had to be taught their roles; and a large number of dragon's tears had to be secretly gathered – by whatever means necessary. Once all that was achieved, they had to watch and wait, ready to deploy their forces as soon as their enemy appeared.

Flying free!

The jubilation in Soo's voice as it sounded in Ico's mind was proof of the bird's success in delivering her deadly cargo on target. The sparrowhawk soared up and away, out of danger, and the moment of truth had arrived. The waiting was over.

Ico's keen eyes followed the downward path of the stone, a tiny glint of green in the fierce sunlight. Soo's timing had been perfect; the tear fell so that it would intercept the head of the swarm and Ico concentrated fiercely, remembering the

unique crystalline signature of its construction, and counting
down to the precise moment . . .

Now!

Ico shut her eyes and sent out a strong, tightly focused
pulse of energy. She felt the crystal respond, sensed the self-
destructive reaction begin, and shivered involuntarily at the
remote implosion as the warmth was suddenly drained from
the distant air. Instantly the valley was full of sounds; the
thin high screams of fireworms, Soo's painful screech as she
caught the echoes of her partner's telepathic outburst, the
excited cries of other birds as they followed and launched
their own attacks, and – faintly – the voices of the hidden
Firebrands, each now concentrating on their own tasks.

More tears were falling now, released by crows, hawks and
buzzards – all the larger birds who were capable of carrying
them in beak or claws. Ico sensed more implosions in and
around the swarm, and the tortured screams of the fireworms
doubled in volume. It was clear that the attacks were causing
them considerable distress, but would that be enough? They
had been caught by the initial assault exactly where Andrin
had planned – far enough from the hiding places of the
scavengers to leave them safe from frostbite, but close enough
for them to follow up quickly. But from where Ico stood it was
impossible to tell whether the entire swarm had been trapped
by the sudden cold. It only needed a few to escape unaffected
and the consequences would be terrible, especially as Andrin
was down there. He was never one to shirk the responsibilities
of leadership. If Ico could have projected her love, then
Andrin would have walked encased in impregnable psychic
armour, but her magic was not capable of such feats, no
matter how much she might wish it so.

The first phase of the battle was over. All around her birds
were returning to their partners and Soo landed lightly on a

rock beside Ico, ready to accept another crystal and return to the air for a further sortie if necessary.

Did we trap them all? Ico asked anxiously.

I'm not sure. Some of the others were not as accurate as me. Soo's contempt for slower and less agile birds was obvious.

Who were best?

Fia, Tir and Osa, the sparrowhawk replied promptly, unsurprisingly naming three of her own species.

Get them airborne again, with more crystals, Ico ordered, placing one at Soo's feet. *We may need you to follow any worms that break away.*

Soo chattered her response and rose into the sky with a few quick beats of her wings. Within moments, three other sparrowhawks were wheeling with her. Above them, still circling slowly, Ayo watched over the valley. Although she could not communicate with him directly, seeing the eagle relieved some of Ico's fear; if Andrin were in any danger, Ayo would have reacted. There was movement amid the solidified waves of lava, but Ico could make no sense of what was happening. She had done all she could for the moment. It was up to Andrin and the scavengers now.

'Our turn soon,' Andrin said to the boy crouched beside him. 'Are you ready?'

'Yes.'

The fire of battle was in his brother's eyes. Mendo was only fourteen years old, but he could be as fiercely stubborn as any of the Zonzomas family, and it had proved impossible to keep him away from this fight. In the end Andrin had given way, determined to keep his brother near to him at all times.

Are there any worms still flying? he asked silently.

No. Some are dead, some lie still, others move slowly on the ground, Ayo reported. *You must be quick now.*

'Let's go,' Andrin said aloud. He put his fingers to his lips and blew a shrill two-note whistle. Then they were running, Mendo close behind him, treading in his brother's footsteps as he had been taught. The lava was fragile and treacherous in places. At some spots the surface was so thin that it could not bear a man's weight, but would plunge him down into darkness, twenty paces or more. Such a fall was always fatal; if the impact did not kill, then the heat and lack of breathable air below soon would. It took time and dedication to learn the safe routes through this unforgiving landscape, but Andrin was as much at home here as in the docklands of Teguise. He seemed to absorb energy from the volcanoes.

As he ran Andrin was vaguely aware of the other scavengers, all converging on the site of the attack. They carried blunt instruments – hammers, clubs, iron spades – but there were no knives or spears to be seen. Long and painful experience had taught the people of Tiguafaya that the fireworms were impervious to blades or spikes, no matter how sharp. Their grey leathery skin simply could not be cut from outside, merely stretching away from such an attack and then springing back into shape. However, they could be crushed, especially when they were cooling after a long absence from the boiling mud holes that were their homes.

Andrin was first on the site, and he took in the extraordinary scene at a glance. Several fireworms, presumably those that had been closest to the detonating crystals, lay shattered upon the rock, their icy remains beginning to steam in the sunlight. Others lay rigid in the still cold air, while a few squirmed upon the ground, moving in slow motion. They were huge, some of them as long as Andrin's forearm and as thick as his wrist, a grotesque parody of the harmless earthworm. They had no features except almost invisible 'mouths' at either end. They were eyeless and did not react to light or sound, apparently seeking out their prey by smell or some other unknown sense. They were wingless too, and their being able to fly was a mystery. In motion they seemed to 'swim' in the air with a rapid wavelike action, but now they were crippled and apparently helpless. The sight of them made Andrin feel nauseous, and filled him with a murderous rage. The fireworms had been a plague upon his people, responsible for countless agonizing deaths, and now he finally had the opportunity for some measure of revenge.

'Take the ones that are moving first!' he called to the others, who were approaching with varying degrees of caution. 'And count your kills. We need to be sure we've got them all.'

The scavengers moved forward to begin their grisly work, most concentrating on the central area, others scattering to search for and deal with any splinter groups.

Andrin brought the iron head of his sledgehammer down on one of the sluggish worms, and felt a hot surge of vengeful satisfaction as its skin split from within, discharging an amorphous grey ooze of half-frozen mush. The creature gave a tiny whistling sigh and expired. One down, Andrin thought, and moved on to the next. Beside him, Mendo shouted gleefully as he pounded one of the rigid worms with his own mallet, smashing it into smaller and smaller pieces.

'Enough!' Andrin commanded sternly, disturbed by his brother's frenzy. 'Move on.'

Mendo gave him an almost resentful, bright-eyed glance, then obeyed.

Within moments all the exposed fireworms had been dealt with, and the air was filled with a vile stench as the sun's heat began to thaw out the corpses. Two of the creatures had fallen or managed to crawl into deep fissures in the rock and it took some time to drag them out and finish them off. By then, in answer to a summons from some of his colleagues, Andrin had moved on to a nearby site where another, smaller part of the swarm had fallen – and the slaughter continued.

Eventually it seemed that their work was done and the

various group leaders counted up the kills from each of their teams and brought the results to Andrin. Others continued the search, just in case.

'So what's the tally?'

'Thirty-five,' Andrin replied angrily. 'Which means there are two left somewhere. Did you include the ones that were already dead?'

'Yes, but we made sure we only counted them once,' one of his companions replied. As he spoke he glanced around, receiving nods of confirmation from the others.

Andrin looked skyward.

Can you see any worms moving? he asked.

No, came the answer from above. *None of us can.*

Andrin told the others what the eagle had said.

'Do we go after them?'

'Into the tunnels?'

'No,' Andrin decreed, making an instant decision. 'It's too dangerous. We've done well, and I don't want to spoil things by taking unnecessary risks. Call your teams and let's get out of here before the last two revive.' *Let the other birds know we're pulling out,* he added to Ayo.

As the scavengers split up, Andrin looked around, suddenly aware that he had not seen Mendo for several minutes. He swore under his breath, then called the boy's name. There was no answer. Some of his colleagues hesitated as they began to leave the area, but Andrin waved them on. Mendo was his responsibility.

There was the sound of rock cracking and shifting some distance away and Andrin cursed the carelessness of whoever had caused the slide, hoping that no one would be injured – and hoping above all that it was not his younger brother.

Ayo, do you see Mendo?

No. He went into a tunnel downwind of you.

'Stupid little . . .' *How far?*

Fifty paces.

Andrin set off, furious now, vowing never to take the boy
on a mission again until he learnt to obey orders. He found
the entrance to the lava tube and peered within, shouting
his brother's name. The air inside was warm and faintly sulphurous and the tunnel narrowed rapidly so that within
a few paces the darkness was complete. He was about to go
in anyway when Ayo's voice sounded urgently inside his
head.

A second swarm is coming.

Are you sure? he asked stupidly. Fireworms hardly ever
swarmed twice in the same day. *How many?*

Twelve. Heading straight for you.

Tell Ico to use the rest of the crystals, he said, knowing Ayo could
pass the message on via Soo. *Intercept them as soon as possible.*

He shouted Mendo's name again but there was no response
and, bowing to the inevitable, he turned and ran. To stay
where he was would be to invite death. He could not take the
chance that the birds' second attack – this one unplanned –
would be as successful as the first, and could only hope that
Mendo had also had the sense to withdraw. At least the other
scavengers would be well scattered by now and would soon be
out of immediate danger.

Soo and her comrades swooped towards the second swarm,
each of the linked humans watching their flight carefully.
They all knew that precision was vital this time. With only
four crystals they could not hope to disable the entire swarm,
but at least they should be able to slow it down enough to
give the scavengers time to complete their escape. Some of the
other birds were taking wing, but would come too late to
have any real effect. Everything depended on the sparrowhawks.

Ico saw Soo dive, the others following her at carefully timed
intervals, and heard her exclaim as she released the stone. Al-

ready tired from her previous effort, Ico summoned up all her mental strength and prepared to unleash the chilling power. She did not hear the footsteps behind her until it was too late. The tip of the knife blade felt cold as it rested against the side of her neck.

'No magic, witch!' whispered a harsh voice. 'Or you die.'

CHAPTER TWO

Ico froze, shock and fear shattering her concentration. The dragon's tear fell harmlessly to earth and the swarm flew on, even as Soo's disbelieving cry sounded in her mind.

'Good girl,' growled her captor. 'I can sense telepathy, so please don't think you can trick me. You're in enough trouble already.'

Ico's brain was working furiously now, but the dagger at her throat was unanswerable. She dared not even speak.

'Turn around.' The blade was withdrawn and she turned murderous eyes on her assailant. There were soldiers everywhere, the flashes on their uniforms designating them as White Guards, the elite unit who answered directly to the Senate. Their approach had been almost silent, and in any case the Firebrands had not come prepared to fight human foes. All Ico's companions were under guard, quiet now and looking at her.

'If our friends down there have come to any harm because of what you've done—' she began.

'You'll what?' he cut in, smiling contemptuously. 'Use your magic to punish me?'

Ico was beginning to think clearly again now as the choking fumes of her rage slowly dispersed.

'We were fighting the fireworms, Captain.' She had recognized his badge of office and emphasized his rank derisively. 'And we were winning until your thoughtless intervention. Don't you *want* us to stop them? Whose side are you on?'

'You're far more dangerous than the dragon spawn,' he snapped back. 'They won't trouble us if we leave them alone.'

'How can you say that?' she cried. 'Haven't you seen the bodies of their victims?'

'A few peasants,' he answered dismissively. 'No one important. It's a small price to pay for—'

'You're a fool, Captain. And you're deluding yourself if you can't see how great a threat the worms are. They've already wiped out whole villages, and they're getting bolder all the time. What will you do when they fly into Teguise?'

'That will never happen. This is just scaremongering.'

'Were you born stupid, or is it something they teach you at the Academy?'

For a moment the soldier's dark features contorted with anger, his lips drawn back over white teeth, but then he sighed and his face became a cold, hard mask.

'You are the ones using magic,' he said, each word clipped and precise. '*You* are the ones who will bring the wrath of the dragons down on us all. So I hardly think you should accuse *me* of stupidity.'

'But that's nonsense.'

'The Senate has decreed—'

'The Senate is blind!' Ico declared. 'Those pitiful old men can't see beyond their own perfumed gardens.'

'That's treason.'

'It's truth! Magic is our only hope.'

'Keep talking, witch,' he said, smiling. 'In front of these witnesses.' He waved an arm at all the onlookers. 'Every word is yet more proof of your guilt.'

'Guilt? What guilt? There is no crime in magic, no treason in trying to protect ourselves from our real enemies.'

'There are unspoken laws that are more important,' he replied implacably. 'Tradition—'

'Are you conveniently forgetting that magic is our oldest tradition?' Ico asked, trying hard to match his coolness.

'That was long ago. We know better now.'

Ico's half-formed retort went unspoken as Soo's voice interrupted her thoughts.

The second swarm has stopped at the site of the first attack, she reported. *They're not following your flock.*

Ico's relief was immediate and joyous.

Andrin? she asked quickly.

He is clear – and coming towards you.

Tell him to stay away. We can look after ourselves. She knew that Andrin would not like her instruction but saw no reason why he or the other scavengers should become embroiled in this mess unnecessarily.

'What's going on?' the captain asked sharply, his free hand raised to his ear as if he could detect some faint echo of the conversation. 'What are you doing?'

'Nothing.'

'Don't lie to me!' The knife was poised again, its point now resting under Ico's chin. He pressed gently, forcing her to tip her head back. 'No more magic, do you hear?'

'I hear,' she whispered, hoping Soo would have the good sense to keep quiet.

'I should kill you now, save us all a great deal of trouble.' The soldier's voice was pitched so low that no one else heard his venomous words.

'I wouldn't advise it, Captain,' Ico said awkwardly. 'Do you know who I am?'

'Oh, we know who you are. All of you. We've been watching you for some time. Do you think your little games have gone unnoticed?' He lowered the blade again and stared at Ico with the eyes of a fanatic. 'Some of this rabble don't know any better,' and he gestured disdainfully towards the Firebrands, 'but you're a disgrace to your family and your guild. Your father would have made senator years ago if it wasn't for your recklessness.'

Ico's heart sank as she wondered whether the accusation was true. As far as she knew her father had never harboured any political ambitions, and was content to remain a master of his craft. Had Ico's mother lived she might have pushed him into trying for public office but she had died ten years ago when Ico, her only child, had been eight. With his wife gone, Diano Maravedis had given up most social activity and immersed himself in his work, only emerging to make an effort on behalf of his beloved daughter. Ico realized that they had seen little of each other in recent months.

'My father is not responsible for my actions,' she said eventually.

'More's the pity,' the captain remarked disgustedly. He had obviously tired of the whole business, and now turned away from Ico. 'Search them all,' he ordered his men. 'If you find crystals or any other talismans, bring them to me.'

The Firebrands submitted to the thorough search unwillingly but without open resistance, following Ico's lead. They watched in silence as the precious stones were placed in a leather pouch and taken to the captain.

'Now get out of here, all of you!' he shouted. 'Go back to your homes and try not to be so witless in future.' His tone betrayed his doubts about whether his advice would be taken. 'Go on, before I change my mind and throw you all in gaol.' As the others began to move off he turned back to Ico. 'As for you, young lady, I suggest you choose your friends rather more carefully in future. You're playing a remarkably dangerous game.'

'It's no game,' she told him before she turned away.

'That's the first sensible thing you've said today,' was his parting comment.

'Did that bastard hurt you?'

'No.' Ico rubbed the spot under her chin where the captain's knife had left a red mark but not broken the skin.

'I'd have killed him if he had,' Andrin breathed.

'That sort of talk will get us into even more trouble.'

He snorted angrily.

'They should be treating us like heroes,' he exclaimed, 'and yet they look on us as outlaws! We discover the first thing in years to give us a chance against the worms – and prove that it works – yet all we get is threats. It'd be funny if it weren't so bloody infuriating.'

'Patience, my love. We're not going to give up now, whatever the Senate says. Eventually everyone'll see that we're right.' Ico was glad that Andrin had had the sense not to intervene. If the confrontation had escalated into violence, the consequences would have been even worse – and far-reaching.

Having escaped the watchful gaze of the soldiers, Ico had doubled back towards Andrin, and the couple had found each other at one of their regular meeting places. This was a small hollow at the centre of an 'island' – a patch of old ground which had survived when all around it had been inundated by lava. Although it was a dry and dusty place, some plants grew and there were brightly coloured lizards and strange insects who lived in their own tiny universe, cut off from the rest of the world.

'Did you get all the first swarm?'

'Most of it. There were two we couldn't account for.'

'And everyone got away all right?'

'I think so. It was panic stations for a while after we spotted the second swarm, but they weren't interested in us. Apart from that there were a few minor injuries and one of the crows froze to death when she got too close.'

'Whose?' Ico asked, knowing the grief that the loss of a linked bird would cause the human half of the team.

'Fayna's,' Andrin replied. 'Will you . . .'

'I'll talk to her,' Ico promised. 'Where's Mendo?'

'On his way home, I hope.' A flicker of worry showed in Andrin's piercing green eyes. 'No one's seen the stupid little brat, but he knows his way around the badlands. Ayo's still quartering the valley just in case, but he's seen nothing. Hang on a minute.'

Ico waited, wondering where Soo was, while Andrin conversed silently with the eagle.

'Ayo says it's all clear now,' he reported. 'The worms have returned to the mud pits. They won't come out again so close to sunset. He'll be able to fly lower.' He fell silent abruptly as he noticed the expression on Ico's face. 'What's the matter?'

'What colour are Mendo's boots?' she asked.

'Yellow. Why?' He was fretting now.

'Soo's just seen something at the mouth of one of the tubes. It's probably nothing, but—'

'Is it him?'

'She can't tell. There are fumes. She can't get close enough.'

'Let's go. Can she guide us?'

In spite of their youthful agility and detailed knowledge of the terrain, it took them almost half an hour to reach the entrance to the lava tunnel. Above them Ayo and Soo circled and, apart from occasional directions, the birds were ominously silent. The opening was new, formed when a thin slab of rock had collapsed inwards. The air here was thick and fetid, the stench of sulphur and the clamminess of steam overlaid by the reek of putrefying flesh. At first Andrin hoped this last was coming from the remains of slaughtered fireworms, but when he reached the mouth of the tube and looked within his gorge rose and he cried out in despair.

Mendo's body lay deep within the twisting cave, only half illuminated by the slanting rays of the setting sun, but there could be no doubt of his fate. Ico came up beside Andrin, glanced inside, then put her arms about her lover and hid her face in the folds of his shirt. For a long time neither of them moved, then Andrin stirred.

'Stay here,' he whispered in a choked voice.

'Don't go in there.'

'I need to see,' he told her, and slipped away.

Crouching, he edged down the tunnel, testing his footing carefully and trying to breathe as shallowly as he could. Mendo's corpse lay twisted on the jagged floor. Most of his clothes had been burnt away, leaving only scorched rags, and the flesh below was horrible to see. Half his face was gone, collapsed in upon an empty skull, but what remained showed enough terror to confirm that he had died in appalling agony. One or more of the fireworms had caught him and burrowed inside, devouring the soft flesh and organs within. All that was left was a grotesque, pitiful travesty of a human being – tatters of flesh and burnt skin and a few wisps of singed hair. His bones showed through in places, and they were blackened and charred. His hammer lay beside the body and nearby were the vile remains of two squashed fireworms.

Fighting both nausea and tears, Andrin took one last look around, then stumbled out to rejoin Ico. She saw his grief and moved to comfort him, but he waved her away and clambered on to the top of the tunnel.

'What are you doing?'

He did not answer and she soon recognized his purpose. After testing out the rock with his boots, Andrin stamped once, then jumped back. There was a sharp crack and the lava shivered, then with a sucking rush a section of the roof of the tube crashed in, burying Mendo under a mass of black rock. Andrin clambered slowly over to join her.

'I didn't want anyone else to see him like that,' he explained quietly.

Ico said nothing. Having seen other victims of the fireworms, she understood. Moving Mendo's body would have been next to impossible, and this was as close to a decent burial as he had any right to expect.

'Not much of a grave, is it?' Andrin said softly.

'We can come back and mark the spot if you like.'

'No. This is enough.'

He seemed calm now, almost peaceful, but Ico could sense the stresses within, the emotions that would soon spill out like lava erupting from a volcano. Anger, hatred, guilt and sorrow were all seething below the surface and would have to be granted release sometime.

'Can you tell what happened?' she asked.

'No, but I can guess. He was trying to be a hero.'

Like his big brother, Ico thought, but said nothing.

'He must have gone after the last two worms, the stupid, ignorant little fool.' Andrin paused, swallowing hard. 'He got them too, but the second swarm must have caught up with him. And I was too far away . . .'

'You mustn't blame yourself,' she said quickly, seeing the pain in his eyes. 'No one could have saved him.'

Even as she spoke she knew her words were a lie – and saw that Andrin knew it too.

'You might have done – if the guards hadn't intervened,' he said bitterly. 'I have a score to settle with that captain.'

CHAPTER THREE

'I'm sorry,' Andrin said again, then ran out of words.

As he watched his parents, he felt a mixture of pity and disgust and wondered resentfully – not for the first time – what he had done to deserve being born into such a family. Mendo had been the only one with any spark of life, and now he was gone for ever. With him had gone Andrin's only hope of escape.

The air in the cluttered, dingy room was stale, in spite of the open shutters, and Andrin found himself longing to be with Ayo in the clean wind far above this dismal scene. His parents' reaction to the news of the death of their younger son had been depressingly predictable. His mother, a thin, bird-like creature, had exclaimed once, her hands fluttering, then collapsed, sobbing hysterically. When Andrin had gone to try to comfort her, she had flailed at him, spitting and wailing, and he had retreated. Since then her weeping had become less violent and she had fetched herself a flask of cheap rum and a cup. Ordinarily she would have tried – ineffectually – to conceal her drinking from both her husband and son, but she was beyond caring now, beyond any semblance of dignity, and she sat snivelling, tipping her blotched and raddled face back every so often to gulp directly from the flask. The cup lay discarded on the floor. She had been pretty once, Andrin remembered, but poverty and the steady erosion of her fragile self-esteem had worn away the surface beauty, leaving only a lifeless skeleton. And even that was crumbling now.

By contrast his father was a solid, brooding presence, his still handsome face turned to wordless stone. Jarrell Zonzomas was a large man. In his prime he had been the strongest stevedore in all Teguise, an instantly recognizable figure in the docklands community. He had been widely respected, perhaps even feared, by most men and had had many ardent female admirers. Neither his marriage nor the birth of his sons had wholly reformed his wild, irresponsible life style – but illness had. Although the wasting disease had worked slowly, its progress had been inexorable. Jarrell's pride and obstinacy had made him deny it for many months, but by the time of the accident that had crushed his left leg beyond any hope of repair, he was already a shadow of his former self.

Since then his life had been confined to the chair where he sat now, staring blankly into space. He left his seat only when absolutely necessary, hobbling painfully to the privy on crutches, and disdainfully ignoring any offers of help. The rest of the time he spent in bitter, habitually silent contem-plation. When he did speak it was usually to complain or criticize, and his harshness constantly wounded all his family – but especially his wife. His muscular frame had degenerated over the years and he was now grotesquely fat, his skin pallid and coarse, and his lungs wheezed noisily. The sight of Andrin, who had inherited Jarrell's startlingly pale hair as well as his tall, impressive physique, often seemed to bring pain to his dark eyes, as if he saw in his son all he had been and would never be again. Fate had cheated him – and he usually made sure that everyone around him knew it. But at this moment his expression was unreadable. His only outward reaction to the news of Mendo's death had been to grow even more still.

'I told you it would cause trouble, getting mixed up in all this magic,' he muttered eventually.

Beside him his wife whimpered, fresh tears rolling down her cheeks. Jarrell had made no attempt to console or even touch her.

'Can't you be quiet, Belda?' he snapped. 'What's the point of blubbering? There are worse things than dying young.'

At this his wife looked as though she would begin weeping with renewed force, but instead she took another deep draught, turning bright, hate-filled eyes on Jarrell's impassive face.

Andrin was finding it hard enough to keep his own emotions under control without having to witness his parents' mutual cruelty. He knew better than to try to defend his own role in Mendo's demise – that would only prompt further recriminations – but he was having to stop himself from shouting at them both, from driving home the point that his brother's death meant that he, as the only possible bread-winner, was stuck with them for good. I am destined for more than this, he thought desperately. Why else would Ayo have come to me? His link with the eagle had conferred on him a bizarre kind of status, well above that of an ordinary dock rat, but he could not deny his origins. He might long for freedom, but he would not run away from his responsibilities.

'I despise them, and sometimes I hate them,' Andrin groaned. 'And then I hate myself for hating them. I couldn't wait to get away and come to you.'

Ico took his hand and held it, knowing that he needed to talk but, for once, she was not sure what to say in return. They were in the garden of the home she shared with her father, a colourful, flower-filled retreat by day which became a dark, scented hiding place when, as now, darkness fell. Andrin was still slightly breathless, having run all the way from the narrow streets of his home near the harbour to the opulent open spaces of the merchants' quarter. The town of Teguise, the only one in all Tiguafaya large enough to proclaim itself a city, was the land's capital and home to almost half its population. It was here that all the country's main institutions had grown up – the Senate, the various guild headquarters, the military academy, a small university and several schools as well as all the necessary adjuncts of trade – warehouses, markets, crafthouses of all kinds and financial treasuries. Its wall enclosed many extremes; vast wealth and abject poverty, indulgence and malnutrition, silk sheets and filthy straw. In some areas violence and fear were normal aspects of life; in others the greatest danger came from the sharp spines of specially cultivated cacti. Like most cities it had grown by accretion, expanding way beyond its original boundaries in haphazard fashion, so that now it had become an endlessly variable labyrinth which was far more than the sum of its parts. Andrin, one of the few who had the confidence to move freely anywhere in Teguise, knew its secrets better than most. He had lived there all his life, discovering many of its dangers and pleasures as a child, and for all its undoubted iniquities, he knew it was the only place he would ever truly be able to call home. However, such thoughts were far from his mind at that moment.

'Why?' he asked hopelessly, looking up at the stars through the vine-covered trellis above them. 'Why did it have to happen? If only I'd—'

'We've been through all this,' Ico cut in. 'You were Mendo's brother, not his keeper. He had a mind of his own and he knew the dangers. What happened wasn't your fault. It was an accident of war.'

'But if—'

'It happened, Andrin. We can't change it. Don't you think I wish it had been different? But we have to go on. The only

way we can make Mendo's death mean something is to prove
that he didn't die in vain.'

Ico watched her lover closely. Although she saw the sense
of what she was saying register, the lines on his face remained
severe.

'That's going to be difficult if we have to look over our
shoulders for White Guards all the time,' he told her bitterly.

'I never said it was going to be easy.' Ico paused. 'But we go
on. That's all we can do.'

Andrin nodded.

'Captain Chinero has a lot to answer for, even so,' he said,
and his eyes glittered with the thought of revenge.

Although his voice was calm, Ico caught the suppressed
rage beneath the quiet words.

'Chinero?' she queried. 'You know his name?'

'It wasn't hard to find out. He's already been bragging
about what happened. Just let me catch him alone . . .'

'No! The last thing we can afford is a vendetta – and nothing
he's done, no matter how thoughtless, justifies murder.'

'What *he* did was murder!' Andrin countered angrily.

'He couldn't have known what would happen.'

'Of course he knew. There were fireworms everywhere. If it
hadn't been Mendo it would have been someone else.' He broke
off, his voice choked.

'Killing Chinero will achieve nothing,' Ico persisted. 'And it
would give the Senate the excuse they need. We've done
nothing illegal so far, but—'

'That doesn't matter to them.'

'Well, it does to me. Don't stoop to their level. The White Guard
are not the real enemy. They're only following orders. It's the
faceless ones issuing the orders who are really to blame.'

Andrin stared at her, not yet convinced, needing some way
of seeking justice but baulked at every turn.

'Promise me you won't do anything to Chinero.'

He said nothing.

'Promise me, Andrin. Or everything we've worked for will count for nothing. Mendo's death will count for nothing.'

She saw tears form in his green eyes and knew that, at last, he would be able to cry for the brother he had lost.

'I promise.'

She squeezed his hand, knowing he would keep his word and relieved to have caught him in time.

'Mendo's really gone,' Andrin breathed, a look of childlike bewilderment on his face. 'He's really gone. Stupid, stupid, little . . .'

Ico put her arms about him and held him tightly, feeling his chest heave as the tears came. Andrin cried in silence but the tremors wracked his whole body, grief welling up from deep inside. Ico waited, hating each moment of his misery but knowing it was necessary, a first step on the road to healing. At last he grew still and, somewhat ashamed, wiped his face with a sleeve.

'He could be an infuriating little brat,' he said, 'especially when he insisted on following me around. There were times when I could have throttled him . . . but . . .'

'You loved him,' Ico supplied.

Andrin nodded.

'I miss him already,' he said, and shut his eyes as if to trap any further tears.

Ico stretched up to kiss him and, by the time they drew apart, her cheeks were wet too. They looked at each other in silence for a few heartbeats.

'It's taught me one thing, at least,' Andrin told her seriously.

'What's that?'

'I never want the two of us to be that far apart in a dangerous situation.'

'Me neither.'

'I couldn't bear it if—'

'Shhh.' Ico put a finger to his lips, but before she could speak again a voice called from the house.

'Ico?'

She looked up and saw her father silhouetted in the lamplit doorway.

'Ico? Are you out there?'

'I'm coming, Father,' she called, then whispered to Andrin, 'You'd better go.'

They kissed again hurriedly, then he vanished into the shadows as Ico walked slowly towards the light, dabbing at her eyes as she went.

'Was there someone out there with you?' her father asked as she came in. 'I thought I heard voices.'

'No. I was just talking to the plants,' she lied easily, knowing he would not pursue the matter.

'They like that,' he said, accepting her explanation readily. 'Everything grows for you, just like it did for your mother.'

According to Diano Maravedis, everything good in his daughter's character or abilities came from her mother, whose memory had not faded but grown brighter and – although he did not realize it – more unrealistic with each passing year. He was a reticent, soft-spoken man with thinning brown hair and thin limbs, and each time he looked at his daughter he wondered anew how such a scrawny specimen as himself had managed to sire such beauty. He saw the lustrous dark hair, warm brown eyes, small nose and full, wide lips and inevitably credited them all to his dead wife. He saw Ico's lithe, athletic build and graceful movement and attributed them to the same source, forgetting that his wife's had been an altogether rounder, less elegant body and that his own was slight but strong and his fingers, like his daughter's, were nimble and dexterous.

Having had the sole responsibility for Ico's upbringing thrust upon his grief-stricken shoulders ten years earlier, Diano had tried his best to understand his beloved but wilful child, but women had been and remained something of a mystery to him, and he was aware that she kept some secrets from him. Indeed there were aspects of her life about which he knew nothing. He had always trusted her, though, knowing her to be blessed not only with intelligence but also common sense, both of which – in his biased view – she had inherited from her mother. But now he was puzzled, and a strange note in his voice alerted Ico to the fact that her father was worried. It had only been a matter of time before he learnt of the afternoon's events, but she had not expected the news to travel quite so fast.

'Are you hungry?' he asked. 'I can ask Atchen to bring us some food if you like.'

'No. I'm fine,' she replied, thinking that it was just like him to prevaricate when there was something unpleasant to discuss.

'Some wine?' He held up his own goblet. 'This vintage is really very good and you're old enough now to . . .'

'No, thanks, Dodo. Did you want to talk to me about something?'

The use of his nickname – the result of her first childish attempts to pronounce his name – made her father smile, but only for a fleeting moment. He drank more wine and looked down at the marble floor.

'I've just received a rather disturbing message from Senator Kantrowe. It seems the White Guards intercepted some foolish young people in the lava fields, playing with magic, and—'

'And I was one of them,' Ico completed for him, interrupting his sudden rush of words.

'Oh.' He glanced up but could not meet his daughter's challenging stare and dropped his gaze again. 'I thought it must have been a mistake.'

'No. Senator Kantrowe's spies got it right, except that we're not foolish, and we weren't playing. We were deadly serious and using magic to kill fireworms.'

'My goodness!'

'It worked, too,' she went on. 'Or at least it did until the guards messed things up. A boy was killed because of their intervention.' She had no qualms about bending the truth a little to suit her purpose. 'So the great Senator Kantrowe did not tell you the whole truth.'

Her father was obviously disconcerted by Ico's outburst.

'I don't think you should talk about the senator that way. He's a very important man.'

Not to me, Ico thought, but said nothing.

'And isn't using magic rather dangerous?' he went on tentatively.

'Not if it's done properly,' she replied, longing to shout at her father, to tell him not to be so pathetic. 'You never minded when I linked with Soo.'

'Of course not,' he said, rather taken aback. 'Soo is a beautiful creature, and that can do no harm, but real magic . . . that's another matter. The Senate has—'

'The Senate deliberately look the other way and then complain when they can't see anything,' she told him. 'They haven't the faintest idea what's really going on.'

'Steady on, Ico. These are—'

'These are frightened old men looking for scapegoats, anyone to blame except their own incompetent selves,' she burst out. 'And until there are people willing to stand up and say as much in public, we're all their dupes.'

Rendered temporarily speechless by his daughter's vehemence, Diano covered his confusion by drinking again and staring at the last few drops of wine in the goblet.

'Perhaps it would be more prudent . . .' he began, then looked up and found he was talking to an empty room.

CHAPTER FOUR

The hoopoe, whose name was Ero, waddled along the top of the broken fence, his short legs moving quickly so that the whole of his long body rocked from side to side. He stopped abruptly, then probed the rotting wood with his long, slender bill and pulled out a small wriggling shape. His hunger temporarily satisfied, he turned to look at his human partner, who sat beside a tall, light-haired companion. Both boys were staring morosely into the flames of a small fire they had lit using pieces of wood from the waste ground about them. Ero rarely had the patience to listen to – let alone appreciate – human explanations of events, but he was sensitive to the moods of his partner even when he did not understand them. He decided to cheer him up.

You whistle, I dance, he sent hopefully.

Not now, Ero, Vargo replied wearily, but looked up none-theless.

The hoopoe had carefully raised a foot so that its talons faced forward and he stood, swaying a little, on one leg, his head cocked to one side. For some reason this pose always caused humans some amusement, but this time Vargo only smiled half-heartedly and shook his head. Undeterred, Ero bobbed his tail feathers and performed a few halting steps, only subsiding when there was no response.

I'm more handsome than his eagle, he remarked, feeling the need to assert the importance of his position.

Of course you are, Vargo replied fondly. *But Ayo is stronger and can fly higher.*

But he can't do this. Ero proudly fanned his crest, the golden brown feathers tipped with black and white, and turned his head back and forth to show it off to the best advantage. *Can he?*

No, Vargo admitted, trying not to laugh. *I need to talk to my friend now*, he added, hoping Ero would take the hint.

I know when I'm not wanted, the bird muttered sanctimoniously.

With that he exploded noisily into the air. The firelight illuminated the vivid black and white stripes on his broad wings, and his dipping, dancing flight made him look like some giant, exotic butterfly. Both boys watched his progress until he swooped down to some unknown destination and was lost in the darkness.

'He's getting restless,' Andrin said.

Vargo nodded.

'He'll be on his way in a month or so.'

They relapsed into silence for a while, each thinking vaguely of faraway places, unseen lands. Human tides moved more slowly than those of migrating birds. Vargo could already sense the approach of winter – not in the weather, which would remain hot and dry for some months to come, but in his own personality. The changeover time, that twice-yearly period of confusion, would begin soon – and he already had more than enough on his mind.

Vargo Shaimian was unique among the Firebrands and, as far as they knew, among all the people of Tiguafaya, in that he was linked to not one but two birds – both only temporary visitors to his homeland. Ero came in summer, returning south to the great open plains of an unknown continent when the days grew shorter, and was replaced each winter by Lao, a sandpiper curlew, who arrived with others of his kind from the north. In contrast to Ero, Lao was a shy, plain bird whose aristocratic bearing made him seem aloof and wary. When linked to either of his partners, Vargo's own character often took on aspects of the birds' identities but when both were present, as happened for a short time each spring and autumn, he often felt lost, uncertain even of his own feelings and quite unable to explain them to anyone else.

For most of the year, however, the linking was simple enough and his friends found it easy to tell which bird was in residence. In summer, under Ero's influence, Vargo tended to dress flamboyantly, act unpredictably and, whenever possible, find humour in any situation. His music was lively, energetic and designed for dancing, his agile fingers skipping over the strings of his lute. In winter, with Lao, his romantic nature turned to melancholy, his clothes were the colours of earth and stone and he took to playing beautiful, sad melodies on his viol, the drawn-out notes echoing the curlew's soft chirruping cries. In either phase his music was Vargo's life's blood, created for himself but giving pleasure to all who heard him play or sing. His talent was unquestioned and, in spite of his humble origins, he was now an apprentice to the prestigious Musicians' Guild. No one who knew him was in any doubt that full membership would soon be granted.

Vargo had been abandoned as an infant, and had grown up in the harsh conditions of a penurious orphanage, escaping only by dint of his own courage and his gift for music. His parents, it was assumed, had been travelling entertainers who had had no use for the encumbrance of an infant, and it was from them that he had inherited his instinctive skills. But it had been his own determination and the endless hours of practice that had brought about his present expertise.

Andrin and Vargo had met when they were four-year-old harbour urchins, and had become friends instantly. In the decade and a half since then the bond between them had grown progressively stronger. Apart from Ico, Vargo was the most important person in Andrin's life and he was the third, unacknowledged leader of the Firebrands. The trio spent a good deal of time together and if Vargo felt excluded by the close nature of the lovers' relationship he never complained, seemingly content with his role – sometimes clown, sometimes poet, always faithful. To anyone else he appeared something of a loner, and few people knew him well. Only the most observant saw past his music and his singular appearance – the tangle of brown hair, the pale grey eyes and expressive mouth – to the dual personality within.

'When will Lao's flock arrive?' Andrin asked.

'Soon. They're on their way. I can feel them getting closer. So make the most of my happy period. Before long I won't be able to think straight. And then I'll be miserable.'

The forced light-heartedness of his words fooled neither of them. The day's events had cast a pall over their spirits that even Ero's presence could not hope to dispel. Vargo had been one of those rounded up by the soldiers, and had only learnt the full horror of what had happened some time later.

'I've found out where Chinero is quartered,' he said quietly, half afraid of what Andrin might do with this information but unwilling to try to influence him.

'I'm not interested in him,' Andrin replied flatly.

'But I thought—'

'Forget him. He's just a puppet. It's his overlords in the Senate who are pulling the strings. They're the ones who're really responsible for what happened.'

Vargo nodded, recognizing the imprint of Ico's cooler reasoning in his friend's words. As always, thinking of her gave him a pang of longing, half pain, half pleasure, the familiar yearning that he could never mention, except in jest.

'You're right,' he said, feeling relieved. 'We've more important things to think about.'

'Next time we'll make sure there are no guards anywhere near before we start,' Andrin went on grimly. 'So we can concentrate on fighting the real enemy.'

'It's going to be some time before we have the chance,' Vargo noted glumly. 'It'll take an age to replace all those crystals.'

'We'll find a way,' his companion answered confidently. 'The important thing is, it worked! And we proved we can succeed as a team. There's no way we're going to give up now.'

'Agreed. But we'll have to be careful. If they're watching us . . .'

'Let them watch. We've done nothing wrong.'

'That's not how they see it.'

Andrin dismissed this with a wave of his hand. 'I'm more worried about why there was a second swarm,' he said. 'It's going to be hard to plan ahead if that sort of thing keeps happening.'

'They must have been responding to our presence,' Vargo hazarded.

'But not for food. They only came across Mendo by chance, and made no attempt to follow the rest of us.'

Vargo noticed the small catch in his friend's voice but tactfully ignored it.

'So do you think they could have somehow been aware of the attack? Were they checking on what had happened to the first swarm?'

'Perhaps they felt the sudden cold. Or sensed the others dying,' Andrin said thoughtfully.

'Either way, the reason for their coming might not be important,' Vargo concluded. 'What *is* crucial is what they were doing. If they're capable of learning from the encounter, they'll be much more dangerous next time. We could start out as hunters and end up as prey.'

They sat in silence for a while, considering this alarming prospect. Andrin tossed another handful of twigs on the fire. Although the evening was warm and they had no need of its heat, the flickering glow was comforting. The gentle breeze carried with it many scents – all the animal smells of a crowded city – which mingled with the woodsmoke. Somewhere an owl hooted mournfully and, out of sight, Ero answered with his own faintly ridiculous call – hoo-poo-hoo. Vargo and Andrin glanced at each other.

'At least one of us has kept his sense of humour,' Andrin commented bleakly.

'Ero just doesn't have much ordinary sense,' his friend added.

'Or we have too much.' Andrin knew he ought to go home, but the idea made him feel quite sick. The thought of returning to that sordid house and the empty bed in the room he had shared with his brother was too much for him. He would rather stay out all night. At least that way he would not have to sleep – and thus risk the dreams that would follow.

'Do you want a drink?' Vargo asked, sensing the other's mood.

'No money.'

'I can sing for our supper. There are still a few taverns I haven't been thrown out of. Come on, let's go and get drunk. It'll do you good.'

Thinking of his mother, Andrin wasn't so sure, but he stood up slowly, stretching cramped limbs. Anything was better than going home.

'All right,' he said. 'Just don't expect me to join in the choruses.'

'And have all the dogs in the neighbourhood singing with you?' Vargo said. 'No thanks.'

Howling at the moon, Andrin thought, glancing up at the night sky as he fell into step beside his friend. Sometimes that's all we can do.

***

The door opened a crack and a suspicious face peered out. Then, having seen who it was, Fayna's father threw the door wide and beckoned the visitor in.

'Come in, Ico. I'm very glad to see you. Fayna came home this afternoon in a terrible state, and we haven't been able to get a sensible word out of her. Would you . . . ?'

'That's what I came for. Sorry it had to wait until the middle of the night.' Ico nodded to Fayna's mother who regarded her anxiously from the bed on the far side of the room.

'She's in her room at the back. Do you know why she's so upset?'

'Ria was killed today. Losing a link suddenly like that can be devastating.'

Fayna's parents exchanged a glance. Neither of them had any feel for magic, and so the bond between bird and human was a mystery to them. They were not stupid or insensitive; it was just that, like so many people, they had no idea how it felt to be linked, nor of the desolation caused by its loss.

'I'll do what I can,' Ico promised, crossing to the bedroom door and knocking gently.

There was no response, but she went in anyway. Fayna was lying face down on the bed, still fully clothed. Despite the lateness of the hour Ico knew she was not asleep.

'Hello?'

Fayna stirred at the sound of the unexpected voice and pushed herself up on her elbows. Her eyes were red and swollen from crying. 'What do you want?'

'I thought you might need someone to talk to.'

Fayna glared up at Ico. 'What good will talking do?'

Ico was not surprised by the antagonism in the younger girl's tone. It had been her own plan that had resulted in Ria's death.

'It might help you to mourn, and to realize that losing your bird is not the end of the world.'

'That's easy for you to say,' Fayna remarked bitterly. She swung her legs off the bed and sat on the edge. Ico sat down beside her, putting an arm round her thin shoulders. Fayna grew rigid at the touch but soon relaxed, accepting the offer of comfort.

'I know what you're going through,' Ico said softly.

'How can you? Ria's the one that's dead, not Soo.'

'I know, but Soo is not my first link. Birds don't live as long as we do, and we have to get used to them moving on.'

'It would have been all right if she'd died of old age,' Fayna whispered, 'but this . . .' She broke down and began weeping again.

'The shock isn't as great,' Ico told her, 'but it's just as hard to accept.' She spoke from personal experience, remembering Soo's predecessor vividly.

'But it . . . it was horrible,' Fayna breathed, when she was able to speak again. 'I *knew*. I felt all cold inside, as if I was being frozen. I was yelling at her, telling her to get out of the way, but she was too slow.'

'She died in a good cause,' Ico went on. 'She was brave, and now you need to be too. Once you've found the link you never truly lose it. There'll be another bird for you.'

'There'll never be another one like Ria,' the girl protested loyally, but there was a small note of hope in her voice nonetheless.

'Of course there won't,' Ico agreed. 'But they're all wonderful, in their different ways, and when you're ready, keep your mind open. One of the other crows will step forward for you.'

'You think so?'

'I know so. Haven't you caught snatches of their thoughts before?'

'Yes, but . . . but I thought they were just coming through Ria.'

'You'll see. Your link will be complete again sooner than you can imagine.'

'You're not just saying that?' Fayna asked doubtfully.

'I swear it. You're special, and the birds have too much sense to let your link go to waste.'

They sat quietly for a while, until at last Fayna seemed calm. Eventually she sighed, and for the first time her voice held an intimation of sad acceptance.

'Why me?' she asked. 'No one else lost someone they loved.'

'It was just an accident. There was no reason for it.' Ico did not tell her than Andrin had lost his brother. She would find out about Mendo soon enough. For now she needed all her strength for herself.

Fayna's next question surprised Ico, and reminded her uncomfortably of her conversation with her father.

'Will we get into trouble because the guards caught us?'

'No,' she replied, with more confidence than she felt. 'We weren't doing anything wrong.'

'Then why did they—' Fayna began, but got no further.

From far away came an ominous rumbling, which grew closer with horrifying speed. The whole house shook with its force. Although the earthquake lasted only a few moments, it was terrifying nonetheless. Fayna clung to Ico but then, as soon as the tremor passed, she jumped up and went to the window. Flinging the shutters wide she stared out at the western sky and gasped.

'Our magic *did* annoy the dragons,' she whispered in terror. 'Look!'

Ico went to join her, and her heart sank as she looked out. Half the heavens had been painted the colour of blood.

CHAPTER FIVE

Teguise was many miles from the centre of the firelands, but even from such a safe distance the eruption was a spectacular and frightening sight. However, for the people of the inland villages it was a truly terrifying experience. In the last few decades there had only been minor volcanic disturbances, which had invariably been preceded by telltale signs. Wells would dry up, warm springs would grow hotter, lakes would change colour – and all eyes would turn towards the mountains as the word spread. Such portents allowed the inhabitants of the interior to make preparations for evacuating any threatened area, reluctantly abandoning their carefully nurtured vines and fig trees. This time, however, the only warning had been the tremor, and the eruption had followed on its heels so quickly that there had been no time to react.

The first explosion tore away the entire summit of a small mountain known as the Dragon's Tail, and produced a bulging column of smoke that glowed against the night sky. For several hours afterwards flame and burning rock shot into the air, accompanied by a constant angry roaring. Flashes of lightning illuminated the ever-growing cloud from within,

40

and the hollow booming of thunder was added to the volcanic growl. Blobs of molten stone solidified in midair, then plunged back to earth, raining down in a deadly hail. Floods of incandescent lava poured out from the newly formed crater and spread as rivers down to the valleys below, engulfing all in their path. At first the lava flowed quickly, like rolling water, but later – as it cooled and the eruption began to die down – it became more viscous, the consistency of honey, the red streams now studded with black.

When morning came it seemed that the worst was over. The flow of new lava had slowed, and the outer reaches were moving only very sluggishly. One village had been completely inundated, with only a few of its residents lucky or prescient enough to survive but, for the most part, the volcano had contented itself with destroying a few vineyards and adding new layers to already barren rock. Even so, the giant cloud still towered above the land. It would be several days before it dispersed, and in the meantime ash fell from the sky, coating every surface with a soft grey blanket. Roofs had to be cleared promptly before they collapsed under the weight of the ash, and the air itself seemed thick and choking, but these were minor hazards compared to the potential devastation that had preceded them. By noon the residents of the interior had begun to relax a little. It was then that the Dragon's Tail lashed out with one final vindictive assault.

The cone was no longer spewing forth lava or spraying burning rock into the air, but within its smoke-filled crater there was a sudden collapse, a rush of movement as a second cloud burst forth with explosive force. This time it did not rise into the sky but hugged the contours of the land like an avalanche. The fiery mixture of toxic gas and glowing particles moved with incredible speed, incinerating or melting everything in its path. Such clouds were known as 'the shining breath' and – unlike the slower lava flows – there was not even

the faintest hope of escape from its fatal touch for anyone
unlucky enough to be stranded in its often unpredictable
path. Many more people died almost instantly, their lungs
seared and their clothes and skin burnt away as the cloud cut
a dark swathe across one of the valleys before finally running
out of energy.

Although that truly was the end of the eruption, its
aftermath was to last for some time. For many days men
watched the mountains with renewed suspicion and fear, and
wondered whether this was the start of a massive upheaval –
such as the great series of eruptions more than a century ago
which had, quite literally, changed the face of the land. And
they looked for reasons for the unexpected catastrophe.

The volcanoes had always been central to the life of Tiguafaya.
It was because of their fearsome reputation that the vast,
elongated triangular peninsula had been uninhabited for so
long. A few rough tracks had passed through the mountain
range that separated the region from the rest of the world, but
these were virtually impassable and used only by the most
determined or foolhardy travellers. Eventually, however, the
area had been colonized by a group of religious exiles who
needed somewhere to live in peace, desperate to escape
persecution for their unorthodox beliefs.

The land which was eventually to be named Tiguafaya
formed the southern tip of a vast continent. It had been remote
even before a particularly violent sequence of eruptions, some
five centuries earlier, had destroyed the only roads into the
area, effectively cutting it off from all communication other
than by sea. At the time the settlers took this as an omen,
symbolic of their chosen renunciation of the godless ways of
other people. For some it meant justification and peace of mind,
but it also meant hardship for all. Their often professed desire
for self-sufficiency was put to the test.

Over the centuries that followed, religious freedom had ironically become less important than the simple need to survive in a hostile environment. Further eruptions caused periodic havoc and, although major upheavals only occurred once or twice each century, the ever changing, treacherous nature of the land made progress slow. However, the pioneers were hardy and they adapted to their new conditions, finding both land and sea to be unexpectedly bountiful if treated with respect. Most of the original settlements, including Teguise, were sited along the east coast, sheltered from the prevailing winds and occasional storms that blew from the Great West Ocean. Because of this, and because of the difficulties of travelling by land, many of the colonists became seafarers. Gradually a fleet was built, starting with individually owned boats, then expanding to larger vessels as communities saw the need not only for fishing but also for trade, and pooled their resources. Eventually, after the discovery of rare and valuable gemstones in the firelands, such trading vessels became doubly important and some ships were built purely to protect the others and their vital cargoes. Thus the Tiguafayan navy was born.

At the same time, the settlers learnt how to make the most of the apparently barren soil, together with the excellent climate, to cultivate a wide range of foodstuffs, even utilizing the water-absorbing properties of volcanic gravel to make the most of early morning dew and the moisture in the wind. Fruits, vegetables, cereals and cacti were all raised with increasing success by dint of hard work, careful husbandry and experience. Sugar cane and grapes provided the raw materials for rum and wine, and goats were raised for their milk and meat. Later, camels were imported from southern lands and these inelegant but practical animals adapted well to their new habitat.

Prosperity enabled the community to grow and to devote

its energies to aspects of life other than mere survival. Music and other artistic pursuits flourished, and this helped forge a common bond between the various villages and settlements, eventually leading to a formal alliance of all the people of the firelands. A ruling council, known as the Senate, was set up as the governing body of this new nation, to meet the needs of a growing political sophistication. Several trade guilds were already in existence by then – transporters, farmers, wine-makers, jewellers and so on – and, naturally enough, the first senators to be elected were senior representatives of these organizations. Over the years the members of the Senate had come to be regarded as the aristocracy of Tiguafaya, and they and their families enjoyed various privileges in addition to considerable wealth. Other guilds were formed – bankers, educators, lawyers – as an increasingly hierarchical society evolved, and the most powerful dynasties grew so entrenched that certain positions on the council became hereditary. Over time the Senate became innately conservative, and less responsive to the needs of the people as a whole.

Later, when various troubles beset Tiguafaya, the country's leaders became increasingly unpopular with some sections of the population – especially the self-styled Firebrands. However, not even the most rabid of the Senate's opponents could justify blaming them for the volcanic nature of their homeland. Nor could they be held responsible for the capricious whims of the firelands' other inhabitants, whose presence had played an important role in defining the history and culture of the land. The dragons of Tiguafaya were a law unto themselves.

'"Our magic *did* annoy the dragons,"' Ico quoted. 'That's what she said.'

Andrin said nothing, but his expression was one of pure disgust.

'It's just a coincidence,' Vargo said.

'I know that,' Ico agreed, 'but if even one of our own is thinking like that, how many others are going to be convinced?' She had been dismayed to hear Fayna talk as she had, and had done her best to persuade the other girl that the two events – their attack on the worms and the eruption – were not connected. Fayna had eventually seemed convinced, but her instinctive reaction was symptomatic of the Firebrands' underlying problem.

'It couldn't have worked out any better for the Senate if they'd stage-managed the whole thing,' Ico added.

'Or any worse for us,' Vargo agreed glumly.

The three friends were sitting together in the shade of Ico's garden, considering all that had happened in the last twenty-four hours. The eruption had been an impressive sight from Teguise, but, other than a light film of grey dust, the city had not suffered directly. It would be some time before the details of the damage to the interior were known, but they were more concerned for the future of the Firebrands.

'Whatever the truth of the matter,' Ico went on, 'the Senate will make sure everyone knows about our attack. They won't even have to blame us for the eruption. The implication will be obvious.'

'The dragons are taking revenge for our presumption,' Vargo said.

Ico nodded. 'Trespassing on their magical preserve,' she added. 'And using it to fight their spawn.'

'That's such crap!' Andrin burst out.

'Of course it is, but—'

'The worms are nothing to do with the dragons,' he went on angrily. 'Even the birds know that!'

'You don't need—' Ico began, but he interrupted her again, unable to contain his fury.

'The Senate are scared of their own shadows. We had magic

before we even knew of the dragons – and that bloody volcano would have blown no matter what we did. It's got nothing to do with the dragons. Is the whole country mad? No one's even *seen* a single dragon for decades. It's absurd.'

'You're preaching to the converted,' Vargo told him quietly and Andrin fell silent, the angry colour in his face fading slowly.

'We know all that,' Ico said, after a short pause. 'The question is, how do we stop everyone believing the Senate's propaganda?'

'You'd think they'd use common sense,' Vargo said. 'After the mess the Senate have made of things, why should anyone believe those old farts?'

'Because they play on people's fears,' Andrin replied, rational now.

'And on their religious faith,' Ico added. 'Common sense can't hold out for long against that.'

'They've already rewritten history several times,' Andrin commented bitterly. 'What's one more lie? Trying to ban magic is insane, but if you accept their warped view of the past then it makes a horrible sort of sense.'

'I wonder what it was really like?' Vargo asked wistfully, always the dreamer. 'When the first settlers came here, I mean. What did the dragons really look like? And what did they make of men?'

'They probably just ignored us,' Ico answered. 'If the old stories are even half right, they're so big and so powerful we must have seemed completely insignificant to them.'

'I'd like to see one, just once.'

'Forget the dragons, will you!' Andrin snapped. 'Leave them to history, where they belong.'

Long ago, when the first colonists had discovered that the nearby mountains were inhabited by huge flying serpents, it had almost meant the end of their hopes of building a new life. However, such was the pioneers' determination that they were prepared to risk even these neighbours. Indeed, some even saw them as protective spirits, guarding the new-found freedom of the immigrants.

As it turned out, these vast and terrifying creatures had had little direct effect on the people, but were nevertheless regarded with awe and credited with godlike powers. To the pioneers the fire and smoke of the volcanoes became 'dragon's breath', and indicated that the ancient beasts were angry. To pacify them they made sacrifices and prayed, deifying the dragons and immortalizing them in countless legends. Even the mountains themselves became part of the mythology, with specific peaks being named after parts of the beasts' anatomy, so that one became the Dragon's Head, another the Dragon's Spine, and so on. Over the years these places acquired a mystical significance of their own, as if some prehistoric giant had actually turned to stone and formed the mountain range.

Reliable descriptions from those early days were hard to find, but it was generally agreed that the dragons were black in colour, their scales as resilient as steel and that they resembled gigantic winged lizards. Other details varied from tale to tale; some said that they walked upright on two legs, like birds; others that they had four legs which ended in huge talons, with each claw as big as a full-grown man. Their immense wings were reported variously as being covered with metallic feathers or unfolding like the membranes of a bat. Their eyes were described as red fires or orange slits, and were credited with being able to hypnotize any man with a glance, or even turn living creatures to stone or ash. Fire was supposed to spring from their nostrils or from between twin rows of massive teeth and, given their natural habitat, it was assumed that they drew this power from the volcanoes about them.

As the years passed, the dragons' presence was gradually taken for granted and, as they seemed willing to coexist with man peaceably enough, their influence declined until they were no longer regarded with such reverence. Eventually they were seen less and less, until the only glimpses of them were at night – and these only flashes of colour in the sky, deeper shadows among the stars. For young people like the Fire-brands, the dragons were creatures of legend and nothing more, but that made them all the more alluring to Vargo. In spite of Andrin's instruction, he could not dismiss the images from his mind. In his dreams he played music for the dragons and one day, he was firmly convinced, he would do so in the real world.

CHAPTER SIX

Senator Tias Kantrowe looked back on the events of the afternoon with considerable satisfaction. For once the Chamber had been almost full, with even some of the most reluctant members in attendance. The political grapevine was all aquiver, its tendrils snaking into every quarter of Teguise. Great matters were afoot, so even the lazy and the complacent had been roused from their usual indifference – and had come to hear what he had to say.

In the event, Kantrowe's speech had been a model of patience and tolerance, apparently made more in sorrow than in anger. His audience had been surprised, and many were disappointed not to hear the expected fireworks, blistering condemnation and vengeful oaths. Instead they had listened, innocently bewildered, to reasoned arguments and calm reassurances. Magic was the lawful heritage of the people of Tiguafaya, he had said. If some chose to abuse their privilege, then the only legal recourse was to try to persuade them of the foolishness of their ways. That was their country's tried and tested democratic system. Even though they faced perils enough from outside, Kantrowe and his colleagues would carefully consider how to deal with such internal problems before any action was taken. As one of the later speakers had commented, it had been a truly statesmanlike performance. The senator smiled at the memory; they had been so easily fooled.

Of course it had been simple enough to prompt the required response from the floor. A few of his like-minded cronies had not needed much persuasion to get the ball rolling – and it had soon become an avalanche of indignation. The previously unstated connection between magic and the volcanic activity was referred to again and again; righteous pleas were made for stronger measures to be taken on behalf of the less fortunate; and finally, amid noisy scenes, a chorus of approval was given to the proposal to confer emergency powers upon Senator Kantrowe and the White Guard so that the matter could be dealt with swiftly and ruthlessly. Kantrowe had accepted the responsibility gravely, and with a show of reluctance, hiding his secret jubilation. At the end of the debate he had retired to his own chambers, and now awaited certain colleagues. Once they joined him the real work could begin.

First to arrive were two elderly senators, whose influence and patrician status outweighed Kantrowe's carefully concealed dislike of the old bores. He greeted them warmly, but looked forward to the day when their usefulness would be over. Next came Mazo Gadette, a young man whose cadaverous appearance and thin, reedy voice concealed a devious intellect and passionless ambition. In spite of his youth and lesser family status, he had risen quickly, becoming one of President Marco Guadarfia's aides the previous year. Guadarfia was well respected but old and infirm now – some would even say senile – and was less of a force than he had been earlier in his term of office. His aides had already wielded his authority as if it were their own on many occasions, and their manoeuvring to ingratiate themselves with his possible successors had begun some time ago. Kantrowe and Gadette had sought each other out, both seeing advantages in the alliance.

'You took your time, Mazo.'

Gadette took the comment at face value, not reacting to the senator's conspiratorial smile.

'Drawing up such documents takes time,' he said. 'And the President is slow to read and even slower to write these days.'

'But he *has* signed it?'

'Of course.' The young man handed Kantrowe a parchment, which had Guadarfia's scrawled signature next to his seal at the bottom.

The senator glanced at the decree, noting with amusement that some self-important scribe had made small amendments to the text drafted by Kantrowe himself in anticipation of these events. The essence remained unchanged, however. It was a mandate of almost limitless potential.

As Kantrowe finished reading, the last member of what had become known as the inner council entered the room. At forty years of age Deion Verier was one of the youngest senators, but it was already obvious that he was destined for high office. His family was immensely rich and that, combined with his dashing appearance, gave him an unshakeable self-belief that bordered on egomania. He had gained a reputation as a merciless opponent, and although ugly rumours about his private life circulated periodically, no one had yet dared voice them in his presence. Kantrowe was one of only a very small number of men who knew which of the lurid tales were true, and his knowledge gave him an unbreakable hold over Verier – who might otherwise have been regarded as a danger to the security of the inner council. The newcomer slumped into a chair.

'Wine,' he ordered imperiously. 'All this talk makes my throat dry.'

Gadette moved to fetch the drink but Kantrowe waved him back to his seat and, to Verier's obvious surprise, waited on him himself. Senator Kantrowe was nominally an appointee of the Wine-Makers' Guild, the trade in which his family had made its name and fortune, and his cellars were unmatched in all Tiguafaya. Of course, it had been many years since the Kantrowes had relied solely upon their vineyards. The clan now controlled many businesses, both financial and mercantile, as well as several huge estates, and their influence reached into almost every sector of Tiguafayan life. With Kantrowe's appointment to a position in charge of all matters relating to the country's defences, their grip had grown even stronger.

Verier tossed back the contents of the goblet and held it out for more, staring defiantly at his host.

'This is an excellent vintage,' Kantrowe said mildly as he poured again. 'It should be savoured.'

The younger man grunted, but took the advice.

'As we should all savour this moment,' Kantrowe went on. 'Now that we have been *forced* into this unfortunate action . . . we must, of course, be extremely *thorough*.'

The other faces in the room reflected his smile with varying degrees of malicious enthusiasm.

'We'll put a stop to this menace once and for all,' one of the elder statesmen said.

'So we just ban all magic?' Verier asked bluntly.

'Of course not,' Kantrowe replied patiently. 'You might as well try to ban all thought.'

'We ban all *unofficial* use of magic,' Gadette said.

'Exactly,' Kantrowe responded, congratulating himself again on the choice of this particular ally. 'That way we can decide who is fit to use such power responsibly, and for what. We don't want to limit our own options. There may come a time when *we* want to use the techniques discovered by the Firebrands.'

'Surely you can't mean that, Tias?' one of the old senators exclaimed. 'We've already seen where that road leads. Do you want the whole country engulfed?'

Kantrowe shrugged.

'Circumstances change,' he said. 'Who knows? Perhaps the dragons wouldn't notice a few, rather more discreet spells. And if the fireworms ever get as far as Teguise . . .'

'That'll never happen!'

'Of course not.' His tone was soothing now. 'But thinking ahead can do no harm.'

'What about the birds?' Verier asked. 'Are the links illegal now?'

Kantrowe sighed. 'That wouldn't be very practical, would it? Many people depend on their links for their livelihood, and anyway, most don't consider it real magic. We'll make the proclamation vague enough for any interpretation we like – and it will still be more than enough to make the Firebrands tip their hand.'

'Vague or not,' Gadette chipped in, 'there are going to be some objectors.'

'I know. It'll be useful to see who comes crawling out of the woodwork. Did you see any obvious dissenters during the debate?'

'Nothing obvious. The usual quota of blank expressions . . .'

'Most of which were because there were blank minds behind them,' Verier remarked contemptuously.

'But nothing outright,' the aide went on, ignoring the interruption. 'The majority will go along without too much complaint, but there were a few I couldn't read.'

'Who?' Kantrowe wanted to know.

'Maciot.'

'As always,' Verier commented. 'I've never trusted him.'

'Who else?'

'I'll give you a list.'

Interesting, Kantrowe thought. Mazo is being remarkably discreet, even in this company. Does he know something I don't? Aloud he said, 'We'll deal with any difficulties as they come up. I know we've got to appease the waverers. So we'll make it clear that this is a temporary measure, intended to deal with a specific problem.'

'The Firebrands,' one elder added fervently. 'The sooner we put them in their place the better.'

'Agreed,' Kantrowe said. And this, he added silently, is only the beginning.

Senator Alegranze Maciot kicked off his boots and whistled softly. He was immediately answered by a soft chirruping, and a small dark shape flew in the open window. The bird's wings flashed in the slanting sunlight as it landed on the back of a couch, and Tao regarded his human partner with jewelled eyes.

You were a long time. The bird sounded vaguely resentful.

It was quite a show, Maciot replied. *The whole thing was stage-managed by Kantrowe, of course. The gods know what he's really up to. But I don't like it. Whatever it is.* He slumped down among richly embroidered cushions and sighed deeply. *It's all a stupid game.*

Then why did you go?

I don't know.

It wouldn't be because you love games – and happen to be rather good at them?

You're smarter than any bird has a right to be, Maciot answered, laughing. *However did I get stuck with you?*

It is I who should be asking that question, Tao remarked primly. *Where would you be without me and my kind to carry your messages?*

Where indeed? Alegranze reflected privately. The Transporters' Guild was responsible for long-distance communications and the conveyance of goods throughout all Tiguafaya. Without birds like Tao, his linked mirador chaffinch, their job would be a great deal harder.

I am always in your debt, he conceded, and wondered for the umpteenth time what exactly Tao got out of their relationship.

But don't become too sure of yourself. If Kantrowe gets his way I'll wager that just talking to you like this will be a punishable offence.

Don't be absurd. Even humans can't be that stupid.

I wouldn't bet on it. Anyone who is tainted with magic is in for a rough ride. Especially the Firebrands.

Why?

You must have heard. Birds gossip even more than we do.

Perhaps. But I'd like to hear your version.

Smiling but obedient, Maciot related what he had been told about the attack on the fireworms and subsequent events.

Of course Kantrowe was careful not to say they were connected, but everyone jumped to the obvious conclusion.

It's only obvious if you have the brain of an insect, Tao said sarcastically.

You seem very sure. It's a hell of a coincidence.

Magic is older than this land, older than your race or mine, older even than the dragons, the bird stated, his tone now that of an impatient lecturer. *It is a force of nature that we are allowed to borrow. We pay a price for such gifts, but not in that way. If the dragons are angry then magic is not the reason. It is not their sole preserve, nor can it ever be. And to imply that this attack on the fireworms is responsible is even more nonsensical.*

Tell that to the people who lost their homes.

Tao clicked his beak in annoyance at such illogicality.

If they choose to live in the shadows of volcanoes, they should accept the risks that go with it, not look for scapegoats, he said indignantly. *The worms are our enemies, the dragons are not. Look at me. How can you doubt that I come from the same stock? My colouring, my wings . . .*

Your fiery breath . . . Alegranze teased.

Long ago, the chaffinch went on with exaggerated patience, *before even the first eggs were laid by the sky, the shape of all winged creatures was there, waiting in the air. Since then we have travelled different paths but—*

I know. I believe you, the man cut in. *You all share a common ancestry with the dragons.*

And the worms do not! Tao stated emphatically. *They have no wings. They kill our young, burn our nests. We are not warlike, we do not kill our own for sport. The fact that so many of us were willing to help in the attack is evidence enough.*

Even so, it was a reckless thing to do, Maciot said. *Most of the Firebrands are no more than children. Youth disguises a lot of stupidity, but in the end they must have known it would provoke some reaction. Now it's coming. And they're not going to like it.*

CHAPTER SEVEN

The sun had set more than two hours ago, and Tias Kantrowe was alone again. He sat in his office, staring into space and contemplating the progress of his plans. A dull orange glow was provided by a single oil lamp, its initially pungent smell now unnoticed. The shutters were still open, revealing a view over the moonlit rooftops of the city. Occasionally moths fluttered by, but did not enter the room – as if the attraction of the light was counteracted by some other force.

The senator was motionless, his broad face set in a half smile. He was a restless man, his own seemingly inexhaustible supply of energy keeping him in constant motion, but for the moment he was content merely to wait. There was still business to conduct but, even if that had not been the case, he would have been in no hurry to leave. His official chambers were in a private eyrie on the topmost floor of the Vestry, the monolithic building in the heart of Teguise whence the government of the country was organized. In spite of the lateness of the hour, Kantrowe had no thought of returning to his home and family. Neither was he in the mood to visit any of his mistresses, young women who were less boring than his wife of twenty years but who, in their mercenary ways, were just as demanding. On this night the pleasures of the flesh paled into insignificance beside the intoxicating allure of intrigue.

A precise, three-tap knock on the door brought him out of his reverie.

'Enter!' he called. He already knew who it was.

Mazo Gadette came in and, although he tried to conceal his distaste, his gaunt face twitched as he sensed the vaguely fishy odour of the burning oil. Kantrowe was glad to see Gadette show a sign of human weakness, and wondered briefly why the aide looked so emaciated. He had never seen Gadette eat or drink, but knew that within the thin body there was a strength of purpose few men could match. Perhaps Gadette regarded sustenance, like sleep, as a luxury he could easily forego.

'Is all ready?' Kantrowe asked, waving the aide to a chair.

'The scribes are completing the last few copies,' the younger man replied. 'They will be checked and ready within the hour. The night watch is on standby and Captain Chinero has been summoned. He will be here shortly.'

'Excellent.'

'The proclamation will be posted in all quarters of the city well before dawn,' Gadette went on, his tone neutral, 'and couriers will set out at first light to every village worth the name.' Having completed his report, he took a handkerchief from his pocket and dabbed at his nose. Kantrowe caught a faint waft of perfume, and smiled.

'As always, Mazo, you are a model of efficiency.'

'I endeavour to give satisfaction,' Gadette replied without a trace of self mockery. 'Is there anything else we need to discuss before Chinero gets here?'

'Several matters, but they can wait until he's on his way again. In the meantime, I want to know whether you think the proclamation will achieve the desired results.'

'Undoubtedly. The Firebrands are not all simpletons, no matter what some people would like to believe. The Maravedis girl, for instance, will recognize its implications at once.'

The name caused Kantrowe a spasm of hatred as old feelings resurfaced, but if Gadette noticed he gave no sign.

'And then?' the senator prompted.

'They will have no choice. They can either capitulate or fight. Either way we win. They can't hope to match our forces.'

'You're ignoring the possibility that they carry on in secret.'

'I doubt they have the patience. There are some very hot heads among them. And, if necessary, it would not be difficult to provoke them. In any case, there is little they can achieve in secret. Magic tends to make a spectacle of itself.' Gadette paused and, in as much as his face could ever betray any emotion, he looked at Kantrowe with a certain amused curiosity. 'Forgive men, Senator, but you must surely know all this for yourself.'

'I value your opinion, Mazo. And you can speak with greater candour when no one else is present.'

The aide nodded, his expression resuming its habitual neutrality. Only his pale eyes revealed that he had picked up the senator's hint.

'I have the list we discussed.'

'Amazing,' Kantrowe said, genuinely impressed. 'I had not expected anything in writing so soon.'

Gadette handed over a scroll and Kantrowe unfurled it, glancing at the names recorded there in tiny, spider-like script, each entry accompanied by a concise note. Although the senator had spotted several detractors himself, some came as a surprise and he marvelled at the young man's powers of observation. The aide had watched the debate from the onlookers' gallery and had recorded the reactions of dozens from among the crowd. Not only that, but his notes included relevant quotations and, in some cases, background information.

For a brief moment Kantrowe felt a flicker of unease. Gadette's network of informants must be almost as omniscient as his own, and the senator wondered how many of his own secrets were already known to the aide. He let nothing of this show in his face, however, and merely made a mental note to stay on his guard. Such efficiency was dangerous.

'I will soon have more information on some of them,' Gadette added, reinforcing Kantrowe's conviction. 'I'll let you have a further report as soon as possible.'

'Good. I may have some questions of my own once I've had a chance to study this properly.'

The aide nodded, as if he had been expecting as much.

'For now,' Kantrowe went on, 'I am curious about this particular entry.' He pointed to the name of the brother of one of the inner council's elder statesmen, and Gadette glanced down at the paper.

'His son is reported to be talented,' he said. 'He is linked, it seems, but only to a small, common bird – so the family have never made much of it. I'll have more details soon.'

'You did well not to mention it in front of the boy's uncle.'

Gadette bowed his head slightly, acknowledging the compliment.

'I do not wish our allies to become afraid of magic,' Kantrowe added. 'Merely of its misuse.'

'Of course,' the aide replied. 'Magic is a commodity like any other, subject to the laws of supply and demand.'

A man after my own heart, the senator thought, but said nothing. Both men were fully aware that they should soon have an effective monopoly in this particular commodity.

The sound of heavy boots in the corridor outside alerted them to Chinero's arrival, and they postponed any further discussion. After the captain had confirmed the arrangements for the distribution and display of the proclamation, Kantrowe regarded the soldier thoughtfully.

'One last thing, Captain. I think it unlikely that there will be any overt opposition to this measure in the immediate future. However, should there be any spontaneous expression of public *support* for the move, I would like to feel that such demonstrations would be allowed to go ahead unhindered. If such an outpouring of feeling were to take place – in the merchants' quarter, say – then of course I would expect your men to prevent any serious damage to property, but it would be a mistake to suppress such righteous indignation. You understand?'

'Perfectly, Senator.'

'Good.' Kantrowe sat back in his chair.

When Chinero did not stand or make ready to leave in spite of this obvious dismissal, he raised his eyebrows.

'Is there something else, Captain?'

'I have news, Senator, which may not have reached you yet.'

'Go on.'

'There's been another big pirate raid in the south.'

'Damn.' Kantrowe frowned. 'Where?'

'Caldera Rada. First reports say that the entire town was overrun.'

'Do we know which group is responsible?'

'There's nothing definite yet, but I think it's almost certainly the Barber.'

Kantrowe and Gadette glanced at each other, though their expressions gave nothing away.

'The local militia did the best they could, but they were obviously outmanned,' Chinero went on. 'The settlements nearby have asked that we send troops to protect them from further attacks.'

'The White Guard are to remain in Teguise,' the senator stated firmly. 'Your responsibilities are here.'

'Yes, sir. Can we spare any regular units?'

'I think not at present. If we move too many men south, more important targets will be left undefended.'

'And the western division is helping with the effects of the eruption,' Gadette put in.

Kantrowe nodded gravely.

'Tell them we'll do everything we can, and that resources will be made available to them as soon as possible, but for the time being they're on their own. Tell them to prepare the inland retreats.'

'Yes, Senator,' Chinero replied obediently, although he could not hide his disappointment.

When he had left, Kantrowe and Gadette regarded each other solemnly, each deep in thought. Their earlier mood of euphoria had vanished.

'Not the best of timing,' the aide commented quietly.

'No.'

'Has there been any word from Zophres?'

'Not yet.'

'I wonder if we can really trust any of them.'

'That's what Jon is supposed to be finding out.'

'It's a dangerous strategy.'

'I know that!' the senator snapped, then sighed and grinned apologetically. 'But we must find some way of resolving the situation without another major conflict. I've no wish to set us back another thirty years. I've worked too hard to organize this, and it's our best chance. At worst it'll sow seeds of doubt in the minds of various pirate leaders. If they end up fighting amongst themselves it'll take the pressure off us.'

'And at best?'

'We solve the problem overnight.'

'Madri tried to do that,' Gadette pointed out.

'Yes, but with brute force. He played right into the hands of those savages. Credit me with a little more subtlety.'

'Of course, Senator.'

'The gods forbid that history should remember me in the same breath as Jurado Madri,' Kantrowe concluded earnestly.

Tiguafaya had begun to suffer from pirate raids more than two centuries earlier, the marauders being attracted to the land by its increasing prosperity and lack of military expertise. The first to suffer were merchant vessels but, as these targets found ways of evading the pirates, the coastline came under increasing threat. For a long time the land raids were little more than an infrequent nuisance. However, as the buccaneers grew more organized and aggressive, the settlers began to retaliate, building warships and funding a permanent navy to protect themselves. Fortifications were erected in the larger ports, manned by raw but enthusiastic bands of recruits to the newly formed army. Although these efforts were successful for a while, the pirates were relentless in their pursuit of profit and debauchery. Trade gradually became more difficult, and the country's resources were badly stretched.

The turning point had come thirty years ago when, in a huge battle against several enemy fleets, the Tiguafayan naval forces, under the command of Admiral Jurado Madri, had been almost totally annihilated, leaving the firelands suddenly vulnerable. The only thing that had saved them from being overwhelmed was that, having won the victory together, the pirates were unable to agree on a division of the waiting spoils and their alliance fell apart – leading to conflict between their various factions and a return to incursions by smaller forces.

Nevertheless, the defeat had had major consequences for the demoralized people of Tiguafaya. Admiral Madri, who had been the country's most widely respected military leader, survived the battle but was forced to retire in disgrace and had disappeared from sight. The entire community had been left in a state of shock, and the feeling that emerged was one of understandable caution and conservatism. They now lacked the collective willpower or leadership to challenge the pirates at sea, and so the navy had never been rebuilt. During the last few years the number of ships had risen again, but these were mostly short-range fishing boats, with only a few sleek merchant vessels designed to outrun the reavers.

Overseas trade had inevitably been drastically reduced, and

Tiguafaya had been forced to become self-sufficient once again. This presented considerable opportunities for some, while others suffered a great deal. As more of the country's resources were concentrated in fewer hands, the already hierarchical society became more divided and extreme.

Defensive efforts continued on land, concentrating at first on protecting the seaports from raiders, but even these measures came to be neglected in some less important regions. The threat of the fireworms had diverted much attention, leaving some people caught between two deadly enemies. However, many more were blind to the nature of the crisis. From the relative security of Teguise, and their own fortified family estates, the senators seemed complacent and, in the face of the continuing dangers, discontent grew.

At the centre of this unrest were the Firebrands.

CHAPTER EIGHT

The noise began as a distant growl, a muted rhythm of drums and marching feet combined with the rumbling voice of a many-tongued crowd. It moved forward relentlessly, like a spring tide, each wave of sound bringing it closer to its final destination until it broke with the sudden crashing fury of a storm.

Asleep in her first-floor bedroom, Ico sensed it first in her dream as an expanding invisible presence, a physical force. A threat. Then, as the resonances grew, she caught the edges of crude music, a rattling mockery, and – still dreaming – realized what was coming next.

The tumult burst upon her, catapulting her into wakefulness and out of bed in one terrified movement. The sheer volume of noise was incredible, so shocking that she could hardly breathe, but the worst of it was that she knew beyond doubt that the braying cacophony was directed solely at her. Her instincts told her what her scattered thoughts could not; this thunderous din was a pointing finger, a focus of anger, resentment and blame. The chivaree had come for her.

'What's happening?'

Ico started violently at the voice and the touch on her

shoulder. Unheard amid the clangour her father had entered the room and now stood behind her, to one side, his lips close to her ear. She turned, saw his pale, anxious face and felt a momentary surge of irritation at his perverse bewilderment. Wasn't it obvious?

'Someone's idea of justice!' she shouted, relenting a little. 'Or revenge. It amounts to the same thing.'

Diano still looked confused, but then understanding crept into his dazed eyes and his lips moved. Ico could not hear what he said over the continuing bombardment, but she had no need to. He had mouthed just two words. 'The magic.'

They were both standing facing the shuttered window, and their gaze returned to it now. Ico stepped forward, pushing herself against the pressure of sound. Her father made an ineffectual attempt to hold her back, perhaps fearing that she was about to open the shutters, but unable to bring himself to move. Ico had no intention of doing anything so stupid, but she had to see something. She needed her enemy to have a face.

Looking between the downward slanting battens of the shutters, she saw the plaza below divided into horizontal strips, but it was enough. Even in the silvery pre-dawn light it was obvious that there was quite a crowd. They were a mixed lot – men, women and children of varying degrees of wealth and status. Some wore worn and tattered clothes, while others were dressed in well-to-do finery, but their faces all bore the same exultant expression of purposeful hatred. That was what united them, that and their deranged 'music' – the chivaree.

This was the antithesis of art, a travesty, a deliberately violent and harsh expression of disapproval. It was the music of chaos. Their instruments were metal pans, pokers, cleavers, bones and wooden trays, all of which were clashed and hammered at random. Rude horns, a few drums and shrieking human voices added to the uproar, and the entire throng seemed to vibrate and sway, trapped in a hypnotic, febrile dance of their own making. Although they were locked in a sort of manic trance, most eyes were fixed upon the Maravedis house, watching for any sign of reaction – and ready to increase their efforts if any was seen.

At the centre of the mob stood the jongleur, in his gaudy, striped costume. He had led them here, capering through the streets at the head of a bizarre procession, and danced frenetically now, elastic limbs flying in all directions as if he were directing the pandemonium. He, like some of the drummers and horn players, was a professional who could be hired to orchestrate such demonstrations, and Ico wondered who his current employer was. The rest of the crowd were just along for the ride, for the excitement, whether or not they genuinely deplored Ico's supposed crime.

The pounding went on and on, but she found it impossible to retreat to another room, somewhere that might be marginally quieter. She too was held by the awful spell – and in any case, a small part of her was still observing keenly, registering faces. She had also noticed some soldiers, White Guards, on the periphery of the gathering, watching but making no move either to stop the protest or to join it.

At last Ico noted a small reduction in the level of noise, and wondered what this presaged. The drums were silent now and the jongleur was gesturing for quiet. His followers obeyed slowly and reluctantly until eventually a strange hush descended and all eyes turned to their figurehead. He now struck a comical pose, standing on tiptoe, one hand cupped by his ear as if he were listening for a response from the house itself.

'Oh, Ico!' he called. 'Ico Maravedis!' After a short pause, he turned aside and said in a stage whisper, 'Do you think she's still asleep?'

This prompted laughter and a few ribald comments, but the jongleur silenced the crowd with a slicing motion of his hands.

'Perhaps all that magic wore her out,' he suggested, to more laughter and some angry shouts. 'Or perhaps she's awake but hasn't the courage to face us.'

Don't rise to the bait, Ico told herself as she listened to the cries of agreement. He's trying to provoke you. But her hands rose to the catch on the shutters as if of their own volition.

Behind her, her father hissed, 'No!' and she froze, having forgotten that he was even there.

'Come away from the window,' he pleaded, but she still did not move.

'I should sing now!' the jongleur shouted. He began to chant in a falsetto voice, posturing ridiculously. His colleagues punctuated his words with the absurd buzzing sounds of mirlitons, adding to the comic effect.

'Making magic was so tiring,
But it set the dragons firing.
My name's Ico, I'm so clever,
Houses burning, well I never!'

A thud of drums brought the verse to an end, and silenced the laughter all around as the jongleur's expression changed from vacuous to coldly serious.

'But I won't!' he cried, 'because this really is no laughing matter.' He paused, gauging the angry muttering of the crowd. 'Our countrymen, our friends, our kin, have *died* because of the arrogance of a silly, spoilt girl.' The muttering rose again, much louder now. 'She is not brave enough to face us and see our anger!' he yelled. 'So let her *hear* it instead.'

The outburst of noise this time was like an explosion, shaking the walls of the house. The incensed chivaree banged and shouted with renewed vigour, apparently determined to continue for some time. Ico had taken an instinctive step back when the din started again, and she was glad of it a moment later when the shutters clattered and shook and a few pieces of debris fell into the room. A ragged cheer went up outside, rising above the racket. Someone had pulled a clod of earth from a nearby garden and hurled it at the window. Others followed, the soil bursting on impact, and a few stones ricocheted off the bedroom walls.

'Come away, Ico,' her father urged, tugging at the sleeve of her nightgown. 'Before the shutters give way.'

She went with him, her mind reeling, too shocked to resist. They took refuge in Diano's workshop, the inner room of the ground floor, where the noise was still loud but not so overwhelming. Ico stared at the familiar benches, the neatly racked tools, the storage boxes and ledgers, but nothing seemed real. Only the sound that was making the floor vibrate had any substance, and the words of the jongleur's song ran round and round in her head. She had expected some public censure, some misunderstanding, some anger . . . but not this. Not this.

Her father was speaking, but at first his words did not register. He was watching her anxiously and seemed to expect some response, but she had no idea what to say. She was still trembling.

'They'll be gone soon. The guards will send them on their way.'

Ico nodded, even though she knew the truth was nothing so comforting.

'You see now that Senator Kantrowe was right?' her father went on. 'Meddling with magic *is* dangerous.'

She wanted to deny it, to tell him not to be so stupid, but she could not. She didn't have the strength, and her tongue would not work. They stood quite still for a time, just listening, praying that the house would not collapse around them, and Ico finally began to recover her wits.

'How did that rabble know where you live?' Diano said.

Ico wondered how he could be so naive.

'It went on for more than an hour. I thought I'd go mad.'

'Couldn't you have snuck out?' Vargo asked. 'At the back?'

'And risk being seen?' Ico replied. 'They probably had lookouts posted, and that singer had got them so worked up . . .'

'Don't call him that,' he said quietly. 'Jongleurs are not musicians.'

It had been near midday before Ico had been able to escape, both from the house and from her father's unwanted advice. She had gone to the crumbling, abandoned concert hall, hoping to meet Vargo there, and had not been disappointed. He had been practising alone, as was his habit.

'So why did they leave in the end?'

'The guards moved them on,' she admitted. 'But not until they were running out of energy. Perhaps some of our neighbours complained.' She smiled weakly at the thought. 'There are soldiers everywhere now.'

'Are you . . .' he said awkwardly. 'Are you all right now?'

'Yes . . . I think . . . I'll admit it shook me up for a time, but . . .'

'You know this is only the beginning,' he said. 'If we go on . . .'

'We must go on!' she exclaimed. 'I'm more certain of that than ever.'

He almost asked her if she was really sure, but bit his tongue, realizing that it was a ridiculous question. He had never seen her more determined, in spite of her ordeal.

'Have you seen Andrin?' he asked instead.

'No. Not yet. I'm hoping he'll come here. If he did go to the house he had the good sense not to call, and I left your sign on the pavement. It won't take him long to figure it out. Soo's been looking for Ayo too, so he should find me, one way or another.'

'And until then you can make do with me,' Vargo remarked cheerfully.

'I couldn't ask for a better friend,' Ico replied fondly and kissed his cheek.

'Sometimes I wish he'd never come. Then I'd have you all to myself.'

'Don't say that,' she told him. 'Not even in jest.'

Vargo found he couldn't meet her eyes then, afraid not only of what he might see but of what he might give away. To cover his confusion he looked down at his lute and played a bright arpeggio. The notes echoed and whispered in the rafters above. When he glanced up again she was gazing through a hole in the roof at a small patch of blue sky.

'Is Soo coming?'

'No. I'm just thinking.'

'What about?'

'I'm wondering how we can beat them,' she answered. 'The Senate, I mean, Kantrowe and his lackeys.'

'By being right. And proving it,' Vargo said.

'We've done that and it made no difference! They have all the resources – money, people, power. What chance does the truth have against that?'

'Enough people know the truth in their hearts,' he said. 'They just don't want to admit it yet. They're scared – and you can't blame them for that.'

'But we're so insulated here in Teguise,' Ico complained. 'If they only knew how bad it is in the rest of the country . . .'

'They will. Eventually.'

'By then it might be too late. We have to tell them and *show* them that we can fight back.'

'A demonstration?'

'Of magic, yes. Right here in the city.'

'How? What?'

'Oh, don't bother me with details,' she snapped, then laughed. Vargo joined in, but her laughter had an edge of hysteria and he felt distinctly uneasy.

'I've no idea what we can do, but we must do *something*,' Ico persisted.

Vargo's eyes widened as a thought occurred to him.

'Why not in the very heart of the city?' he said. 'In the Senate itself.'

'You're mad.'

'No, just picture the scene,' he went on, clearly inspired now. 'What if we smuggled a live fireworm into the chamber and set it loose – only for Soo to swoop in through a window and drop a crystal, and for you to freeze it before it ate too many senators?'

Ico burst out laughing again, but did not get a chance to respond. Vargo was in full flow now.

'Think of the panic, the terror, and then the heartfelt gratitude. Ico Maravedis saves the entire Senate from gruesome death! I'd like to see them hush that up.'

'Knowing our luck,' Ico said, 'someone would have shut all the windows. Or we'd freeze the President to death.'

'Have you no faith?' Vargo exclaimed, grinning. 'We're the Firebrands, we can do anything.' He played a flashy sequence of chords, then a jaunty little tune, and ended by spreading both hands wide. From somewhere above came the sound of fluttering wings and a joyous call of hoo-poo-hoo. 'You see, even Ero agrees.'

'Leaving aside certain practical difficulties in this otherwise admirable plan,' Ico said, smiling, 'do you really think they'd let us get anywhere near the Senate building? They've always been one step ahead of us.'

Their merriment slowly faded in the shadow of that uncomfortable truth.

'I can't help feeling that the repercussions of our attack aren't over yet,' she said quietly. 'Even if the chivaree was organized by someone in the Senate, it was still a public reaction – or at least that's how it'll be seen. I want to know what the *official* response is going to be.'

'I—' Vargo began, but got no further.

At that moment the door crashed open and Andrin strode in, brandishing a crumpled poster that bore an official seal.

'It's unbelievable!' he exploded, in a voice half strangled by rage. 'Have you *seen* this?'

CHAPTER NINE

It took them a long time to calm Andrin down. This was in part because the proclamation had shocked them too, although both Ico and Vargo recovered some degree of objectivity rather more quickly than their friend. But the main reason was that Ico was still feeling tired and irritable after her own experiences that morning. She almost lost her temper several times but somehow managed to remain composed, recognizing her lover's greater need while at the same time resenting having to make the effort. She did not even mention the chivaree, knowing that this would cause Andrin's rage to spiral out of control, and Vargo too remained silent on the subject. Illogically, Ico wished that the musician would not be so tactful. If he had spoken up, then she would have been given an excuse to air her own grievances, to let Andrin know that he was not the only one who was suffering, but Vargo followed her lead, trying to dissuade his friend from doing anything foolish. Even though the white heat of Andrin's rage eventually grew somewhat cooler, he had only to look at the proclamation for it to flare up again.

'I mean, listen to this!' he exclaimed in disbelief. '"Magic is only to be used in pursuance of official business or such trade as is officially countenanced." What the hell does that mean?'

'Anything they want it to,' Vargo commented cynically.

'It's all couched in such *reasonable* terms,' Andrin went on furiously, 'but it's not! It makes me want to burn down the Vestry.'

'That's just what they want,' Ico said in alarm. In his present mood she knew Andrin was quite capable of arson. 'They're trying to provoke us into doing something stupid so they can punish us legitimately.'

'But we won't be able to do *anything* if we obey this,' he protested. 'Listen. "The crystals known as dragon's tears are to be considered restricted merchandise with immediate effect. Stocks must be registered, and any dealings without a specific licence from the Chamber of Defence will be subject to the same penalties as for other contraband." And this,' he added, stabbing at the text with an accusing finger. ' "Misusing magic . . ." *Misusing!* Can you believe that? ". . . to attack any living creature is prohibited." '

'They're making it perfectly clear that it's us they're warning,' Vargo said.

'There's no need to state the obvious!' Ico snapped, then, seeing his crestfallen expression, she relented and her tone softened. 'But it's even more devious than that. It doesn't mention fireworms, just lumps them in with camels, goats, dogs. Who could argue with that?'

'Fireworms aren't living creatures,' Andrin burst out. 'They're monsters, evil . . . things.' Words failed him.

'There's no mention of dragons, either,' Vargo said thoughtfully.

'There's no need,' Ico replied. 'They know everyone will jump to the same conclusion. We have to persuade people it's not true.'

'How?' Andrin demanded.

'I don't know.' Her reply was terse.

There was a short silence, broken only by the sound of rats

skittering under the floorboards. Andrin was the first to speak again, and Ico was relieved to hear that his voice was a little calmer now.

'The worst thing of all is this, right at the end,' he said, shaking the proclamation. '"Further measures will be taken if necessary." Sounds so innocuous, doesn't it?'

'But, in effect, it gives Kantrowe a free hand to do whatever he likes,' Vargo agreed.

'Exactly.'

There was another pause, longer this time, as they each contemplated this alarming prospect.

'So what do we do now?' Andrin asked eventually.

'I don't see that we have any choice,' Vargo replied. 'We have to lie low for a while.'

'And just give in to them?'

'Of course not,' Ico said. 'But what good will getting ourselves arrested do?'

'This is illegal!' Andrin exclaimed, waving the poster again.

'No, it's not,' she told him wearily. 'Look at it, look at the President's seal. It's the law. And the mere fact that you've taken it down already makes you a criminal.'

'They can't do this,' Andrin hissed, shaking his head. 'People won't stand for it. This is supposed to be a democracy. We came here to escape such tyranny.'

'That was a very long time ago,' Vargo pointed out.

'But it doesn't alter the principle!' he shot back. 'Has everyone forgotten our past? The tradition of universal magic is the touchstone of our society. It's fundamental to all our beliefs. How *dare* Kantrowe try to suppress it!'

'In times of trouble people aren't interested in the past,' Ico argued. 'They want solutions now.'

'But that's what we're offering!'

'Yes. And they'll realize it eventually, but for now Vargo is right. We have to be careful, learn to play Kantrowe at his own game.'

'I don't want to be like that corrupt bastard,' Andrin declared vehemently.

'And that's one of the reasons I love you,' Ico told him, smiling for the first time in what seemed like hours, 'but you must see the sense in lying low just now.'

'I don't see what sense there is in doing nothing,' he said stubbornly.

'It won't be for long,' she promised, 'but we must be discreet, at least for a while.'

Andrin said nothing, and clenched the poster in his fist. Then, changing his mind, he smoothed it out again, folded it up and slid it inside his shirt.

'Well, I'm not giving up,' he said coldly. 'I've got to do *something*, so you'd better decide whether you're with me or not.'

Ico was too horrified to respond. How could he doubt her loyalty? Was she to be condemned for speaking the truth? Although she knew it was his frustration and anger talking, his words were still like icy daggers in her heart.

Even Vargo was left speechless as Andrin turned away and strode towards the door.

'Where are you going?' Ico cried, finding her voice at last.

'To the docks,' he replied shortly, without turning round. 'I must do some work or I'll lose the job for good.'

'Promise me—' she began, but he was gone, and she was left staring fixedly at the empty doorway.

Ico was angry as well as worried by the time she returned home. Vargo had tried to reassure her, to persuade her that Andrin would not do anything reckless, but he had clearly had his own doubts about his friend's intentions. Neither of them had made any attempt to follow him, knowing that they could never match his pace while he was in this mood, and after a short while they had gone their separate ways.

Ico had walked quickly to the merchants' quarter. Several

people had glanced her way, including some of the soldiers who were still patrolling the area, but thankfully no one had tried to speak to her. She arrived determined to do her part to preserve what was left of the Firebrands' mission, and headed straight for her own small workshop, which adjoined her father's. To her dismay she found Diano standing at the entrance, waiting for her.

'Where have you been, young lady?'

'Out. Walking.'

When it became clear that she would offer nothing more, Diano's expression grew stern.

'I hope—'

'You hope what?' she cut in belligerently. 'That I haven't done anything foolish? That I'm not meeting the wrong sort of people? What?'

Diano could not meet his daughter's fierce glare, and he looked down at a letter in his hands. Ico's nerves were frayed almost beyond breaking point. She wanted to push past him into her study but held herself back, waiting for the response she knew would not come.

'Have you heard about the proclamation?' her father asked eventually.

'Yes.'

'Do you have any dragon's tears in your store-chests?'

'A few,' she admitted, knowing that he would never believe her if she said there were none. It would be too blatant a lie.

'I need to include them on my manifest,' he said, still not looking at her. 'The number of stones, their weight and quality.'

'I'll give you a list.'

'Perhaps we should do it together?' he suggested nervously.

'Why? Don't you trust me?' she asked sharply.

'Of course, but . . .'

'But what?'

'This is the law, Ico.'

'I've done nothing wrong, Father,' she pleaded, pushing her

anger aside in an attempt to appear convincing. 'I said I'll give you a list, and I will.'

He looked up at last, and she stared resolutely into his eyes until he gave way and nodded.

Left to her own devices, Ico worked quickly and by the time Atchen served them dinner she was able to give her father a short list of all the crystals that remained in her workshop. The rest had been secreted temporarily in her bedroom until a more secure hiding place could be found. It seemed to Ico to be a pitifully small cache but, at least for the moment, it was all the Firebrands had left in their armoury.

After Ico left him, Vargo knew he could no longer hope to concentrate on his music, and so for once in his haphazard life he acted decisively. Calling to Ero, he instructed the bird to fly to the docks, seek out Andrin and make sure that he was actually working, and not getting into trouble. The hoopoe had difficulty with the concept of work, but eventually seemed to understand and flew away. Vargo immediately set off himself, trudging through the dusty streets to the tavern where he rented a tiny attic room. The inn was called The Camel's Hump, and catered for a rough clientele, mostly dock rats and sailors from the nearby harbour. Even so, Vargo's music – with which he often paid his rent – had been known to quieten even the most unruly crowds. He was treated with a respect that bordered on awe by several burly regulars, who could be relied upon to protect him from any strangers inclined to violence or ridicule.

On this occasion he slipped in the rear entrance, via the kitchens, not wanting to be delayed. After locking away his precious lute, he left again and made his way inland through the maze of streets until he came to a ramshackle area in the shadow of the city's western wall. The people who lived here were a strange and shifting group, comprised of all kinds of misfits, artists, wanderers and criminals. Most of the shelters were of flimsy construction, as if emphasizing the temporary nature of the residents, but even by the general standards of the quarter, Famara Ye's home was especially rickety. There were horses in other parts of the city who lived in greater luxury than she did. Most of the citizens of Teguise would have considered the crooked wooden building to be no more than a hovel, and yet Vargo loved the place – and the woman who lived there.

She was his mentor, the one person who had recognized his latent talent and, sometimes at great cost to herself, had encouraged and nurtured his music and thus enabled him to escape from the brutal poverty of the orphanage. He owed her more than he could ever repay – even if she had been willing to accept anything – and he still went to her whenever he was troubled or in need of advice. For him she was an oracle, a source of wisdom and comfort, as well as an incomparable teacher.

Famara had many talents. In the old days she would have been called a wizard but that title, once a mark of great respect, had become discredited and had almost fallen out of use. She was one of the few who still retained much of the ancient magical lore and, had she been of an entirely different character, could have used her skills to acquire both status and wealth. As it was she used them simply for the benefit of others and was quite content to stay in her own poor home, nearly destitute but never friendless. Vargo was not the only one in her debt, and those she had helped did not forget.

In her time Famara had also been a remarkable musician, and had passed on many of her secrets to pupils she found worthy. She was old and infirm now, and no longer performed herself, but she took pleasure in her protégés and scolded them unmercifully if they ever squandered or abused their gifts. It was one of Vargo's greatest regrets that he had never known her in her prime. Her voice was like gravel now, a throaty rasp that she rarely raised above a whisper, but as a young woman she had reputedly sung with a pure tone that could charm birds from the trees, reduce grown men to tears and add lustre to the stars. Her fingers were gnarled with arthritis and she could no longer play her beloved lute but, even so, on the rare occasions when she could not get her ideas across verbally, she would grab her pupil's instrument and send a few exquisite phrases spinning into the air. Each time she did this, pain made her breathing ragged and she took a long time to recover, but everyone who heard her was staggered by the artistic alchemy of those tortured hands. Vargo knew he could never hope to match her as she had been at her peak, but her inspiring example had made him resolve to be the best that he could. Every time he played, no matter what the occasion, his music was dedicated to her.

When Vargo reached the shack he knocked softly on the wall, then pulled aside the heavy blanket that acted as her door and peered within. As his eyes grew accustomed to the gloom he saw a thin and rumpled shape lying on the truckle bed on the far side of the room. Famara lay so still that for one terrible moment he thought she might be dead, but then she stirred and two bright, pale grey eyes peered back at him.

'Come in,' she croaked, then coughed. 'You're always welcome here, Vargo. You know that.'

'Are you all right?' he asked, hesitating still.

'Of course,' she replied truculently. 'Old people sleep at odd times, that's all.' Her words were harsh but she was smiling, so Vargo tied back the curtain and went inside. Famara sat up and then edged her legs over the side of the bed, wincing as she did so.

'Can I get you something?' he asked solicitously.

'Stop fussing and tell me why you're here,' she replied. 'What's happening in the world?'

Vargo could tell that she was in pain, and wondered why she never used her talent to heal herself. Many others had benefited from this aspect of her magical abilities, and there was a jar full of dragon's blood crystals on the shelf behind her. These translucent red stones were formed when drops of resin from the cauldron trees solidified in air. These stunted but tenacious trees grew only in the firelands and the dragon's blood crystals, like amber, were known to have great healing properties when handled by a wizard. As always, Vargo was dismayed by Famara's neglect of her own wellbeing, but he knew better than to argue with her, especially when she was in her present belligerent mood.

'A proclamation has been issued,' he said, coming straight to the point. 'Have you heard about it?'

Famara shook her head slowly, her wispy grey hair floating about her head.

'I've not much time for politics,' she remarked.

'This one is about magic,' he said, and went on to tell her everything he could remember about the decree.

Famara listened in silence, only the rising colour in her cheeks and the glint in her eyes betraying her growing indignation. When Vargo explained what had precipitated the Senate's action, the old woman's expression grew even more concerned.

'Well, this is a pretty pickle you've got yourselves into,' she commented.

'I know. The question is, what do we do now?'

Famara gave no sign of having heard him. Her mind was far away, pursuing other thoughts.

'Bloody cheek,' she muttered.

'What?'

'There was a time – and not so very long ago at that – when we were respected, even honoured.'

Vargo assumed that she was referring to wizards, and did not interrupt.

'Healers, advisors, practical men and women who did what others could not, by sheer force of will. Who was it solved the problems of irrigation, found the underground streams and lakes? Who was it discovered the treasures of this land and demonstrated their power? Who talked with the dragons, rode the air, interpreted omens?'

She looked at her visitor then, but he knew she neither needed nor expected any answer.

'Magic is a force of nature, like the wind or the tides,' she went on. 'All we could ever do was focus it with our minds, give it substance and purpose. But that took training and discipline as well as talent. Is it any wonder the lore is dying out, when there are easier ways to live, ways that don't involve personal sacrifice?'

Her words were tinged with bitterness now, and Vargo felt he must say something.

'Some of us are trying.'

'Yes. You're a good boy, Vargo, and I wish there were more like you. But it's too late now. You can't turn back time. It had gone too far even when I was a little girl. The last of the great wizards was long dead, even then.' She paused, sighing. 'It's all so different now. Even the birds remember it better than we do. No one understands what a great privilege it is to be linked, no one. And that's the least of it. We're all so ignorant. And now it's come to this – a proclamation!'

Her distress was obvious. For Famara the world had become an emptier, less interesting place. Vargo could think of nothing to say.

'Perhaps they were always bound to win in the end,' she mumbled, 'these men who think laws and money and possessions rule their lives, who call themselves realists when truly they deny half of what is real. And they drag us down with them—'

'No. There must be a way . . .' he cut in, dismayed by her pessimism. 'We can't give in without a struggle.'

Famara smiled weakly.

'You're right. Don't listen to the ramblings of a foolish old woman. All is not lost yet.'

'So what should we do?' he asked, encouraged.

'I haven't the faintest idea.'

Her frankness all but demolished his remaining hopes, and they sat in silence for a while.

'Play for me,' she said at last, indicating her own lute with a crooked finger.

Vargo did as he was told, picking out a quiet melody of his own invention.

'I taught you well,' she commented as the last note died away. 'Now play something more lively.'

He obeyed, weaving intricate dancing rhythms from the strings.

'I shall have a word with Marco,' Famara stated determinedly over the music.

Vargo stopped playing.

'Marco Guadarfia? The President?' Although the idea seemed incredible, he could picture her doing it. Even dressed in rags Famara was the equal of any man, no matter how exalted.

'He's an old friend of mine,' she explained. 'He'll listen, if his mind hasn't been addled by the fools about him.'

'I don't think he's the true centre of power in the Senate any more,' Vargo said carefully.

'I've guessed as much,' she replied, 'but he used to value good advice once and he might again. The title must still count for something.'

'How will you—?' he began, but Famara signalled for quiet.

'I need to dream,' she said. 'And you need to go. Your bird has been looking for you for some time and is getting fretful. I'll guide him here, but he'll only talk to you.'

Vargo did not question her. Laying the lute aside reverently, he kissed the old woman's soft cheek and slipped outside, closing the curtain behind him. Her voice, muffled and faint now, following him.

'Never stop dreaming, Vargo. Never. Dreamers are the only true realists.'

CHAPTER TEN

Ico was dreaming. She was being pursued by a swarm of singing fireworms, running through narrow city streets that should have been familiar but which had become an empty labyrinth, full of unexpected dead ends, serpentine twists and absurdly sharp corners. Music rang discordantly in her ears, making it impossible to think. Although she ran as fast as she could, the swarm was gaining steadily. The doors and windows she passed were all securely locked and shuttered against her but then, above the tumult, she heard a faint scratching and turned towards it in sudden hope. Tired and afraid, she dragged herself towards the sound, knowing it meant escape.

She awoke in the pitch darkness of her bedroom to find that she could still hear the scratching. She sat up, her heart pounding, with all sorts of horrors crowding her brain. Was someone trying to break in at her window? Was this a prelude to a second assault by the chivaree? The noise was certainly coming from the shutters, but seemed too tentative for it to be a burglar. Anyone who had gone to the trouble of climbing up to the window ledge would surely not let a few wooden struts hold him up for long.

The scratching stopped for a moment and Ico held her breath, then jumped as someone tapped sharply three times. She made a quick mental inventory of the room, trying to think of something she could use as a weapon, and then told herself not to be ridiculous. If there really was an enemy out there, he would be vulnerable; one push would send him crashing to the pavement below.

The tapping was repeated, but it seemed now to be polite rather than aggressive. Who could it be? She almost called out but thought better of it, not wanting to reveal that she was awake. Instead she slipped quietly from her bed and tiptoed across the room until faint bars of silver moonlight showed her that she had reached the window.

There was a flicker of movement outside and the shutters vibrated again. After the second tap Ico threw the catch and flung the shutters wide, hoping to catch the intruder off guard. A huge white shape reared up, filling the entire frame of the window with startled movement, and Ico stifled a scream. Then – as the motion settled and the shape resolved itself – she breathed a huge sigh of relief. Ayo stood upright on the ledge, his massive wings no longer fluttering for balance but folded into his sides. He looked like a ghost, his feathers glimmering softly in the faint light, but his eyes were sharply focused and faintly accusing.

'What are you doing here?' Ico whispered, then leant out past him to scan the plaza, expecting to see Andrin. The square was empty and still and she drew back, feeling disappointed and annoyed. Ayo dipped his square head, his hooked bill seeming to point down. Ico looked and saw a scrap of cloth that lay on the window sill next to the eagle's fearsome talons.

'Did you come to bring me this?' she asked, picking it up.

Ayo could not reply directly, but gave her a clear enough answer by launching himself into the air and flying away with heavy, inelegant wingbeats. He had evidently completed his mission.

After the darkness of her room, the moonlight seemed almost bright and Ico had no trouble reading the few words that had been daubed onto the cloth. 'Talk on the roof' it said and underneath, as though it were an afterthought, the single word 'Please'. It was an apology, and Ico smiled, her spirits lifting. They could never stay angry with each other for long, and on this occasion Andrin's need for reconciliation had produced an even more imaginative response than usual.

Stopping only to pull a shawl round her shoulders, Ico made her way out on to the landing, where a lamp burnt low. Her father had gone out that evening to attend an emergency meeting of the Jewellers' Guild and had evidently not yet returned. That meant there was only Atchen to worry about, and as her quarters were on the ground floor there was little chance of disturbing her. Even so Ico moved carefully, her bare feet making no sound on the cool marble, and climbed the ladder that led to the skylight. Pulling back the bolt, she pushed the trapdoor upwards and emerged on to the flat roof.

Andrin was waiting for her, his face pale and beautiful in the starlight, and she felt a surge of affection that turned swiftly to desire as he took her hand and lifted her up beside him. Held tightly in his arms, she instantly felt safe and knew that she was loved.

'I'm sorry . . . for what I said,' he whispered awkwardly. 'I should never—'

'Shhh.' She had heard all she needed.

'You know you mean more to me than anything, more than all of this,' he persisted. 'If the sun never shone again I'd still be happy as long as I was with you.'

'I know,' she said softly. 'I feel the same way.'

'Even when—?'

'Enough!' she commanded and silenced him with a kiss.

'I have a surprise for you,' he told her when they eventually drew apart.

He led her across the roof to where a rug lay spread out next to the eastern parapet. Beside it were a bottle, a goblet and several small wooden dishes filled with food.

'A midnight feast,' he announced. When she didn't respond, he added anxiously, 'Are you hungry? I've got some of your favourite things.'

Ico found to her surprise that she was ravenous. She had had little appetite at dinner, and in fact had given food little thought during the last few days. Now, presented with this typically romantic gesture, she found her taste buds reawakening.

'This is wonderful. You're spoiling me.'

'That's my job,' he replied, grinning.

They sat down and as Andrin poured wine, Ico inspected the food. There were chunks of bread, small fillets of pickled fish, slices of cheese, tiny tomatoes and apricots. She wondered idly how he had managed to get it all up to the roof. It was not the first time they had met there, but she still did not know how he was able to climb up without being seen or heard by anyone.

'Try this,' he said, handing her the cup.

She sipped, and shivered with pleasure. The wine was dark, fragrant and delicious. She knew at once that it was one of Tiguafaya's finest vintages and that its price was way beyond what Andrin could afford, but she had no intention of asking where he had got it. There was a good chance that it had been stolen, but she did not care.

'Wonderful,' she repeated.

They ate in silence for a time, feeding each other choice morsels and taking it in turns to drink from the goblet. Ico savoured every mouthful and felt a warm contentment spreading through her. With all the terrible things that had been happening recently, and with the uncertainty that hung over their future, it was reassuring to know that there could still be moments like this.

Neither of them spoke until they were eating the last of the apricots.

'Why didn't you tell me about the chivaree?' he asked softly.

'It didn't seem important,' she replied, picking the least contentious of the answers that had sprung to mind. 'We had other things to think about.'

'And it would have made me even more angry,' he added, with uncharacteristic insight.

Ico did not bother to deny this, but instead took his hand and squeezed it.

'The last thing I wanted was for you to do something stupid on my behalf.'

'I can't think of a better reason,' he told her. 'When I think about those moronic—'

'They did me no harm,' she said quickly. 'They were just being used, like everyone else.'

He nodded, though the resentment still smouldered in his eyes.

'Why pick on you?' he asked.

'It's obvious, really. I was the one Chinero recognized and my family is well known.'

'I suppose so,' Andrin conceded morosely. 'But it's still not fair.'

Ico could only marvel at his protectiveness. Considering his own loss, how could he decide that her losing a few hours sleep was unfair? She would gladly have put up with much worse to save him from the grief of Mendo's death, but she knew better than to express such thoughts.

'How did you find out?' she asked instead.

'It's being gossiped about everywhere. You know what the docks are like, rumours spread faster than rats.'

'So you did go to work then?'

'Yes. I've got to keep that job, so I have to show my face every so often. And it kept me out of trouble,' he added sheepishly. 'I thought you'd know that already.'

'How could I?'

'From Vargo? I saw Ero at one of the quays, spying on me. That bird doesn't know how to be inconspicuous. I assumed Vargo had sent him to check that I really was working.'

'He didn't tell me,' Ico said, wishing she had thought of asking Soo to do the same.

'He's a good friend,' Andrin commented.

'The best,' she agreed.

They lay on their backs, side by side, watching the slow tide of stars and listening to the faint sounds of the slumbering city.

'I'd better go,' Andrin said eventually. His efforts had been intended purely as an apology and although he ached to touch her, he would wait for her to take the initiative – if she chose to do so. But it had been some time since Ico had had any doubts about how the night would end.

'Not yet,' she said firmly, and began to unbutton his shirt.

Ico was woken by unexpected noise a second time that night, but this time it came from inside the house. She had returned to her bedroom and fallen almost immediately into a deep and dreamless sleep, while Andrin disappeared into the night as silently and mysteriously as he had arrived. But now, less than an hour later, she was awake again and listening to footsteps coming up the stairs. Her father, ordinarily the quietest of men, was making no attempt to move silently. Not only that, but she heard him muttering to himself as he passed her door.

Impulsively she jumped out of bed and went out on to the landing. Diano stopped in his tracks and slowly turned round to face her. Even in the dim light she could see that his face was flushed, his eyes unnaturally bright, and he was moving very carefully, with an exaggerated grace. At the same time Ico caught the strong, unmistakable scent of rum and saw the stains on his clothes. His unspoken motto of moderation in all things had obviously been set aside for once. He was hopelessly, resoundingly drunk.

'What're you lookin' at?' he asked defiantly.

'Are you all right?'

Diano laughed, but it was a far from happy sound.

'Oh, yes! I've jus' been through the mos' humiliatin' night of my entire life, so *of course I'm all right!*' He was shouting now and Ico felt first alarm, then pity and finally anger.

'What happened?' she asked coolly.

'The Guild meetin' was a shambles. Ev'ryone complainin', shoutin' an' screamin'. Paperwork! Liberty! Outrage! Half of 'em blamin' the Senate, an' half of 'em blamin' me.'

'You? Why you?'

'Because of my daughter!' he yelled, waving an unsteady finger in her direction. 'An' how'm I supposed to defend you when you're so damnably proud of what you did? Answer me that, my girl.'

'I can defend myself.'

'Can you?' He laughed again. 'Can you really? Well tha's good, because I've had enough.'

'Obviously,' she replied caustically. 'Your solution is to get drunk, is it?'

'At least then I can try and forget this mess,' he shot back. Then suddenly all the fight went out of him and he buried his face in his hands. 'Oh gods, what have I done? It would never have come to this if your mother was still alive.'

'At least she would have supported me, instead of running away,' Ico snapped, not sure whether this was the truth, but needing to punish his betrayal.

'Am I such a bad father? Did you have to disgrace me so?' he cried.

'I've done nothing—'

'Then why is all this happening?' he demanded. 'The chivaree and this accursed proclamation are just the beginning. Do you know what they're saying now?' All at once he appeared completely sober, even though he was obviously close to tears.

'What?' Ico asked, as her heart filled with foreboding.

'If there are any further eruptions, then there are various . . . things that they'll do to try and appease the dragons.'

'That's absurd! What things?'

For a few moments her father did not answer. Shame and bewilderment showed on his face as the alcohol raced around his brain.

'All sorts of things,' he mumbled. 'But surely it's just rumours. The Senate would never allow it.'

'Allow what?'

'Sacrifices,' he replied in a hollow, tortured whisper. 'Human sacrifices.'

CHAPTER ELEVEN

Jon Zophres had experienced – and mastered – more professions in his thirty-six years than most people could have managed in two complete lifetimes. At various times he had been a seaman, a slave-trader, a wrestler, a mercenary, an explorer, a gambler and a spy. He had seen and done things others only dreamed about, always restless, always learning, but now he had returned to his first love, the sea. He was captain of his own ship, the *Dawn Song*, the fastest and most beautiful vessel to sail the Inner Seas, and he had recently undertaken a delicate task, one which appealed to his inquisitive spirit and which would test his hard-won skills to the full. As Kantrowe's envoy he would be free to use his own initiative – as long as he produced results. It was an invigorating challenge.

Zophres did not need to work. Having already accumulated a substantial fortune he could, if he had wished, have spent his remaining days in pampered luxury in any one of several city ports. He would not have lacked for company. He was in excellent health, handsome, witty and rich. He was also known to be lucky. Adventures had a way of following him around, and although some of these had inevitably involved violence – he had seen more than his fair share of battles and had killed many foes with his own hands – he had never even been scratched. There was not a scar anywhere upon his lithe, well-muscled body, and this well-known fact contributed to his reputation as invincible. No one in their right mind picked a fight with Jon Zophres.

In his whole life he had been hurt only once, many years ago, and then it had not been by a fist or blade but by the invisible weapons of passion. A woman, the only one he had ever loved, had scorned and rejected him, openly betrayed his devotion and laughed in his face. He had vowed then never to allow himself to become so vulnerable again, and he had kept his promise. Women were now no more than necessary playthings, to be used, discarded and then forgotten. In spite of this, there was never any shortage of female volunteers to share his bed. But when it came to the important things in his life – voyaging, sport, conversation and drinking – he preferred the company of men. And men such as those who sat beside him now were especially welcome, for they saw themselves as his equals and had almost as many tales to tell.

To his right was Galan Zarzuelo, whose name was synonymous with piracy in many lands. It had been his father, also called Galan, who had led the pirate fleet which had defeated Admiral Madri's Tiguafayan navy some thirty years earlier, but if anything the younger man's reputation was even more fearsome. Anyone who made the mistake of calling him 'junior' was liable to find himself forced to eat part of his own body – an ear perhaps for a single slip, his liver if he were stupid enough to repeat the offence.

To Zophres' left was the second pirate chieftain, Vicent Agnadi, known to all as the Lawyer. He had acquired this title because one of the tales – and there were many – about his origins claimed that he had earned his living as a legal advocate before turning to a more stimulating and rewarding career. He had retained it because of his way of enforcing his own unique brand of justice upon his enemies, or even upon any of his own men who disobeyed his wishes.

Both men were deeply suntanned, dressed in colourful but serviceable clothes and, like most of their men, wore their hair long. Their only distinguishing marks were their jewellery. Zarzuelo wore a huge gold brooch of intricate design at his neck and several rings on his fingers. Agnadi had a necklace of sharks' teeth, and a silver amulet on each wrist. Both carried jewelled daggers in their belts. The sailors ranged behind them all wore swords, but had been forbidden to draw them on pain of death while their leaders were in conference.

The meeting should have been attended by the third leader of the 'brethren of the islands', as the pirates liked to call themselves, but the Barber had chosen to stay away. Zophres was disappointed by his absence. No one even knew the Barber's real name, and he was the most enigmatic of all the buccaneers.

The serious talking had not yet begun; their host, Zarzuelo, had organized some entertainment. The three men sat side by side in carved wooden thrones on the high stern deck of the pirate's flagship, the notorious, black-sailed *Night Wolf*. From this vantage point they had an unobstructed view over most of the lagoon, which was enclosed by a broken circle of islands formed by a volcanic eruption more than a thousand years before. Many other ships, including the *Dawn Song*, were moored in these quiet waters and all eyes were currently focused on a flat square raft of bare wood that floated in open water in the midst of the fleet. Two outriggers lay at opposite sides and in the bows of each stood a man who stared ahead, ignoring the oarsmen behind him.

'This is something of a grudge match.' Zarzuelo was obviously enthusiastic. 'Something to do with a woman, no doubt. I'm told they are evenly matched, so it should be a good fight.'

Zophres nodded, while Agnadi merely smiled as though he itched to say something but resisted the temptation. Their host raised his glass, which was full of the honey-flavoured rum he had been sharing with his guests. Those watching in the boats saw the signal and both craft shot forward, then steadied so that the two contestants were able to step aboard the raft simultaneously. As the boats withdrew to an agreed distance, the two men, now alone in their arena, eyed each other, their stout legs set wide, arms flexed in readiness for the first moves.

From a distance they could almost have been twins. Both were fair haired, both tall and heavily built. They were unarmed and wore only knee breeches, their oiled muscles shining in the strong sunlight. They began moving, circling warily, their bare feet testing the boards and the motion of the raft as they shifted their weight. Some spectators shouted encouragement to one champion or the other, but the combatants paid no attention. They were intent only on each other.

'They fight for the honour of their crews?' Zophres asked, seeing that the respective outriggers bore the names of two of Zarzuelo's ships, anchored nearby.

'Yes. Such rivalries increase efficiency, wouldn't you say, Vicent?'

'Perhaps,' Agnadi replied noncommittally, his eyes never leaving the spectacle.

'Are there rules?' Zophres enquired.

Zarzuelo laughed.

'The brethren of the islands do not live by rules,' he stated proudly. 'We are the only truly free men.'

'Then how is the winner decided?'

'When one of them is in undisputed possession of the raft.'

'So all they have to do is throw the other into the water?'

'And ensure they do not climb out again,' his host replied, smiling.

'I see,' the envoy said, his interest rising as the gladiators drew closer, feinting and testing each other's reflexes. 'And if one yields?'

'It is not usual,' Zarzuelo answered complacently. 'The boats will only go to their aid if they are unconscious in the water, and then it may be too late.'

'Too late?'

'There are sharks in the lagoon. It adds a little spice to the contest.' He sounded smug.

'You'll see the fight take on a new urgency if either draws blood,' Agnadi added with an expectant grin.

A shout went up as the contenders made first contact. One of them had ducked low and dived towards his opponent, intent on grabbing hold of his breeches and throwing him. The other had evaded the thrust, and got in a blow with his fist to the back of the aggressor's neck before losing his balance. Both men fell heavily, making the platform rock in the water, but they were on their feet again in an instant.

From that moment on the contest was relentless, each attack countered and used as a springboard for the next assault. The speed and brutality were impressive, but eventually the violence took its toll and the pace slackened until trickery and deception took the place of speed and strength. By then each man was clearly bruised and battered from all the punches, kicks and falls, but they still seemed evenly matched. Then, after a brief wrestling match, one man landed awkwardly and there was a crack that was heard even above the cries of his onlookers. As he rose to his feet his right arm hung uselessly at his side, obviously broken. His opponent moved in to take advantage and landed two vicious blows to the face, producing spurts of blood from nose and mouth. Concerted groans were heard from the wounded hero's ship, while his opponent's comrades cheered. The end was only a matter of time now.

The cheers and groans died away to a whisper before being renewed – but in reverse. For a moment Zophres could not make out what had caused this change of attitude, but then a sudden movement caught his eye and he understood. In the injured man's good hand there was now a blade, so thin that it seemed no more than a sliver of light – but deadly nonetheless. It had evidently been secreted in the man's breeches and only brought out at a time of absolute need.

There are no rules here, Zophres thought, resolving to keep his wits about him at all times. If such a manoeuvre was not only condoned but actively admired, then he was indeed in dangerous company. The pirate chiefs were now leaning forward eagerly, anxious for the kill, and their wish was soon granted. The unarmed man put up a spirited fight, but his anger at being tricked made him careless, and even facing a one-armed foe he was soon bleeding profusely. The knife completed its work and the victor kicked the torn body of his adversary into the water, where no one but the sharks paid it any attention.

'Excellent, excellent,' Zarzuelo commented approvingly, and looked directly at the envoy.

'Most enlightening,' Zophres agreed, and knew that they understood each other.

'To business then,' their host decreed. 'We'll go to my cabin.'

Under normal circumstances the details of Kantrowe's proposal could have been laid out in a few minutes. However, Zophres knew that with these men such an approach would not do. They required drama, ceremony and elaboration, not a business meeting, and he had done his best to oblige. They had listened quietly for the most part, only interrupting to make inconsequential remarks or add titbits of gossip, but now that the envoy had come to the end of his proposal, the real work would begin.

'When an arrangement has clear benefits for both parties,' he concluded, 'I can see no reason for delaying an agreement.'

Agnadi clearly wanted to speak, but tactfully left their host to reply first. Zophres had taken stock of the two pirates' characters and decided that the Lawyer was the more dangerous, even though he commanded smaller forces. He was certain that the shrewder questions would come from him.

'I think perhaps Senator Kantrowe does not understand us very well,' Zarzuelo said gravely. 'We are free men.' With a sweep of his arms he indicated the unlimited scope of their independence. 'We are not bean counters or tax collectors, to be content with a *percentage* of other men's enterprise. What are you offering that we cannot take for ourselves?'

'This arrangement would enhance your freedom, not deny it,' the envoy replied confidently. 'Apart from those exceptions I outlined, your dominion would be absolute, unchallenged. What greater freedom could you want? We do not seek to deny your way of life, but to enrich it – in every way. The obligations you undertake will be paid for in good faith, to the benefit of all. What free man would not choose a measure of luxury to set beside adventure?'

Zarzuelo nodded, trying to appear wise, but the uncertainty in his eyes betrayed him. Although he had the wits and guile of a hunting animal, his politics were defined by swords, not words. In the silence that followed, Zophres was acutely aware of their surroundings, a mixture of ostentation and barbarism. The cabin was furnished richly, with gilt and silk much in evidence, but nailed to the wall were two human skulls and the air in the room was foul – a bestial stench overlaid with a decaying sweetness that had turned Zophres' stomach when he first came in. In the corner of the room was a cage containing a parrot, with brilliant green and red plumage, which had blinked once as the men entered, then apparently gone to sleep as if bored with the entire affair.

After the silence had lasted long enough for his intervention to be acceptable, Agnadi cleared his throat.

'You've not answered Galan's question,' he said mildly.

Zarzuelo winced slightly at the familiar use of his forename. He had often wished to acquire an appropriately grand or bloody nickname but, in spite of his efforts, it had not come about. In his annoyance at this apparent snub – wasn't he a greater leader than the Lawyer or the Barber? – he had surreptitiously tried to promote himself as 'King of the Pirates', but his efforts had been in vain. His followers were genuinely too independent to countenance a king of any kind, and all he had earned were a few other names that were never repeated in his hearing.

'What question?' the envoy asked innocently.

'What are you offering us that we cannot take for ourselves?' the Lawyer repeated.

'Power – and a share of what you cannot take, the wealth of Teguise itself.'

'You think Teguise is beyond the reach of our sword arms?' Zarzuelo asked indignantly.

'Our defences are strong,' Zophres replied, choosing his words with care. 'It would cost you a great deal to gain a fraction of what I am offering you.'

'What guarantees do we have that Kantrowe can deliver all he has promised?' Agnadi went on. 'He is not President, after all.'

'The Senator is the power behind the Presidency. Guadarfia is old now and reliant on younger, bolder men. Kantrowe will make good all his promises if you deal with him fairly. But he would make a formidable enemy.'

Both pirate chiefs laughed, but it seemed a token effort, something they felt they ought to do.

'Threats?' Zarzuelo enquired.

'Not at all,' the envoy replied smoothly. 'I am merely trying to allay your doubts. There are uncertainties in your position, after all.'

'What do you mean by that?' his host demanded.

'You two have always been rivals. How can we be sure you can work together?'

'If it is worthwhile, that will not be a difficulty,' the Lawyer replied.

'We're here, aren't we?' Zarzuelo added.

'And the Barber is not,' Zophres pointed out. 'Without his cooperation can *you* guarantee your half of the bargain?' He knew he had taken a risk in mentioning the Barber's name, but it was worth it to see the momentary flash of anger in even Agnadi's calm eyes.

'He will not stand against us,' Zarzuelo stated in a tightly controlled voice.

'And nor will Senator Kantrowe's colleagues be able to interfere. The reins of power are in his hands now. We are both in a position of strength. Doesn't it make sense to be allies?'

'We hear some of your opponents at home are using magic,' the Lawyer said.

Zophres was taken by surprise, but recovered quickly.

'Magic has always been part of our people's heritage, but it is not a significant factor now. What remains is a pale shadow of former glories. And we are taking steps to ensure that what is left will soon be in our hands.'

'Tell me more,' Agnadi said, grinning.

'It's really not important,' the envoy went on. 'But if you wish I should be able to report more fully the next time we meet.'

'*If* we meet,' Zarzuelo put in.

Zophres bowed his head in acknowledgement.

'I sincerely hope we do.'

'And how is your battle with the fireworms going?' the Lawyer asked.

'It's under control. But one of the advantages of this agreement would be to allow us to divert more of our resources to the problem before the menace spreads. It's in no one's interest to have any part of the country overrun by these creatures,' he added with heavy emphasis.

Zarzuelo and Agnadi glanced at each other and nodded, the first sign of genuine cooperation that Zophres had noted.

'We have enough for now,' their host said.

'Then I will return to my ship and let you discuss the matter,' the envoy said, recognizing his dismissal. 'Send word if you need further clarification.'

'We should need no help in reaching our decision,' Zarzuelo replied, as if resentful of the implication, 'if everything you have told us is true.'

'I am a man of my word.'

'Good, because should there be any dispute I have a record of everything that has been said here.'

Both the other men looked at him in surprise, and Zarzuelo smiled.

'Olivina,' he said, 'what was our guest's answer to the question about fireworms?'

The parrot opened its eyes and shuffled sideways on its perch. '"It's under control,"' it began, even mimicking Zophres' tone. '"But one of the advantages—"'

'Enough.'

The bird fell silent. For a few moments all was quiet, apart from the natural creaking of the ship, then all three men burst out laughing. It had not even occurred to Zophres that the parrot might be linked, let alone that it had the unique ability to recall and re-create human speech. He laughed as if he did not have a care in the world, but privately he was cursing his own stupidity. He had underestimated Zarzuelo and that could prove fatal. Even the Lawyer had been taken aback.

Some time later, when Zarzuelo was alone in his cabin, he turned to the bird again.

'Well, Olivina. What do you think? Was our good friend Jon Zophres telling the truth all the time?'

'No,' the parrot replied. 'Some of what he said was lies.'

'Good,' the pirate said. 'I would not trust a man who told the whole truth at a first meeting.'

CHAPTER TWELVE

They came in ones and twos, creeping silently along darkened alleys when once they would have walked openly in larger groups, talking and laughing. In the two days since the proclamation had been posted a new atmosphere had enveloped the city, and it had affected the Firebrands more than anyone else. They were cautious and afraid now, aware that many were blaming them for their country's ills. Strangers were regarded with suspicion, soldiers with outright horror, while some of the youngsters even found themselves questioning their own beliefs. This self-examination had a polarizing effect. While a few of the Firebrands began to lose faith, others became convinced that what they were doing was not only right but absolutely necessary. Opposition had only made them more determined and, in some cases, fanatical. The situation was becoming more volatile by the hour, and it was a relief when the message from Andrin was finally broadcast, calling them all to meet at the old concert hall three hours after sunset. Now at least they could clear the air and settle what they were going to do.

Under normal circumstances the Firebrands rarely gathered together in large numbers. There was no formal structure to their organization but, as was natural for a group formed by common interests and opinions, there were several sets of friends who saw each other regularly. Even when it was necessary for them to act as a whole – such as the preparations for and execution of the attack on the fireworms – they tended to work in smaller teams. Go-betweens kept everyone up to date with what they needed to know. Overall the Firebrands were a disparate bunch, with many diverse personalities and from all levels of society. They were united by a dissatisfaction with the way the country was being run, together with a fascination for magic and legend, and the fact that almost all of them were among those few chosen by the birds to be linked. Many proudly wore flashes of colour on their clothes, designating the species of their avian partners, but in the last few days all but the most wilful had kept these hidden from view.

Andrin's summons had asked them all to proceed with caution and to ensure that they were not followed, an element of clandestine behaviour that had excited some and frightened others. The derelict hall was ideal for their purpose, standing amid other dilapidated and untenanted buildings in an area ordinarily deserted after dark. Soo and several other birds of prey circled in the darkness above, using their excellent night vision to watch for any unwanted intruders. Technically there was nothing illegal about what the Firebrands were doing, but in the present climate it was better not to take any chances.

In the event it seemed that there was no attempt to infiltrate or spy upon the meeting and, with the birds still keeping a lookout, Andrin decided it was time to begin. As he stood up, thirty or so faces immediately turned towards him expectantly. It was less than a third of their total number, but he knew that several small groups had sent representatives to argue their case rather than risk them all attending. Others, especially many of those who lived beyond the walls of Teguise, had simply been unable to get there in time. But his fears about being deserted had proved groundless. There were relatively few unexplained absences. Even so, it seemed a pitifully small gathering when he considered the forces pitted against them.

As Andrin took out the poster, unfolded it and held it up, a hush fell upon the hall. Even the birds in the rafters grew silent and still.

'Is there anyone here who hasn't read this?' he asked. Then, realizing that several of his companions could neither read nor write, he added quickly, 'Or been told what it says?'

No one spoke. They were all familiar with the proclamation, but seeing it there in the dull candlelight heightened the already considerable tension.

'It's pretty obvious that they're trying to put us out of business,' Andrin went on. 'The question is, what are we going to do about it?'

'Fight back,' one hothead stated promptly.

'What with?' someone else queried. 'We haven't even got any crystals now, thanks to the White Guard.'

'We can get more,' the other retorted belligerently.

'Wait a moment,' Andrin cut in. 'Now, more than ever before, we must stay calm and clear-headed.'

Ico smiled inwardly at this, but kept her expression neutral, wishing she could believe Andrin capable of following his own advice.

'They're trying to provoke us, and it makes sense to do not what your enemy wants but what he would like least,' he added.

'Which is what?'

Andrin did not answer the question directly but looked round from face to face, assessing the mood.

'Can we agree that what we *can't* do is just give in and do as they say?'

'Damn right!' someone said and others nodded, while a few looked uncertain.

'Do we have any choice?' one of the doubters asked. 'I mean, we could all end up in gaol – or worse.'

'And anyway, what can we do?' someone else added.

'We can do a lot!' the hothead shouted. 'We're not all cowards!'

A flurry of accusations and angry denials flew back and forth as tempers rose, but Andrin soon restored order. His physical presence was something he occasionally used to great effect, and the room grew still when he yelled at them to stop. His short hair seemed to glow in the dim light, as if he were giving off white sparks.

'We should save our energies to fight our real enemies, not amongst ourselves,' he told them fervently. Then, looking directly at the doubters, he said, 'There *are* things we can do without risking our liberty or our lives – if we stay calm. I'll never accept that we have no choice but to surrender, but we can't rush in like a camel in heat.' He transferred his gaze to the hotheads. 'We can't afford mistakes, or we'll put ourselves and each other in danger.'

'So what *do* we do?' a calmer voice asked.

Andrin took a deep breath. After much discussion with Ico and Vargo, he had a mental list of practical measures. He felt happier about some of them than others, but what mattered now was how he presented them to the Firebrands. If they were to be successful, cooperation was absolutely vital.

'All right. There are several things we can do, and it makes sense to divide them up between us, depending on our skills and those of our birds.'

He hesitated, seeing Fayna looking hopefully up at the birds in the roof. Her loss reminded him of his own, and he felt anger twist in his gut. He suppressed it and the grief that went with it, knowing he must remain focused.

'First of all we have to collect more crystals,' he said, starting with the most practical matter of all. 'We've proved we can use them effectively against the worms and, sooner or later, I promise you we will again.' There was some muttering at that, and he added firmly, 'Of course we'll have to be more circumspect than before.'

'Some of our methods weren't exactly legal last time,' Vargo chipped in, provoking smiles and a little laughter.

'Exactly,' Andrin said, not appreciating the interruption but nonetheless grateful for the small release of tension. 'Ico's going to take charge of that.'

'Are you sure she's the best one for the job?' someone asked. 'Won't they be watching her more closely than anyone?'

'We're all under suspicion to some degree,' Ico replied. 'If I can't do what's necessary then I'll pass the responsibility on to someone else, but until then I'm the nearest thing we've got to an expert, and I have access to a lot of information via my father. It'll take more than a few chivaree to keep me from playing my part.'

Her voice was calm and determined, and her words drew nods of approval from the gathering. They had all heard of the visitation, and knew she had more to lose than most.

'The next thing is magic itself,' Andrin went on, taking advantage of the newly resolute mood. 'We can't hope to match the Senate forces if it comes to a battle of brute strength. Magic is our one real hope – and we need to develop it as fast as we can. We've covered a lot in the last few months, but there's a lot more still to learn.'

'How? We're never going to get near the old books now, are we?'

'There are ways,' Vargo replied. 'And anyway, the most important lore has never been written down.'

'Vargo is going to oversee the research,' Andrin said. 'He's done a lot already, as you all know.'

'I'll explain what to do when the teams have been sorted out,' the musician added. 'Remember, although using magic may be illegal now, learning about it isn't.' He grinned.

'But you must still be very careful,' Andrin warned.

'When we're finished we should at least be able to plan a few practical jokes,' Vargo said. 'Turn Senator Kantrowe into a frog, that sort of thing.'

Andrin laughed dutifully with the others, but wished that his friend wasn't so influenced by Ero – who could be heard calling from the rafters. He resented Vargo's flippancy at such a serious time. Glancing at Ico he saw her watching him and smiled. *We need to laugh sometimes,* her expression said. Then she nodded, encouraging him to go on.

'Apart from that, we watch and learn,' he said. 'When we come to make our next move we must be sure what we're doing, so we need teams to study the fireworms, to see if their swarming patterns have changed at all. We need timings, routes, habits, places where they emerge or congregate, anything that'll help us do the job properly next time.'

'And the White Guard?' someone suggested. 'Do we watch them too?'

'Of course. If they're watching us then we need to know when, where and how, in what numbers, when their duty hours change, and so on. That's the only way we can hope to avoid their interference.' Andrin paused, and the silence was awkward. Everyone knew what the soldiers' interference had cost their leader last time. Realizing that he could not bear it if they were to begin offering condolences, Andrin went on. 'We need to know how they react to various situations so we can arrange some diversions if necessary.'

'Know your enemy.' There was a low murmur of voices, and glances were exchanged as ideas began to form.

'Beyond that we have to face the Senate's propaganda,' Andrin continued. 'They would have you believe that everyone thinks the same way they do, but it's not true. We must tell our side of the story as widely as possible, gauge what support we might have if—'

'Support?' What support? People are *blaming* us for everything.'

'That's why we need to set the record straight, let everyone hear the truth, not just what Kantrowe and his cronies want them to hear.'

'We can hardly start posting proclamations!'

'Why not?' Vargo asked impetuously. 'A few lines of comic verse could be quite effective—'

'I think perhaps we'll leave that option for later,' Andrin cut in, controlling his irritation with difficulty. 'For now we need to talk, first with those we can trust, then widen the range. It wouldn't do any harm if some of the rumours were started by us for a change.'

'Instead of this nonsense about human sacrifices, you mean?'

'It may not be nonsense,' another speaker warned. 'Let's face it, the timing of that eruption did us no favours. If everyone thinks we've made the dragons angry, what's to stop people trying to appease them?'

'It'll never happen.'

'Don't be so sure. It was accepted practice not so long ago.'

'This is insane!' Andrin burst out, unable to remain silent any longer. 'The whole idea is repulsive. Haven't enough people already died because of the fireworms, without giving them more?'

'But the Senate says that it's the people who provoked the dragons by fighting against the worms who should be blamed if we have to appease them.'

'That's right,' someone else agreed. 'We're getting the blame for that too.'

'Look, we all know the dragons were not responsible for the eruption,' Ico said reasonably. 'They have nothing to do with the fireworms. What we must do is convince enough other people so that we won't be threatened by such vile ideas.'

'People are afraid to speak out against the sacrifices,' a worried voice persisted, 'for fear they might be chosen as an example to others.'

'It won't happen,' Ico stated. 'Not even Kantrowe is that barbaric. He's just trying to frighten everyone.'

'And he's succeeding. People are already talking about how the sacrifices are to be chosen.'

'Let me guess,' Andrin remarked scornfully. 'Convicted criminals?'

'That's one idea.'

'Which means us if we get caught.'

There was a pause as everyone considered this.

'I heard they were thinking of using newborn babies,' Fayna said. 'Only girls, of course.'

'Gods! That's sick,' Ico hissed, trying not to let her rage overcome her completely.

'Or a lottery,' another Firebrand went on. 'Can you *imagine?* Anyone could be condemned. It'd cause absolute panic.'

'And they'll be looking for scapegoats.'

'All this just makes it even more vital for us to get our point across,' Andrin said, trying to regain control of the meeting. 'Let's get organized into teams now, so we all know what we're doing.'

If only it were that simple, Ico thought ruefully. Still, we have to do something or we'll all go mad.

As she moved forward to talk to those who would be helping her collect the new supply of crystals, Soo's voice sounded urgently in her mind.

There's a stranger outside the hall.

Where?

By the tall window at the back.

How long has he been there?

I'm not sure, the sparrowhawk replied, uncharacteristically vague.

Why didn't you warn us earlier?

He just appeared, Soo answered. *From nowhere.*

CHAPTER THIRTEEN

As soon as Ico passed on Soo's information, Andrin acted swiftly and decisively but without haste. He and Ico were both aware of the need to move quickly, but if they had simply blurted out a warning the ensuing alarm would have caused panic and would probably have allowed the spy to escape. Stealth was necessary if they were to capture him. After a whispered conference Andrin called several young men to him and quietly issued instructions.

'What's going on?' Vargo asked as they moved off, but Ico signalled for silence.

'We need to keep the meeting going, but just talk about something unimportant,' she whispered, her voice pitched low so that it would not carry to anyone outside. 'How about some music?' she added more loudly.

'I'm sure you don't want to hear my old songs again,' Vargo replied, playing along.

Others, catching on, began to suggest song titles, and it became a deceptively lively discussion as Andrin and his team crept towards various doorways.

'I haven't even got my lute with me,' Vargo protested as

everyone waited tensely – and then there was no need of further subterfuge.

At a signal from Andrin he led the way out of the main exit while others slipped out of side doors and ran to cover all possible escape routes. Their footsteps alerted the intruder, but he made no attempt to flee and cowered deeper into the shadows. Moonlight glinted on several drawn blades as the Firebrands closed in.

'Don't hurt me,' the stranger whined. 'I'm only the apple taster, taster.'

The shrill words silenced Andrin's intended challenge and his followers hesitated too, their knives wavering in midair.

'I only came to hear the beautiful music, music.'

'Who are you?' Andrin demanded harshly. 'What are you doing here?'

'My name is Angel, I think,' the man replied, sounding doubtful. 'I taste the apples.'

'What's he talking about?'

'I've no idea,' Andrin said. 'Someone fetch a light. I want to see what he looks like.'

One of the Firebrands went back inside and returned with a candle, shielding the flame with a cupped hand. Moving closer to the intruder so that the flickering light played upon his face, he came to an abrupt halt and gasped. Several of the others echoed his surprise with sharply indrawn breaths. The man that crouched beneath the window looked less like an angel than anyone they had ever seen. His face was disfigured, twisted so that one side of his mouth was lower than the other. His eyes were mismatched, one wide and staring, the other a squinting shadow, and his nose was covered with bulbous growths that made it look like a misshapen bunch of diseased grapes. His hair grew in irregular clumps and his clothes were little more than dusty rags. He kept so still now that, in the half-light, he looked more like a gargoyle than a human being.

For some time no one knew what to say, then Andrin

sheathed his dagger, stepped forward and offered the stranger his hand.

'Here,' he said. 'Get up. I won't hurt you.'

After a few moments fearful hesitation, Angel reached up and allowed himself to be pulled to his feet. His limbs were crooked too, as if warped by some terrible disease, but once standing he seemed to gain a little confidence.

'Is it wrong to listen to the beautiful music?' he asked timidly.

'Not if that was all you were doing.'

'I only taste apples. Everyone says that's all I'm good for.' The faint touch of pride in his voice was almost comical, but no one laughed.

Others were coming out of the hall now, curious to see what was going on.

'Is everything all right?' Ico asked.

'You tell me,' Andrin replied. 'Angel here says he only came to listen to music.'

'Music?'

Angel nodded.

'Beautiful, beautiful,' he said. 'Like the delicious apples.'

'This is obviously a man of taste,' Vargo declared. 'Anyone who thinks my playing is like the best fruit can't be all bad.'

There was some uneasy laughter among the Firebrands.

'He's harmless,' someone at the back said.

Andrin turned to see who had spoken and Nino Delgado came forward, threading his thin, wiry body through the crowd.

'You know him?'

'Yes. I've seen him a few times in the badlands. Among the people of my village he is something of a legend. He lives wild, like a hermit.'

'Tasting apples?'

'He's a little mad,' Nino said gently. 'We give him food sometimes. He loves fruit.'

'What's he doing here, in Teguise?' Ico asked.

'I've no idea. Why did you come to the city, Angel?'

'To see the ships sail,' the disfigured man replied, 'but then the music caught me and they disappeared.'

'What disappeared?' Andrin asked.

'Everything.'

It was clear they weren't going to get much sense out of him.

'Well, there isn't going to be any music tonight,' Vargo told him eventually. 'So *you'd* better disappear.'

'Go on,' Andrin confirmed. 'You can't stay here.'

Angel looked around, his grotesque face clearly troubled, then set off at a surprisingly fast pace, his bow legs propelling him down the alley.

Is anyone else nearby? Ico asked Soo. *Is he going to meet anyone?* She was still a little suspicious.

There's no one, the sparrowhawk replied. *Shall I follow him? Yes.*

As Angel reached the corner of the alley which would take him out of sight of the watching Firebrands, he seemed to spin round suddenly and the air shimmered. Several of the onlookers blinked.

'What was that?' Vargo said.

He's gone. Soo sounded angry and confused.

What do you mean? Ico responded.

He's not there any more. He just vanished.

Keep looking, Ico said, though she knew the search would be fruitless.

'Come on. Let's get back to business,' Andrin said, and led the way back into the hall.

Ico followed more slowly, unwilling to share Soo's intelligence with anyone else yet. She had no idea what it meant. Could Angel's madness be an act? Was it possible that he was really one of Kantrowe's agents? Ico didn't believe this, but the doubts nagged at her and she found it difficult to concentrate on the job in hand. Had it been luck, craft or magic that had enabled Angel to evade Soo's watchful gaze? She decided to make a point of talking to Nino later, to try and calm her fears. One thing was certain, at least; there was more to Angel than met the eye.

While their human partners were meeting down below, the birds in the rafters held a council of their own. As was usually the case when so many different species were present, it was a chaotic and sometimes acrimonious affair. The birds that flew in flocks – sparrows, finches and so on – all chattered loudly at the same time, while the larger, more solitary creatures eyed their lesser brethren with disdain. Ayo was not present and Soo was on duty elsewhere, so neither of the acknowledged leaders was there to lend some order to the proceedings. As a consequence, to the despair of some of the more thoughtful birds, nothing was decided and the only thing they could agree on was to wait and see what the humans suggested.

When the disturbance caused by Angel's appearance interrupted what little debate was still going on, no one noticed an iridescent black chaffinch swoop down through the hole in the roof and alight on one of the rafters before crossing the room to perch next to Ero. The hoopoe was frankly bored, wondering why he had bothered to come. Not all the linked birds were there, and he felt it beneath his dignity to discuss important matters with pigeons and crows. And as for the sparrows . . . Ero shuddered.

However, the newcomer was a different matter and Ero looked at him with unashamed curiosity.

'Nice sheen,' he remarked, referring to the mirador's sleek feathers.

'Thank you. Your plumage is very fine.'

'Yes, isn't it.' Ero raised and lowered his crest in acknowledgement.

'Have they decided anything?' Tao asked, nodding his beak towards the Firebrands below.

'I haven't been listening,' Ero replied dismissively. In fact Vargo hadn't told him anything yet.

'Were you there when we attacked the fireworms?'

'Of course,' the hoopoe said proudly. 'Weren't you?'

'I was . . . on another mission. Top secret. But I was sorry to miss the big event. What really happened?'

'I led the attack,' Ero began, and proceeded to give his attentive audience a fanciful, self-serving but not too inaccurate picture of the fateful battle.

Tao listened closely, discounting much of the hoopoe's transparent self-aggrandizement, but asking several questions about various aspects of the operation. When he had learnt all he could he moved on to other birds, but found most of them rather more suspicious of his unknown presence. Their reticence made it difficult for him to find out what was going on with the humans and so eventually Tao flew away, leaving Ero to preen and practise little dance steps in time to his own singing.

Towards the end of the meeting, when most of the practical details had been decided, the talk turned to the dragons and their supposed connection with the volcanoes. As usual Andrin argued vehemently that such a connection did not exist, aware that even some of his own followers had been influenced by such nonsense. As he grew more passionate, Ico watched him, feeling a mixture of love and unease. Seeing him like this, she found it hard to believe that he could stick to his own resolutions concerning the immediate future. He was so easily roused that she dreaded to think what might happen if there was another eruption or – the gods forbid – anyone was actually sacrificed. She pushed such dreadful thoughts aside.

'It wouldn't surprise me if there weren't any dragons left,' Andrin declared, provoking some exclamations of disbelief. 'They haven't been seen for ages, after all. Nino, you live in the heart of the firelands, near where the dragons are supposed to live. Have you ever seen one?'

'No.'

'You see!'

'But my father has,' Nino added. 'And I believe they're still there.' His dark eyes regarded Andrin steadfastly.

'Perhaps they're hibernating,' Vargo suggested, and made loud snoring noises.

'I don't see how anyone could sleep through an eruption,' the girl next to him remarked, smiling. Allegra Meo was the small, pretty daughter of a fisherman and she had, somewhat to Vargo's surprise, volunteered to help him with his magical research. She was one of the few Firebrands who was not linked, and it seemed an odd choice, but she had been insistent.

'Let sleeping dragons lie,' Vargo intoned solemnly.

'I'd almost be glad if there *were* another eruption,' Andrin said seriously, 'so people could see it had nothing to do with our attacking the worms.'

'You wouldn't say that if you lived in the interior,' Nino responded heatedly. 'All you get here is a bit of ash. We get lava flows, rocks crashing through the roof, and clouds of poison gas. I can run faster than most, but sooner or later I'll get caught too.'

'I'm sorry. I didn't mean . . . ' Andrin shrugged apologetically. 'But surely you don't believe the dragons *cause* eruptions?'

'No,' Nino replied slowly, drawing the word out. 'But this land holds secrets older than any one of us, from a time before men ever came here.'

Soon after that the Firebrands went their separate ways, slinking like rats in the darkness, each with their own hopes and fears hidden beneath a newly acquired sense of purpose.

CHAPTER FOURTEEN

'Madmen sometimes have a kind of wisdom we can't understand,' Nino said. 'And Angel is very gentle. We have nothing to fear from him.'

'He still scares me,' Ico admitted.

They were walking slowly through the dark, deserted streets. Soo had not managed to locate Angel after he had disappeared, and felt much anger and shame because of this. When Ico had mentioned it to Nino, he replied that his own link, a peregrine falcon called Eya, had sometimes had the same problem – and no one could fly faster than him.

'We all fear what we don't understand,' Nino said now, 'but after all, madness and magic are not so very far apart. It's all in the mind, and who's to say which is better?'

'Don't say that,' Ico replied, laughing. 'I have enough to worry about without wondering how close I am to going insane.'

'I don't think you need fret on that score,' he told her. 'You're the sanest person I know.'

They strolled on in silence for a few paces, at ease in each other's company, but still keeping a wary eye on every shadow.

'Where does Angel live?'

'No one knows. He's more familiar with the cave systems than most, but he comes and goes.'

'How did he . . . become so disfigured?'

'I don't know. His appearance never seems to bother him, so he's probably always been that way.'

'Poor man.'

'I don't think he's unhappy. Many people in my district have reason to be thankful to him – for all his ugliness he has our respect, even love.'

'Why?' Ico asked, intrigued.

'Midwives are always glad to see him at a birthing,' Nino replied. 'They say he drives away any evil spirits that might try to enter the newborn baby. Most people think that's just superstition, but I'm not willing to dismiss it out of hand. It's certainly true that every birth he's attended has gone well.'

Ico looked sceptical.

'But that's not all,' Nino went on. 'I've seen him stand in front of a lava flow about to destroy a village, and tell it to stop or turn aside. He's completely fearless, and he's saved at least three places like that.'

'The lava *obeyed* him?'

'Yes. Of course it could have been going to stop anyway, but . . .' He shrugged.

'Even if it was a coincidence, he was still very brave,' Ico commented. 'No wonder he's earned your respect.'

'Very brave or very stupid,' Nino amended. 'Sometimes it amounts to the same thing.'

'Either way, I'm beginning to think we shouldn't have sent him away,' she said. 'Angel sounds as though he'd be a useful ally!'

I was lucky to get that much, Tao remarked at the conclusion of his report. *The hoopoe was the only one willing to talk.*

And you didn't find out what was decided at the meeting? Maciot asked.

No.

Try the hoopoe again in a few days. There's a chance he'll tell you more then.

That depends on whether his human is as silly as he is, Tao stated scornfully.

The musician?

Yes.

Did you try the Maravedis girl's bird?

Of course. Soo is much too superior to pay attention to the likes of me, the mirador replied, sounding mildly offended. *And she's too intelligent to answer questions from a stranger.*

What about the eagle?

He wasn't there. I've no idea where he is.

And you say their security was good?

There were several birds patrolling the area. It took me some time to get past them. Only one human came close, and they caught him easily enough.

Who was it?

No one I know. Odd-looking fellow, from out of town I think.

So Kantrowe's people weren't aware of the meeting then, Maciot deduced thoughtfully.

Can't have been, Tao agreed. *They'd surely have tried to spy on it or break it up if they did.*

Unless they've already got an agent inside the Firebrands' organization.

It's possible, the bird admitted doubtfully. *If that's the case, I wouldn't like to be in his shoes if he was caught. They wouldn't take kindly to traitors.*

I didn't think you wore shoes, the senator remarked, yawning. *Thanks, Tao. Goodnight.*

Aren't you going to tell me what you've been up to?

Another time. I need to go back to sleep.

Huh! Tao clicked his beak. *Anyone would think I was just your slave.*

The bird flew out of the open window, a darker streak against the night sky, leaving Maciot with the echoes of his telepathic grumbling whispering in his head. The senator smiled fondly, then settled himself again. He was alone in his large, comfortable bed and the house was perfectly quiet, but sleep would not come. His mind was too active for him to relax, and he almost wished he had not sent Tao away. The news of just how successful the Firebrands' attack had been had come as something of a shock. He had known they had done some damage, but the foresight and precision they had shown told of intelligent and resourceful minds at work. If Kantrowe tried to destroy them completely he might get more than he bargained for.

For his own part, Maciot had been quietly canvassing the opinions of his fellow senators and other influential citizens. What he had found was encouraging. Not everyone had been taken in by Kantrowe's performance, and many people were as horrified by the subsequent developments as Maciot was himself. Even so, the majority still supported the proclamation. He would have to tread carefully – especially when that weasel Gadette was around – but if he decided to oppose some of Kantrowe's less palatable measures, he had reason to hope he would not lack support.

However, he still could not decide whether aligning himself with the Firebrands, even without any direct contact, was a good idea. They were clearly still active, in spite of the tacit threats made against them, but their methods were dangerous. Maciot had left the brazen recklessness of youth behind him years ago – or told himself so, at least – and he had no wish to be caught in the undertow when and if the Firebrands' ship sank. If he were ever to choose the manner of his death, it would not be by drowning.

Morning found Vargo in a state of muddleheaded panic. This was partly due to lack of sleep, but uppermost in his mind was a sense of dismay at the responsibility he had taken on. What had possessed him to volunteer to coordinate their search for magic? He was a musician, not a wizard. Where was he even supposed to begin?

The sight of Ero's gaudy plumage only reinforced Vargo's feeling of inadequacy. Even with his eyes closed, immersed in some unimaginable avian dream, the hoopoe looked ornate and comical. We're entertainers, Vargo thought helplessly, not investigators. As if in response to the private thought, Ero raised and lowered his crest without ever waking up. He showed off even in his sleep. Nevertheless, the display made Vargo smile, and he began to feel a little better about the day. And now that he thought about it, his starting point was obvious. Famara would know what he should do.

He rubbed his eyes, threw off the sheet and sat naked on the side of the bed. Ero woke at the movement and called softly in greeting. Vargo stood up, careful not to hit his head on one of the beams that ran across the ceiling of his tiny room, and stretched.

We've got work to do, Ero.

Not dressed like that, I hope, the bird responded, sounding disgusted. The hoopoe had never quite worked out why humans shed their feathers so often. Especially when it made them look so repulsive. *Are we going singing?*

No. This is more important than music, Vargo said, hardly believing that he was able to express such a thought. *The meeting decided—*

That was so boring, Ero interrupted. *The only good bit was when that black bird asked me about killing the worms.*

What bird? One of the crows?

No. I'd never seen him before, but he enjoyed my story.

You'd never seen him before? Vargo was instantly alarmed. *What was his name?*

I don't know, Ero answered sullenly, sensing that his link was upset but not understanding why.

So he wasn't linked to one of the Firebrands?

No. But he liked my plumage.

What did you tell him?

About the attack, when I carried the crystal and—

Nothing about what was being discussed at the meeting?

No. That was boring, the hoopoe repeated.

Vargo breathed a sigh of relief. Even if, as he suspected, this mysterious black bird was linked to one of Kantrowe's men, the damage might not be too great. He would have to warn the others that the old concert hall may no longer be a safe venue, but other than that their secrets were safe – if Ero was telling the truth. Vargo made the hoopoe go over exactly what he had told the other bird until he was satisfied.

Listen, Ero. This is very important. If you see that bird again, find out what his name is and who he's linked to, but don't tell him anything about what we're doing. Understand?

Yes, yes, yes, the bird responded huffily.

Vargo could only hope that his message had sunk in. It was quite possible that Ero would have forgotten it all by the next day. Then he remembered that the hoopoe would soon be flying south, migrating to warmer climes, and felt a wave of sadness as he realized that his unreliable but amusing companion would soon be gone.

A knock at the door interrupted Vargo's thoughts and he tensed, then realized it was almost certainly his landlord wanting the overdue rent – or the promise of some music instead. However, when he unlocked and opened the door and found himself face to face with Allegra, it would have been hard to determine which of them was more surprised. As Vargo saw the colour rush into the girl's cheeks he recognized his predicament, and felt his own face begin to burn. He turned away quickly, grabbed the sheet and twisted it round himself. As he straightened up again he banged his head painfully against a beam, and fell on to the bed in a dishevelled heap. Still seeing stars, he heard Ero's mocking call and – to his acute embarrassment – Allegra's helpless laughter.

'I'm sorry,' she gasped, still giggling. 'I didn't mean to intrude. Are you all right?'

'Yes,' he replied, rubbing his head. 'What are you doing here?'

'I found that book you wanted.' She held up a thick, dusty volume. 'You remember, the one my grandmother used to read aloud. Some of the pages are stuck together, I'm afraid, but most of it's all right.'

'You don't waste any time, do you,' he said, recovering a little of his composure and taking the proffered book.

'Not when there are important things to do,' she replied, her eyes downcast. 'Are you going to see Famara today?'

'Yes.'

'I'd like to meet her some day,' Allegra hinted.

Vargo thought for a moment.

'I'd better go alone this time,' he said, hoping she would understand.

'Of course.' She was trying hard not to sound disappointed. 'I've got plenty of other things to do.'

'Be careful,' Vargo advised her. 'And thank you for the book.'

Allegra nodded, smiled briefly and left, closing the door carefully behind her.

Well, that was a very elegant performance, I must say, Ero commented.

You could have warned me, Vargo shot back exasperatedly. *I didn't have any clothes on!*

Does that mean you have to mate with her now? the hoopoe asked, all innocence.

When Ico woke, the house seemed unnaturally quiet. She got up and opened the shutters and found that the square below was empty, although at this hour there was usually some activity. It was almost as though her home was now a source of plague, somewhere to be avoided at all costs – and in a sense it was. Ever since the chivaree's visit, Ico had known she could not hide. Her family was being shunned by some people and carefully watched by others.

She dressed slowly and went out on to the landing, hoping to escape the oppressive atmosphere without being detected. Her father was sitting hunched up on the top step of the stairs, his head in his hands. He kept perfectly still, not reacting to the sound of her emergence, but he had to be aware of her presence. Although Ico had not seen much of him during the last two days, she knew he had been drinking intermittently but heavily ever since the unpleasant guild meeting. She had heard him crying on occasion and shouting angrily at others, and had suffered Atchen's reproachful stares whenever they met, but her mind had been full of her own concerns. Now, however, she felt stirrings of pity. Diano seemed to have grown older and smaller, and to find him sitting here was so out of character that, somewhat belatedly, she scolded herself for not having been more considerate. She sat down on the stairs, squeezing between her father and the banisters, but he still did not stir.

'Are you all right?' she asked softly.

'My head hurts,' he groaned.

The alcohol had finally caught up with Diano. Remembering her own first hangover and how terrible she had felt, Ico realized that for a man of his habitual moderation the aftermath of his prolonged binge must be equally devastating.

'It'll wear off,' she said encouragingly.

'I feel awful.' He looked up at last and although he was dry eyed, his unshaven face was haggard and very pale.

'That's funny,' she replied, making an effort to smile. 'You look great. Come on, let's go downstairs. You need something to eat.'

'No food. I . . .' He shut his mouth abruptly.

'Whatever you say.' She put an arm around him and helped him to stand and then, one painful step at a time, they made their way to the kitchen.

The smell of freshly baked bread almost made Diano gag, but he was too weak to resist when Ico set him down on a stool and began bustling about. There was no sign of Atchen. Ico decided she had probably gone out to market, which made things easier.

After infusing some herbs, she set the steaming bowl down in front of her father and made him drink. At first he sipped gingerly and reluctantly, but before long he began to feel marginally better, and eventually finished the entire draught. As she poured out more tea Ico noticed that a little colour had returned to her father's cheeks.

'Thank you,' he whispered hoarsely, and looked at her directly for the first time. 'Ico, I—'

'Shhh,' she hissed, cutting off the words she would rather not hear. 'Drink. I'll make us breakfast.'

He did as he was told, his eyes following her like a devoted dog. His meekness sometimes annoyed her intensely, but now she was grateful and felt a welling up of concern – and love. She knew she had been the source of much heartache for her father, and was certain she would create a good deal more before too long, but his helplessness had aroused in her a protectiveness she had thought long dead.

Eventually, still without speaking, she coaxed him to eat and watched as he struggled to overcome his revulsion and found that the food continued his slow recovery.

'I think, perhaps, I may not be going to die after all,' he said, smiling weakly.

'It'll take more than a few drinks to finish off a Maravedis,' she told him, then wished she had said something – anything – else. Her words, as she had realized too late, would inevitably make Diano think of his wife and the illness that had deprived them of her long ago.

'I've done my best,' he said quietly. 'Your mother always understood you better than I did. Are you so ashamed of me?'

'Of course I'm not,' she assured him. 'And I know it's been difficult for you. I can't be easy to live with.'

'But your mother—'

'My mother was a lovely person,' Ico cut in, wondering why she, like her father, could never bring herself to use the dead woman's name, 'but sometimes you think too much of her and too little of yourself.'

He considered this in silence for a while, stifling his instinctive response.

'Do you think all this would have happened if she—'

'I can't answer that, Dodo. All I know is—'

'You have to do what you believe in,' he completed for her.

'Yes,' she said, surprised. 'I'm sorry if I've hurt you. I never meant to.'

'Just be careful, please,' he begged. 'I couldn't bear it if I lost you too.'

'You won't,' she told him confidently, then wondered whether this was a promise she would be able to keep.

CHAPTER FIFTEEN

Morning found Ayo far to the south, at a place where the mountains had flowed down to the sea. Unusually for the eagle he had been flying all night, soaring on the updraughts as the sun-baked land cooled, releasing the day's heat to the sultry night air. He had been drawn there not by duty or instinct but by a need he could no longer explain, a memory that had outlived its natural span.

Below him the landscape had been carved into fantastic shapes by the forces of nature. When the lava had met the sea the black rock had twisted and writhed, sending columns of exploding steam high into the air. But that had happened more than a century ago, and now the coastline was a treacherous labyrinth of caves and inlets, buttresses and flying spray. Even beneath the swirling water there was turmoil as the tides swept in and out, with the sharp-edged reefs so dangerous that they had earned the name 'the Dragon's Teeth'. Many ships had been lost there, torn apart in those deadly jaws, and any sailor worth his salt steered a course well out to sea.

To the unskilled eye the terrain looked completely barren, the only discernible growths being the grey-green lichen that was the first plant life to reappear on the surface of the lava fields. But Ayo knew better. There were hidden pockets of soil where prickly bushes grew, where lizards and insects congregated and rabbits burrowed. In a few places there were even some stunted trees, wild figs and cauldrons. And the ever surging ocean provided an endless supply of fish. It would certainly be possible for an eagle to live in such a place.

Ayo glided with his broad wings – spanning the height of a tall man – spread out, the feathers at each tip splayed like the fingers of two huge hands. He was the ruler of the skies, and his shape and shadow cast an instinctive pall of fear over all the creatures below. Even when he no longer rode the air effortlessly but propelled himself forward, the power of his heavy, ponderous wingbeats was awe-inspiring. And then, in the pale light of sunrise, he saw the luminous green glint of the lake that was his destination and, with relief, he folded back his wings. Streamlined now, he dived, the onrush of air screaming in his ears but making hardly a ripple in his perfectly aligned plumage. Ayo screamed back in greeting.

The eagle had begun his journey the day before, flying southwest from Teguise towards the Lower Firelands. His course had taken him directly over the small, circular crater of a long-dormant volcano, which was the closest mountain to the city. It had been adopted long ago as a trysting place for lovers, and was now a shrine to such emotions.

According to the legend, there had been a young couple – Bertin and Orzola – among the first settlers in the area. They had been passionately in love with each other, but their families had forbidden their marriage. In desperation Bertin had gone down into the crater, collected dozens of white stones and arranged them to spell out his lover's and his own name in huge letters that could be read from the rim of the old volcano. Then he had persuaded Orzola's father to come and look at his handiwork, in the hope that seeing the huge effort he had put into the project would convince the older man of his sincerity and worth. Instead, his prospective father-in-law had been incensed at what he took to be a public insult to his daughter. He turned on the defenceless Bertin and stabbed him, leaving the young man to bleed to death where he lay. It was some time before the now frantic Orzola discovered what had happened and completed the tragic cycle. Under cover of night she fled to the crater, found her lover's body and saw the ghostly glimmer of their names in the darkness below. With his head cradled in her arms she drank poison.

The next morning her father found a message scrawled on the wall of his daughter's bedroom. To his immediate horror it read, 'He who loves should live. He who doesn't know how to love should die. He who obstructs love should die twice.' Orzola's last wish was granted, for something inside her father died at that moment and he spent the rest of his life filled with unbearable regret. The lovers were buried side by side, and over the years their names had become synonymous with unconquerable love. They were still united by the white stones, and over the years had been joined by many other couples, who had placed their own names there as a sign of commitment. The base and sides of the crater were now covered in writing.

Ayo knew that Andrin and Ico's names were somewhere down among the lines and swiggles he could not even begin to decipher, but he flew past, ignoring the monument to human emotion. He was headed towards another, far greater mountain. Pajarito was a huge peak of tumbled red and ochre stone with a deep but lopsided crater facing east, which lay surrounded by the vast lava fields that it had produced. Life was harsh there, but to all birds it was a place of special significance, a place where the voices of the sky spoke to the land. They went there hoping to be deemed worthy enough to hear the echoes of those voices, and to have their questions answered by the sometimes enigmatic oracle.

Ayo settled on a boulder near the centre of the great tilted bowl and called once – a harsh, challenging sound, but made with reverence, not anger. Pajarito answered in whispers and tiny, windblown murmurs from the rock itself. Ayo heard and, although it was less than he had hoped for, he was satisfied, knowing he would learn no more. He did not regard the answer as ambiguous, merely misplaced in time. Understanding would come in due course. Until then he would keep his own counsel. There were some secrets he kept even from Andrin.

From there he had turned to the southeast, heading for the coast again. The ocean was his main hunting ground, and he always felt more at ease when it was in sight. When darkness fell he listened to the faint roar of the waves far below and was comforted by the sound. Moonlight glittered darkly on the surface of the water as he turned south to follow the line of the shore.

He made only one more detour, this one unplanned, when he saw the dark shapes and faint lights of several ships. There were eighteen of them in the fleet, and such a large armada was unusual. Ayo swooped down to take a closer look, knowing that Andrin always welcomed news of such movements. He was soon in no doubt that these were no innocent traders or fishing boats. Even from a great height he could see many men sleeping, huddled on deck. There were far more on board than was necessary for an ordinary crew – a sure sign of aggressive intent – and he did not really need the confirmation provided by the flags that fluttered from the tallest masts. A white skull above crossed cutlasses on black cloth was the mark of the pirate leader known to the humans as the Barber.

The ships were moving very slowly, with few sails set. They seemed in no hurry to reach their destination but they were heading north, and Ayo knew that if they kept to that direction they would eventually reach the city of Teguise. The eagle noted all this but felt no immediate need to turn that way himself. He considered flying low over the leading vessel and letting the sailors see him. Seamen were notoriously superstitious about large white birds, and in the past Ayo's mere presence had been enough to induce considerable panic, but he was under a stronger compulsion now. As he gained height again and continued south, the fleet was soon lost to sight.

Some hours later dawn came, and then the sun, making the eagle's feathers shine while the land and sea below still lay in shadow. The world reawoke beneath him, and he was ready.

Ayo's dive ended in a fast, flat curve just above the emerald waters of the lake, his scream echoing from the serrated cliffs that loomed above it on three sides. The shock waves of his flight created ripples in the glass surface, so that the reflections of earth and sky above wavered and fragmented.

To the fourth side of the lake, beyond the whale-backed pebble beach, lay the sea, with the ever present rhythm of the foaming surf and hissing shingle adding to the resonances of the cove. The tide was full now and the tiny island, that Ayo remembered so well, was some forty paces from the nearest dry land, although at low tide it was just possible for a human to walk out to the rock dry-shod. Not that many tried; Elva was sacred territory. Even though Ayo could have reached it easily, no matter what the state of the tide, he would never dream of alighting there. The island was forbidden to the birds. There were no nests on her ledges and not even the raucous, wheeling seagulls who populated the nearby cliffs would dare perch anywhere on her slopes.

But Ayo had no thoughts of Elva now. This place – the cove, beach and lake – were painfully familiar. At one time they could easily have been his home. The hunting was good – the lake always swarmed with fish – there were trees nearby which were suitable for nesting; and here, far from any human habitation, there was little danger of being disturbed. And it was here, four years ago, that he had met Iva.

Their courtship had been elaborate. He had had to prove to his potential mate that he was worthy of her, brave and strong and skilled. He had hunted for her, skimming down over the lake or sea, his legs extended so that his fearsome talons could pluck the fish neatly from the water, while he flew so close to the surface that his tail feathers flicked up shining arcs of spray. He had brought the trophies to Iva, letting her eat her fill before satisfying his own hunger.

He had also demonstrated that he could defend his territory against all comers. Ordinarily his warning cries had been enough, but he had twice had to test his courage and strength against other males. To do so he had locked talons with the intruder high in the air, and then the two birds had whirled round, cartwheeling like crazed dance partners as they spiralled down towards the earth or sea below. The first to lose his nerve and fly free, avoiding the potentially fatal crash, admitted defeat and fled. Ayo had been victorious both times, knowing in some fierce, primeval part of him that Iva was worth any possible sacrifice, and had escaped without injury.

Only then would she allow him to come closer, to preen her feathers, to share in her joyous flight on the winds that rose from the cliffs. He had been lost in his desire, his admiration of her brilliant white plumage and consummate elegance, and he had set out to build a huge nest.

It was then that he had heard Andrin's alien voice. Although it had been far away, it had sounded loudly over the rustle of the sea, over the calls of other birds, even above Iva's plaintive, bewildered cries. Ayo had felt his mind slowly tearing apart, but had known from the beginning that this was a summons he could not ignore. Even now, at the very core of his being, he knew that if offered the same choice again he would not have acted any differently.

Once he had left the cove he had known that he could never really return, but he had nonetheless made the pilgrimage once a year, a private homage to what might have been. Strangely enough these visits never took place in the spring, when the mating urge was at its strongest, but in autumn, when their unborn fledglings would have been leaving the nest, embarking on their own adult lives. Ayo had not questioned this, but simply accepted his instincts and flown south, without hope. He had never seen Iva again, never even seen any other eagle in the area, in spite of the fact that the lake was still a perfect hunting ground. The cove was empty now.

The momentum of his dive over the lake carried him up and away, until he turned, catching the wind perfectly and hung in the air, almost motionless. For an instant his ever vigilant yellow eyes were blind. She came to him then, linking talons in joy rather than challenge, as they had done so long ago.

And there, quite alone, Ayo danced in the sky with the ghost of the most beautiful white eagle in all the world.

CHAPTER SIXTEEN

The slaves came ashore in chains. They looked fearful and dejected, and kept their heads down, uncertain whether they were exchanging one hell at sea for a worse one on land. Even so, as Remonnet watched their steady progress up the beach, he was pleased. This shipment looked in better condition than most. Poor food and relentless toil reduced many slaves to worthless wraiths before they ever reached their destination, but these were well muscled still, broken in spirit but not yet in body. Master Verier would be pleased.

The privateer, whose ship was now anchored in the secluded bay, stood beside Remonnet. The chamberlain knew him only as Snake, and because this was the first time he had ever dealt with him he had taken no chances, bringing a strong escort of soldiers, some hidden behind rocks further inland in case reinforcements were needed. The chamberlain was naturally cautious. The fact that he had lasted more than a decade in the service of Senator Deion Verier was proof enough of that, but this night's work promised to be very profitable, and Remonnet was confident that even his demanding and unpredictable master would be well satisfied.

Slavery was technically illegal, but conditions in the northern mines were such that few free men were willing to work in them, so the discreet importation of labour was necessary as well as economically sound. In addition, the price that had been agreed with Snake was a perfect use of resources. The dragon's tears had suddenly become more trouble than they were worth in Tiguafaya, although they were still obviously valued highly abroad. A month ago the quantity demanded would have been exorbitant. Now it constituted a bargain.

'I trust you approve of the merchandise,' the privateer said confidently.

'They appear adequate,' the chamberlain replied grudgingly.

Snake laughed.

'You're a hard man to please. Think how much silver those strong arms will dig up for you.'

'They need to,' Remonnet said. 'We have paid a generous price. The crystals are of excellent quality.'

'I know,' Snake replied, smiling. He had inspected every jewel before restowing them in their casket. 'So we both stand to profit. That's only fair, don't you think?'

Remonnet said nothing, wondering just how well informed the trader was. The chamberlain did not like his smile. It was too complacent, almost smug, even though he had been as good as his word so far.

The last of the slaves were ashore now, watched by their overseers and the guards. In the fading light of dusk they looked dispirited as they waited for their masters to decide what would happen next. Remonnet could not guess where they came from; their skin showed all shades, from lava black to the pale sheen of the moon, and they were dressed in an eclectic assortment of rags. All that united them was their subservience.

'Sixty men, all fit to work, as agreed,' Snake declared. 'We will leave them in your tender care and take our price now.'

He signalled for one of his own heavily armed men to come and collect the casket, which lay open on a flat rock between the two leaders. Before he could move, however, a strange, flapping figure darted from the shadows into the open, making straight for the crystals. Several hands went instinctively to the hilts of their swords and knives, each side suspecting treachery, but then Snake laughed and even the stone-faced chamberlain smiled. It was clear that the intruder was only a young boy – and an idiot. His clumsy movements and his fat, moon-shaped face marked him as a harmless lunatic, a figure of fun. Snake's laughter had made the boy falter but his slanted eyes kept returning to the casket, irresistibly drawn to the glitter of the jewels within.

'Get out of here, Magpie!' one of the soldiers called. 'This is none of your business.'

'You know this creature?' Snake asked.

'Yes,' Remonnet replied. 'He's addled headed and wild, but he has his uses.'

'Really? Why would he follow you out here?'

'He's drawn to shiny things. We sometimes use him for prospecting.'

'So, you like pretty stones, eh, Magpie?' the privateer asked, holding up a crystal.

Magpie nodded solemnly, his eyes following the hypnotic glint of the dragon's tear, and shuffled forward nervously when Snake beckoned him. The crystal was placed in his outstretched hand and immediately Magpie held it close in front of his face and wailed. It was an eerie sound, half animal howl, half crooning love song. Some of the onlookers grimaced, while others put their fingers in their ears. Some of them laughed.

'You want it?' Snake asked.

Magpie looked uncertain, as if he did not understand the question, and fell silent. His gaze went from his hand to the casket, to the privateer and then back again, so that his large head seemed to wobble unsteadily.

'Well, you can't have it,' Snake exclaimed abruptly, snatching back the stone. 'It's mine!'

Magpie's keening began again, this time giving voice to the pain of loss, while all around him the cruel laughter rose once more.

'Now scram, you little runt!' Snake yelled, waving his arms.

The boy turned and fled, his awkward gait prompting further merriment. Snake tossed the crystal back into the casket, shut the lid and turned the key.

'Let's go.'

The two groups separated, still watching each other warily. The sailors, one of them carrying the precious box, returned to the boats which had been drawn up on the beach, while Remonnet's guards began to move the slaves into lines to begin their march inland.

Ico crouched in the tiny cave to the north of the bay. She had chosen this vantage point because, while offering concealment, it also afforded an almost unrestricted view of the water between the beach and the open sea. The slaves were all on their way now and out of sight, but the sailors seemed to be in no hurry, still settling themselves into the boats as they prepared to row back to their ship. Ico scanned the entire panorama, looking for Andrin, and was reassured when she couldn't see him.

Beside her Magpie stirred and sighed gustily. He had been shivering when she had intercepted his headlong flight, but now he seemed to have forgotten all about the incident – and that worried Ico. There were things she needed him to remember.

She had hated putting him through such an ordeal, and felt a violent dislike of the men who had treated him so callously. For all his simplicity and lack of grace Magpie was a gentle soul, deserving respect. But what could she expect from men who dealt in slavery, the ultimate degradation of humanity? She had known that Magpie would be the object of ridicule and disdain – in fact she had relied upon his not being taken seriously – but she had not seen how else she could achieve her objectives. Perhaps, she thought hopefully, such derision flowed around Magpie like water off a duck's back. At least that part of the process was over now, and they could move on to the next stage of the operation.

Ever since she had learnt – from jewellers' gossip – that Deion Verier's family were hoarding dragon's tears, she had been certain that they would be used for something unpleasant. When one of the Firebrands in the north had discovered that a new batch of slaves were expected at the mines, she had put two and two together. A plan had begun to form, and now it would only be moments before it was put to the test.

'Can you do it, Magpie?'

He looked at her blankly, eyes wide, and her heart began to race.

'You remember what we talked about. The crystal. It's soon now.'

'But I'll hurt it,' he said doubtfully.

'Yes, but we can save the others, all those beautiful stones,' she replied. 'The bad men will take them away if you don't, and you'll never see them again. We don't want that, do we?'

This idea made Magpie frown, and his lips pursed as he shook his head. Ico glanced out at the bay. The boats were all on the water now, moving unhurriedly towards the ship, with the one carrying Snake and the crystals ahead of the others.

'Now, Magpie,' she urged. 'Do it now! I'll help you.'

She took his hands and felt his internal struggle. The signal formed agonizingly slowly, the resonance exact but reluctant. The boy's mind was remarkably open, easy to read, and when his telepathic pulse was at last sent out Ico was able to sense it and lend it a little of her own strength and protection. Out in the bay the dragon's tear that Magpie had held, unconsciously recording its unique internal structure, began to disintegrate.

Snake, seated next to the casket, was the first to feel the sudden eviscerating cold. His hand, resting possessively on the lid, caught the worst of it and he screamed as his skin cracked and the blood in his fingers froze. He scrambled away from the piercing chill, still howling as the frigid waves began to spread. The other men in the boat could feel it now, and they stopped rowing. There was a grinding sound from beneath the bows as seawater turned to ice and scraped along the keel.

'Get away!' Snake yelled. 'Or we'll freeze to death!'

The sailors needed no further urging. They dived overboard and began swimming frantically towards the other boats. Snake, handicapped by his crippled arm, was slower than the rest but, even while he thrashed about in the rapidly cooling water, his brain was burning white hot. Remonnet had tricked him! Booby-trapped the casket somehow. He knew that the crystals were supposed to absorb heat when they were destroyed, but he couldn't work out how the process had begun. Nor did he know if just one crystal was responsible for the damage, or whether the reaction, once started, would spread to all the others. If it did, it was entirely possible that the whole bay would soon be turned into a saltwater glacier. Fear leant him strength, and at last he reached one of the other boats. He was pulled aboard and sat shivering, cradling his numb, disfigured hand and watching his boat from what he hoped was a safe distance. It was now at the centre of its own small, ever shifting iceberg.

Time passed and although the ice spread no further, the boats still kept their distance, their crews not convinced that the danger was over. Some of the sailors thought they saw a dark shape slither over the side of the ice-encrusted boat but no one said anything, certain that no living creature would be foolish enough to venture into the heart of such cold.

Some way inland, on the road that led eventually to the Verier estates and their infamous mines, the slaves trudged in unison. The soldiers were at ease now; the dangerous part of the transaction was over and they were looking forward to the evening's revels once their prisoners were safely stowed in secure barracks. Even Remonnet, walking at the rear, allowed himself a little smile of congratulation.

Their mood did not last long. At a sudden loud yell from one of the slaves, there was unexpected movement everywhere. Manacles fell away and chains broke as the entire column turned upon its captors. Concealed knives appeared in calloused hands, and the iron links that had bound them now became weapons, wielded by the 'slaves' as they made their concerted bid for freedom. Taken entirely by surprise, many of the guards went down without striking a single blow. Others put up sterner resistance, but the eventual outcome of the fight was never in doubt. A few soldiers escaped, fleeing into the night, but most, including Remonnet, were killed. As soon as the treachery became obvious the chamberlain had tried to run, but two of the prisoners made a special point of hunting him down. He asked for no mercy, and received none.

When it was over, the surviving slaves – in reality members of Snake's crew – retraced their steps to the bay, laughing and congratulating each other not only on the fight but also on their acting abilities. It had been a pleasure to put one over on that snobbish chamberlain. They arrived back at the beach, where they were expecting their comrades to be waiting to pick them up, and were surprised to see the boats milling about in the middle of the bay. Soon all but two began pulling towards the shore. As the bogus slaves climbed aboard they were told what had happened, and all eyes turned to where Snake was now cautiously edging towards the ice-rimmed boat.

'Get in and see if there are any left,' Snake ordered as they came alongside. One of his men scrambled to obey, testing the floating ice that cracked beneath his boot, then jumping over the frozen gunwale. He fell heavily, catching a foot on a plank that had sprung loose under the pressure of the ice, then righted himself and gingerly touched the casket. It was icy cold, but his hand suffered no harm. Holding the key with a cloth, he turned it and pushed back the lid. Moonlight glinted on the pile of stones within, and they shone with a liquid brightness.

'They're here,' he reported.

'Good,' Snake grated savagely through the pain of his injured arm. 'Pass it over.'

The lid was closed and locked again and the two boats drew closer by knocking away the fast thawing ice with their oars.

Before long they were all back aboard ship. There the casket was stowed in Snake's cabin, and as they left the harbour the ship's surgeon amputated the captain's ruined hand, promising to fit him with an impressive hook when the tar-covered wound healed. For two days Snake lay in a delirious stupor, wracked with pain when he was awake and by wintry nightmares when he was asleep, but he eventually recovered sufficiently to take the key in his remaining hand and peer into the casket. What he saw filled him with rage, but then he began to laugh so hard that the crew thought he had gone quite mad.

Inside the box were dozens of ordinary pebbles, such as could be found on any beach, and a little seawater. His double-cross had been matched by another. Snake had no idea how Remonnet had managed the switch, but admired his opponent's expertise. And he smiled to think of the price the chamberlain had paid for his perfidy.

By the time Snake discovered his loss, Ico and Andrin were back in Teguise with their prize. They were jubilant. In one fell swoop they had restocked the Firebrands' armoury, and had done so in a way that could not be connected to them. They were still not sure what had happened after the slaves had been exchanged, although it was obvious there had been some fighting. But no matter what had happened, Deion Verier was hardly in a position to complain about his loss of the crystals, as trading the dragon's tears was now as illegal as buying slaves. And the slave-traders were hardly likely to appeal to the authorities either. So as long as Ico kept this new cache secret from prying eyes, the entire enterprise had worked to perfection. In fact the only drawback was that they could not tell anyone about their success, at least for the time being. Magpie was the only one who could betray them, and even if he remembered events accurately, very few people ever took him seriously. And so, for now, only Ico knew how the crystals had been acquired by her partner.

Andrin had waited at the water's edge, among rocks at the side of the bay, for over an hour before the meeting between Remonnet and the slave-trader took place. His whole body, including his hair, had been plastered in dark grease which acted both as a disguise for his pale colouring and as protection against the cold of the disintegrating crystal. Once Magpie had done his work, Andrin had swum out to the drifting boat, underwater for the last hundred paces, and slid on board, pouring the crystals into an empty muslin bag and replacing them with pebbles he had brought with him in another. Then he had closed the casket again and slipped back into the sea. He had returned to the shelter of the rocks and in due course, under cover of nightfall, had rejoined Ico. They had hoped their subterfuge would buy them enough time to get away from the bay, but in the event it had worked better than they could have anticipated, and they had watched gratefully as Snake's ship sailed away.

They had rewarded Magpie with one of the crystals, to his great delight, and had left him in the care of friends at a village on the way back to the city.

Although the raid had been wonderfully successful, they returned home to find that other members of the Firebrands had been busy too. Senator Kantrowe, it seemed, was not going to have things all his own way.

CHAPTER SEVENTEEN

Although the Presidential Palace in Teguise had been designed to intimidate visiting dignitaries, it had little effect on Famara. Great marble halls, processional rooms lined with tall columns and graceful porticos were all so much stone and air as far as she was concerned. She appreciated the coolness because the sun's heat troubled her these days, but was left unmoved by the grandeur of her surroundings.

She followed the uniformed servant to one of the smaller chambers which were set aside for private conferences, noting as they walked how their footsteps echoed in the hollow spaces. The palace was quiet now that few foreigners came to Tiguafaya and the President himself was not involved in the everyday running of the country. Famara remembered that it had been very different when she was a young mage, a welcome guest at any of the receptions or dances that had seemed so frequent then. It had been at one of these celebrations that she had first met Marco Guadarfia. He was not yet president, of course, but the dashing young man had already been elected to the Senate at the tender age of twenty and was clearly destined for great things. But that was a long time ago, and the world, Famara mused, had looked very different then.

The usher showed her in and left without ceremony. Guadarfia was sitting, propped up by a mountain of cushions, with his head tipped back, eyes closed and mouth hanging open. He was snoring softly. A goblet sat on a small table in front of him and a book lay open in his lap. The room had a heavy, faintly musty air that Famara found unpleasant. She was not shocked to see how thin and frail her old friend had become. His failing health was common knowledge after all and, being old herself, she was well aware of the toll that the passing decades extracted from the human body. Even so, she was saddened to see a once vital and tireless man reduced to such feeble quiescence.

She coughed, but when this produced no reaction she crossed the room and tapped him on one bony knee. He woke with a splutter, and for a moment there was only confusion in his eyes. Then he gathered his wits about him and smiled.

'Famara? Is it really you?'

'Of course, you old fool. Who else would come to see you when it's so hot?'

She stooped to kiss both his cheeks, then took the chair at the other side of the table. He had made no effort to rise but his pleasure at seeing her was obvious.

'You used to like the warmth,' he remarked fondly. 'I remember you dancing all night.' The nostalgia in his voice was a poignant reminder of all they had once done – and would never do again.

'And you,' she replied tartly, 'never used to be so sentimental.'

'It comes with age.'

'Like wisdom?' she asked, smiling.

'Perhaps. Beyond a certain point . . .' He shrugged. 'Would you like something to drink? Wine?'

'Tea. Wine doesn't agree with me any more.'

He reached for the cord which hung from the wall and pulled sharply. A bell rang in a distant room.

'Are you not well?' he asked, concerned now.

'As well as anyone our age has any right to be.'

He nodded, understanding.

'I find that wine is one of life's few remaining pleasures. I would not be without it.' He picked up the goblet and sipped as if to demonstrate his allegiance.

Some time later, after the herb tea had been delivered and they had exhausted their small talk, Marco looked his guest in the eye.

'Now, are you going to tell me why you've really come to see me after all this time, or do I have to drag it out of you piece by piece?'

Famara had not thought him capable of such directness, and prepared to revise her opinion of the old man. Were there still times when his mind was as sharp as ever? Was he just humouring her? Or was his indolence a complete sham? She decided to test the limits of their relationship before coming to the real point of her visit.

'Most of our contemporaries are dead. Do you think we've outlived our usefulness, Marco?'

'Perhaps,' he replied heavily, then reconsidered. 'No, not you. Your skills are too valuable.'

'And what about yours?'

He thought for a while, then shrugged in a gesture of resignation.

'Experience must count for something, I suppose.'

'Then you've not become Kantrowe's puppet?' she asked bluntly.

'No.' There was a flicker of anger in his watery eyes now. 'But he is an able man, with all the energy and strength I lack. And he loves and honours Tiguafaya.'

'As you do?'

'Yes.'

'It's said he loves himself and his own power more.'

'Powerful men make enemies. You should not pay heed to rumours.'

'Then you support the recent proclamation?' Famara asked. 'That was Kantrowe's doing, was it not?'

'Of course I supported it,' he said heatedly. 'I would not have put my name to it otherwise. But it was never meant to be directed against those such as yourself. The responsible use of magic is not condemned. It is these foolish young—'

'The Firebrands?'

'Yes. Surely you see the difference? They don't care what harm they do, and such vanity is dangerous when allied to power.'

'And what if it is not vanity?' she asked calmly.

'You would defend them?' He was obviously surprised.

'They represent hope.'

'They represent anarchy!'

'So to control *them* you attack all magic? Does that strike you as reasonable?'

'I explained before—' he began.

'But don't you see?' Famara cut in angrily. 'Whatever your intentions, this has handed control of all magic to Kantrowe, and I'd like to know what he intends to do with it.'

'He will act in the best interests of the country,' Marco replied stubbornly.

'Will he? Perhaps he's acting in his *own* interests.'

'Why do you slander a man you do not know?'

'Oh, I know him,' she said emphatically. 'Better than you think.'

'I've had enough of this.'

He did indeed look even more tired and pale now. He reached for the bell pull but before he touched it the door opened and a gaunt man came in. The President looked at him with a mixture of relief and surprise.

'Mazo. Good. I was about to ring for you. My guest is just leaving.'

'Very well, sir.' Gadette switched his death's-head gaze to Famara, but she did not move.

'It used to be easier to get an appointment to see you, Marco,' she said, wondering how long the aide had been listening outside. 'With all the bureaucracy surrounding you now, it's taken me days to get this far. Don't ignore good advice when it's offered.'

'The President is quite capable of discerning good advice from bad,' Gadette observed acidly. 'Now, if you will follow me, madam.'

Still Famara did not rise but remained staring at Marco, who refused to meet her eyes. She leant forward, picked up the bowl which was still half full of cold tea and cradled it in her hands. Moments later tendrils of steam began to rise from the liquid, which then began to boil vigorously.

'Madam, please!' the aide exclaimed.

'Famara, no!' Marco cried.

The last of the tea evaporated in a sudden flare of blue-green fire, making both men jump. Famara set the bowl down carefully and stood up.

'Will the dragons punish me too?' she enquired caustically. 'Or are they a little more selective in who they decide to turn against? There's a lot of nonsense being talked in the name of reason at the moment – and you know it, Marco. Don't make your age an excuse for not doing the right thing.'

'I could have you arrested for this,' Gadette told her.

'*You* could?' she retorted, glancing at him with contempt. 'Isn't the President master within his own palace? Who are you to usurp his authority?'

'I—' Gadette began, then thought better of it and glanced at Guadarfia for guidance.

'Take her to the gates and let her go,' the old man said wearily. 'And make sure she doesn't come back.' He still would not meet Famara's gaze and she went without another word, having said all she had come to say. She had no idea whether it had done any good, but she felt better for trying.

Gadette left her at the palace entrance, and his parting words were meant as a warning.

'In his place I would not have been so lenient.'

'What's the matter, young man?' she grated. 'Are you afraid an old woman might upset your plans?'

As she glared at him, he had the uncomfortable impression that she knew more about him than she ought. He would set his spies to keep an eye on her, just in case.

'Leave now,' he told her, doing his best to sound disdainful, 'before I change my mind and have you thrown in gaol.'

Famara turned away, muttering something under her breath that he could not catch. Irritated, he almost went after her, but then turned back abruptly. Soon all her kind would be in thrall to his whim. Her pathetic demonstration of magical talent was nothing beside the power he would wield before too long.

'Of course, it was Famara who got us started,' Vargo said. 'But we've come a long way since she pointed us in the right direction. All my team have been working very hard.'

'But discreetly?' Ico asked.

'Of course. They all know the risks and we've been careful, but a few of the best sources are sympathetic to us.'

'Or pretend to be,' Andrin said cautiously.

'We have to trust some of them or we'd never get anywhere,' Vargo countered. 'And why would anyone lend us their books if they didn't want us to learn from them?'

'You have some of the old records?' Ico exclaimed.

'Yes. Several,' the musician replied proudly.

'Where are they?'

'Various places. We didn't want to put all our eggs in one basket.'

'Is there anything we can use?' Andrin asked.

'Depends what you want to use it for,' Vargo said, 'but there's plenty that seems feasible. When Famara learnt that you'd discovered a way to trigger the crystals telepathically she got very excited. She said that if we could do that, then we'd mastered half of all magic – focusing the power of the mind.'

'So what's the second half?' Ico asked.

'Shaping power from other sources and making it do what we want.'

'What sources?' Andrin asked. 'Crystals?'

'They're the most obvious, but there are hundreds of others.'

'Such as?'

'The volcanoes, the sea, certain trees and plants, fire and wind and the memories of stone, anything old that has absorbed magic from earlier times. Famara says that magic is all around us, but only becomes useful when we can recognize and control it. Which is where the power of the mind comes in,' he added, tapping the side of his head.

'And the dragons?' Ico prompted.

'They were the most potent beacons of all,' Vargo said, 'but it needed the most experienced of the old wizards to harness their potential – and even then it was apparently very dangerous. If even half the tales I've read in the books are true—'

'Forget dragons,' Andrin cut in. 'I want to hear about something we can use, something practical.'

'Illusions,' his friend replied promptly.

'What do you mean? What illusions?'

'I'll show you,' Vargo said, smiling. 'I'm not the only one who's been busy the last few days. We've planned a small demonstration for this afternoon. It should be quite interesting.'

CHAPTER EIGHTEEN

Lookout duty at Roncador Point was one of the least popular assignments among the soldiers of the White Guard. Although it was no more than an hour's march south of Teguise, the circular stone tower seemed remote and vulnerable. It was built upon the top of tumbled cliffs that formed the tip of a narrow headland, and was surrounded on three sides by the sea. It commanded a spectacular but unchanging view, and a vigilant sentry would be able to spot any ships in the southern approaches to the city long before they were ready to enter the harbour. The White Guard in Teguise could then be warned of any sign of hostile intent, either by sending a runner or a carrier pigeon, or by lighting a beacon.

In fact, most soldiers considered the whole exercise to be a waste of time. Pirates had never dared attack the capital, and were much more likely to amuse themselves by surrounding the lookout tower itself. At these times the occupants' only option was to draw up the ladder that led to the second-floor entrance – the first two storeys had no doors or windows – making themselves virtually unassailable but entirely dependent on their own supplies of food and water. In such a case they must hope either that the pirates grew bored and gave up the attempt, or that the tower was relieved by outside forces. Either way it was not an enjoyable experience, especially as some pirates had become adept at cheerfully shooting down the carrier pigeons and roasting them over their camp fires. There was little to do at Roncador Point at the best of times, but being confined to the cramped quarters indefinitely on strict rations was liable to unhinge even the most phlegmatic guards. However, most cycles of duty passed uneventfully, without such trials, and were merely endured with as much stoicism as the six-man teams could muster, counting the days until their replacements were due.

The morning shift was only an hour old, but the two men stationed on the roof of the tower were already finding the time dragging. The tedium had made the younger of the pair garrulous.

'Gods, this is pointless,' he sighed, glancing over the parapet at the empty, glittering ocean. The sun was still low in the sky, spreading a blinding streak of gold across the water. 'If our defences in Teguise are so badly organized that they can't react to their own lookouts, what good will any message from us be? I think they only keep this place on out of habit.'

'Just two more days,' the sergeant replied. ' Then it's back to the city.' He had no need to list the amenities offered by Teguise – and singularly lacking at Roncador Point. To dwell on them would be to invite even more discontent. The end of a tour of duty was always the worst time, but although the sergeant was as fed up as his men, as platoon leader he was responsible for keeping up their morale.

In the rooms below the two men who had been on night watch were sleeping while their remaining colleagues were engaged in a long and occasionally acrimonious game of dice. The resident pigeons strutted in their cage and cooed incessantly. The soldiers found this intensely irritating.

'I've lost count of the number of times I've been to this godforsaken hole, and I've never seen anything worth reporting,' the young soldier grumbled.

'There's a first time for everything,' the sergeant observed conscientiously.

'If you ask me, we've better things to worry about than pirates just now,' the younger man went on. 'Like the Firebrands.'

'They're just kids. And anyway, Kantrowe's got them on the run. They haven't done anything for days.'

'That's what worries me. The gods know what they're planning next. Chinero should have locked them all up.'

'The captain had his orders, same as we do,' the sergeant added philosophically. Privately he agreed with his companion, but it was not done to criticize officers in front of the men.

The soldier caught the hint in his superior's tone and dropped the subject, aware that he had already been granted more leeway than usual in speaking so freely.

'Is that a sail?' he asked, squinting and shading his eyes as he glanced to the southeast.

The sergeant looked, saw nothing and was about to say so when their half-hearted surveillance was interrupted by an urgent cry from below.

'Hello! Anyone there?'

The guards crossed to the inland side of the tower and looked down. On the path below, looking back up at them, was a young man. He had obviously been running – his face was red and sheened with sweat, and he was breathing heavily.

'Worms are coming!' he gasped. 'Help us.'

'Where?'

'Betancore,' the man replied, naming a village some way inland.

The sergeant was relieved. For a moment he had wondered if the fireworms were headed for the point.

'We can't help you!' he called. 'You know the drill. Get everyone inside, secure the houses and wait them out.' It was inadequate advice and he knew it, but there genuinely wasn't anything else he could do.

'No, no. You don't understand,' the runner pleaded, his eyes wide and his tone desperate. 'It's just not worms. There are magicians with their birds headed to meet them.'

'Mages?' The sergeant was aghast.

'Yes.'

'Do they have crystals?' the soldier asked.

'I don't know. Please hurry. We have to stop them.' He had no need to explain why.

The sergeant made his decision.

'We're on our way!' he shouted, then turned to his companion. 'Rouse the others. I must send a message to headquarters.'

'We're going out there when worms are flying?' the soldier asked, the colour draining from his face.

'Yes. Get moving.'

As the younger man obeyed, scrambling down through the trap-door in the roof and yelling to his comrades, the sergeant wondered what message he should send with the pigeon. This situation did not fit any of the prearranged, colour-coded bands that could be wound round the bird's leg, so he would have to improvise. In the end he used an orange ring, for an unspecified emergency, and set the pigeon free. After circling for a few moments it headed northwards, and the sergeant set about completing his arrangements. All the men were awake now, and had gathered their equipment.

'Paulo, you're the fastest here. Run back to the city. They should already be mobilized, but won't know where to go. We need reinforcements to Betancore fast. Got that?'

'Yes, sergeant.' The guard looked relieved. None of the men fancied coming face to face with fireworms, and his athletic ability – which in the past had earned him some dangerous assignments – now seemed like a godsend. He began to discard his heavier gear, while the others watched enviously.

'The rest of us are going back with the villager,' the sergeant went on.

'He's already gone,' one of the others reported, having been watching from one of the slit windows.

'Well, we know the way,' their leader replied dismissively. 'If the Firebrands are really set on doing anything this stupid, we've got to stop them. And if we do, Chinero and his superiors will be *very* pleased with us. So let's go!'

The pigeon's arrival in Teguise caused much consternation. The receiving sentry went straight to Captain Chinero who, as duty officer, set the military wheels in motion. Within a remarkably short time more than a hundred guards were mustered at the southern gates, ready to embark on any possible sortie, messages had been sent to senior officers and to Senator Kantrowe, and an extra detachment had been detailed to keep watch from the harbour in case of an attack by hostile shipping. Runners were already on the way, following all possible routes to Roncador Point so that news of the exact nature of the emergency could be ascertained as quickly as possible. All this activity was watched with considerable interest – and some unease – by the citizens of Teguise, many of whom were wondering fearfully what might have triggered such urgency.

Within half an hour Paulo and the runner he had met were reporting breathlessly to Chinero; moments later the White Guard were on the move.

When the sergeant and his men arrived at Betancore the village seemed deserted, and this was confirmed by a quick house to house search.

'Now what?' one of the men asked nervously. They all knew that if the residents had fled it was because they feared that the fireworms would be coming that way. And, unlike many of the citizens of Teguise, most members of the White Guard had seen how people died at the hands of the creatures.

'We've got to find the Firebrands and stop them before they do anything stupid,' the sergeant replied.

'Where are they?'

'There's only five of us . . .'

'Reinforcements will be here soon,' he assured them. 'This is our chance to be heroes.'

'Just so long as it's not dead heroes,' one of his charges muttered.

'Spread out,' their leader ordered. 'Find the local vantage points. Chances are they're west of us. Whistle twice as soon as you see anything. Now move!'

Military training overcame their fear, and they set off as ordered. The first thing they spotted were some birds, hawks of some kind, hovering and circling in a group. Moments later movement was seen on the ground below and, obeying the signal, the soldiers moved forward purposefully, running over the small cultivated fields and then picking their way across the lava fields beyond. One of them fell awkwardly as the rock gave way beneath his boot but the sergeant ordered the others to go on, ignoring their comrade's pleas for help.

The pursuit seemed to last for ever; every time they appeared to be drawing close enough to intervene, the mages were further away again, allowing only tantalizing glimpses of themselves amid the outcrops of stone. The birds too always seemed to be out of range, almost as if they were deliberately taunting the soldiers. The men ran deeper and deeper into the firelands, sweating profusely and growing angrier by the minute. At last they came to the crest of a ridge, looked down into the black gully ahead of them and saw their quarry clearly for the first time.

And then the screaming began.

'Crystals!' the sergeant yelled. 'Come on, we've got to stop this!'

They ran forward again as, in the distance, the hawks swooped down, releasing tiny green sparks that fell to the ground below. The birds' masters seemed oblivious to the approach of the soldiers, concentrating on the task in hand, but the sergeant roared out a battle cry and his men followed suit, hoping to distract them.

They succeeded. There were eight of the Firebrands present and, as they turned to watch the guards advance upon them, the distant screaming became less insistent. The mages all wore masks, and were apparently unarmed. They did not move, either to hide or run away, but just stood staring at their would-be attackers through the eye slits of their colourful disguises.

With swords drawn, the four soldiers drew closer, each yelling threats and imprecations against magic.

'We don't want to kill you!' the sergeant called hoarsely, 'but we will if those birds drop any more crystals or if the screaming starts again.'

None of the Firebrands spoke or moved as the soldiers caught their breath. They were beginning to be disconcerted by the mages' apparent acquiescence, and suspected a trap.

'Over here!' the sergeant yelled. 'Together. Where we can keep an eye on you. And get those masks off.'

There was still no reaction, and he was about to reinforce his words with the flat of his blade when one of his men shrieked in terror. Several fireworms had just flown into the hollow and were heading straight for them.

'No!'

'Kill them!' one of the guards shouted, pointing and threatening one of the magicians with his sword. 'Do it!'

A sparrowhawk sped overhead, there was a cracking sound and a wave of cold, and the fireworms shrivelled and fell to the rocks below.

'You bastards!' the sergeant roared, and made a grab for the nearest Firebrand, intending to rip away his mask.

But the soldier's hand passed right through the young man's head without encountering any resistance, so that he staggered and almost fell. As he exclaimed in horrified disbelief, all eight masked figures shivered out of existence. The petrified guards were left alone in a silent, empty landscape.

CHAPTER NINETEEN

'Oh, that was wonderful!' Vargo laughed. 'I wish I could've seen the look on their faces.'

'Very impressive,' Andrin agreed soberly, 'but are you sure it was wise?'

'What do you mean?'

'We've made the White Guard look very foolish. That's a dangerous game to play.'

'And even if they can't prove it, they're still going to blame us,' Ico added.

'And admit how they were duped?' Vargo said, his pleasure fading now as doubts crept in.

The three friends had watched the entire performance from the rim of a nearby crater. They had been too far away to see many of the details but, now that they were back in the city, it was the general principles that interested them most.

'So none of what the soldiers saw was real?' Ico asked.

'It was all real, in a sense,' Vargo replied, regaining some of his enthusiasm. 'Just not when or where they saw it. Most of the illusions came from our memories, but naturally we enhanced them a bit to make the scene fit the situation.'

'You mean *you* were taking part? How...I never noticed...' Andrin was astonished.

'I did the fireworms,' the musician stated proudly. 'Realistic, weren't they.'

'And you're saying that anything we've experienced can be reproduced as visions?' Ico asked.

'In theory, yes. Of course we can't do everything yet – there hasn't been that much time – but we're learning fast. Memories give us a solid base to start from, but eventually we ought to be able to use anything we can imagine. There'll be no limits to what we can do then, but that's still a long way off. In the meantime, the most important thing is that we're getting better at drawing the power we need from sources around us.'

'So memories aren't enough on their own?' Ico said.

'No. Although they shape the images, we need more energy to project them over distance and make them visible. The principle involved is the same as the signals to the dragon's tears, but it's more complicated.'

'And I suppose the more people there are watching the harder it is,' Andrin guessed.

'Funnily enough, the opposite is true,' Vargo replied. 'The more people in the audience the better the illusion is. I don't understand why exactly, but I think it's because their belief in what they're seeing reinforces the vision so that it actually becomes stronger. If there was a really big crowd the cascade effect would probably be amazing.'

Ico did not spare the time to consider this surprising claim. There were still too many questions to be asked.

'How many people did it take to do it?'

'Six, including me.'

'So you worked as a team?' she said. 'Each handling a different aspect of the illusion?'

'Yes. It's easier that way. Theoretically one person could do it all, but even if any of us had been confident – or powerful – enough to try, it would've been much too tiring. It's exhausting enough as it is.'

Ico nodded, remembering how tired she had been after completing her experiments with the crystals, creating and refining the technique.

'Isn't coordination a problem?' she asked.

'Practice helps,' Vargo replied, 'but when you're all concentrating on one goal, strange things start happening. It's hard to describe unless you've experienced it, but it's almost as if you become part of something bigger. One mind. Everyone noticed that when we began rehearsing. It was weird and uncomfortable at first. Some people were too frightened or embarrassed to share their thoughts, so it wasn't easy. In the end we just chose the best of us, pooled our ideas and accepted our limitations.'

'Where were the others?' Andrin asked.

'Below us, on the crater slope. Far enough away from the site to be safe, but not so far that the power needed would be too great. There were limits to what we could do convincingly.'

'And where did the power come from?' Ico asked.

'Each of us has a talisman now, something through which we can syphon magic wherever we find it.' Vargo held up a silver brooch in the shape of a large ring, studded with golden brown stones. 'This is mine. Famara gave it to me. It's very old, and there are more memories stored inside it than I'll ever be able to see.'

'So the power is actually in the talismans?' Ico took the brooch and weighed it in her hand. Although it felt heavy on her palm, she sensed nothing unusual.

'A little bit, but not much,' he replied. 'Storing energy is a skill we haven't even begun to master yet. The talismans act as a focal point for magic, though, so that we can use it from any source. And it's all around you – once you know where to look.'

'I can see I've got a bit of catching up to do,' Ico remarked. 'You've learnt such a lot!'

'My services as a teacher are yours to command,' Vargo stated, smiling. 'And I think you'll find my rates quite reasonable.'

Chinero had left the questioning of the sergeant until last, but the man's story tallied with that given by each of the other lookouts, and the captain was now left to mull over the implications. When he and the detachment of Guards had reached Betancore there was nothing to be seen or heard, and it had been some time before their search had revealed the angry and bewildered platoon. They had clearly been through a harrowing ordeal, and it was some time before the full picture emerged.

'This man, who said he came from Betancore, would you recognize him again?'

'Yes, sir.'

'But he didn't say the mages were members of the Firebrands?'

'No, sir. But who else could it have been?'

Who indeed? Chinero thought resentfully. Aloud he said, 'The entire population of the village was absent, not because of fireworms, but because the son of their head man was getting married to a girl in Hilario, three miles to the south. None of them was aware of any movement by the worms or of sending a runner to you.'

'I had no reason to doubt it at the time, sir,' the sergeant replied defensively.

'Hmm. Was the runner real, or was he another illusion?'

'I couldn't say, sir. He seemed real enough to me.'

'But it turned out to be a wild goose chase in the end.'

'Yes, sir.'

Chinero glanced at the veteran, who stood foursquare,

staring fixedly into space beyond his superior officer, and knew that he was not the one to blame for this fiasco. After a long, uncomfortable pause, the captain decided that he had heard enough.

'You did what you thought best, sergeant. Had the emergency been genuine, your initiative might have paid off handsomely. As it was, we've all been made to look rather foolish. No blame to you. It might have been better, however, if you had not left the tower entirely unmanned.'

'I realise that, sir. I take full responsibility.'

In their haste, the tower had been abandoned, unlocked and with the ladder in place. Seeing this, some pirates from the Barber's fleet had come ashore, ransacked the place and then set it ablaze. All that was left now was a stone shell, with a blackened pile of still-smoking embers inside.

'I'm putting you in charge of the rebuilding,' Chinero said. 'I expect it to be completed within six days.'

'Yes, sir.' It was less of a punishment than he had anticipated.

'Dismissed.'

The pirate fleet was still in the area, but had not come any closer to Teguise. Nonetheless, a careful watch was being maintained. The last thing they needed now, Chinero thought, was a full-scale battle against outsiders. They had enough trouble coming from within.

He took a deep breath and set out to make his report to Kantrowe. He was not looking forward to the experience.

After Chinero left, Kantrowe, Deion Verier and Mazo Gadette sat in silence, none of them wanting to look at either of the others.

'They're getting more adventurous,' Gadette said eventually.

'Assuming it *was* the Firebrands,' Verier said.

'Of course it was,' the aide stated. 'But we can't prove it.'

'We don't need to,' Kantrowe said, suddenly becoming animated. 'We'll simply teach them the consequences of such effrontery.'

'What do you have in mind?' Gadette enquired.

The senator told him and, after a while, the mood of the meeting improved dramatically.

'I'll see to all the details,' the aide concluded happily.

'Good,' Kantrowe said. 'Is there anything else we need to discuss?'

'There is one thing,' Gadette replied. 'Famara Ye visited the President yesterday.'

'What did that old bat want?' Verier asked.

The aide gave them a report of what he had overheard and what he had subsequently learnt from Guadarfia.

'She's trying to stir up trouble, and I wouldn't be surprised to find that it's linked to the Firebrands. I have her under observation now.'

'Good,' Kantrowe said. 'Do you think she'll have had any influence on Marco?'

'He was rattled, no doubt about it, but—'

'He knows where his best interests lie,' Verier completed for him. 'He won't do anything stupid.'

'Even if he tries, there's little danger from that quarter,' Kantrowe said complacently. 'There've been rumours about his ill health for so long now that no one would be surprised if he were to die soon. It would only take a little nectar in his wine. His palate's so addled he wouldn't even taste the poison until it was too late.' He laughed. 'Let's hope it doesn't come to that. Leave him to me. Anything else?'

'Yes,' Verier said, his face darkening as he remembered a grievance of his own. 'I got word last night that my chamberlain and several of my men had been double-crossed and killed by pirates. I thought we were supposed to be talking to those sea-scum.'

'Am I to take it that Remonnet was involved in some sort of illicit trade with these pirates?' Kantrowe asked mildly.

'What of it?' Verier answered defensively. 'That's irrelevant now.'

'Do you know whose men they were?'

'They were privateers,' Verier admitted. 'The captain calls himself Snake.'

'So Zarzuelo and Agnadi wouldn't necessarily have any influence over them,' Kantrowe pointed out.

'No, but if we had a pact with them they'd be protecting us from vermin like this. It's an outrage, and those responsible should be punished. Why hasn't Zophres been back to us yet?'

'All I know is that the negotiations are taking some time, but he should be here soon.'

'And in the meantime, bastards like the Barber and this Snake character are running amok!'

'Patience, Deion. Perhaps you'd better find other ways of procuring labour for your mines until we've got this sorted out.' Kantrowe sounded amused.

'This is no laughing matter,' Verier raged. 'I paid good money for nothing, and Remonnet was one of the best men I ever had.'

Not if he was stupid enough to get himself killed like that, Kantrowe thought, but did not voice his opinion.

'You'll have your revenge in due course, never fear,' he assured his colleague. 'And if our other projects come good you may not need as many slaves soon.'

Although Verier's expression revealed his doubts, he said nothing more. There was a knock at the door.

'Come.'

The door opened and Jon Zophres put his head round the corner.

'My ears were burning,' he said. 'I hope what you were saying about me wasn't too complimentary.'

'No chance of that,' Verier growled.

The envoy came in, still grinning, and slumped into a chair.

'Well?' Kantrowe demanded. 'Do we have an agreement?'

'Not yet.'

'Then what are you doing here?' he asked coldly.

Zophres was not to be intimidated. 'If I'd stayed any longer they'd have taken it as a sign of desperation, of weakness,' he explained confidently. 'I think each of them was waiting for the other to make the first move.'

'And the Barber?' Kantrowe asked curiously.

The envoy shrugged. 'He wasn't there.'

'We know that!' Verier snapped. 'He's been raiding villages in the south again, and now he's not far from Teguise.'

'Some of his men burnt the watchtower at Roncador Point this morning,' Kantrowe added. 'It looks as though he may be the rogue element.'

'Surely we can turn that to our advantage?' Gadette suggested quietly.

'Probably,' Kantrowe agreed. 'We need this alliance, but only as a temporary measure. I've no intention of letting those thieves keep everything we've promised them, and if we can start them fighting amongst themselves . . .'

'So I should press Zarzuelo and the Lawyer to agree, even if the Barber won't get involved?' Zophres asked.

'Yes,' Kantrowe answered, sounding more confident now. 'It'll be perfect. The Barber will give them something to think about so they won't get too big for their boots and, in due course, it shouldn't be too hard to prompt a little antagonism between our various friends.'

'Consider it done,' the envoy said emphatically. 'Now tell me what's been happening here. I bet it's been really dull while I've been away, risking life and limb.'

CHAPTER TWENTY

The two house sparrows had fallen to the floor where they rolled and fluttered, feet locked together and beaks clashing. The chattering of the entire clan rose to new heights as they watched the fight, so that Vargo and Famara could hardly hear themselves think, let alone speak. The birds were perched on every available surface in the hut, and the racket they made defied belief. Responding to a request from Famara, the tribe's matriarch flew down and separated the two warring males, giving each a sharp peck of her own. They retreated reluctantly and sullenly, but did not question Tek's authority. The noise level in the shack fell slightly.

Thank you.

Men! Tek complained. *They're worse than fledglings sometimes.*

Now could we have a little quiet, please? Famara asked.

Of course.

At a particularly strident call from their leader, the sparrows fell silent for a few moments and then, because complete quiet was impossible, resumed their chatter at a muted level.

Vargo had not been aware of the exact nature of the conversation, only of its results, and he smiled now, looking round at the relatively subdued clan. There must have been fifty of them in the hut, either perching or hopping about in their familiar jerky way. Each one of them was a compact bundle of energy, cocky and cheerful but nervous too, and in such a confined space their overall effect was comical and almost overwhelming. And yet they also displayed a kind of exuberant respect; only the very young ever disgraced themselves by defecating on Famara's furniture – and they were instantly reprimanded by their elders in such a way that the offence was never repeated.

Vargo could only pick out a few individuals and thought of the tribe almost as one creature, but it was clear that, even though they all looked similar – their colouring was predominantly brown, with the males having white cheeks and black necks – there were distinct personalities here. Famara knew them all, although she sometimes found it difficult to keep up with the newest arrivals when fledglings joined the group, but even she knew it was impossible to remember all their names. Her actual link was Tek, the matriarch, who was old and a little decrepit herself, although she remained a fierce and steadfast leader who stood no nonsense from her tribe. Famara rarely had need of her link these days, but when she did she had long since accepted that the others would all come with Tek. They were as much a part of her as were her wing feathers. Had Famara wanted to, she could have communicated telepathically with any of the sparrows. However, to do this would have been to invite madness, as the concept of talking as a conversation – as opposed to verbal warfare – was alien to them as a group, and she would not have been able to prevent the mind-numbing barrage of them all speaking at once. So Famara restricted her empathy to Tek alone, shielding herself from the others. For the sake of convenience she referred to the other birds as Tek Two, Tek Three and so on, in order of the tribe's hierarchy.

Compared to humans, sparrows do not live long, but whenever a matriarch died the most senior female took over the position and became the new link with Famara. The old woman could not recall how long this particular Tek had been with her, but it would be a sad day when she died. She had been perhaps the wisest and most valuable of them all, although every one had brought some special memories. Then again, Famara mused, it won't be too long before *I'm* gone, and then the clan will revert to being wild again. It was a melancholy thought.

'Now at least we can talk,' she told Vargo, pushing aside her preoccupation.

'Yes,' he replied, smiling. 'I'd have thought someone like you would have linked to a bird with a more musical song.'

'Oh, there's music in their songs,' she said fondly. 'It's just hidden below the noise. I've no complaints. They've taught me a great deal over the years.'

'Such as?'

'Teamwork, companionship, the importance of freedom *and* order, opportunity and alertness . . . I could go on, but this isn't what you came to talk about.'

'No, it's not.'

He fell silent then, unwilling to return to the contemplation of his own problems. In the relative quiet he could hear Ero's footsteps as he marched about on the thin roof, and was glad that the hoopoe had chosen to remain outside. The gods knew what he would have made of the sparrows. It could have—

'Daydreaming again?' Famara enquired softly.

'What? Oh, sorry. I just don't seem to be able to do anything right at the moment.'

Famara knew that he was referring to more than his current distraction.

'The path you've chosen was never going to be an easy one,' she said. 'Magic can be a harsh mistress.'

Vargo nodded.

'I know,' he said heavily. 'I accept that. We all do. We've been working really hard and I think what we've achieved in such a short time is incredible, but . . .' He hesitated, fighting annoyance and wondering whether it should be directed at himself or someone else. 'Even the demonstration, when we put almost everything we've discovered into practice, seems to have caused more problems than it solved.'

'How so?'

'I mean, we've learnt so much,' he went on, oblivious to the question, 'not just my team, who actually produced the illusions, but we had Firebrands watching every move the White Guard made. Timings, numbers, routes, everything – just what Andrin wanted, in fact. It'll be invaluable knowledge whenever we want to create a diversion, but all he seemed concerned about was that we might have provoked Kantrowe into even more vigorous action.'

'Making your enemy look a fool is not always wise,' Famara commented, 'no matter how satisfying it may be.'

'That's just what Andrin said,' Vargo admitted disappointedly. He had secretly been hoping that Famara would vindicate him, tell him he had done well and that Andrin was being over-cautious, but he knew in his heart that this was not the case.

'You're just learning the hardest lesson of all,' his mentor added. 'Magic isn't the answer to everything; it won't solve all your problems. It's just a tool and, like any other, it's only as good as the craftsman who wields it. A hammer is good for knocking in nails, but it's also possible to bash your own thumb with it.'

Vargo winced at the idea.

'You think that's what I've done?'

'I don't know. Only time will tell. What I *do* know is that your heart is in the right place – and you have made remarkable progress.' Vargo's spirits rose at the obvious pride in her voice. He could ask for no better reason to persevere than Famara's tacit admiration.

'Besides,' she went on, 'you're not the only one whose recent efforts might have unfortunate repercussions.'

'Why? What's happened?' he asked, worried now.

Famara told him about her abortive visit to the Presidential Palace.

'I lost my temper with the silly old fool, which would've been all right if we'd been alone, but an aide called Mazo Gadette was there by then, and he's a nasty piece of work. Marco won't do anything. I reckon he'll just try to forget the whole thing, but Gadette may not be so amenable. You have to choose your enemies even more carefully than you do your friends.'

Vargo thought about that for a while.

'What do you want me to do?' he asked eventually. 'Are you in any danger?'

'I'm not worried about myself,' she replied dismissively. 'Harming me will always be more trouble than it's worth, but I don't want anyone else getting into hot water over it. You especially.'

'Me?'

'You're here, aren't you? Did you notice anyone watching outside?'

'Only some of the locals.'

'Good. They look out for me, not that there's any need. Did anyone follow you?'

'I don't think so.'

'Well, keep an eye out when you leave. If I'm being spied on, you'll automatically become suspect too. And you don't need that at the moment.'

'I'll be careful,' he promised. 'We're all on our guard just now. But are you sure you don't want to move somewhere safer?'

'I'm as safe here as anywhere,' she told him. 'Don't fuss.'

'You know I'd do anything . . .' he began, but stopped when Famara gave him an expressive glance.

'Is there anything else you want to discuss?' she asked after a pause. 'Because I'm tired. I've been tired ever since I made that tea explode yesterday.'

'You made your tea explode?' Vargo exclaimed. 'You didn't tell me that!'

'It was only a few dregs, and it was a mistake,' she added defensively. 'I'd already made my point. I was being stupid, showing off to prove I could still do it – and then I hardly had enough energy left to get home!'

'Explode?' he repeated incredulously. 'Really explode?'

'Yes, really,' she said impatiently. 'And making something actually happen – no matter how trivial – takes a lot more strength than making someone *think* they saw it.'

'True magic,' he whispered longingly.

'Yes, and very silly of me it was too,' she replied. 'Let's drop the subject. Was there anything else?'

'There is something,' he admitted, then hesitated, 'but if you're tired . . .'

'Well?' Famara demanded when he didn't go on. She tried to flex her fingers, which were aching intolerably now, and found them almost rigid.

'I'm in love,' Vargo said softly.

'About time too,' she remarked, forgetting her pain instantly.

'I've been in love for a long time . . .'

'But?'

'It's Ico.'

'Ah.'

'I pretend it's just a joke, and that's all she thinks it is. The worst thing is that I can't even tell her the truth.'

He looked up nervously then, and the mixture of hope and confusion in his face made Famara want to weep.

'What do you want me to tell you?' she asked gently.

'I don't know. I know she loves me, but like a brother – and sometimes she despises me. Yet when I look at her I . . .' He broke off, too ashamed to continue. And then, as if determined to purge himself of all his most loathsome thoughts, he forced himself to go on. 'I've even wondered if she would turn to me if Andrin were ever killed. How can I *think* that? He's my best friend!' Vargo's self-disgust was painfully apparent.

'I doubt she'd want anyone at all under those circumstances,' Famara said. 'And you'd be fundamentally too decent to offer her anything more than genuine concern and comfort.'

'I wish I could believe that.'

There was a pause, as Famara looked at him with genuine sympathy.

'You don't make life easy for yourself, do you?' she observed.

Vargo laughed, a sharp, unhappy sound that provoked the sparrows into a fresh wave of excited chattering. They quietened slowly.

'Why now?' Famara asked over the din. 'Why have you never told me this before?'

'I felt so stupid. But with everything that's happening, I thought I might not get the chance again. We could be killed any day. Ico, Andrin, me . . .'

'And my own demise is long overdue,' she added cheerfully.

Vargo looked up, stricken, then saw her smile and his tension eased.

'You'll outlive us all,' he said.

'I hope not,' she replied honestly.

'I'm sorry. I should never have told you. It's my burden—'

'I'm honoured by your trust,' Famara interrupted. She almost added that he was like a son to her, but held her tongue, knowing that this would increase his embarrassment. 'But it seems to me that Andrin and Ico are as close as Bertin and Orzola. Separating them would be a deadly business.'

'I know,' Vargo conceded miserably.

'Hasn't anyone else caught your eye?' she asked mischievously. 'After all, you're an attractive, talented young man. Plenty of girls would be glad—'

'No. Nobody,' he cut in. 'What would be the point? All I'd see would be a pale shadow of her.'

'So you won't give anyone a chance?'

'I can't.'

'Oh well, they say suffering is good for the soul of an artist,' Famara observed flippantly. 'So at least your music should benefit.'

Vargo smiled in spite of himself.

'Anyway, why are you asking advice from a shrivelled old wreck like me?' she asked.

'There's no one else I . . . Please never mention this to anyone.'

'It's our secret,' she promised, crossing gnarled hands over her heart.

'Besides . . .' Vargo hesitated. 'Didn't you ever . . . when you were younger?'

Famara laughed, a hoarse, throaty sound that Vargo thought must have been very sexy once.

'You want the juicy details of my sordid past?' she said, enjoying his instant blush. 'Oh, I had my fair share of suitors and lovers. But that's ancient history. It was just a game then.'

'So there was no one special?' he persisted. 'No one you wanted to stay with?'

'One, perhaps.'

'Who?' he asked, then knew what she was going to say before the answer passed her lips.

'Marco.'

'Why didn't you marry him?'

'He asked me, but we were both too busy at the time and we grew apart. And then it was too late.'

'I wish you had married him,' Vargo said earnestly. 'Tiguafaya would be a very different place now if you were in the palace.'

'You are presumptuous, young man,' she told him haughtily, 'although your loyalty is appreciated. But people don't usually get married for political reasons.'

Someone's coming. Ero's voice sounded loudly inside Vargo's head, startling him.

Do you know who it is?

Famara, sensing the conversation even though she could not hear it, kept quiet.

The one who saw you featherless, the hoopoe reported.

Vargo sighed with relief, and answered Famara's unspoken question. 'It's a friend. Allegra Meo. She's one of my team. Can she come in?'

'Of course. Your friends are my friends.'

Vargo pulled back the curtain and beckoned to Allegra, who was standing a few paces away, looking around uncertainly. When she saw him she smiled, obviously relieved.

'I was beginning to think I was in the wrong place,' she said. 'Why does Famara live in this dump?'

'Because it's my home and it has all I need,' the mage herself replied from the gloomy interior. 'Come in, my dear.'

Allegra ducked inside and took in the cluttered surroundings as best she could, showing no surprise at the gathering of sparrows.

'I'm sorry,' she said, embarrassed. 'I didn't mean . . .'

'It's all right,' Famara assured her. 'It *is* a dump, but I'm comfortable here.'

Ero waddled in through the open doorway, looking about self-importantly. He eyed the clustered sparrows disdainfully, then hopped up on to a small table, scattering several birds as he did so. The clan, who had been temporarily silenced by uncertainty over the new arrivals, protested loudly, then settled back into their habitual low prattling.

Seeing no other available space, Allegra sat down cross-legged on the floor.

'It's a pleasure to meet you, ma'am. Vargo's told us all so much about you.'

'Hell's bells,' Famara laughed. 'I've not been called that for more years than I care to remember. My name's Famara, young lady, so use it.'

'Yes, Famara,' she responded, brightly obedient. 'You can call me Cat.'

'Cat?' Vargo looked puzzled.

'It's what the other kids used to call me when I was little,' she explained. 'My friends still do. Allegra, Ally, alley cat. See?'

'You never told me that,' he said.

'You never asked.'

Famara watched the exchange, noting how much more knowing the girl was, even though she was the younger of the two. The old woman had warmed to her immediately. *You're a fool, boy,* she thought, *if you can't see what's under your nose. Ico's not for you, but this one could be for the asking.*

Allegra had stretched out a hand towards some of the frankly curious sparrows, and one of the braver birds had hopped onto her finger. She laughed with delight at the touch of the tiny feet and soon the clan had adopted her, alighting on her shoulders, arms and legs, and chirruping happily. Ero watched the entire scene with an air of outraged disgust and hooted in protest, but no one took any notice of him.

'Well, Allegra, you're the first cat to have that effect on my tribe,' Famara commented. 'Are you linked?'

'No.' The girl's pleasure faded for a moment. 'I'd like to be, but I know you can't just choose something like that. It has to happen of its own accord.'

'You're young,' the old woman reassured her. 'There's still time.'

'Al . . . Cat is proving a very valuable member of the team, even so,' Vargo said loyally.

'I'm not much of a mage,' Allegra admitted. 'Without a link to teach me, the idea of telepathy seems so strange, and I can't grasp the idea of mental focusing. But I'm still trying – and I'm pretty good at research, aren't I?' she added, looking at Vargo.

'The best,' he replied promptly. 'She's tracked down no end of information.'

'That's why I'm here,' she said. 'I know where there's another of the old books. It's owned by a man named Giavista Martinoy. He won't let us take it away, but we can read it at his home if we want to. Oh yes, and I found another reference to flocks of birds just like these.' She carefully indicated her living blanket.

'The nets?' Famara asked.

'Yes. You know about that?'

'A little.'

'Of course,' Allegra said, with obvious chagrin. 'I'm sorry, I'm not usually so stupid. We've found several references in the old archives, but the one I came across this morning is the most extensive yet. I couldn't make head nor tail of it, but I was hoping Vargo might. It was something to do with spreading magic out.'

Famara nodded as the other two looked at her expectantly.

'It's been a long time since I used anything like that,' she said, then paused, thinking. 'When someone is linked to one bird within a tightknit group, as I am, there are certain types of magic that can be projected via all the members of the clan, as if they made up a single telepathic network. That way the effective range of the spell can be greatly increased.' Seeing the blank expressions on the faces of her guests she added, 'Look, I may not be able to explain it very well, but I can show you.'

'No,' Vargo protested. 'You're tired enough already.'

'Whatever gave you that idea?' his mentor asked innocently. 'Watch.'

Famara closed her eyes and for several heartbeats nothing seemed to be happening. Then a tiny spark of golden light began to blossom in midair, in the centre of the room. Moments later Tek flew up and through the glow, followed rapidly by other members of her tribe. As each sparrow flew on a spectral trail of gold was left behind in the air, so that it soon seemed that the entire room was filled with a delicate, shimmering filigree.

Vargo and Allegra watched, both enchanted and awestruck, as the birds continued to add to the pattern, but it was all too much for Ero. He jumped down and hid under the table, deliberately closing his eyes to the spectacle.

'Enough,' Famara commanded eventually, and the sparrows settled. The golden spider's web gradually faded from view, leaving only a ghostly memory in the air.

For some time no one spoke. Even the clan was silent. Ero emerged slowly from his hiding place.

'That was amazing,' Vargo whispered eventually. 'Beautiful.'

'Do you think we could apply it to the use of crystals?' Allegra asked excitedly, coming out of her reverie.

'I don't see why not,' Famara replied.

'So when a tear implodes, the birds could take the cold and spread it out like a fisherman's net?'

Famara nodded.

'They could shape it so the worms couldn't escape. We'd catch more that way.'

'Wouldn't it be dangerous?' Vargo asked. ' For the birds, I mean.'

'Perhaps,' the old woman replied. 'You'll need to experiment carefully. Are many of the Firebrands linked to clans?'

'A few,' Vargo said. He was less enthusiastic about the idea than the two women, foreseeing several problems, but he was glad that the ideas were still flowing.

'We should go,' Allegra said, seeing their hostess yawn suddenly.

'I am very tired now,' Famara conceded. 'Shake those little beggars off before you try to stand up.'

Allegra did as she was told, dislodging the birds who had settled on her again. For a few moments the air was full of movement, feathers and cries of outrage. Then the whirlwind abated and the visitors made their farewells, Allegra shaking Famara's hand and Vargo stooping to kiss her cheek.

'She's wonderful,' the girl said when they were out of earshot.

'Yes,' Vargo replied absently, his mind elsewhere.

'What is it?' Allegra whispered.

'We're being followed,' he said. 'Don't look back. Two men in grey shirts.'

'What shall we do? Split up?'

'No. We'll lose them. I'll wager I know this quarter better than they do. When we turn the next corner, be ready to move fast.'

They reached the junction, turned left, then ran as fast as they could. They turned left again into a tiny alley, dodged through a gateway, crossed a small, overgrown garden, climbed over a low wall and slipped into another lane on the other side. Once there Vargo led them into an alcove where they waited, huddled close together in the shadows. Time passed slowly, but there was no sign of their pursuers.

'I think we lost them,' he said cautiously, peering up and down the lane.

Allegra nodded, her eyes bright with excitement.

'Let's go and see this new book then,' Vargo suggested.

They set off, congratulating themselves on the ease of their escape. Neither of them noticed the raven mirroring their course from above. Nor did they see the single man in a black shirt, who followed at a discreet distance and glanced every so often up at the sky.

CHAPTER TWENTY-ONE

The sensible part of Ico knew that she should not have gone out during the hours of daylight. However, the obstinate part had decided that she'd be damned if she would let prejudice and ignorance force her to live like some timid, nocturnal creature. She had never been one to run away from a fight but now, as she saw heads turn to watch her walk past and heard the whispers start, she began to have second thoughts. There was antagonism and even a little dread in some of the looks she received, but she did her best to ignore them. Other Firebrands had told her of the public anger directed at them but, apart from the chivaree, she had not yet experienced it personally. She had been able to dismiss that horrible incident as having been planned – and probably paid for – by Kantrowe and his associates, but this was different. The feeling directed towards her now was uncomfortably close to hatred.

Her problem was that, in the minds of the citizens of Teguise, she was the embodiment of the Firebrands. Ever since Chinero had intervened in the attack on the fireworms and the story had spread throughout the city, her well-known face had been publicly associated with the supposedly irresponsible rebellion.

For a time she had worn her notoriety like a badge of honour, only too glad to stand up for what she believed in, but as the situation became more fraught and the stakes rose higher, she had tempered her pride with a little realism. Of the many courses of action outlined by Andrin at the meeting seven days ago, the battle for the respect and support of the people of Tiguafaya was the only one in which little or no progress had been made. And, sooner or later, that failure was bound to affect their cause.

'Hey, missy! You off to freeze more worms? Get us all killed?'

The spiteful voice came from a group of people she had just passed, and the outburst was accompanied by mocking laughter and angry mutterings. Ico did not stop walking, did not turn round.

'You should be ashamed of yourself!' a woman called after her. 'You've no respect.'

Other voices were raised now that the spell of silence had been lifted.

'Slut!'

'The guards should've locked you up.'

'And thrown away the key!'

Ico tried to ignore them, keeping her pace steady with difficulty. When the sound of running footsteps came up behind her her nerve broke and she glanced round, wondering whether hostility was turning to violence and she would have to defend herself. In fact it was only a small boy who pelted past her, keeping his head down and not even looking at her. As Ico went on the boy ducked into a tavern on the corner ahead, and she felt a new wave of disquiet. Moments later her fears were realized.

A group of men, some of them obviously drunk, spilled out into the road ahead of her and spread across the entire width of the thoroughfare. All eyes were upon her but, although their silence was intimidating, Ico knew she could not turn tail now. She slowed her pace and picked out the ringleader, a burly figure who stood a little in front of the others, feet firmly planted, arms folded. His stare was the most intense and malevolent of all.

'We don't want your sort here,' he stated coldly.

Ico stopped and looked at him directly, uneasily aware that others were gathering behind her to watch the confrontation. This was a part of the city she did not know well, and there were unlikely to be any friends among the small crowd now surrounding her.

'What sort is that then?' she asked as boldly as she could.

'You know very well,' he snarled.

'Bloody witch!' one of the drunks yelled, provoking shouts of agreement.

'Shut up!' the ringleader snapped, and his followers grew silent again. 'Do you deny you've been fooling about with magic?'

'We're not fooling about with anything. We're serious—'

'Answer the question!' he roared.

'I did. Magic is—'

'Evil, stupid shit!' he shouted, his face contorted with rage. 'My brother *died* because of your meddling.'

'It wasn't meddling. What we did—'

But he was determined not to let her answer.

'What you did was stir up a dragon's nest, and my brother's entire village was burnt to ashes. What's it like, being a murderer?'

This time Ico did not even attempt to defend herself and, as their leader had obviously had his say, others joined in, hurling insults and accusations. The air seemed to grow thick with malice, and Ico knew that it would take only a tiny spark for it to explode. She had to do something. But what? Her own feeble magical skills were worse than useless here. What little she might achieve that way would only inflame the situation further. There had to be a rational solution to her predicament but, as she bore the torrent of abuse as stoically as she could, she could not think of one. She found herself looking from man to man, trying to see if there was violence in their eyes, searching for any sign of concealed weapons. Get a grip, she ordered herself. No one's going to murder you. Their threats are just drunken bluster.

Driven by some desperate instinct, she held up both hands and to her astonishment the throng fell silent almost immediately. Although the atmosphere of ill feeling remained, there was something else in the air too and, as she swallowed hard, wondering what she was going to say, Ico recognized it as fear. They were afraid of her! That was why they had only been able to face her in the safety of numbers.

'You've had your say!' she cried. 'Will you allow me mine?'

'Why should we?' someone called.

'Because you don't know all the facts,' she answered. 'Because you've only heard what the Senate wants you to hear.'

'At least Kantrowe has our best interests at heart,' the ringleader said defiantly.

'Are you sure?' she asked, and went on, ignoring the muttering her question had provoked. 'Since when has the Senate cared about the poor? Why hasn't Kantrowe done anything about the fireworms? They've killed far more people than the volcanoes, yet nothing is done to stop them. And when we try, they prevent us from doing the job properly. Does that sound as though they're acting in your best interests?'

No one answered, and she took advantage of the silence to weigh up their mood. Although they were still angry, they seemed less certain now. None of the faces before her was familiar; she had been afraid that some of the paid agents from the chivaree might be among this group, but she recognized none of them. Their grievances were genuine, if misguided.

'You're exaggerating,' another onlooker claimed. 'The worms aren't that big a problem, and Kantrowe will deal with them when necessary.'

'Yeah, all you've done is make things worse!'

'And made the dragons crazy. They hadn't bothered us for years until *your* efforts.'

'They still haven't,' Ico pleaded. 'Has anyone even *seen* one of them? Volcanoes can erupt at any time, not just because the dragons are supposed to be angry.' Looking at the ringleader and raising her voice over the new round of muttering, she added, 'I'm truly sorry about your brother, but I had nothing to do with his death. Surely he must have told you about the worms? About how serious a problem they were becoming?'

The burly man shook his head.

'And he'll never get the chance now, will he?' he replied implacably.

'We should feed *you* to the dragons!' someone shouted. 'Kill two birds with one stone.'

'Why leave it to them?' another voice asked. 'Let's teach her a lesson ourselves.'

A blade glittered suddenly in the late afternoon sunlight. Shouts of encouragement mingled with exclamations of shock, and Ico knew she had reached the point of no return.

'Don't come any closer!' she commanded, pointing an accusing finger at the knifeman. 'I don't want to hurt you!'

The man laughed, but there was an edge to the sound, and Ico hoped her bluff would work. In the event she was fated never to find out because, as her would-be attacker moved closer, his head became the centre of a whirling hurricane of feathers and talons. Soo had come to defend her link, and had brought several other sparrowhawks with her. The man flailed wildly, screaming even though he remained unharmed, while other birds swooped and dived nearby, discouraging anyone else from joining the attack.

Ico was grateful for their protection, but knew it was still a dangerous moment. If the crowd associated the birds with magic, their mood would become even uglier, and Soo and her comrades would be no defence against a determined assault. She began looking for a means of escape, only to find the onlookers drifting away of their own accord. The knife was nowhere to be seen now, and the shouting had all but ceased as the hawks continued to circle above the street.

What's happening, Soo?

Soldiers coming.

A new wave of hopelessness, close to despair, swept over Ico. Was she to escape one enemy only to fall into the hands of another?

Six guards were in sight now, marching purposefully towards her, hands on the hilts of their as yet undrawn swords.

'Clear off, you lot, before I sling your arses in gaol!' their leader yelled. 'Show's over!'

'Why don't you arrest *her*?' one last heckler suggested, but the authority and self-assurance of the soldiers overcame their resistance and the crowd melted away.

Ico stood alone, wondering what would happen next.

We're still here, if you need us, Soo told her.

Not yet, she replied. *But stay close.*

'You seem to be having a little trouble, miss,' the platoon leader remarked with a condescending smile.

'It wasn't of my making, sergeant.'

'I'll take your word for it. Can we escort you anywhere?'

This was the last thing Ico had expected, and the surprise must have shown on her face. The guard smiled again.

'We're charged with protecting *all* the citizens of Teguise,' he said. 'Even the irresponsible ones. Where are you going?'

'Home,' she answered truthfully. 'The merchants' district.'

'I know where it is. Would you like us to come with you?'

'No . . . No, thank you. I'll be fine now.'

'Just be more careful in future,' he advised.

As she ran off, Ico was aware of the sound of laughter behind her, but she was too relieved to care about the soldiers' ridicule. The book she had been out to collect was small, and had fitted inside her blouse easily enough, but during her confrontations – both with the drunkards and then with the guards – she had been afraid they would notice it and investigate. The volume in question contained the collected wisdom of an ancient wizard, and its discovery would have been unfortunate, to say the least.

'Are you sure you want to stay here?' Andrin asked. 'Everyone knows where you live, and if it's getting dangerous . . .'

'Where would I go?' Ico answered. 'Besides, I can't hide for ever.'

'You could come and stay with me,' he said, then paused. 'But things are so awful at home right now I'm rarely there myself.'

'You can't expect your parents to get over Mendo's death so soon,' she told him gently, 'especially when you haven't yourself.'

'It's not just that,' he replied sombrely. 'They're eating away at each other like acid. It's unbearable.'

'I'm sorry.'

'Don't be. We've more important things to worry about,' he said, resolute now. 'I know you can't hide for ever, but I think it would be better if you did for a while at least. Vargo and I can keep you up to date with everything that's happening.'

'All right,' she sighed, although she had no intention of giving up her active involvement in the struggle. There were ways of travelling without being recognized. After all, Andrin had had no trouble coming to her house undetected, entering via the roof under cover of darkness. They were sitting together now on her bed and, in her present mood, Ico did not care if they were discovered.

'Do you think we're doing the right thing?' her lover asked unexpectedly. 'I mean, can we finish what we started?'

The uncharacteristic note of doubt in his voice dismayed Ico, but she knew how he felt. The same thought had crossed her mind more than once.

'Of course we can. We've come too far to back down now.'

'What if they were right?' he persisted. 'What if Kantrowe really *is* doing what he thinks is best?'

'Perhaps he is, in his own warped view of things,' she

replied carefully, 'but that doesn't change a thing.'

'We know better?'

'Yes. The Senate are looking after themselves and to hell with anyone else – as usual. They've had their own way for too long. Something has to change.'

'You're right,' he said wearily. 'I know it. But I get scared when things like this happen. What if Soo hadn't been around, or the soldiers hadn't turned up when they did?'

'Enough what ifs!' she told him. 'I'm here, I'm safe, and I'm going to stay that way.'

'See that you do.'

They sat in silence for a while, taking comfort in just being close, touching.

'I should go.'

'Oh.' She was disappointed. 'Can't you stay?' she asked softly.

'Here?' His green eyes lit up at the prospect, but then he shook his head. 'You don't need any more problems. And we should both get some rest.'

He kissed her, and then, after she had checked that the landing was clear, he climbed up on to the roof and disappeared into the night. Ico returned to her room, wishing he could have stayed longer, and went back to the contemplation of her talisman. It was a necklace of silver, set with seven deep red dragon's blood stones. It was beautiful and, as one of the first major pieces of jewellery she had ever created, it still held a special place in her affections. She had chosen it – or rather it had chosen itself – as her talisman because of this close connection and the magical potential of its stones. They were held to have great healing powers, and Ico dearly wanted to use her talent to heal and not to harm. Looking down at the mysterious translucence of the gems, she remembered her pilgrimage back to the old, twisted cauldron tree whence the sap had originally come. She had shown the necklace to the tree in silent homage, asking for its blessing, and had felt a sense of approval, even joy. There was never any question of selling the piece after that, even though in purely commercial terms it was a valuable item.

It was not the only time Ico had been back to the point of origin of stones included in a particularly important creation – such reverence had become a habitual element in her craft – but it was the best remembered still. And now she hoped to put those feelings to good use. But before she could do that she had much to learn.

The book she had brought home was written in elegant but archaic prose, with many references she did not understand, but there were occasional passages of fire and light that illuminated the mysteries she was pursuing. She was particularly intrigued by a section about dragons. She had only had time to skim through it earlier, so she turned to it again now, intent on studying it more closely.

The process proved to be more than a little frustrating. The long-dead wizard seemed to have taken great pleasure in writing in riddles, and his prose could also be irritatingly self-important and patronizing. There was no clear advice about how the dragons – 'those salamandraical beacons of magical felicitude', as he put it – could be contacted or even located. There was no hint as to how their power could be utilized, although it was abundantly clear that the mage himself took this for granted. And then there were a few sentences that were tantalizingly close to the longed-for clarity. Three in particular aroused her curiosity and she spent hours puzzling over them, battling against her growing need for sleep.

'Men, not dragons, have adiactinic scales upon their eyes, but even the blind can see with their inner orbs.' Did that mean that searching for dragons needed more than mere sight? Were the inner orbs supposed to be the mind? And if so, did magic play a part in actually finding the dragons, as well as in all their other interactions with mankind?

'The grey amphistomes consume fire, but do not corrupt the land unless they are themselves corrupted.' Ico had no idea what amphistomes were, but thought this might refer to the fireworms. If so they were certainly corrupted now, so what had been responsible?

'Elva, Mistress of Wings, is a part of the land and apart from the land; wait and speak softly beyond the earth's breathing, and you will be answered.' It was typical, Ico thought, that when a possibly helpful instruction was included, it was couched in such enigmatic terms. Who or what was Elva? Was it – she? – an oracle of some sort? These were certainly questions Ico would like to have answered. Of course, dragons were not the only creatures with wings, and she decided to ask Soo if the name Elva meant anything to her. For all her efforts, this was the only positive step she could think of to further her understanding.

She was about to put the book aside and see whether her dreams might hold the solutions to any of the wizard's riddles, when the sound of a commotion downstairs reached her ears. Opening her door, Ico heard Atchen arguing with someone who sounded distraught. She went halfway down the stairs and recognized Vargo's voice.

'Let him in, Atchen!' she called. 'I'll come down.'

The housekeeper reluctantly did as she was told, muttering about the rudeness of visitors in the middle of the night as she returned to her own quarters. Ico waved Vargo ahead of her into the empty workroom, hoping her father had not been woken.

'Famara warned me, and I still messed it up!' the musician wailed. 'I'm so useless.' His face was pale but shiny with perspiration.

'Calm down. Tell me what's happened.'

'Giavista Martinoy's been arrested.'

The name meant nothing to Ico, and at her blank look Vargo hurriedly explained that Martinoy owned a book of magic that he and Allegra had been to look at the day before.

'It wasn't much use, but someone must have followed us to his house and now he's been arrested. This is all going much too fast for me. I can't cope.' He glanced at her then, and noticed for the first time that she wore only a thin nightdress. He quickly looked down again. 'I had to talk to someone and I couldn't find Andrin.'

'What makes you think you were followed?'

'We saw them,' he replied dismally. 'I thought we'd lost them, but we obviously didn't.'

'What was Martinoy arrested for?' she asked, fighting to stave off a sense of panic.

'Possession of the book, of course. And they found a piece of jewellery containing dragon's tears that he hadn't declared.'

'They can't do much to him for that,' Ico suggested optimistically.

'Who knows what they can do?' Vargo replied. 'But one thing's certain, they're making it obvious that helping the Firebrands is bad for your health. It's going to be even harder after this.'

Ico had to admit that he had a point.

'What I don't understand,' the musician went on, 'is why they arrested him and not us? What are they waiting for?'

'I don't know,' she admitted, then told Vargo about her own unnerving experience that afternoon. 'If they'd wanted to arrest me, that was the perfect opportunity. I even had this book hidden under my blouse.'

'It doesn't make any sense,' he said helplessly.

'Perhaps they didn't follow you to Martinoy's house,' Ico said. 'Perhaps they got a tip-off from another source.'

'Not very likely, is it? That would be quite a coincidence.'

'Well, we'll have to be extra careful from now on,' she concluded.

Vargo gave her a bleak look.

'And just wait for them to come for us next?' he said.

CHAPTER TWENTY-TWO

The tiny black dot in the sky would only have been visible to those with particularly keen eyesight, but to Nino it was as clear as the newborn day. And to him it was more than just a dark spot; it was movement, glory and a promise. He watched as it grew larger, almost imperceptibly at first, then with incredible speed. Eya's flight was arrow-straight and purposeful, so fast that it defied belief, and with the bird's approach Nino felt his heart swell with admiration and love. In only a few moments the peregrine falcon had covered the distance it would have taken Nino almost an hour to walk – and it had been effortless, a single long dive from high in the infinite blue dome of the early morning sky.

As Eya drew close – his wings spread and tipped back to slow his breakneck pace – he swooped up, then glided down to alight on a jagged rock beside his link. The whole manoeuvre had been an exercise in grace and beauty, and it was one that never failed to take Nino's breath away, no matter how many times he witnessed it.

At rest the peregrine was a solid, impressive bird. His upper plumage was pale grey, while underneath it was almost white, with a touch of colour added by the vivid yellow of his fearsome curved beak and taloned legs. Eya squatted down, motionless now, his head hunched down into powerful shoulders. He could remain perfectly still like that for hours if he so desired, with only his ever watchful eyes remaining mobile.

Anything? Nino asked.

A shining towards the setting sun, near the red marks at the base of the slope, Eya reported.

Crystals?

Perhaps.

Thank you. We'll send Ca to check.

Nino turned to his human companion. Lechuza was his maternal grandfather and, in spite of his age, was still sprightly. Even so he tired quickly these days and had acquired the useful habit of being able to catnap almost anywhere at a moment's notice – and he was asleep now. He had been a prospector all his life and knew the firelands of the interior as well as any man alive, which was why Nino had been glad to have him come along – even though he restricted the pace at which they could travel.

To minimize the distance they would have to cover on foot they had devised a system that made the best use of their links. First Eya would scout out a large area, using his speed and peerless eyesight to pick out any interesting sites. Then Ca, Lechuza's linked magpie, would be sent to investigate, and only if he reported that any of these looked promising would the humans begin to trek over the lava fields. This method cut out much unnecessary effort, and made the process of finding deposits of dragon's tears or other gems much faster.

Ca, with his breed's natural attraction to shiny objects, had a matchless instinct for the special glow that came from crystals, even when the majority of the stones were buried beneath base rock. Like Lechuza, the magpie was old now, but he still took pride in his work and over the years he had been responsible for many important – and lucrative – finds. The vast expanse of the firelands was not his natural habitat, but he had grown to know its secrets and respect its ways, so that now he could advise on routes for his human partner.

Nino and his grandfather had come to this particular area, which was remote and barren even by the standards of the interior, precisely because it was so seldom visited. Their prospecting had to be done in secret; if they were successful, only part of the haul would be declared to the government officials who had visited their village recently to ensure that everyone was aware of the Senate's proclamation. The rest would go into a suitable hiding place as part of the Firebrands' supplies for the future. So far, however, they had not been very successful and, even though their stocks of food and water were running low, Nino was determined to make one last effort before they gave up and went home. He had not been back to Teguise since the meeting, and was therefore not aware that Andrin and Ico had captured a large supply of crystals only a few days before. He shook the old man gently.

'Grandpapa, wake up.'

'What?' Lechuza shared his grandson's light, wiry physique and dark complexion, but his thick hair and short beard were mostly white now, as if he had been gradually bleached by the sun.

Nino told him about Eya's sighting, and Lechuza relayed the information to Ca. The magpie rose, swung his tail to and fro, took several long, springy bounds and then rose into the air in a flurry of quick wingbeats, iridescent blue feathers flashing amongst the black and white.

'I reckon it'll be about an hour's trek,' Nino said. 'Will you be all right with that?'

'Of course,' his grandfather answered gruffly. 'I'm not on my deathbed yet, you know.'

'I know,' Nino said, grinning.

There were few paths here, unlike the less isolated parts of the lava fields where men drove camels between settlements, carrying water, hay or crops. This journey would be difficult and possibly dangerous, taking them even further from home, and so was not to be undertaken lightly. The surface of the land here varied greatly, even within a relatively small area. In places the lava lay in desert swathes of black gravel or sand. This was generally easiest for travel, even though it was wearisome because boots slid backwards or sank with every step, but there were dangers even so. In spite of the fact that these lava fields had been formed more than a century ago, there were still some hot spots, where the temperature of the rock rose dramatically – especially if you were foolish enough to dig even a few handspans beneath the top layer. In places, these vestigial remains of the eruption's heat were marked by strange, convoluted patterns, swirls of red, orange and yellow in the stones. Many people believed these to be trails left by fireworms or even the signatures of dragons, and so they were generally shunned. Although Nino did not share these superstitions, he nonetheless treated such signs with caution and always listened to Lechuza, who claimed to be able to read them like omens.

In other areas the lava was a solid mass, either smooth and ropy, like frozen waves, or razor-sharp and irregular. It was almost impossible to walk on the latter type, but the former provided excellent footing. Yet even here there were pitfalls, as not every surface was as solid as it appeared and the caverns below could be very deep. Steering a safe course was a hard-earned skill.

Other hazards were more easily recognized. Chimneys of lava – tall pointed cones where hot gases and steam had once gushed into the air – were called 'dragon's horns' by the local people. Most were long dormant, but in recent times they were approached with caution because fireworms had been known to rest inside them, taking advantage of the residual heat.

Ca returned, and after a short conversation with his link, Lechuza announced that there was a sizeable deposit of dragon's tears there for the taking.

'Must have been exposed by the wind or a landslip,' he added. 'I've never seen anything worthwhile round here before.'

'Let's go,' Nino said enthusiastically.

They set off, picking their way through the broken terrain, each hoping that this find would indeed justify the four-day trip. Even if the morning shadows had not pointed the way, it would have been easy enough for them to navigate on old lava such as this. The first plant life to return after an eruption was always the lichen, which only grew on surfaces that faced northwest so that they could absorb moisture from the prevailing winds. As a consequence the rock appeared bare in one direction, while in the other everything was covered by the pale green growths. This made it possible to navigate even in the most inhospitable or unfamiliar areas.

They were less than a quarter of the way to their destination when they came across a sharp-edged hole that revealed the entrance to a lava tube beneath the surface.

'That's new,' Lechuza announced. 'The recent eruption must have shaken this place up more than we'd thought.'

As Nino peered inside, he saw a faint glow within. Knowing that the birds could not be induced to go underground, he decided to investigate himself. He climbed down carefully, testing each foot and handhold, and then stooped to follow the course of the tube itself. The slanting rays of the sun gave him some light for a distance, and then he lit one of the precious sulphur-tipped tapers and went on into the deepening gloom. Although the ceiling of the tunnel was irregular, the walls were smooth, with several horizontal lines running along them at different heights. These showed where later, more fluid lava had continued to flow after the outer rock had solidified. It was a familiar sight, but one which never failed to remind Nino of other places, other times.

He had been barely two years old when the last major eruptions had begun, and they had stopped only a few days short of his fourth birthday. The lava flows had gone on for so long and had remained so constant that people simply got used to them. The horrors of the initial explosions, with their clouds of burning gas and smoke, did not return after the first few traumatic days; because the slow red oozing of the lava was constant, it was seen as less dangerous and people returned to their homes. One of Nino's earliest memories was of his grand-parents dancing at midnight by the light of the molten rock as it rolled by. He and his mother had watched, torn between delight and anxiety, as Lechuza and his wife had swung closer and closer to the radiant flow. It had been a matter of honour to see who could get nearest – and his grandparents had almost always won, their stately, traditional movements punctuated by flamboyant wheels, dips and turns. Nino could still hear echoes of the music now, even though no one had danced like that for many years.

Smiling at his own nostalgia, Nino proceeded gingerly, always testing the floor ahead and creeping even closer to the glint that had enticed him in the first place. The air grew fetid. If he went too far into the tunnel he would be unable to breathe at all, but he was too experienced to take such a risk.

At last he reached the spot he had been aiming for, and was rewarded by the sight of a small seam of excellent crystals. Wedging the taper in a crack, he took out his hammer and spike-chisel and began to loosen the main area. He worked slowly and with a delicate precision; unless he was careful some of the best crystalline structures would be damaged. He was almost finished when he heard his grandfather calling.

'What?' he yelled back. 'I can't hear you.'

'The dragon's breathing again!' Lechuza replied urgently. 'Get out of there!'

Nino knew that this was the old man's fanciful way of saying that a new eruption was imminent. Lechuza had a sixth sense about these things, an ability that Nino had inherited in some measure. He hesitated, sensing the tension in the ground, the waiting, but he could not feel even the slightest tremors. Perhaps the old man was losing his grip.

'Come on, boy!' Lechuza shouted angrily.

'I'll just be a moment,' he called back, and set his chisel in place again. He was close to retrieving the dragon's tears, and did not want to lose them.

At that moment the earth shook. The tube's walls, roof, even the floor, vibrated and from somewhere in the distance came the dreaded sound of rock falling as well as his grandfather's unintelligible cry. The taper fell and went out, and Nino was half blinded. Cursing his own stupidity he ran, crouched over, dropping his tools and banging into overhanging shelves of rock. Behind him the tube was disintegrating with a noise like two mountains grinding against each other, but he could see daylight ahead of him and scrabbled on desperately. At last he arrived at the opening, reached up and found his hand grasped in both of Lechuza's. The old man helped him up and they stepped back from the edge, then looked at each other for a moment, both breathing hard. Nino nodded in wordless apology as they waited for the tremor to subside. All around them the firelands creaked and trembled but then, as the earth beneath their feet grew still, there was another sound, a deep, ominous rumbling. They both turned to look at the mountain they had been heading for.

The lava surged up over the rim of the crater in one gigantic red wave. Only moments later it poured down the slope, as if the earth itself was bleeding, inundating the place where the birds had seen the crystal deposit. Then the stream split into several burning tributaries, each moving more slowly now but deadly enough for all that. The two men stared in awe rather than horror.

'I should have sensed it earlier,' Lechuza said.

'No matter,' Nino replied. 'We've time yet. We should head north.'

'No, southeast. There's high ground there.'

'The main flow is headed that way. Even if the plateau isn't overrun, we could easily be cut off.' Nino hated to argue with the venerable old man, but this time he was sure he was right.

'You're wrong,' Lechuza insisted. 'And going north will take us even further from home.'

'It doesn't matter. It'll keep us alive. Come on. I'll pick you up and carry you if I have to.'

An hour later, they sat on high ground to the north, well clear of the lava that was still flowing like crimson honey, albeit sluggishly. They could both see that the island Lechuza had suggested as their refuge had indeed been overwhelmed. The old man's head was in his hands, his spirit broken, knowing that his instincts would have killed them both.

'It's time I retired,' he stated sadly.

Nino felt a surge of pity, but did not pretend to disagree. He felt no pride in having been proved right, but perhaps it was time for the mantle to be passed on.

'Well, Grandpapa. We've a long walk home ahead of us. Shall we make a start?'

Lechuza stood up without a word, shouldered his pack and trudged off. Nino followed, wondering how long the volcano would continue to burn. At least they won't be able to blame the Firebrands for this eruption, he thought. We should be grateful for small mercies.

Behind them the column of smoke rose up to the heavens.

CHAPTER TWENTY-THREE

'Health, love and money – and time enough to enjoy it.'

Kantrowe could not help but smile whenever he saw the Tiguafayan motto emblazoned on the circular frieze around the Senate chamber. It was a simple-minded sentiment, but had served his country well in times of prosperity. Now, for many, the words had a hollow ring. In periods of political uncertainty and economic hardship it was absurd to expect the motto to apply to everyone. And if what the gods ordained benefited only a privileged few, then so be it – as long as Tias Kantrowe was one of the few.

The formal preliminaries of the session had just been completed, and all eyes had turned his way. He rose to his feet slowly, his expression grave.

'Honoured President, gentlemen, may I first extend my thanks to you all for making time to attend this hurriedly convened meeting. When you hear what I have to report, I am sure you will realize that your efforts are not only worthy but absolutely necessary. We have some difficult decisions to make.'

He scanned the room, and was gratified to see that he held

the complete attention of everyone there, both on the floor of the chamber and in the spectators' gallery.

'You will have heard rumours of how, two days ago, the White Guard were tricked into leaving Teguise because of a fake magical attack on some fireworms. I am here to tell you now that such gossip is untrue.'

Although his voice rang out with unmistakable conviction, his words provoked gasps of surprise. Most of those present had either seen evidence of the soldiers' mission for themselves, or had been given eyewitness accounts by others. How could Kantrowe deny it had happened?

'Before I explain what really took place, I need to reassure you all that this incident, serious though it was, did not affect the security of Teguise. The capital's reduced garrison was by then on full alert, and their numbers were still more than adequate to defend our city against any foe. Your lives and property, and those of all our fellow residents, are the paramount concern of our defence forces and that will always be the case.'

His audience shifted impatiently and whispered, many of them giving their neighbours an occasional sidelong glance. Kantrowe seemed to be contradicting himself now, so what was the real story?

The senator decided it was time to put them out of their misery. 'This was a *genuine* attack on the fireworms,' he stated emphatically, 'using dragon's tears, in direct contradiction of the recent edict of the President and this assembly. It was no illusion, no trick, in spite of the fact that some might wish us to believe it so. I do not deal in rumour but in facts, and the evidence found at the site is incontrovertible. Our investigators discovered pieces of the fireworms' dead bodies. These have since decayed and become noisome, and I do not wish to defile the Senate chamber with such foul carrion. But the guards also found this.'

He took a small muslin bag from his pocket, loosened the drawstring and tipped the contents on to the desk in front of him. A pale, grey-green powder trickled out, forming a small pyramid on the wooden surface, and raising a tiny cloud of dust in the sunlight that slanted down from the high windows.

'This, gentlemen, is the worthless residue left behind when dragon's tears crystals are destroyed, releasing their forbidden cold.'

When the renewed commotion that his demonstration had roused died away, Kantrowe went on. 'The only use of *illusions* was to enable the perpetrators of this vile deed to escape when our soldiers intervened, at great risk to themselves, thus preventing an even more serious incident. Magic *was* used, and as such it was a thoughtless and heinous crime, but if it had not been for the prompt action of the White Guard it could have been much worse.

'Furthermore, far from preventing the ravages of the fireworms, this second regrettable attack seems to have prompted even more. Reports are coming in that the village of Cangrelos, only a few miles from Betancore, has been destroyed, with its entire population killed and virtually all its buildings burnt to the ground.'

He paused to let this last piece of sobering news sink in, then played his trump card. 'And of course, as we now know, this wholly irresponsible action has resulted in another eruption!'

Kantrowe smiled inwardly as he recalled his first sighting of the distant column of smoke that morning. Fate had conspired to provide him with the perfect complement to his fabrication. It could hardly have been better suited to his purpose, but he kept his expression indignant, careful not to let his real emotions show on his face.

'Thankfully, this upheaval has been relatively minor and as yet there are no reports of any casualties, but if further proof were needed that our recent proclamation was not only well advised but absolutely vital, then this is it. You need only look to the western sky to see for yourselves!'

He pointed dramatically, even though the horizon was quite invisible from inside the chamber. Everyone there, he knew, had already seen the ominous grey tower rising from the firelands – and the reason for its appearance was now fixed in their minds.

'You see the depths to which the enemies of Tiguafaya are prepared to sink,' he declared righteously. 'And I am sure I have no need to tell you who is responsible.'

There was a further rumble of outraged muttering, in which the word 'Firebrands' featured prominently, and Kantrowe moved swiftly to take advantage of this groundswell of belligerence.

'Regrettably, I am now of the opinion that some harsher measures are needed to curb this menace. Accordingly, a new proclamation is being readied, under the powers granted to me recently. Among the items to be included are the following.' He began to tick them off on his fingers. 'One; the provision of a register of all linked persons, so that we can separate the legitimate use of avian telepathy from the illegal acts we have witnessed recently. Two; details of increased penalties for anyone breaking the authorized code of magic as set out in the earlier proclamation, together with some clarification of that code. Three; confirmation that the military authorities now have the emergency powers of arrest and/or imprisonment of anyone suspected of such illegal acts, without the need for any formal charge. Four; a list of people the authorities wish to detain for questioning.

'The exact wording of these decrees is still being determined, and other items may yet be added, but I have told you the most important details. None of these measures is pleasant, and I trust that their implementation need only be temporary, but they are all necessary for the security of Tiguafaya.'

Kantrowe scanned the faces before him, knowing that Mazo would be doing the same from the gallery. He noted those senators whose expressions were unreadable, but saw that the majority were either nodding or reacting in a generally favourable manner. He would compare notes with Gadette later, but for now he had one last scheme to set in motion.

'Lastly, I want to address another area where rumours have been rife, and that is the possibility of appeasing the dragons with sacrifices. I personally find these ideas most distressing, and state here and now that no such barbaric events will take place unless both the Senate and the people of Tiguafaya as a whole are overwhelmingly in favour of such a measure. I can only emphasize that this must be as a last resort, one which I have no wish to accept, even if historically it was once common practice. This country has come a long way since such times and, no matter what hardships face us now, I hope that we can remain civilized. I only mention this because I am sure other members of this chamber will want to voice their opinions on the matter.'

With that the senator relinquished the floor, allowing the debate to begin.

Senator Alegranze Maciot had stayed until the end of the session, but had not contributed to the ensuing argument. Many had voiced their reluctant support for the limited use of sacrifices, while others had merely urged caution and more reflection before such a drastic step was taken. No one had stood up and stated the obvious fact that the whole idea was utterly repugnant. The moderates had won the day, in part because no one could agree on a suitable method for choosing the victims, but it was clear to Maciot that the reprieve was only temporary. As soon as the idea had been mentioned officially, even if just as a remote possibility, it had become obvious that its eventual acceptance was inevitable – unless some other, as yet unknown solution could be found to the problem. A problem which, in Maciot's mind, was illusory.

Kantrowe's very clever. If the Senate decides to go ahead with the sacrifices, he'll appear to have been forced into it against his will.

And then, Tao replied, sounding as disgusted as his link, *for all his supposed reluctance, he'll use it like any other political weapon – against his enemies.*

Exactly. Not only that, but by ending his speech the way he did, he made sure that the following discussion would be about the sacrifices and not much else, Maciot added. *The precise details of his new proclamation were conveniently hidden behind a smoke screen. The President is helpless, the Senate is easily led, Kantrowe is in charge and we're going to be living under martial law. And the gods know how easy it'll be to abuse those circumstances for someone of Kantrowe's sensibilities.*

These are dangerous times, the mirador remarked.

My friend, Maciot replied, *you never spoke a truer word.*

'Why don't we just round them all up?' Verier asked. 'There's nothing to stop us now.'

'No, no,' Kantrowe replied. 'We must balance our actions to our needs. On the one hand we must be seen to be strong, to be tackling the problems the people are most concerned about. But on the other hand we need the Firebrands to learn a little more.'

'But . . .'

'We don't have enough talents of our own,' Kantrowe explained, 'and this way they'll do our work for us. When we finally decide to crush them, we'll have a ready-made task force.'

'How do we know we'll be able to trust them even then?' Verier said.

'There are ways to ensure cooperation. I am sure you are no stranger to some of them. But this is a long-term project, remember. We must proceed cautiously. No one outside this room must know of our plans. *No one.* Agreed?'

Verier and Mazo Gadette, who were the only others present, nodded.

'We can't afford to leave it too long, though,' Verier warned. 'Cangrelos was *not* one of the places we'd earmarked for depopulation.'

'I'm aware of that,' Kantrowe retorted, irritated by his associate's habit of stating the obvious.

'So can't we speed up the process?' Verier persisted.

'Not if we wish to remain discreet,' the older man replied patiently. 'If we betray ourselves now, we could end up being skewered by our own swords.'

'But in the meantime the Firebrands go on destroying worms.'

'Not enough to be significant. Besides, how can you expect us to learn how to control the fireworms for our own ends without a certain amount of experimentation?'

'Think too of the prospects for gain once they're under our influence,' Gadette added encouragingly. 'Great areas of the country ripe for exploitation without the need to even consider the local population – because there won't be any!'

'And we'll be able to thumb our noses at our pirate friends,' Kantrowe went on. 'They'll be left with a deserted wasteland, while we retain all the important resources of the land.'

'I never misprized our goal,' Verier said, grinning now. 'Merely the time it's taking to reach it. Patience is not one of my more prominent virtues.'

'I wasn't aware you had *any*,' Kantrowe remarked drily.

Verier laughed.

'I try to avoid them whenever I can,' he said, 'but I will play your waiting game. This time.'

'Good.' Kantrowe turned to Gadette. 'What news from the western mines?'

'Mixed,' the aide replied. 'Some of the results have been encouraging. In others, the worms vanished without a trace and without producing anything worthwhile. But they're still working on it.'

Kantrowe nodded.

'If this unexpected bonus turns out to be as profitable as I think it will, we'll all be very much richer before too long. And Deion, my friend, you will no longer need to risk good men while trading for slaves.'

Verier scowled at the reminder of his loss, but said nothing.

'So, back to the list,' Kantrowe declared.

'Ico Maravedis?' Gadette asked.

'Yes, she has to be on it,' his master decided. 'She's their figurehead, and no one would take us seriously if she was not included. Put her at the top, and then we'll go through the rest together. Choosing who to leave out could be crucial, especially as we want to start divisions within their ranks. But, for our own sakes, we don't want to break them completely.'

'At least not yet,' Verier finished for him.

CHAPTER TWENTY-FOUR

In the grey hour just before dawn, when all life is at its lowest ebb, the soldiers came. Overriding the shrill protests of Atchen and the feeble threats from Diano, they ran up the stairs and burst into Ico's room. They found it empty, her bed unused.

The soldiers searched the entire house, tore her bedroom apart, but still they found nothing. No sign of her, no evidence of where she might be. They questioned her father and the maid, gained nothing from their frightened and angry ignorance, and left. The violated house grew still and quiet again.

He had never seen snow, and yet the endless icy wasteland below him was too real to be just imagination. It was so white it was almost blue, dazzling in its purity and its emptiness. The wind was the only living thing in this place.

The sun dipped and flickered and the burning plains were now a smoky red, so hot and dry that any movement raised clouds of choking dust into the shimmering air. His horizons were vast, yet there was no sign of any lava fields, nothing familiar. He saw everything through a wavering heat haze, which made the sparse vegetation and the exotic creatures seem even more outlandish.

There was music too, beautiful in fragments but with no cohesive structure. Joyous one moment, mournful the next, it was like dancing at a funeral.

Night came. Not night. He was in a cave. Glimmering light fell from torches held by his invisible companions. Crystals glowed inside the different colours of the rock, some of them like fire. The air was warm but not hot. If this was the inside of a volcano, then it was very old and sleeping now.

He moved, walking silently down the twisting corridors of stone, occasionally having to stoop or turn sideways, but always finding a way through. He sank deeper and deeper into the labyrinth, until he came to a huge cavern, rising up far above his head and down below his feet so that he teetered on the edge of vertigo. Bending down, he stretched out beyond the ledge on which he stood and his fingers touched water. As the mirrored surface rippled, the canyon below was revealed as a mere reflection of the dome above. The water was only a handspan deep.

A sudden wrenching shift seized him. Although he was in the same place, he was now looking up from far below – *inside* the mirror. Lying on his back, he felt drowsy, and just before he sank into a sleep within sleep he felt the lure and the terror of the unknown. I don't know where I'm going.

He was answered by only darkness and the smell of frying mushrooms.

'Why should I trust you?' Ico asked.

'I think you've already made that decision,' Maciot pointed out. 'Otherwise you wouldn't be here.'

'I'm only here because Soo persuaded me to come. I trust her.'

'And she in turn trusts Tao, my link.' He indicated the mirador chaffinch, who was perched in a corner of the room. 'Why should we not extend each other the same courtesy?'

'Tao came to our meeting, didn't he?' Ico said, recalling Vargo's description of the bird Ero had talked to. 'We thought he was spying for Kantrowe.'

'No. For me.'

'What do you want?'

Maciot laughed. 'Many things,' he replied. 'One of the things I do *not* want is to see you in Kantrowe's hands.'

'But you're a senator,' she said suspiciously.

'Not all senators are the same,' he assured her. 'There are others who think, as I do, that our exalted leader is carrying his obsessions too far. Tiguafaya deserves to remain a democracy.'

Although Ico made a derisive sound, she was feeling easier in this strange man's company now.

'Oh, I know it's not perfect,' Maciot went on. 'No system ever is. There will always be those who wield more influence than is their due, but what we had was still preferable to a military dictatorship. We must agree on that, at least.'

It had taken Ico most of the night to reach the senator's house, moving only when the streets were empty, and avoiding patrols with the help of the birds above. When the warning had come that she was in immediate danger, she had not believed it at first. But Soo had been insistent, and so Ico had fled her home, bringing nothing but the clothes she stood up in, her talisman and the wizard's book. She was glad she had had the foresight to hide the Firebrands' new store of crystals elsewhere.

When she had arrived at Maciot's house, he had ushered her inside himself and – so far – had given every sign of dealing with her in good faith. He had told her of Kantrowe's speech, the subsequent debate and the certainty that hers would be one of the names on the White Guards' list, and had asked for nothing in return. He had offered her food and drink, a bed to sleep on and the use of his home for as long as she required it. She had refused all but the last – for the time being.

'When will the arrests start?' she asked quietly.

'I'd be surprised if they'd not begun already.'

'I must warn the others. I can't stay here doing nothing.'

'You of all people cannot go out now,' he warned her. 'The birds will pass the messages on. We don't know who else is on that list, but if they keep their wits about them they'll have a good chance of eluding the guards.'

Ico was certain that Andrin's name would be on the list, and her frustration at not being able to go to him was unbearable. In times of crisis they should always be together. Even so, she saw the wisdom of leaving it to the birds. They could move unhindered and, for the most part, unnoticed about the city. Soo was abroad now, raising the alarm.

'Tell me,' Maciot said. 'Am I right in assuming that Kantrowe lied about your latest attack on the fireworms?' Her expression had told him as much earlier, though she had said nothing at the time.

'Of course. There was no attack.'

'I wonder where he got the crystal dust. It looked genuine to me.'

'Probably from the first attack. It was real that time.'

He caught the note of pride in her voice and nodded, thinking that Kantrowe had a naive but formidable enemy in this spirited girl.

'And it worked?'

'Yes. We're not—'

She was interrupted as Soo announced her return by pecking at the shutters. Maciot let the sparrowhawk in and, in terse, unemotional phrases, she described the raid on the Maravedis house in the early hours of the morning.

My father? Ico asked.

He is unharmed, but distraught, Soo reported.

Have you seen Andrin?

No, but word has been passed to Ayo.

In spite of this one small measure of good news, Ico felt a cold numbness growing inside her. She glanced up at the man to whom she owed her liberty. In her eyes, beside the fear and worry, was the gratitude she could not express in words.

'You are welcome to stay here for as long as you need,' Maciot repeated. 'This is a large house, with many hiding places – though my status should ensure there is no immediate danger. Later, when the situation is clearer, you can decide what to do.'

Ico nodded. Whatever her future held now, one thing was certain. She could not go home again.

He opened his eyes and stared at the beam directly above his bed. The grain of the wood seemed beautiful, almost poetic. It made him want to laugh and cry at the same time. Nothing else made sense.

Where am I?

He tried to think, to rationalize his chaotic thoughts. And failed, as an even more fundamental question occurred to him.

Who am I?

There were no answers anywhere, just flashes of nonsensical existence, chimera and fragments of sound. The images of his dreams seemed infinitely more real than anything around him now. Except for the mushrooms; even though he could only smell them, they were surely real.

He's arrived, hasn't he?

The voice in his brain sounded loud and disgusted, but it gave Vargo a lifeline, a connection to the life of this confused stranger he had become.

He always makes you stupid, Ero grumbled. *And he's no fun!*

Lao had arrived.

With that realization, everything began falling slowly into place. Vargo was in his room at The Camel's Hump. The smell from the kitchens was the cook preparing breakfast, and even the dream images made sense now. Or at least most of them did. Vargo pushed the ones that still puzzled him aside, knowing that he had shared, however vicariously, in the migratory experiences of his two links. There was beauty and wonder in both.

I suppose you'll be getting that horrible screechy saw box out now, Ero said caustically.

Vargo shook his head. He felt too befuddled still, too divided, to contemplate playing either his lute or the instrument that Ero referred to, the viol that had been locked away for the summer. Lao's viol.

Somewhere outside, but close now, was the sandpiper curlew, a shy and aristocratic bird whose soft, melancholy calling echoed the sad romanticism of Vargo's winter music. It was the time of disorientation; the days when his overlapping personalities made him indecisive, muddleheaded and emotionally unstable. During this time he usually hid from the world, even from his friends, knowing that he could contribute nothing while he was in such a state – but he did not have that option now. He would have to do the best he could, hope to control the violent changes of mood, and not let anyone down. His feelings were reinforced a moment later when Lao appeared on the sill of the skylight and then fluttered down to perch near Ero. The two birds eyed each other scornfully.

Lao held his head high and chirruped softly in greeting. His dark summer plumage was already fading to the pale shades of winter, and he gave the impression of fragility. His slim neck, pointed head and downward-curving bill were matched by the elegant curve of his neat body and his long wader's legs.

You're early, Ero remarked accusingly.

The sky-voices choose their own times to call us, the sandpiper replied. *Are you so deaf you do not hear them yet?*

I hear them better than you. And I sing better. And—

Quiet, both of you, Vargo cut in. *I've no time for this.*

Although he was already in a state of mind close to despair, he was also filled with a bloody-minded determination. He could not afford to surrender to self-pity or to the divisive influence of the birds, because he was sure that he would soon need all his wits – or whatever wits he could muster – about him. The one sudden certainty in all the confusion in his head was that something terrible was destined to happen that very day.

CHAPTER TWENTY-FIVE

Andrin lay on his bed and listened to the bickering of his parents, the usual round of recrimination and deliberate cruelty separated by silences that were even worse. Whenever they grew quiet he tensed, waiting for the next inevitable outburst, the next exchange of poisoned barbs in their endless war of attrition. Worse still, he waited for the sounds of violence – the smash of breaking crockery, the impact of flesh on flesh, the scattering of furniture when his mother fell to the floor. He knew he should intervene, try to help heal the worst of their self-inflicted wounds, but he was too weary, too disgusted and too angry to make the effort. They were beyond his help now. Although he pitied them, his love had long since been extinguished by contempt.

Another silence, longer than usual, made it impossible for him to lie there so he got up and began to dress. He knew that unless he took the coward's way out, and escaped via the window, he would have to go through the room where his parents were before he could leave. If he was lucky they would try to drag him into their petty arguments, ignoring the possibility that he might have concerns of his own, and he would then be able to speak his mind, voice his own frustrations. More likely they would simply watch him in silence, their eyes accusing him as he prepared to desert them for another day. The fact that the money he earned was their only means of sustenance was never acknowledged, and Andrin neither wanted nor needed any thanks for doing his family duty, but his parents' resentment of his so-called freedom rankled.

He was greeted by shards of flying pottery as he entered the living room. Belda, her haggard face already flushed with drink even though the morning was only a few hours old, had hurled an empty bowl at her husband. As usual her aim had been abysmal, and she had hit the wall beside Andrin's door. He ducked instinctively, flinging up his hands to protect his face, then looked at his mother. She stared back uncomprehendingly as Jarrell laughed, mocking her.

'Trying to kill our other son now, are you? Like you killed the first?'

'I . . . I . . .' Words failed her and she burst into tears.

Andrin snapped. Leaning over his father's chair, he grabbed his collar and dragged him forward so that their faces were practically touching. The momentary astonishment in Jarrell's eyes gave Andrin an illusory sense of satisfaction. Even as a cripple his father possessed an intimidating physical presence, and Andrin had never confronted him in such a way before. It felt good.

'Ma had nothing to do with Mendo's death!' he shouted furiously. 'Nothing! You understand?'

'She might as well have done. Look at her, the drunken slut.'

Andrin shook him, as a dog might shake a rat, so that Jarrell's heavy head rocked back and forth.

'Have you ever thought that if you weren't so cruel to her she might not drink so much? You're a self-centred bully and . . .' He threw his father back into the chair in disgust and turned away to find Belda watching him timidly, almost fearfully.

'You shouldn't talk to your father like that,' she whispered.

'If you go on drinking like this you'll kill yourself,' he told her as gently as he could. 'If you want to stop, we'll help you.'

'He won't,' she hissed bitterly. 'He wouldn't help me do anything. All he—'

'We'll both help you,' Andrin said firmly. 'But you have to help yourself first.'

'Maybe I don't want to stop. Maybe I'd be better off dead.'

'That's your decision,' he replied, all compassion spent.

He left the house without another word, leaving behind a silence even more profound than usual. The relief he felt at his escape was enormous, even if it was tinged with guilt. Once in the street he wondered where to go. His recent preoccupation had meant he had not worked much recently, and the family coffers were almost empty, but such considerations meant little to him at the moment. He sensed that other, greater issues would soon claim his attention, and the sight of Ayo gliding down towards him only reinforced that feeling. There were few people about in this part of the town, but those who were abroad watched the great white eagle with something approaching awe, and Andrin felt a flow of lofty pride – which vanished abruptly at Ayo's first words.

I have a message from Soo. She said to tell you that Ico is safe.

Safe? He was instantly alarmed. *Safe from what?*

I don't know.

Where is she?

At the house of Senator Alegranze Maciot.

Who?

Ayo repeated the name, but it still meant nothing to Andrin.

Who is he? Do you know where this house is?

Soo will know, but she said you must not go there until nightfall.

Why not?

It is too dangerous. She said that Maciot is a friend who must not be compromised. Once it is dark and you can approach unseen, then she will lead us there.

A whole day of wondering and worrying stretched out before Andrin like a never-ending chasm, but he knew there must be good reasons for the instruction. He also knew that he would find the wait unbearable.

You're sure she's safe there?

Soo said so.

Can you get a message to her?

Of course.

Tell Ico to be careful, that I'll see her as soon as it's dark, and that I love her.

As Ayo wheeled away and set off in search of the sparrowhawk, Andrin became aware that he was the object of some interest. Several onlookers, including a pair of White Guards at the end of the street, were staring at him. He strode away immediately, losing himself in the maze of alleyways, not really thinking about where he was going. His mind was full of uncomfortable speculation. Who was Alegranze Maciot? What could a senator – of all people – want with Ico? Was he really a friend, or was this some kind of elaborate trap? And, above all, what had happened to make Ico take refuge with a stranger?

Instinct had taken him towards the derelict hall, but before he reached it he was hailed by name and turned to see Vargo running towards him. As the musician drew near, Andrin noted his dishevelled appearance and the strange, almost demented look in his eyes.

'Have you heard?' Vargo asked breathlessly. 'The White Guard raided Ico's house in the night.'

Although Andrin now had the answer to one of his questions, he still did not know how Ico had been warned, or by whom.

'They came up empty-handed, though,' Vargo added, when his friend did not speak. 'At least that's what I heard. Do you know where she is?'

Andrin nodded.

'She's safe,' he said, hoping it was true.

'Thank the dogs . . . I mean gods.' Vargo did a little dance on the spot, then became still, his face sad.

Andrin noticed the odd inflections in Vargo's voice, took in the fact that the buttons of his shirt were fastened wrongly, and saw that he wore a boot on his right foot and a sandal on his left. Even for the musician this was unusually eccentric. It did not take Andrin long to jump to the obvious conclusion.

'Lao's here.'

'Yes. Great timing, huh?'

'Are you all right?'

'I'll have to be. There's more news too,' Vargo added with evident reluctance.

'Other raids?' Andrin guessed, his heart sinking.

'Not that I know of, but I wouldn't be surprised. As soon as they arrested Martinoy I thought the chances were that it was the first of many.'

'What's the news, then?'

'Fireworms destroyed Cangrelos yesterday. Everybody there was killed.'

'Everybody?' Andrin swore softly under his breath.

'So I'm told.'

They were both well aware that two members of the Firebrands had lived in the devastated village.

'Perhaps people will start to believe us now,' Vargo added. 'Can you smell mushrooms?'

'What?'

'Sorry. I just don't seem able to . . . Never mind. There's more, I'm afraid.'

'Go on,' Andrin said heavily.

'There's a new proclamation due, which is supposed to include a list of people wanted for questioning. And the Senate debated the possibility of sacrifices last night.' Having completed his report, Vargo began whistling a disjointed tune.

Andrin was almost too stunned to respond. Too much was happening too fast.

'Where did you hear all this?'

'It's common gossip in the market places.'

Andrin set off immediately, his long strides leaving his friend behind. Vargo tried to follow, and almost tripped over his own feet. It was as though his body had decided to start walking before his brain was ready to coordinate his muscles. When he caught up he was out of breath again, and alarmed by Andrin's obvious intention.

'Do you think this is wise?' he asked. 'I mean, you'll probably be on that list.'

'You too,' Andrin replied, not slowing his pace.

'Then shouldn't we be a bit more cautious? Going to Manrique Square could mean we're walking into a trap,' Vargo said, naming the largest of all the city's market places.

'Well, we'll find out, won't we?' Andrin said, uncaring. 'I have to see for myself. And there has to be more to it than that. If they're going to arrest us, why haven't they done it already? And why warn us by publishing a list? It doesn't make sense.'

There wasn't much that was making sense to Vargo just at that moment. But he could see that Andrin had a point, so hurried on beside him. No one paid them much attention as they approached the bustling heart of Teguise, even though they made a bizarre pairing. There were more than the usual number of soldiers on the streets, but they did not appear to be doing anything out of the ordinary, and Vargo began to wonder if the rumours he had heard were true. Perhaps they had been delusions, brought on by his divided mental state.

The broad avenue that led to Manrique Square was lined with palm trees, and stall owners had set out their wares between them, trading in all kinds of food, as well as trinkets, pottery, metalwork and leather goods, but few people were buying now. The centre of attraction was a large notice board, where the earlier proclamation had now been joined by another. People were clustered around this, those closest shouting details to those on the edges of the throng. By the time Andrin and Vargo had pushed their way to the front, they already knew the gist of what it contained. But they had to find out who was on the list.

Andrin stood in front of the board, and the crowd drew back a little as they recognized his need, his anger and the pent-up violence within him. Some people evidently recognized the boy who was linked to a white eagle, and Andrin heard them whispering. He did not care. His eyes were fixed on the list and on the name that stood at its head. Even though he had expected nothing else, seeing Ico's name there in black and white made him feel as though his heart were pumping iced water instead of blood, and for a time he could read no further. The game was over; the war had begun.

When he forced himself to look down, skimming over the two dozen names, he was puzzled, angry – and a little relieved. Although several Firebrands were there, as well as a few people Andrin did not even know, neither his nor Vargo's names featured in the neatly printed column. He turned to glance at his friend, who was open-mouthed, clearly as bemused as he was, but horrified too. Then the reason for Vargo's distress became clear. The last name on the list was that of Famara Ye.

'I . . . I . . . I must go to her,' he stammered. 'Tell her about this . . . this clay promotion. I have to tell her.'

He turned away and ran off, his ill-assorted clothes flapping around him, and the crowd parted to let him go. Silently furious now, Andrin reached up and ripped the poster from the tacks that held it in place. Ignoring the murmurings of the onlookers, he set off again, the crumpled proclamation in his hand.

Moments later he entered Manrique Square, part of the tide of humanity that was flowing into the market place. It was nearly noon. Although trade was slackening off, there were still a great number of people there, searching for late bargains before the stalls closed for their proprietors to take a siesta during the hottest part of the day. On this occasion, however, there was more than trade going on.

On an unladen cart in the centre of the square, a man stood, shouting and gesticulating. He had attracted a large audience, many of whom were either heckling or asking questions in what had become an open debate.

'The Senate is full of bullshit!' the speaker yelled. 'They're cowards. They know what has to be done, but they haven't got the guts.'

'So who has?' someone called. 'You?'

'Yes, me!'

'But only beer guts,' another heckler shouted, provoking considerable laughter.

'Laugh all you want,' the speaker sneered, 'but the dragons will kill us all if we don't show them we're sorry. What's the use of proclamations? The Firebrands don't understand words. We need action!'

'What kind of action?'

'Sacrifices! That's what they did in the old days, and there was never any trouble then.'

'Who would you have die?'

'Easy,' he replied. 'The Firebrands. They're the ones causing the trouble. They broke the law. They should be the ones to pay.'

There was a noisy interlude as several arguments broke out among the crowd. High above, a white eagle and a sparrow-hawk circled, watching.

In the square, silence fell as a young man leapt up on to the cart, pushed the speaker unceremoniously over the side and held up a crumpled poster. Although several people moved to throw the interloper down, a huge white bird swooped threateningly over their heads, and then settled on the seat at the front of the cart to stand guard over his link.

All eyes were on Andrin as he began to speak.

CHAPTER TWENTY-SIX

'Sacrifices won't solve any of our problems!' Andrin cried, his voice carrying easily around the square. 'It would just make murderers of us all!'

He knew even as he spoke that he was being reckless, that he was in the grip of a kind of madness. The fires had been banked up inside him for a long time now, but with this day's events the pressure had become too great to contain. All he could do was try to control the explosion, direct it to some purpose. Today had been the final straw. First there had been the miserable encounter with his parents, then Vargo's seasonal idiocy and the unwelcome news he had brought – the fireworm attack, the second proclamation and the real possibility of sacrifices. On top of that was Andrin's intense frustration at not being able to see Ico, and his uncertainty about her safety. And finally, this moronic speaker, sprouting his lies and vitriol, had been more than he could bear. His self-control had been gradually worn away until at last he felt he had nothing to lose. He knew it was not a logical conclusion, and that it had been reached by purely emotional means, but that did not make it any less real. Remaining silent was no longer an option.

He had already thought of several ways of putting his thoughts into words; instinctively, he chose the most dangerous.

'I am one of the Firebrands!' he shouted. 'And I am proud to say that, because we truly have the best interests of Tiguafaya at heart.' Overriding the wave of protest provoked by his words, he went on, turning as he spoke so that every section of the crowd saw the fire in his eyes. 'There have been many lies told about us, lies invented by people who find our honesty a threat to their cosy way of life, their pampered, uncaring existence, while others suffer the consequences of their indolence and greed. Ask yourselves, what have we actually done that is so bad? We've tried to lift our country out of the stagnation it's fallen into, we've tried to revive some of our old and treasured values and traditions, and we've tried to protect innocent people from a terrible, senseless death. That's what we've actually *done*. Everything else that's been ascribed to us is a product of speculation, of vindictiveness, or of pure fancy. Where are these dragons we're supposed to have annoyed? Has any one of you even seen them?'

He was inspired now, the words coming from deep inside him without the need for conscious thought. He was possessed by a fervour that was close to arrogance, assuming that all who heard him must be convinced. He was a beacon of truth. He was blind. And he did not see the movement at the outer edges of the ever growing crowd as several White Guard patrol units began to encircle his position at centre stage, cutting off all means of escape.

Ico was alone in the senator's house when Soo arrived with her urgent and horrifying news.

'How could he be so stupid?' she exploded.

I think he believes he can convince them all.

That's crazy. We must stop him.

It's too late for that.

Then I have to help him at least.

I don't see what you can do, Soo argued. *If you go out you'll be in danger yourself.*

That doesn't matter, Ico replied, looking around, wild-eyed.

She found a hooded cape that was too big for her, but which would hide her from prying eyes, and threw it on. Leaving Maciot's house by the front door, she set out to run the short distance to Manrique Square. With the hood flapping in her eyes, and having to hold the cape up to stop her tripping over its hem, her progress was erratic, but she had the sense to slow down when she reached the entrance to the market place. There were several soldiers on duty there, but none of them paid her any attention. All eyes were on the commotion near the centre of the square and, even from a distance, Ico could pick out Andrin's distinctive hair and hear his voice raised above the noise of the crowd.

She tried to get closer, but the press was so great it was impossible to make much progress. She had no idea what she could do to help him, and eventually settled for climbing on to the end of a stone water-trough so that she could see what was happening more clearly. From her vantage point she could make out the uniforms of the White Guard, who now blocked all the exits and who also formed a ring within the crowd, a ring that was slowly tightening, like a noose. And yet Andrin was still speaking, clearly oblivious to his imminent capture.

Andrin's speech had been impassioned and articulate, and it was as much a tribute to his fluency and obvious conviction as it was to Ayo's intimidating presence that, after the initial flurries, no one had tried to oust him from the cart. He had used several of the arguments that Ico had employed when faced with the drunken gang, but he had expanded on them at some length. He had questioned the motives of Kantrowe and the Senate, and challenged the supposed links between the fireworms and the dragons, between the dragons and the eruptions; he had argued persuasively against the persecution of the Firebrands and anyone else involved in magic, and had painted a dark picture of the horrors of martial law, of the denial of freedom and of the inevitable injustices that would follow. He had emphasized the abhorrence that all decent people must feel at the very idea of human sacrifices, and ridiculed the idea that such abominations would prove effective. And throughout all this he had dealt easily with several hecklers, slapping down their arguments, demanding proof or even solid reasoning to back up their accusations, and even provoking laughter in some of the spectators by mocking their more extreme opinions. In doing so he gained many friends as well as enemies and, even though he still held centre stage, the debate had become heated in many other sections of the throng, in some instances to the point of violence.

His evident sincerity had made quite an impression on the gathering and, by the time he finally began to run out of words, there were as many calls of support as of opposition. The impassive presence of the soldiers was the only note of ominous quiet in the thunderous music of what was now a major disturbance, with all the potential to turn into a full-scale riot. The guards moved forward steadily, grim faced, and those around them became nervous and fell silent. Others tried to call out a surreptitious warning, but their voices were lost in the general tumult. In any case, Andrin was lost to them now. He was flying, drunk on his own rhetoric, invincible.

'We can't let them get away with this!' he called, his voice hoarse now but still rising above the hubbub. 'We must make our voices heard. Let them know what we think, what we want, before it's too late. We don't have to stand for *this*!' He held up the proclamation, still crushed in his fist.

'Here!' The urgent voice sounded from the jostling crowd around the cart.

Andrin looked down and saw a young man holding up a flaming taper, his eyes reflecting a fervour that matched the Firebrand's own.

'Burn it,' the stranger urged. 'Burn the proclamation!'

Andrin stooped to accept the torch, and smiled his thanks.

'Here's what I think of this proclamation!' he declared. Holding it out at arm's length, he set it alight, only letting the last piece fall when almost all of the parchment had turned black. Some onlookers cheered, while other shouted angrily in protest as the flames swept upwards. Then the dark fragments and a few sparks were caught by the breeze and wafted into the air. Andrin stamped on the final embers.

This last, most flagrant act of defiance was too much for the soldiers. At the command of their captain, they pushed forward with greater urgency, shoving people aside. A few of the guards even drew their swords, though it was impossible to use them in the crush. Screams and insults filled the air and, at last, Andrin recognized his predicament. He also saw that there was no way out.

Go! he told Ayo hurriedly. *Warn Ico and the others, tell them to follow up on this. We're not without support.*

As the eagle lifted towards the sky with slow, heavy wing beats, Andrin faced his enemies boldly, hardly caring that his part in the war might be over. Others would finish what he had begun here. As the nearest soldiers reached the cart and prepared to climb up, he did not move, but experienced his only moment of regret as Ico's face appeared in his mind's eye. He had to believe that they would be together again before too long but, if that was not to be, she would be proud of his sacrifice. He wished she could have been there to see him.

The first soldier was on the cart now, approaching warily, his sword held at the ready as if he were expecting a fight. Andrin still did not move.

'Don't make this any worse for yourself than it already is,' the guard warned. Then he froze, his eyes locked on the tip of his blade.

A small, impossible wisp of flame was gilding the end of the steel. Suddenly, fire shot up towards the hilt and he dropped it in panic. Andrin stared, equally astonished, as the weapon fell and embedded itself point first into the boards of the cart. The flames still played around the quivering sword.

And then the entire cart, the soldier, Andrin and dozens of people nearby were engulfed in a roaring inferno that struck like a thunderbolt and threatened to sear the sky.

CHAPTER TWENTY-SEVEN

Unaware of events elsewhere in the city, Vargo arrived at Famara's hut gasping for breath and soaked with sweat. He had never run so far so fast in his life, but he knew even before he swept the curtain aside that he had come too late. There was no one inside, and any faint hope that Famara had left of her own accord was soon dashed. The place had been ransacked and several shelves were broken, their contents scattered over the floor. The dragon's blood stones were gone and the bed had been torn apart, presumably in case any other magical artefacts had been hidden there. Worst of all, Famara's lute lay in a corner, smashed beyond repair. Such senseless destruction was beyond Vargo's comprehension. He stared in horror at the twisted remains of what had once been a thing of beauty.

He found himself crying, tears streaming down his face, even as his whole frame was convulsed with manic laughter. He trembled and began to hiccup violently, so that he seemed to be in the throes of some uncontrollable palsy. His vision blurred and he screamed – an ugly, tearing sound. Famara was gone. He should have made her move to somewhere safe. He should

have been there to protect her. And his own visits were probably the reason they had been able to find her. Famara was *gone*.

'There was nothing we could do. I'm sorry.'

The voice came from far away, from another world, and at
first the words meant nothing to Vargo. He had fallen to his
knees without knowing it and looked up now, staring stupidly
at the man who stood in the doorway.

'We usually look out for her,' the man said, 'to see that no
one bothers her, but they came before dawn. Half of us were
asleep, and there were just too many of them. We're no match
for trained swordsmen.'

Vargo slowly made sense of what he was being told.

'It's not your fault,' he managed to whisper. 'Do you know
where they've taken her?'

'No, but I can guess. The Paleton.'

Vargo nodded, using a sleeve to wipe his face. The Paleton
was the city's main gaol, a heavily fortified block of cells
surrounded by military barracks.

'It's a damn shame,' the man said. 'They've no right taking a
harmless old biddy like Famara. We were all in her debt.'

'Me too,' Vargo added quietly.

'By the sound of things she'll not be the only one locked up
for no reason.'

Vargo could only nod again. He had never felt more
miserable or bewildered in his entire life.

The voices swam in her mind like fish in a bowl, going round
and round but never getting anywhere.

'Why doesn't she wake up?'

'Patience. We don't know what happened.'

'She's cold, and her breathing's shallow.'

'There's nothing wrong with her. Don't worry. It's just a
matter of time.'

'Why doesn't she wake up?'

'Patience . . .'

It was dark. She shivered, and tried to open her eyes, but something was stopping her. Her whole body felt so heavy, even her eyelids refused to move. Something had happened. Something . . . She sank down into the welcoming darkness again.

Much later, there was a tiny spark of light. She swam towards it, pushing her way through the darkness that clung to her like black mud, holding her back.

'She's coming to.'

'Ico? Ico, can you hear me?'

She recognized the voice now, and it gave her the strength to shove her way through the black mud, towards the light that grew brighter with each effort.

Ico opened her eyes. It was the hardest thing she had ever done, but it was worth the effort. There, looking down at her, was Andrin. He was smiling now with relief, though the worry still showed in his eyes.

'Are you all right?'

'Just very tired,' she whispered. It was a laughable understatement.

'Sleep, then,' he told her gently. 'You're safe here.'

'Where am I?'

'At my house,' Maciot replied from somewhere above her. 'Where you should have stayed. But then again, if you had, you'd have missed quite a show.'

Something had happened. It nibbled at the edges of her thoughts as she slipped back into the darkness.

The next time she woke it was easier, and this time her memory returned. With it came the knowledge that had eluded her earlier and she gasped, half in awe, half in terror. A moment later Andrin was by her side, all concern.

'What's the matter? Are you in pain?'

She gazed at him, at the near-white hair and the emerald eyes, and was swept by a wave of gratitude.

'You're not burned,' she said.

'No. Nobody was. The fire wasn't real. It was an illusion, but by the time anyone realized that, panic had already set in. It's a wonder no one was crushed to death in the stampede. But that was nothing to what came next.'

'The serpents,' Ico breathed, remembering.

'You saw them too?' he asked. 'Some people didn't, apparently. And what with you fainting . . . But they were magic too.'

'I know,' she said quietly. 'I made them.'

Andrin grew very still, staring at her in disbelief, and for a long time neither of them spoke.

'You?' he said at last. '*You* made them?'

'And the flames,' she confessed. 'It was me, but I never meant . . .'

'Wait a moment. You're telling me that all the magic came just from you?'

'Yes.' Only her weakness prevented her from growing angry. How could he doubt her?

'I think you'd better start at the beginning,' Maciot said, coming to join Andrin at her bedside. 'I want to hear this.'

Ico looked up at him, prey to mixed emotions. She no longer doubted him, and his presence was somehow re-assuring, but she wasn't sure she wanted him intruding on what felt like a private conversation – even if it was taking place in his own home. She tried to put her thoughts in order, but found it difficult.

'Did Soo come and tell you what was going on?' Andrin prompted her eventually.

'Yes. She said that you'd torn down the new proclamation and were making a speech about it in the market place. Oh, Andrin, how could you be so stupid? After what we all agreed?'

'It's a long story. I'm sorry. I couldn't stop myself.'

'You can tell her later,' Maciot put in, then turned back to Ico. 'You took my cloak and set off. What happened next?'

'When I got to the square I couldn't get too close, because of the crowds, but I saw soldiers everywhere, closing in on you. I heard the last part of your speech and saw you burn the poster, and then the guards moved in. I had to do something. I had no choice.'

'So you used magic?' Maciot said.

'But you'd never created *any* illusions before,' Andrin exclaimed, 'let alone anything as big as that!'

'I knew about it in theory, though, and I'd learnt a lot since we got back to the city – from Vargo and from what I'd read.' Ico glanced at the senator to see whether he reacted to the mention of the old books, but he merely nodded, wanting her to go on. 'All I wanted to do was create a diversion, something to give you a chance to get away. I never thought . . .' She was silent again, recalling the sight of those first small flickers and then the incredible surge of power that had followed.

'Well, you certainly succeeded in that,' Andrin remarked in admiration. 'No one was paying any attention to me after what you did.'

'It was Vargo who gave me the idea,' she explained. 'You remember, he told us that the more people who witness an illusion the more convincing it becomes? Well, that's what happened. I only needed to project a tiny image of fire and then, when everyone saw it, it was their belief that magnified it and created that huge blaze. There were so many people watching that it just got out of hand. After a few moments it was out of my control.'

'And that's when everyone panicked, including the soldiers,' Andrin concluded. 'You're a genius!'

Ico smiled wanly.

'And the serpents?' Maciot asked.

'I didn't mean them to appear, but it just sort of happened,' she replied uneasily. 'I'm not even sure whether they came from my mind or the crowd's, or both. I suppose dragons are in everyone's thoughts at the moment, and they're associated with fire, so . . .'

'Even if it wasn't deliberate,' Maciot commented, 'you could hardly have chosen a more effective way of ensuring that no one stayed around to try and capture Andrin. I was right at the back of the crowd, and they scared the hell out of me.'

'It was a mistake,' Ico said. 'I wish it hadn't happened, but the whole thing was out of control by then. I don't even remember much after the serpents first appeared. That's when I fainted, I suppose.'

'Did anyone there recognize you, or realize what you were doing?' the senator asked.

'I don't know. Some people were looking at me very strangely,' she replied doubtfully. 'I think I might have been shouting, but I'm not sure. I do know that I felt as if all the life was being sucked out of me by the flames and those creatures. I nearly blacked out more than once, but the magic wouldn't let go. Eventually I fell, but someone caught me.' She shivered suddenly. 'I remember a face. It was horrible, but his eyes were kind. He helped me, I think.'

'That someone brought you here,' Maciot told her. 'He wouldn't stay or even speak – other than to say that he'd brought you from the market place – and he was the most misshapen creature I've ever seen.'

Ico and Andrin looked at each other.

'Angel?' he asked.

Ico nodded, seeing the grotesque features again in her mind.

'Can he be a friend too?' Andrin wondered.

'Who is he?' their host asked.

They told him about the strange man who had spied upon the Firebrands' meeting, and explained that they knew nothing else about Ico's saviour. How and why he had come to act as he did was a mystery they had no way of solving yet.

'The magic obviously drained all your energy,' Andrin said. 'When I got here you were still unconscious.'

Ico was feeling desperately tired again. The exertion of talking for so long had almost worn her out.

'There is a price to pay for everything,' Maciot observed. 'Even magic, it seems. You should get some more rest.'

Beyond the shutters darkness had fallen.

'I'm going to check on the others,' Andrin told her. 'I had to hide after I got away from the square, until the birds guided me here, so I haven't been able to find out whether Vargo's all right. Famara's name is on the list, and he went to try and help her.'

'What list?' she asked feebly.

Andrin explained about the second proclamation.

'Your name's on it, but mine isn't and nor is Vargo's. It's weird.'

'But Famara's is?'

'Yes, and several Firebrands. I need to be sure they're safe.'

'Be careful,' she said, wishing she was capable of going with him. 'You're a marked man now.'

'I'm not likely to forget it,' he replied, smiling. 'Don't worry about me. Sleep, and recover your strength. We need you.' He kissed her gently. 'I'll be back before you know it.'

Ico was asleep again before the door had closed behind him.

Mazo Gadette stared at his master as the senator laughed uproariously. It was rare that anyone, including Kantrowe, surprised the aide to this extent.

'I thought you'd be furious,' he said. After all, this was the second time in one day that a leading member of the Firebrands had escaped arrest.

'No, no, no. This is wonderful. Don't you see? They're falling apart even quicker than we anticipated.'

'But—'

'You're sure it was her?'

~~'Yes. There were several witnesses—'~~

'And she really used magic, here in Teguise?' Kantrowe went on as if he could hardly believe it.

'Yes.'

'With dragons?'

'According to all the reports they were fire-breathing serpents, but it amounts to the same thing.'

'Wonderful!' Kantrowe repeated. 'The Maravedis girl has played right into our hands. Tell Chinero to find her – and no slip-ups this time!'

He burst out laughing again.

It was a mistake. Andrin remembered Ico's prophetic words as he watched the torchlit streets from a dark alcove. The demonstration flowed through the city like an angry tide, heading for the government district. Their chants and shouted slogans demanded that the sacrifices begin at once.

Whatever he had been able to achieve in Manrique Square had been swept away by the fear induced by the appearance of the illusory dragons – which were being used as proof of the Firebrands' guilt. The last hope of preventing the madness was gone.

'Ico, wake up.' Maciot shook her gently.

She opened her eyes reluctantly, but felt that some of her strength had returned.

'Is Andrin back yet?'

'No, but I think you'd better leave.'

'Why?' she asked, instantly fearful.

'Tao's just brought word that the White Guard are on their way here. Ostensibly it's to check on me for the new register. Admitting that I'm linked isn't a problem – it's common knowledge – but they may make it an excuse to look around. I'd rather not have anything to hide, and you'll probably be safer somewhere else.'

She got up and dressed hurriedly.

'Will you be able to find somewhere to hide until they've gone?' he asked. 'You can come back then of course, if you want to.'

She nodded.

'What if Andrin returns while the guards are here?'

'I'll have Tao keep watch, or get some of the other birds to do it. And if I see Andrin later, I'll let him know what's happened.'

'Will you keep these for me?' she asked, handing him her talisman and the wizard's book. 'It'll make it easier for me to travel inconspicuously.'

'Of course. Do you want my cape again?'

She nodded and a few moments later her cloaked figure slipped out of a side entrance and headed towards the docks, intending to find a place to wait until she could contact Andrin. She had not gone far when Soo appeared in the sky above her. Ico took comfort from the sparrowhawk's presence, and did not notice the raven that flew some way behind her. She told Soo where she was heading, so that a message could be passed on to Andrin if necessary, and warned her about the soldiers approaching Maciot's house.

Ico turned a corner, entering a narrow alleyway, and found her way barred by several soldiers. Others emerged from a doorway behind her, cutting off any chance of escape. Captain Chinero stepped forward and smiled.

'So, Ico,' he remarked pleasantly, 'we meet again.'

CHAPTER TWENTY-EIGHT

Tias Kantrowe looked out over the city from the window of his Vestry office, and toasted the events of the day in one of his very finest vintages. He was delighted by the fact that so many of his plans were coming to fruition at the same time – and saw no reason why they should not continue to do so.

That morning's emergency debate, the second in three days, had gone exactly as he had foreseen. The use of magic in the city, and in such a public and spectacular manner, had forced the senators to show their true colours. He had watched even the more liberal-minded weighing conscience against expediency, and the results had been predictable. The people of Teguise had spoken the night before, needing only a little encouragement to break their silence, and the Senate had now followed suit. The prevailing opinion had been expressed in terms of sorrow rather than anger; given the lamentable events of the previous day it seemed that only drastic action could be relied upon to quell this menace – and the sooner the better. Even so, the arguments had been fierce and had split the chamber.

Most decisions in the Senate were taken by acclamation or, at most, by a show of hands. On this occasion, however, Kantrowe himself had decreed that it should be put to a formal vote. He had done so not because the result was in doubt – it was a foregone conclusion – but because he wanted the official record to show that he considered the matter to be of the utmost gravity. He also wanted there to be no possibility of any subsequent disputes or backsliding. The decision, once made, was to be irrevocable. The vote would also give him the opportunity to study exactly who was resisting the shift of power, and who might therefore be a source of opposition in the future. Knowing his enemies would make them easier to deal with.

One by one the senators had taken the polished stone spheres – which were inscribed with their individual badges of office and the insignia of their respective guilds – and, with all due solemnity, they had walked to the centre of the room. Once there they had placed their sphere on one side or the other of the 'Scales of Justice', depending on whether they were voting for or against the motion. Long before the end it had become clear that the decree would be passed, as one side of the perfectly calibrated balance was already weighted firmly to the floor, but the ceremony had been completed. Kantrowe had been the last to cast his stone – and voted, with every outward sign of reluctance, with the majority.

The official recorder had duly noted the final result, with those in favour outnumbering the objectors by more than four to one, and Kantrowe knew that he had been given leave to begin the sacrifices. He had accepted the responsibility gravely, assuring the chamber that he would act speedily, as required, but with all necessary prudence. As specified, only those convicted of serious crimes would be considered as potential victims, and in every case the President must grant his personal approval before any action was taken. Beyond that, everything was left to Kantrowe's discretion.

The senator smiled to himself and took another sip of wine. It's only a matter of time now, he thought, until I have my long-awaited revenge. And that's not all, he reminded himself, glowing with a satisfaction that bordered on joy. The possibilities for the future seemed limitless.

When Verier and Gadette arrived, their colleague's good humour was immediately made evident. Kantrowe poured them generous measures of wine, and led them in a toast to their success. Gadette, shrewd as always, realized that his master's mood was not entirely due to the result of the morning's debate. He set aside his notes and looked at Kantrowe quizzically.

'Good news?'

'I've had two messages since I returned from the chamber,' the senator replied. 'Both more than satisfactory.'

'Well?' Verier demanded impatiently.

'The first was from Jon Zophres, telling us that the deal is done. Zarzuelo and the Lawyer have agreed to our terms, and have already proved their good faith by defending one of our vessels against some renegade pirates. And they have pledged to seek out the Barber, and either convert him to the cause or destroy his fleet. We'll continue to watch them closely, of course, but it seems that we need not worry about a threat from the sea, at least for the time being.'

'Honour among pirates?' Verier said doubtfully. 'How long before they double-cross us?'

'Long enough for us to be able to deal with them from a position of strength,' Kantrowe replied confidently.

'Will you make an announcement?' Gadette asked practically.

'Eventually, but not yet. This is a delicate matter, and I don't want to divert attention from our other affairs. We can work on the wording of a statement later.'

'Surely you're not going to tell everyone the truth?' Verier exclaimed.

'Of course not!' Kantrowe snapped, and wished that the younger senator was not so vital to his strategy. His occasional stupidity was immensely irritating. As it was, the inner council was now effectively down to just three men. Although the old senators had not been officially notified, their exclusion was self-evident now that their usefulness was over. They would be fed enough titbits to keep them from making trouble, but their hands had slipped from the reins of power. Verier was still needed, partly because of his family's wealth, influence and their huge estates in the north of the country, and partly because as an ally he was malleable. As an enemy he would be extremely dangerous.

'We'll be able to come up with plausible reasons for the troop withdrawals and the dismantling of defences,' Kantrowe explained, 'but we don't want to cause general alarm.'

'They're only peasants,' Verier said. 'Why bother?'

'So are most of the men who work in your mines and my vineyards,' Kantrowe pointed out. 'And we wouldn't want to give *them* the wrong idea, would we.'

Verier held out his goblet for more wine, his expression sullen. 'What was the second message?' he asked.

'News from the west. The latest experiment was a great success – a considerable yield in a very short time.'

'That's more like it,' Verier said, becoming animated again.

'Two miners were killed in the process,' Kantrowe added, 'but that's a small price to pay for such progress. Once we're able to put together our own experience and that of the Firebrands, who knows what we might achieve?'

'Speaking of which,' Gadette put in. 'I have that report you wanted.'

'Go ahead.'

'The boy's name, as you know, is Andrin Zonzomas. He lives with his parents in a hovel near the docks. Neither of them is in the best of health, apparently, but there may not be much leverage there because he doesn't get on well with them. The only other member of the family was a brother, Mendo. He was killed by fireworms, which probably explains Andrin's fanaticism. He's a dock rat, although according to the stevedores he's not been at work much recently. He's linked to a white eagle, which as far as we know is the only one of that species ever to be linked.'

'An interesting young man,' Kantrowe commented.

'There's also a romantic attachment to the Maravedis girl, although he's not remotely in her social class.'

'Even better.'

'A lot of people thought he must have been responsible for yesterday's illusions, but we've no hard evidence that he has any real magical talent.'

'And you're sure it was the Maravedis girl?'

'As sure as we can be,' the aide replied. 'The White Guard are on the lookout for them both now. They won't be able to hide from us for long.'

'Especially as they both seem to be exhibitionists,' Verier remarked caustically.

'Perhaps we should leave Zonzomas alone for a while,' Kantrowe mused. 'See what he does. If he's one of their leaders, then we may need him to keep their efforts going. With regard to the worms,' he added for Verier's benefit.

'He certainly has a certain charisma,' Gadette admitted grudgingly. 'If it hadn't been for the way his outburst ended, last night's result might have been very different.'

'Who's going to take a dock rat seriously?' Verier said contemptuously. He had been drinking steadily while the other two spoke, and was now growing bored.

'No one,' Kantrowe answered. 'We'll make sure of that.'

A short while later, after some further discussion about the debate and its consequences, Verier and Gadette left to go their separate ways. The aide returned to work and his ceaseless gathering of information, while Verier chose to visit the discreet establishment that was able to cater to all his tastes. He was a valued customer, to the extent that the unfortunate death of one of the girls had been dealt with quietly and anonymously in order to save him from any embarrassment. Kantrowe's wine had given him the appetite for further pleasures – more wine and a good deal besides.

After they had gone Kantrowe received a third message, this one from Captain Chinero. And it contained, the senator thought happily, the best news of all.

While the inner council was meeting in the room above the city, the Firebrands met below. The disused cellar was filthy and dark, but it was the safest venue available to them and the dismal setting matched the sombre nature of the occasion. Their numbers were much reduced. At least seven Firebrands were now incarcerated in the Paleton. Those were the ones they knew about; others were missing, and so had either been arrested or were in hiding, or had fled the city altogether. The remaining group were nervous, some of them obviously terrified, and Andrin felt an acute sense of responsibility. They were all so young, and obviously quite unprepared for the horrible predicament into which they had been plunged. No matter how many times he told himself that it was bound to have come to this sooner or later, he still felt guilty about his part in precipitating the crisis.

They had all heard what had happened in Manrique Square, although some had received somewhat garbled third-hand versions, but it was only Andrin who had been able to tell them the full story – including the part played by Ico. And once the Firebrands had recovered from their awe at her achievement, they voiced their obvious concern.

'Why isn't she here?'

'Is she all right?'

'She's safe for now, but it exhausted her. Once we've finished here I'll go back to her.' Andrin had decided, coldly rational, not to tell anyone where Ico was. The fewer people who knew about Maciot the better, and he did not want to put Ico's safety at risk if more Firebrands should be arrested. 'But I *can* tell you that we have some friends in high places.'

'Not enough, though,' someone said with feeling.

'I know the whole situation is a mess just now,' Andrin went on, 'but we must decide how we're going to respond.'

'It's all very well for you to say that. My name's on that list!'

'Yeah, how do you explain why only some of us are wanted?'

'I can't,' Andrin replied honestly. 'But we're all in this together. Sooner or later they're bound to find out who we all are.' He did not need to specify how.

'Can we try to rescue those in the Paleton?' Vargo asked.

'How do you propose to do that? There are hundreds of soldiers all round the place.'

'Magic,' the musician responded. 'It's our only advantage. There must be a way we can use it to do *something*.'

'That's right,' one of the bolder Firebrands agreed. 'We fooled them before, so why not again?'

'This is different!'

'But we've nothing to lose. We're already fugitives in our own city.'

'We could lose our freedom – or our lives!' one of the objectors protested.

'Freedom may not be worth having soon if Kantrowe has his way,' Vargo said. He whistled softly and Lao, the only bird who had been willing to come underground, answered with an equally melancholy call.

Most of the other links were airborne, on sentry duty, or far away. The Firebrands' discussion went on for some time, with a variety of plans being put forward and then rejected. For his own part, Andrin was not sure they would ever be able to breach the security of the Paleton. Even the wizards of old would have been hard put to do that – and the Firebrands were just a bunch of novices. But he approved of the spirit that made them want to try.

As the arguments began to head towards stalemate and no new ideas were forthcoming, they were all distracted by movement at the top of one of the staircases that led to the outside world. The lookout stationed there opened the door slightly and Soo flew in, alighting next to the startled Lao. There was a brief burst of chatter from the sparrowhawk, then the curlew turned to Vargo, who immediately paled visibly.

'What's happened?' Andrin asked worriedly.

'The White Guard have arrested Ico,' Vargo whispered, his voice weak with dread.

'She's been betrayed?' Andrin exclaimed, silently cursing Maciot and trying, without much success, to retain some semblance of calm.

'Soo says not. She left because there were soldiers coming to the senator's house.'

'Where's she been taken?'

'I don't know. Soo followed as far as she could but they went inside the Guards' headquarters, so there's no telling where she is now.'

The impact of this news was only just beginning to sink in when there was a second arrival. Tao, almost invisible in the dim light, joined the other two birds – and the ensuing conversation obviously caused them much consternation. Andrin was prey to any number of fears, and the ominous speculation among the Firebrands increased at the sight of the unfamiliar bird. Again it was left to Lao to pass on the chaffinch's message, via Vargo. The musician reported as he went along.

'Alegranze Maciot asked Tao here to pass on this message,' he began, glancing at Andrin to see if he knew who Maciot was, but Andrin merely waved at him to continue.

'He wanted us to know that Ico's been captured. She had to leave his house, but was intercepted before she could find another hiding place.'

'We know all that,' Andrin said impatiently. 'Anything else?'

Lao was still faithfully relaying the original message.

'They only found out,' Vargo went on, 'because Angel – Angel? – has apparently been following Ico for some time. Wasn't he—'

'Just get on with it!' Andrin snapped.

'Oh gods, no!' Vargo exclaimed, his face now a mask of absolute horror.

'What?' Andrin demanded.

'Maciot also found out,' his friend replied, speaking with some difficulty, 'that if Ico was captured she . . . she was going to be made the first sacrifice.'

Andrin was frozen, speechless, so utterly petrified that he could not even be certain that he could still breathe or that his heart was still beating. All he could do was silently deny that this was happening, the words echoing in his mind over and over again. No, no, no!

'When?' someone else asked, breaking the shocked silence.

'This afternoon,' Vargo answered helplessly.

CHAPTER TWENTY-NINE

Kantrowe rarely made public appearances, but made an exception in this case – and tried to ensure that as many people as possible knew about it. Criers walked the streets, rousing the populace from their siestas with bells and whistles, and spreading the news. Their announcements were successful and, at the appointed hour, Manrique Square was packed. The crowd stood shoulder to shoulder in the open spaces, while others clung to precarious vantage points in the trees or watched from the windows and roofs of the surrounding buildings. And watching all of them was a strong detachment of White Guards.

Kantrowe entered the arena like a triumphant general returning from a great victory. He was flanked by more soldiers, who cleared a path for him and the bedraggled group who followed him in chains. Climbing on to the hastily constructed wooden platform at the centre of the square, the senator raised his hands for quiet, and the silence spread out around him like ripples from a stone. When he had their undivided attention, Kantrowe spoke.

'This is a sad day for Tiguafaya,' he began, surprising many with his sombre tone. 'You all know that we have faced enemies before, and faced them bravely. But this is the first time that the greatest threat has come from within, from treason among our own people. As is so often the case with such things, the foolish and treacherous acts of the unreasoning few have tainted us all. It is time now to put an end to this madness, once and for all. I have resisted this outcome in the name of common humanity, but it has become inevitable. You, the people of Teguise, have made your wishes plain and today the Senate ratified the use of sacrifices.'

He paused while a storm of noise blew around the square, noting with satisfaction that most people were cheering the decision.

'This is both to appease the great creatures who control the stability of our land and to demonstrate our implacable opposition to any who would cast aside their protection, shatter our peace and create a deadly realm of anarchy.'

He paused again, this time for dramatic effect.

'This is a sad day for Tiguafaya,' he repeated, his voice rising towards a crescendo, 'but because we now choose to stand firm, it is also a day of new hope. And above all it is a day of justice!'

Kantrowe waited until the second wave of noise subsided, pleased by the reaction to his rousing cry, then turned and beckoned to some of the soldiers who stood guard around the platform. They in turn herded eight young people up the steps and on to the stage. Each of the prisoners hung their head, eyes downcast, as they shuffled uneasily into place. The iron manacles around their wrists rattled ominously, and the onlookers at the front of the crowd could see that several of them were injured, either limping or with cuts and bruises on their dejected faces. Their clothes were dirty and seemed to hang from them like wet rags, and they had been stripped of all jewellery. Prompted by their escorts, the eight fell to their knees in a line and waited, heads still bowed. They were a picture of defeat, of utter humiliation.

The crowd muttered and stared, wondering whether the promised executions were going to begin right now, but

Kantrowe waved the soldiers away so that he remained alone on the platform with the prisoners. In doing so he emphasized their subjugation and his own confident superiority.

'These pathetic creatures are Firebrands,' the senator announced. 'Frightening, aren't they?'

The growls of anger in his audience turned to laughter.

'We can mock them now,' Kantrowe went on, his smile fading, 'and it is less punishment than they deserve, but not so long ago these young people were engaged in acts of betrayal which brought danger to us all. Fortunately, as you will hear, they have seen the error of their ways. This is Fayna Bravi.' He pointed to the girl at the end of the line and she started at the sound of her name. 'Come here, my dear.'

Fayna raised terrified eyes to Kantrowe, seemed to flinch at the sight of his smile, and then her expression grew vacant. She got to her feet unsteadily and walked over to stand beside the senator. He put a fatherly hand on her shoulder and she flinched again.

'Why did you join the Firebrands, Fayna?'

'Because I thought—' Her voice was little more than a whisper.

'You must speak louder, so everyone can hear.'

'Because I thought we could do something to help Tiguafaya,' she said in a dull monotone. 'Because they made it sound exciting.'

'But what they did was a mistake, wasn't it?'

Fayna nodded.

'Why was that?'

'We used magic . . .' Her voice failed again.

'Speak up.'

'We used magic to kill fireworms, which was wrong. It made the dragons angry and they took their revenge on all of us, all the innocent people.' The words were tumbling out now, though her face remained inert, her eyes blank. 'Anyway, it was all lies. They hate the Senate and the people who are really trying to solve the country's problems, and this was just spite. I can see that now.'

'So you were misled by your leaders?' he prompted.

'Yes. They were doing everything for their own selfish ends and didn't care who got hurt.'

'What do you mean?'

'My link, my bird, Ria, was killed by their magic.' There were tears in her eyes now.

'How did Ria die?'

'She was frozen when one of the crystals was destroyed,' Fayna sobbed.

'And will you take part in such an action ever again?'

'No, never!' There was real vehemence in her voice for the first time. 'I hate the Firebrands and all they stand for. I'm sorry . . .'

The rest of what she had to say was lost as she began to weep uncontrollably. Kantrowe led her back to the others where, without being asked, she knelt down again. The senator turned back to the now solemn crowd.

'All these others could tell similar stories!' he cried. 'They are tragic victims in one sense, foolish criminals in another, but at heart none of them is evil. Like Fayna, they come from good families, worthy citizens of Tiguafaya, but they have been led astray. What are we to do with them?'

The crowd responded with a great deal of vociferous advice which Kantrowe merely allowed to die away of its own accord. The decision had already been made.

'Each of these wretches has freely admitted their guilt,' he went on, 'but they have renounced their association with the Firebrands and vowed never to use magic again, except in circumstances permitted by the laws of the land. I believe their repentance to be genuine, and have therefore decided to err on the side of mercy. Their shame is punishment enough. They will be returned to their families, free of all charges.'

There were gasps, some dissenting cries and a smattering of applause at this announcement, but the senator allowed no time for speculation.

'They all understand, however, that if they transgress again then the consequences will be extremely serious – as they will be for any members of the Firebrands who remain at large, should they act in any way detrimental to their homeland. Indeed, I would urge them all to give themselves up. If they do so and swear oaths of loyalty to the Senate as these here have done, we will treat them with similar leniency and compassion. If, on the other hand, they continue to resist the legitimate forces of authority, then their fate when they are captured – as they *will* be captured – will be far less pleasant. They are aware, as we all are, of the penalty for treason.'

The muttering in the crowd was becoming ugly. This was not what they had expected. Kantrowe set his face in his most stern expression, and decided it was time to give them what they wanted.

'Mercy is an elastic commodity, but it cannot be stretched indefinitely. There are those to whom the general amnesty I have outlined cannot apply. These are the Firebrands' principals, who have led so many of our young citizens astray. Some of them are still at large, although that situation will soon be rectified. In the meantime, we have already arrested someone who has grievously abused her position in society. She comes from a well-respected family in one of our oldest guilds, and yet she has seen fit to spit on her heritage and lead this vile conspiracy. She has not only broken the law, endangering us all, but she has shown no sign of contrition for her actions. She was responsible for the appalling events in this very square yesterday, when her unaccountable behaviour invited the spirits of the dragons into our city. She is condemned by her own actions and by her lack of repentance. I have the President's approval for her death. Ico Maravedis will be sacrificed to the honour of the dragons, today, at the hour of sunset.'

The throng murmured and cheered. This was more like it. Kantrowe watched and listened without betraying his contempt for the braying, bloodthirsty multitude. He had been working towards this moment for a long time, and allowed himself a small measure of self-congratulation. The Maravedis girl was the perfect choice, an attractive, well-born woman who had obviously helped shape the Firebrands' organization. Punishing her would make it crystal clear that no one, no matter how prominent, who opposed the rule of the Senate would escape judgement. There was also the small matter of the senator's own personal grudge, but that was merely a private bonus; the politician in Kantrowe insisted that it would have made no difference to his decision. He raised his voice again.

'In the distant past the sacrificial victims would have been cast into lava flows or thrown over the cliffs of craters in the heart of the dragons' realm, but we do not have the resources for such an expedition at present. If justice were truly to be served, Maravedis should be left in the firelands so that the worms could devour her and make reparation that way, but this too is impractical. I have therefore decided that the sacrifice will take place here, in Manrique Square, and it seems only fitting that fire should be the means of her death. It will be an appropriate tribute to the ancient powers, as well as an example to us all of the rewards of folly. Return here at dusk and add your prayers to mine, so that our future safety may be assured. And do not fear another abuse of magic. We have taken certain precautions that will prevent any repetition of such illusions. The only flames you will see will be real – and they will bring our salvation.'

Kantrowe looked at the man who sat opposite him, and tried to conceal his unease. Maghdim – a sinister figure in his black shirt – was the only person who could make the senator feel nervous. There were many reasons for this. Maghdim was a foreigner, from some remote land to the east; he appeared to have no interests, no existence, outside his work; his expression never betrayed any emotion beyond the merest hint of amusement – and Kantrowe could never be sure whether this humour was directed at him or at the world in general; and, above all, he understood more about magic than anyone the senator had ever met. The fact that, for some unfathomable reason, Maghdim hated magic with an almost religious zeal and had devoted his whole life to discovering ways of combating it was almost as disturbing as if he had been a wizard. His depth of knowledge could hardly have been greater. And, right now, his expertise was vital.

'Your preparations are complete?' Kantrowe asked.

Maghdim nodded stiffly. He was a man of few words.

'I want no mistakes this time,' the senator added unnecessarily. 'If anything happens . . .'

'They are but children. Do not fear.'

'And you can prevent her from interfering?'

'Of course. She will die.'

'Good.'

For a while the two men sat watching each other, Kantrowe edgy, Maghdim impassive.

'I will go,' the foreigner said, to his host's relief. He had wanted to dismiss his visitor, but had been unable to bring himself to do it.

As Maghdim left, Gadette came in, shutting the door behind him.

'The sooner that man returns to his duties in the firelands the better,' Kantrowe muttered. 'His eyes are like mirrors, but I can't help feeling they see right through me.'

'He's just one man,' the aide replied, meaning that he could be disposed of, just like any other.

'Indeed,' the senator agreed, annoyed at himself for having displayed any weakness. 'But for now we need him.'

Gadette nodded. 'There's someone else asking to see you,' he said, 'but I didn't think you'd have the time – or the inclination.'

'Who is it?'

'Diano Maravedis.'

'On the contrary, Mazo,' Kantrowe said. 'I've been looking forward to this meeting for almost twenty years. Show him in.'

CHAPTER THIRTY

The darkness was so complete that Ico thought she must have gone blind. The stone floor and walls of the cell were rough and cold, and the stale air smelt of dried sweat and urine. And of fear.

When the door had been closed upon her she had explored the space gingerly, by touch, finding nothing beyond the bare outlines of the tiny room. She had assumed that she would be able to see something once her eyes adjusted to the dark, but the absolute blackness was unrelenting.

As was the silence. Even when Ico pressed her ear against the solid wood of the door, there was nothing to be heard, which made her think that she had not merely been imprisoned but entombed. The only voices that still spoke to her were those of memory: 'The guards should've locked you up.' 'And thrown away the key!' They were the only voices she might ever hear now.

She sat, hunched up in a corner, too frightened even to move or make a sound. Time no longer had any meaning. She might have been there for a few hours or a few days, cold, afraid and alone. Madness beckoned, and her imagination began to populate the empty darkness with snakes, spiders and gibbering demons. She sank down into herself, trying to become smaller and smaller, invisible.

The heavy bolts on the far side of the door were drawn back without warning, and Ico jumped so violently that she banged her elbow on the wall behind her. She felt no pain, however, only hope. Anything was better than this impenetrable negation of life. When the door was thrown open, the greasy red light of the torches in the corridor outside was almost blinding, but then the silhouette of a man became clear. He was dressed in black, a shadow on the world, and his presence made the dismal cell seem even more bleak. A chill flowed from him like vapour, tainting the already foul air with dread. He stood quite still for a long time, and Ico found herself paralyzed. She had never met anyone who could come into a room and yet make it seem more empty. It was as if he were human quicksand, sucking everything in and giving nothing back. And then she sensed, rather than saw, his dead eyes – and the empty darkness suddenly seemed infinitely desirable.

'Who are you?' she whispered, surprised to find that her tongue could still shape words.

He ignored her question, stepped forward again and studied her anew. Ico was terrified, realizing that one of the reasons the cell had been so cold and inhuman was that it was like this man. He had spread his sickness into the very stones. There was no trace of magic in either but, more than that, they seemed to be the antithesis of magic, capable of cancelling it out. Even with the talisman her feeble powers would have been useless. Without it she was utterly helpless.

'Get up.'

His words were harsh and strangely accented, and she felt compelled to obey. She stood before him, trembling, and feeling exposed and vulnerable.

'What do you want?'

'Drink this.' He held out a small phial.

She shook her head, fearing poison.

'It won't poison you,' he said, as if he had read her thoughts. 'That would be too generous an end.'

Ico still demurred. She wanted nothing to do with this man. 'Very well.'

He unstoppered the tiny bottle, leant his head back and tipped the entire contents into his mouth. Then, with the speed of a striking snake, he grabbed either side of her head, holding her in a vice. He kissed her violently, full on the mouth. Ico tried to struggle, to beat at him with her fists, but all the strength had been sapped from her limbs and her flailing had no effect. She felt the bitter liquid being forced between her lips, gagged, swallowed. And still the kiss went on, a violation, an obscene mockery of passion.

When he finally relented and released her, she spluttered and retched, wanting to vomit, to expel the vile tincture from herself, but she could not. Nothing was hers to decide any more. Something had died inside her at his touch, and she no longer knew what it was she had lost.

Andrin's disguise had been donned in a great hurry, and any close inspection would have revealed oddities in his appearance. His pale hair was mostly covered by a close-fitting cap, and dark grease had been rubbed into his neck and eyebrows. Fortunately for him, most of the crowd had other things on their minds and he had only to avoid the scrutiny of the soldiers. That in itself was no easy task; there was a great number of White Guards posted all round Manrique Square, and he knew that Kantrowe would have other spies, in civilian clothes, among the spectators. Even so, he could not afford to worry too much about that. He glanced around, checking as far as he could that the other Firebrands were in place.

Andrin had been among those who had listened to Kantrowe's speech earlier in the day, and the spectacle had sickened him.

Apart from the not unexpected but still horrifying confirmation of Ico's proposed fate, the sight of the captured Firebrands and of Fayna's 'confession' had been repulsive. It had been obvious to him that Fayna and the others had been ill-treated, possibly tortured, and that their oaths and her professed guilt had been obtained under duress. He had found it difficult to understand why most of the onlookers had not seemed able to realize this, but as Vargo later pointed out, people often saw only what they wanted to see. The one good thing to come from the senator's performance had been the release of the eight prisoners. That had left Andrin with one less problem to deal with. All that mattered now was Ico.

Ever since Maciot's message had arrived Andrin's emotions had been in turmoil, a mixture of boiling rage and sick fear. Apparently, Maciot had learnt of the decision by calling in a big favour from an employee of some sort at an exclusive club. She had discovered it during the boastful, drunken ramblings of one of Kantrowe's closest associates. Andrin was grateful to Maciot, whom he now thought of as a renegade senator, especially because both he and his contact had taken considerable personal risks to pass the news on. Their intelligence had proved to be all too accurate, but at least it had given Andrin a chance to prepare his response – such as it was.

Although their strategy had necessarily been devised in haste, Andrin had been both moved and gratified by the response of all the remaining Firebrands. Every one of them, even those who had initially been unwilling to take further risks, had immediately put aside any personal concerns and set about planning Ico's rescue. For himself, he would gladly have risked anything, including his own life, for her sake, but he could not have asked others to do the same. He did not have to. They had all volunteered.

And now the moment of truth was fast approaching as the sun sank towards the distant horizon. Andrin's hand closed upon the hilt of the knife concealed within his shirt. He would avoid killing if he could, but would have no compunction should it become necessary. He would save Ico from burning, or die in the attempt. Even so, he knew that weapons and physical courage would not be enough. So much now depended on Vargo – and in his present state, Vargo was hardly dependable.

Kantrowe had come in person to the gates of the Paleton.

'Is everything ready?' he asked the duty officer. 'Then bring her out.'

As he waited, he recalled his conversation with Diano. Ico's father had been surprisingly forceful. For such a perpetually timid man he had spoken out boldly, pleading for his daughter's life, arguing that she had hurt no one and that she did not deserve to die for her youthful indiscretion. However, in the face of the senator's implacable attitude, he had soon lost his nerve and his resolve crumbled. When Kantrowe had explained calmly that the decision had already been made, and that they must make an example of Ico in case others were tempted to follow in her irresponsible footsteps, Diano had broken down altogether.

'But she's all I have!' he had cried. 'My wife is gone. Please, it is in your power to reprieve her. I beg you.'

'You have my sympathy,' Kantrowe had replied coldly. 'But I cannot alter the necessities of fate.'

He had enjoyed watching Diano grovel and weep for a little longer, but then grew tired of his whining. The jeweller had needed assistance to leave the Vestry. It had been a sweet moment.

Now, as Maghdim appeared, with the Maravedis girl walking beside him like an obedient dog, Kantrowe felt a brief spasm of regret that such beauty was to be destroyed. Even with her face drawn and her eyes quite blank, Ico was undeniably lovely. That, of course, was a tribute to her mother, the woman Kantrowe had loved, then hated; the woman who had inexplicably chosen

Diano Maravedis when she could have had Tias Kantrowe. Ico's blood was the culmination of a love that was doubly hateful to the senator – and now it was to be stilled for ever. The long-festering wound to his pride was to be cleansed at last.

The procession moved swiftly through the streets, under heavy guard. More soldiers protected the corridor leading through the crowd to the open area in the centre of the square, which itself was cordoned off by ropes and additional guards. In the middle of this area was a large bonfire, kindling and logs woven into a neat pile around a central post.

There was a macabre festival atmosphere in the square, a mixture of expectancy, awe, horror and vindictive good humour. The noise of the crowd was loud, but it quietened considerably as Kantrowe and his prisoner made their entrance. Everyone saw the dull indifference in Ico's eyes and, in spite of what Kantrowe had said earlier, most assumed that she had finally accepted her guilt, like the other Firebrands. The prospect of dying was bound to give anyone second thoughts.

Everyone watched, mesmerized, as Maghdim led her to the waiting fire and up the steps that had been built into it. She did not resist as he tied her hands and then her ankles to the post behind her. No fear showed in her face; in fact, it seemed that she might not even be aware of what was happening to her.

Few people noticed a sparrowhawk swoop high over the arena and then rear up again as though repelled. Maghdim glanced up, but his face gave nothing away. Ico did not react at all, nor did she stir when he left her alone at the centre of the pyre. She merely waited, like everyone else. Manrique Square held its breath.

'Oh, great dragons!' Kantrowe cried. 'Accept this tribute. If we have offended you, take this as our penance. If we are worthy, protect us. We offer you fire – and a life.'

He signalled to a guard who was carrying a blazing torch. The soldier marched stiffly towards the bonfire and handed the torch over to Maghdim, who waited there still. However, before he could lean forward to set the kindling alight, the scene was interrupted by a strange interloper. No one saw him break through the cordon of soldiers but suddenly he was there, spinning round on crooked legs in the space between them and Ico. Angel sang, his voice a strange mixture of bird song and an animal howl.

Everyone who saw his grotesque, lopsided features was struck dumb. Kantrowe stared, Maghdim eyed him thought-fully and every soldier hesitated. Even Ico raised her insensate eyes to watch him for a moment. Madness has its own fascination, its own glamorous terrors, and the crowd were hushed, their attention momentarily distracted from the business in hand. Angel's song changed to words, but none that made any sense.

'Not smoke, not smoke. I am the apple taster, taster.'

Still no one moved, and Angel stopped his disjointed dance and scuttled like a giant insect towards the bonfire, stopping at its edge.

'Everything went away,' he chanted. 'There's sap in the stones too, stones too.'

'He's got his own bleedin' echo!' someone shouted from the crowd.

Laughter broke the spell.

'Get him out of here!' Kantrowe barked, and several guards ran to obey.

Angel bent to pick up a small piece of kindling, cast one skewed glance at Ico, then meekly allowed himself to be led away. He vanished into the crowd, where his progress was marked by jeering until matters of greater interest reclaimed the onlookers' interest.

'Light the fire,' Kantrowe ordered.

CHAPTER THIRTY-ONE

Vargo had witnessed Angel's bizarre performance, but was as mystified by it as everyone else. For a few moments he had hoped that Ico's strange friend might do something to make the Firebrands' job easier, even if it was only to create a diversion, but those hopes had been dashed when Angel was led away, unresisting. So now it was back to the original plan, and Vargo's stomach lurched as he thought again of what they were trying to do. The news that his beloved Ico was to be murdered in such barbaric fashion had affected the musician almost as much as Andrin, and he had had enormous difficulty in controlling the emotions of both his personalities. Careering between hysteria and almost suicidal despair was not the ideal preparation for a task requiring precise timing and a cool head, but he knew that all the other members of his team – as well as Andrin and Ico herself – were relying on him. So he tried to distance himself from both Ero and Lao, and be only himself. His talismanic brooch was held fast in his left hand and, silently, he asked Famara to guide his efforts.

His first sight of Ico had been a horrible shock. He had expected her to be dejected, angry and frightened, but the empty apathy in her eyes had jolted him badly. Something had happened to her, something appalling. New terrors had crowded into his brain; death, even by fire, was not the ultimate horror. Vargo had pushed such thoughts aside, telling himself that they must rescue her first, then worry about healing her malaise. Even so he had been shaken, but not surprised, when Soo reported, via Lao, that she had tried to talk to Ico and been unable either to get a message through or to provoke any response. Lao's tone betrayed the sparrowhawk's anguish at finding her link both deaf and dumb, but Vargo knew that this would only make Soo even more determined to play her part in the action to come.

And then there was no more time to think.

The man in black, who Vargo took to be the executioner, leaned down and set the torch to the kindling, then quickly walked round the edge of the pile, repeating the process so that it would burn towards the centre from all sides. Smoke began to rise, mere wisps at first, then more substantial billows. Then came the first darting flames – which was the signal for all the Firebrands' efforts to begin. They all knew that their plan walked a fine line between detection and disaster, but desperate measures were necessary if they were to have any chance against such overwhelming odds. And without Soo's ability to contact Ico, the risks were even greater, but that could not be helped.

The birds were the first to act. Like all their kind they were terrified of fire, but Soo would not be denied, and the others were not willing to let her down. So they defied their own fears. Four sparrowhawks dived steeply from the sky, seemingly intent on immolating themselves in the flames. A few soldiers saw them at the last moment and stepped forward, ineffectually brandishing their spears. First Soo, then an instant later Osa, Tir and Fia came to an abrupt, fluttering halt around the edges of the fire, their tail and wing feathers seeming to dip within the flames. The more observant onlookers noticed tiny flickers of green amid the orange – and then the birds flew up again, their mission complete.

The intention had been to place the dragon's tears precisely, then detonate them so that the intense cold would inhibit or even kill the fire. This had to be done carefully so that only the wood was chilled. If they left them too close to Ico she might freeze to death. At the same time, Vargo and his team were supposed to create the illusion of flames and smoke all around Ico in order to confuse their enemies and the spectators, thus enabling Andrin and his followers to move in and rescue her. Their plan was far from foolproof, but it was the best they could come up with at such short notice – and the birds had played their part to perfection. The only problem was that nothing else worked.

At first Vargo thought it must be some side effect of his own divided self. When he sent the telepathic signal to one of the crystals, all that happened was that he set up a series of echoes in his own head, as if the message had somehow been reflected back to him. A quick glance at the others showed that they were experiencing similar difficulties, some holding their hands over their ears with their eyes tight shut as though they were in pain. Those who were trying to create the illusions were having the same problem, merely seeing the flames redouble in their own fevered imaginations but remaining quite unable to project them. In the meantime the real fire was gaining ground, creeping towards Ico who, at last, seemed to have woken up to her danger. She was struggling uselessly against her bonds, wide-eyed and coughing.

'What's going on?' one Firebrand whispered. 'We can't *do* anything.'

'I don't know,' Vargo rasped back. 'Keep trying!'

Their increased efforts led only to more self-inflicted pain – and achieved nothing. But it was then, as his composure threatened to disintegrate entirely, that Vargo saw a faint slippage in the air, a tiny refraction where there should be none. His two eyes seemed to be seeing marginally different scenes, and where they joined there was a kind of interference between the two. A faint, shimmering dome enclosed the fire. It was invisible to everyone else, but Vargo now knew what had been blocking their attempts. What was more, he knew who was creating the shield.

His eyes locked on the black-shirted man, who stood impassively outside the dome, admiring his handiwork. He was clearly more than a mere butcher.

Lao, Ero, help me!

The birds, who were perched on a rooftop some distance away, responded instantly and Vargo felt his internal split widen, his disorientation increase. In the same moment the glittering dome became clearer, more substantial – and Vargo saw its weakness. Instinctively he channelled all his thoughts – and those of his links – through the talisman, unconsciously drawing power from the ancient stones of the square, the trees, the wind, and threw all his strength towards the base of the dome, where it met the ground. The shield of light flared, then buckled, and was ripped to shreds as its internal structure was destroyed. The executioner wheeled round, his calm face showing astonishment for once, and stared across the open space, through the crowd, straight into Vargo's eyes. Vargo was mesmerized, caught in a dark, clinging web, but he was not about to back down now. He would not allow that dome to be rebuilt.

'Do it!' he hissed to the others. 'It'll work now.'

As he spoke he sensed all but one of the crystals begin to disintegrate, felt the waves of cold spread out, slowing the progress of the fire. Then huge sheets of vivid red and orange flame shot up all around Ico – but these, Vargo knew, were not real. The crowd, who were not aware of this, cheered and gasped, seeing Ico now as only a writhing shadow within the inferno. Vargo was vaguely conscious of his team's sudden jubilation and knew that Andrin would be moving into action, but he had no time to worry about either. He was engaged in his own personal war, a battle of wills. The executioner was by far the stronger, but all his energies were negative, all his intentions destructive, while Vargo was purposeful and elusive. Now that the direct connection had been made, the contest would ordinarily have been over in moments. Vargo had only one advantage and, taking his inspiration from the collective magic of Famara's sparrows, he used it to avoid the mental bombardment from his opponent – a barrage which would have otherwise destroyed his mind entirely. Each time the executioner struck out at him, Vargo dodged the telepathic blow by sliding into his other persona and effectively vanishing. It was a weird, disturbing but entirely intuitive process that evidently drove his adversary to distraction. Vargo knew this not because the executioner's outward appearance changed, but because the mental barbs thrown at him became progressively more savage and desperate.

And that's a good sign, he thought, mentally dodging again. As long as I can hold out.

For the first time in his life, Maghdim found himself out of his depth. There was madness in the magic he opposed, a crazed illogicality which was entirely new to him. He could see the boy who challenged him, but could not focus on him. Every time he prepared to strike a crucial blow, there was nothing there. His opponent contained two streams of magic, each divided and dividing still, so that it was impossible to keep track of the various strands, let alone negate them.

Maghdim knew fury and disgust. Magic was anathema to him, and this unknown form was an abomination beyond words. He concentrated solely on combating this new threat, forgetting everything else – including his original purpose. He did not even notice when all the stones of Manrique Square began to belch forth smoke.

Andrin had begun to move as soon as the imaginary flames had leapt up. He was deliberately shielding his mind so that the illusions seemed to him to be pale, half-formed shapes, but he knew that everyone around him saw them as real. The delay while the genuine fire had begun to take hold of the wood had been agonizing, and he had sworn at Vargo under his breath, cursing him for not acting as promptly as they had planned. His relief when at last he was able to go forward was immense; the sight of Ico tied and helpless had been unbearable.

He pushed forward through the last few ranks of the fascinated crowd and prepared to fight his way past the cordon of soldiers if necessary. It was then that he became aware that the pavement below his feet was smoking. Moments later, along with thousands of others, he realized that it was not smoke but mist. The grey tendrils that crept around his ankles were cold and damp – and were soon swirling upwards. While others grew fearful or began to panic at this eerie phenomenon, Andrin merely became more determined, concentrating solely on getting to Ico, unaware of the new sound that had been added to the rising tumult of the crowd. From somewhere distant rose an unnatural wailing, half bird song, half feral howl, and with each note the fog rose higher.

The counterfeit blaze had grown even more fierce and bright now. Had it been real, Ico would have been dead already, but Andrin knew better. As the mist climbed to shoulder height, he waved the others forward, then ducked down himself and slipped between two sentries so that he could run across the open space. The soldiers were as bemused and frightened by what was happening as everyone else, and it was easy for Andrin to avoid detection. Everything had become ghostly within the drifting clouds, but the fire was a beacon, drawing him on.

'Maghdim, what's going on?'

Andrin heard Kantrowe's voice, but there was no reply to his question.

The Firebrands did not stop to think where this unexpected

help might have come from. They simply took advantage of it. Inside the cordon there were many people moving now, but the soldiers were disorganized and the chaos was aiding the rebels' cause. As their enemies chased their own shadows, they moved forward purposefully.

Naturally enough, it was Andrin who reached the fire first. From close to, the flames looked so realistic that had he stopped to gather his courage he might have hesitated. As it was he plunged in without even thinking, trampling over the frozen embers and then the still unburnt wood within. Ico did not react to his arrival and his heart pounded even harder, wondering if he had come too late, especially when he noticed that one section of the pile was blackened and was really burning. But as he cut the ropes that held her, she coughed and opened bewildered eyes before collapsing, shivering, into his welcoming arms.

Andrin lifted her easily, feeling the chill of her skin, and staggered away. The alarm was raised as he carried her from the fire and several Firebrands gathered round, preparing to defend their leaders if necessary. Those in the crowd who could see them cried out in amazement and alarm, having witnessed a miracle and expecting even more spectacles. However, just at that moment, the unseen magical tug of war between Vargo and Maghdim spilled over into the outside world – and instantly created mayhem. Suddenly there were no fewer than seven Icos within the fogbound arena, all identical but all behaving differently. Other spectral figures also flitted within the mist.

Staring around in awe, Andrin was amazed at their realism and even wondered, briefly, whether the Ico he held in his arms was the right one. Such uncertainty lasted only an instant, however, and they made their escape by dodging and ducking in the grey vapour, pushing and tripping the half-blind soldiers as they went. The guards were going crazy;

as soon as they tried to grab one of the Icos she vanished, only to be replaced by another elsewhere. One Ico sprouted wings and flew away out of their grasp; another opened a trap door in the stone floor and climbed down into it. Some of the soldiers tried to follow, but were unable to find any sign of the door. Meanwhile, the real prisoner evaded their clutches by more conventional means.

Somewhere, out of sight, Vargo was laughing, crying and shouting wildly. His words were gibberish and he flailed his arms around, until his companions led him away, still struggling and yelling. He had made use of his unique flaw, turned it into a fractured kind of strength, and in doing so had enabled himself to not only withstand Maghdim's attacks, but to make a few counterthrusts of his own. He had deliberately divided himself even further, duplicating his own thoughts and projecting them in random fashion. And he had won. Overwhelmed by the insane proliferation of bizarre magic, Maghdim had been forced to break off contact before he too was drawn down into Vargo's madness. The executioner had collapsed with exhaustion amid the chaos, allowing Vargo to give full rein to his more fanciful outpourings.

Andrin moved on relentlessly, stepping over the unconscious body of a man dressed in black. Next to him lay the lifeless body of a raven, which had evidently been crushed by the trampling boots of one of the soldiers. A moment later Andrin's eyes met Kantrowe's and held them briefly in a glare of hate-filled enmity, but then they were lost to each other in the ever-thickening fog, and the Firebrands and their prize vanished into the general pandemonium.

When the mist finally cleared, and the unearthly song was silenced at last, there was no one left in Manrique Square and the city was alive with rumours.

PART TWO

The Firelands

CHAPTER THIRTY-TWO

'You rescued *me*, remember?' Andrin said. 'It seemed only fair that I should do the same for you.'

'Thank you,' Ico replied, laughing. 'It was much appreciated!'

'The difference is that you did it on your own,' he added. 'I had a lot of help.'

'But it was still you who carried me out of there,' she reminded him.

The lovers were sitting near one of the entrances to the cave system that was now their home, watching as the twilight faded to night. It was a rare moment of relaxation in what had been a hectic and exhausting month for all the Firebrands. Since that fateful day in Manrique Square, their world had changed beyond recognition. Most of the Firebrands had fled Teguise the same night, many of them without even being able to take leave of their families, and now they lived as outlaws, cut off from everything they had known.

Ico was still coming to terms with what had happened to her – and with what had so nearly happened. The thought of Maghdim was utterly repellent, and she could still sometimes taste the vile tincture on her tongue. By comparison, the fire that would have killed her seemed almost unreal, as though she were recalling someone else's memories – but when she imagined dying in the flames she shuddered and forced her thoughts in another direction.

'I wonder how my father's coping with all this,' she said quietly. She could still hear Diano telling her to be careful. *I couldn't bear it if I lost you too.* She was still alive, but he had lost her anyway.

'The same as everyone else, I suppose,' Andrin replied. 'Most of us had to go without saying goodbye to our families. At least you know Diano won't have to worry about money. If they haven't already killed each other, my parents will probably starve to death without me there to help them.'

'That won't happen.'

'How can you be so sure?' There was a touch of anger in his voice. However much they disgusted him, Andrin still felt horribly guilty about having abandoned his parents.

'You know you had no choice,' Ico told him. 'If you'd stayed, they'd've lost you for good. No matter what happened, they were going to have to fend for themselves.'

'You don't know them,' he said bitterly, and she was silenced by the truth of this.

They sat quietly for a while, looking at the glowing tapestry of stars.

'We shouldn't argue,' Ico said softly.

There was another long pause.

'I have to believe we'll go back one day,' Andrin said eventually. 'We can't live out our lives in these caves, afraid to show our faces in case we're hunted down.'

'We're still fighting,' his lover argued. 'That's the main thing.'

She was acutely aware that the Firebrands had no long-term plan, no view of the future. Although the necessities of survival had made this almost inevitable, they were still all too aware of the lack. They would soon need a fixed goal in order to justify the sacrifices they had made. They had started out full of idealism, determined to bring about change from within. Now they were exiles with, it seemed, little chance of influencing anything.

'Sooner or later, enough people will see that what we were doing was right,' she added. 'Maciot isn't alone in supporting us. Kantrowe will go too far, and then things will change.'

'For the better?'

'That's up to us.'

'But how? We can't just sit here for ever. I wish I knew what to do.'

The self-doubt in his voice worried Ico. She knew she ought to try to rebuild his confidence, but she was permanently exhausted, and it was hard to summon up the energy.

'We need you, we all do,' she told him. 'Everyone looks to you for guidance.'

'I can't think why,' he muttered. 'You're the one who found this place, Vargo's the closest thing we have to a wizard, and Nino understands the firelands better than I ever will. And to cap it all, I'm just about the only one of us who hasn't got any magical talent.'

So that's what's behind all this, Ico thought, angry with herself for not having realized it earlier.

'You don't know that for sure,' she said.

'Then how come everyone else is making progress with it and I'm not? I can't even get a sense of what magic *is*.'

'It's just a force of nature—' she began.

'All around us,' he cut in. 'Yes, I know. Being *told* that doesn't help. No matter how many times it's explained to me, I still can't grasp it. Oh, I can feel the magic when you or someone else uses it. I can even stand aside and watch objectively, but I can't be a *part* of it. What right have I to call myself a leader when those I'm supposed to lead are all better than me?'

'That's nonsense!' Ico exclaimed. 'No one's better than you – and you're the Firebrands' leader because we all want it that way.'

He smiled at her gratefully, though the uncertainty still showed in his eyes.

'What's really frustrating is that I'm sure it's not meant to be this way,' he went on. 'Why would a bird like Ayo have linked with someone who isn't magical? It just doesn't make sense.'

'Have you talked to him about it?'

'We don't seem to have talked much at all recently,' Andrin replied morosely. 'Not about anything important. We've both been so busy, there hasn't been time.'

'Then make time,' she told him firmly. 'Ayo will always be there to help you.'

'I . . .' He made a face. 'I'm afraid he might be disappointed in me. Ashamed, even.'

'Don't be absurd! Ayo would never think like that.'

'I hope you're right.'

'I'm always right,' she announced, with a bravado that was only slightly forced. 'You of all people should know that.'

She was rewarded with another smile, and this time it reached his eyes.

'I love you,' he whispered, and leaned across to kiss her.

As had happened so often recently, Ico found her whole body becoming tense, though she longed to be able to relax. As their lips touched she felt the first, horribly familiar churning and knew it was hopeless. Even keeping her eyes wide open, showing herself who was kissing her, did no good. She drew back, her stomach heaving, and scrambled out of sight behind a fold of rock. Andrin followed more slowly and held her shoulders lightly while she vomited. His sense of helplessness increased, and Ico could feel the tension in him in spite of his gentle touch.

'I'm sorry,' she breathed eventually. 'I'm sorry.'

Andrin lifted her up and looked at her face by the light of the newly risen moon. She looked thin and pale, almost ghostly, and he wondered what had become of the real Ico.

'Isn't it about time you got over that?' he asked, unable to hide his own resentful disappointment.

'I can't help it. I keep thinking of Maghdim, of what he did to me.'

'I know it was awful for you,' he said earnestly, 'but I'm not him. I love you, and I haven't been able to touch you for so long . . .'

'I know. I'm sorry,' Ico repeated, feeling wretched. 'I love you too, and I'm trying—'

'Are you?'

'Yes!' she cried, hurt that he should doubt her about this of all things. 'I am! But I think that stuff – whatever it was – must still be in my blood. As soon as it's gone, we'll be fine again.'

'Are you sure that's all it is?'

'Well, this upheaval's not been good for any of us,' she answered cautiously, after a moment's consideration. 'Danger and exile, having to scavenge for food, the uncertainty . . . it's no wonder we don't feel well. I'm not the only one who's been sick, but we'll all get used to it soon and things will get better.'

She could see in his face that there was something more he wanted to say, and she wasn't sure she wanted to hear it.

'What?' she persisted masochistically. 'Don't you believe me?'

'Of course.'

'Do you think I'm making it all up?' she demanded, angry now. 'That I'm making myself ill just to get a bit of sympathy?'

Andrin did not reply, merely shaking his head and shrugging – which was not enough for Ico.

'So that's it?' she exclaimed. 'That's all the answer I'm going to get?'

'What do you want me to say?'

'Oh, thanks very much! Sometimes I think it's easier to talk to Vargo than to you – and he's crazy half the time.'

'Don't call him that!' Andrin snapped. 'You've no right, after what he did for you.'

They glared at each other for several heartbeats, then looked away, both feeling awkward and remorseful.

'I'm sorry,' they said simultaneously.

Later they lay, side by side, in one of the caverns. Ico could not abide the utter darkness, and so a single oil lamp burned low on a ledge, casting a dim orange glow over the irregular patterns of the walls and ceiling.

'Hold me,' she whispered. 'Just hold me.'

Andrin did as he was told, understanding that this was as close as they could come at the moment. He also knew that she would soon be asleep in his arms – and that he would remain awake for some time, fighting his own demons.

The Firebrands' exodus from Teguise had been a mixture of panic and preparation. Although some contingency plans had been made before the attempt to rescue Ico, a great deal more had been left to chance. Each of them had had to make their own decision about whether to go or to stay and, in the end, all but a few had chosen to go. Fear had been their main motivation, of course; no one could be sure what reprisals would be exacted after Kantrowe was robbed of his intended victim.

Such was the confusion within the city – and especially among the White Guard – that almost all the Firebrands had been able to escape without too much difficulty. But that was only the beginning of their journey. Some rendezvous points had been agreed on in advance, but under cover of darkness, in territory that was unfamiliar to many, there were several mishaps and a few near disasters. However, dawn had found the majority of the refugees together, several miles to the south of Teguise, in one of the endless lava fields. They set lookouts and hid during the hours of daylight as they compared notes, tended injuries and discussed their future options. They were eventually joined by a few stragglers and still managed to avoid detection – even though several detachments of soldiers passed nearby, including some mounted patrols.

The Firebrands were all afraid, and most of them were still struggling to come to terms with the momentous events that had forced them to leave their homes. At this stage everyone looked to Andrin for leadership. Like most of the others, he had been unprepared for the consequences of their once innocent actions, but knew he could not betray any weakness now. Ico was still drugged and only half aware of what was happening, and Vargo was comatose or raving by turns, so the responsibility fell to Andrin alone. His foresight had enabled them to collect the secret cache of dragon's tears before they left the city, and these were now distributed among all the linked Firebrands, but that was the only area in which their supplies were satisfactory. They had little water and almost no food. Although no one felt much like eating yet, hunger would soon become a serious problem. If there had ever been any doubts about Andrin's right to lead them, then his solution to this problem – at least in the short term – swept them aside.

As darkness fell two nights later, he led a small party of scouts into the decimated village of Cangrelos. The fireworms had destroyed many of the buildings, and the place was deserted. None of the neighbouring villagers would have wanted to visit a place of such ill fortune once the bodies of the dead had been buried, and so what had survived the fires remained more or less intact. The Firebrands found limited but welcome supplies of fruit, potatoes, salt and dried meat, and were also able to fill a large number of canteens with water from the village well. In addition, they had been able to equip themselves with other items to help them survive in the open: blankets, oil and lamps, tools, weapons, and much more. When they set out again, continuing their trek south, the entire party was in much higher spirits.

By then Ico seemed to be recovering slightly, taking note of her surroundings for the first time. She was especially pleased when she discovered that Andrin had both her talisman and the wizard's book. He told her that an unknown man – presumably one of Maciot's servants – had caught up with them before they reached the city walls and had handed the treasures over without a word before vanishing into the night. Ico wore the necklace all the time now, often fingering it and drawing comfort from its warmth and weight around her neck. Shortly after putting it on, she began to experience odd visions and fragmentary dreams. Although they frightened her at first, she soon realized that someone – or something – was trying to guide her. Each of the images pointed to a particular way forward, sometimes obviously, sometimes in a more obscure manner, but she began to trust these flashes of intuition when they proved helpful in locating safe hiding places and avoiding possible dangers. Andrin took a little more convincing but, when the nature of her advice proved to be consistently beneficial, he began to rely on it too.

Eight days after fleeing Teguise, the Firebrands reached the cave system that was to become their temporary home – a place Ico had been glimpsing for some time now. It proved to be almost too perfect. The location was all they could ask for. The nearest road was more than three miles away, so accidental discovery was most unlikely. The surrounding terrain was rough – impassable except on foot – but manageable. The ocean was only two miles distant, so the hunting birds, like Ayo, would be able to fish for themselves and for their human companions; nearer at hand were rabbits – which could also be hunted by the hawks or with bows – as well as wild figs, insects, snails and other outwardly unpromising but none-theless valuable sources of food.

Better still were the caves themselves. Not only did they have a plentiful supply of fresh water from three separate underground streams, but the air was clean and they were warm, even at night. Indeed, in a few places the rock was so hot that it formed natural baking ovens. There were many different entrances, spread over a wide area, so that if their hide-out was ever discovered, their chances of escape were still good. In fact, the greatest danger seemed to be that of getting lost in the labyrinth of tunnels and caverns, so Andrin had set some of his team the task of exploring, marking routes and danger spots, and acting as guides for the others.

Now, almost a month after leaving Teguise, these explo-rations were still continuing, though everyone had become familiar with the central section of tunnels and caves. Sleeping arrangements and meal times had been sorted out and, with the basic necessities of life taken care of, the refugees turned their attention to other matters. Their own security was a primary concern, and they had set up a rota of lookout duties, watching all approaches to the caves. This meant that they would have ample warning of any attack by human foes – soldiers would not be able to move quickly in such terrain, and the defenders would therefore have time to prepare to fight or flee – though it would be less effective against fireworms. One of their greatest concerns had been that the caves, which seemed so improbably perfect, might have been home to some of these deadly creatures. So far their investigations had revealed no sign of them, but the possibility remained a worry. Crystals were placed beside all the entrances, each one assigned to particular Firebrands, whose responsibilities were to detonate the stones if their sentries reported any worms in the area. Other crystals were set to guard the tunnels that led to the as yet uncharted parts of the cave system. Although advance warning of any invasion from that direction would be more difficult to obtain, it was the best they could do. As time passed and no fireworms were seen, confidence grew. However, Andrin would not allow anyone to become complacent about their safety, practising evacuations and holding drills to assess their response times to mock attacks.

At the same time, several Firebrands were experimenting with Ico's technique for releasing the crystals' negative energy. After some trials, they had discovered a way of making the implosion a slow, drawn-out process so that although the nearby cooling was gentle, it lasted for hours or even days. Eventually, this team left the caves in search of swarms, and began to test these new options – finding that although the lesser cold was not enough to kill or even injure the worms, it was sufficient to make them change course as they instinctively veered away from even a slight drop in temperature. The possibilities this opened up were still being discussed.

There were now almost seventy Firebrands living in the caves. The original party had been joined by a few latecomers and by those from other parts of the country. Most of these had been guided by the birds – who now made a point of never flying directly to the caves, and never congregating there, so that they did not reveal the location of their links' hiding place. Nino was among the newer arrivals, and his specific knowledge of the ways of the firelands had already proved invaluable. Another was Jair, one of the Firebrands who had been captured, publicly humiliated and then released by Kantrowe. He was the only one of the eight to rejoin the group and, although the torture had broken the spirits of the others, the agonies he had endured – both physical and mental – had only made him more determined to gain revenge now that he was free again.

The later arrivals brought news that was unpleasant but not unexpected. The Senate had branded them all traitors, and decreed that death would be the automatic punishment for joining or even aiding them. The exiles had had very little contact with the nearest villages – it was impossible to trade with dragon's tears, and they had little else with which to barter – but now they kept all visits to an absolute minimum, travelling in disguise by roundabout routes to the fairs and markets where strangers could pass unnoticed, and never going to the same place twice.

Other, less reliable gossip from Teguise told how some of Jair's fellow prisoners had been rearrested, in spite of their oaths of loyalty, and that the entire country was being scoured for anyone with magical talent. Opinion in the city was divided as to why this was being done. Some said that it was so these evil-doers could be properly punished, while others speculated that Senator Kantrowe must have plans to use their abilities for his own ends. No one knew the truth but, as yet, the one piece of news that the Firebrands most dreaded had not been reported.

So far, no one had been sacrificed to the dragons.

CHAPTER THIRTY-THREE

'Will it work?' Kantrowe asked bluntly.

Maghdim regarded his employer with hooded eyes.

'Yes,' he replied. 'If the correct dose is administered.'

'Then you'd better make sure that it is.'

The foreigner said nothing, aware of the implied threat behind the senator's words.

'And you will be able to take care of the madman this time?' Kantrowe added.

A month ago he would not have felt comfortable using such a disparaging tone, but the balance of the relationship between the two men had changed subtly since Maghdim's failure. It had taken him several days to recover from the profound stupor induced by his battle with Vargo, and in one way that was lucky for him. Kantrowe had been enraged by Ico's escape and by the disappearance of almost all the Firebrands from the city, and would possibly have taken out his frustrations on Maghdim, had he not been unconscious. By the time he recovered the senator had regained his self-possession and, because he needed the anti-mage's unique skills, had been prepared to forgive him.

'I will,' the foreigner replied, his voice thick with loathing. 'I will destroy him utterly.'

'How?'

'I shall be prepared for him this time,' Maghdim stated simply, and offered no more.

'Good. So now all we need is a little information.'

'The linkage can be initiated at any time.'

'And he will not be aware of it?'

'No.'

'But you will be able to—?'

'We've been through this already,' Maghdim cut in, his impatience growing. 'You need only say the word.'

Kantrowe smiled, sat back in his chair and pondered the decision.

'Not yet,' he said eventually. 'We should let them continue their work for a while yet. The more they learn, the more we gain.'

The senator studied Maghdim's unresponsive face and, not for the first time, wondered at the man's motivation. He had the feeling that the small fortune that had been promised once the appointed job was done meant little to the foreigner. He was driven by fanaticism, and that was always dangerous, especially as Kantrowe had decided not to tell him the whole truth about his own long-term intentions.

'And what of your new acolytes?' the senator asked. 'Are they ready yet?'

Maghdim regarded him steadily, trying to decide if there was any hint of mockery in his employer's choice of words. In the end he took the question at face value.

'All but one,' he replied. 'And her stubbornness will make her all the more useful when her will is broken. In the meantime, I have learnt much from her.'

'And they will still be reliable,' Kantrowe persisted, 'even when they come to face their old comrades?'

'They will have no choice,' the anti-mage assured him.

And once that is done, the senator thought contentedly, I shall have other tasks for them.

After Maghdim left, Kantrowe fell to thinking about the events of the last month. In retrospect, although he still regretted the delay of his revenge on the House of Maravedis, he felt that the Firebrands' leaving Teguise had actually worked in his favour. Their present location could be discovered whenever he chose, but wherever they were – and there were rumours of their having fled to all parts of the country – they could do no real harm. Their guilt was firmly established in the consciousness of the people, and the exiles were in no position either to defend themselves or to stir up trouble. Although Kantrowe's personal prestige had suffered because of Ico's escape – she and some of her colleagues would eventually pay for that – the senator had good reasons for not exacting retribution from the Firebrands for the time being. And so something else had been needed to restore his status. It had been a simple matter to produce the ideal opportunity.

Kantrowe's suitably incomplete announcement of the 'treaty' between Tiguafaya and the pirate leaders had been greeted with astonishment and then jubilation by the Senate, even by those he knew to be privately sceptical. The news had spread throughout the city, and later the entire country, with amazing speed. Many merchants had already benefited from the new arrangement, and traders were predicting a new era of prosperity. Most common folk rejoiced too, even though the economic benefits would take a long time to reach them – if at all. They simply hoped that it was true, and that they no longer had anything to fear from the sea raiders.

It had then been a small step for Kantrowe to justify the withdrawal of troops from the more remote regions of the southern provinces, and to the dismantling of defences in their ports.

If any of the locals were worried by such imprudent haste,

their voices counted for little in the capital. It was said that the army's efforts could now be concentrated on the remaining threats to Tiguafaya – the young rebels and the fireworms. Quite what actions were to be taken against these enemies was never specified, but it was assumed that Senator Kantrowe would reveal his plans in due course.

Within Teguise itself, where public opinion was not quite so ready to swallow such obvious propaganda, there had been some opposition to Kantrowe's moves, and even some muttering about the possible benefits of the Firebrands' ideas and methods. The senator was aware that this was rumbling on even now, but there had as yet been no open defiance of his policies. Gadette's network of spies were keeping their potential opponents under surveillance, just in case they were foolish enough to try anything.

At the same time, Zophres was keeping an eye on the pirates, making sure that they kept their side of the bargain, Verier was overseeing the building of new ships, and experiments were continuing in the western mines, with a slow but steady increase in their success rate. There had been no more eruptions; in one way this was unfortunate, because it seemed to indicate that the planned sacrifice had been unnecessary, but it was fortunate in another because there was no one left in Teguise to blame it on.

All in all, Kantrowe thought, it's going rather well. And in a few days he would strike the last, decisive blow and seal his domination of the entire land for good.

Diano Maravedis knocked timidly on the door. He felt nervous in this rough, unfamiliar part of the city, but a greater need had overcome his fear. There was no answer so he knocked again, harder this time, and then stepped back instinctively as the door creaked open of its own accord. The air that drifted out was stale and sour, but he forced himself to step back up to the threshold.

'Hello?'

No one answered his hesitant greeting, but he heard a small scuffling noise from the back of the ill-lit room.

'Is anyone there?' he called as he went inside and glanced around.

He almost jumped out of his skin when he saw a huge man sitting in the corner of the room, eyes staring fixedly from his pallid face, but the man did not move at all. Diano was just coming to terms with the unpleasant but obvious fact that the man was dead when the skittering noise came again and he saw a flash of movement in the shadows.

'They're everywhere!' a woman's voice exclaimed suddenly. 'Creeping and crawling, crawling and creeping. Get away!' She screamed, and Diano hesitated again, but he had come too far to back away now.

'Can I help you?' he said, advancing slowly so that he could see the woman more clearly. She was slumped on the floor, trembling and perspiring, her eyes wild.

'Get them off me!' she shrieked. 'Get them off me!'

She brushed madly at her arms and legs, but Diano could not see what was afflicting her. At the same time he smelt the foul odours emanating from her soiled clothes, and saw the broken glass and pottery that littered the floor. He knelt down beside her, feeling pity for this wretched creature, and gently touched her fluttering hand. She jumped violently, jammed her fingers into her mouth and began to cry. Diano felt utterly helpless. He had no idea what to do.

'You'll be all right,' he said absurdly. 'I'll help you.'

The woman looked at him as if seeing him for the first time, her eyes wide.

'I won't hurt you,' he told her soothingly. 'Are you Andrin Zonzomas's mother?'

The question seemed to cause her some confusion, but at last some tiny element of sense filtered through to her brain and recognition showed in her eyes. She took her fingers out of her mouth and spoke in a normal voice.

'Belda,' she pronounced clearly. 'Me.'

'Do you know where your son is? Have you heard from him?'

'He won't eat his food,' she wailed suddenly. 'I give it to him, but he won't eat. He needs his food.'

Diano was confused, but then realized she was not talking about her son. He glanced round at the massive corpse in the corner.

'Should I take him some soup?' Belda asked hopefully. 'He likes soup.'

'He's dead,' Diano said without thinking, then wished he had not been so brutal. 'I'm sorry.'

'Oh,' she said quietly. 'Oh, I see.'

Her acceptance was so docile and so unexpected that Diano didn't know what to say. Belda looked down at herself critically, and tugged ineffectively at her skirt.

'Have the spiders gone?' she asked.

'Spiders?'

'And ants. They're very big. As big as my hand.'

'Yes, they're gone,' he told her, wondering how long she had been living in this private hell.

She tried to stand and Diano helped her up. Together, at her insistence, they went over to the dead man. Although a line of spittle ran from the corner of his mouth, there were no marks of violence upon him. Belda touched his hand and nodded solemnly.

'He's cold,' she observed calmly, then began to shiver again.

'Come on,' Diano said, suddenly decisive. 'You can't stay here.'

He led her, unresisting, out into the street, and back to his own home. Several bystanders glanced curiously at the mismatched couple, but no one interfered. An hour later, after she had been bathed by Atchen, Belda was dressed in clean clothes that belonged to the maid. Although they were much too large for her, they were still a considerable improvement on the stained garments she had been wearing. Diano, who had recently been no stranger to the horrible after-effects of drinking too much, knew a little of what she must have been going through, but Belda's problems obviously went far deeper than a mere hangover. For the time being, however, she seemed calm and relatively lucid. Diano sent the ever-willing Atchen to fetch a physician, then tried to coax his unexpected guest into talking. He explained who he was, and described the rumours he had heard about Ico and Andrin's attachment. Belda did not react to any of this, but when he repeated his question about Andrin's present whereabouts she shook her head sadly.

'He's gone. Mendo and Jarrell are . . . gone too,' she said, faltering on the edge of tears. 'But Andrin's a good boy. He will come back, won't he?'

'I'm sure he will.' It was clear now that she knew nothing useful, but Diano also knew that he was feeling a growing responsibility towards her.

'I hope so,' Belda said. 'Perhaps they'll come back together.' Her sudden smile was far too bright.

'I hope so too,' Diano added. 'Why don't you stay here until they do?'

The sparrows were driving the Paleton garrison crazy. For days now they had been swooping around the prison in a brown, twittering cloud. That such small birds could produce such an incredible volume of noise was astounding, but their remorseless energy was even more astonishing. The racket was making everyone edgy and irritable and, no matter what tactics the soldiers employed, the flock would not go away. Indeed, when a guard had actually succeeded in knocking one of them out of the air with his spear and killing it, the rest seemed to have redoubled their efforts, becoming even more restless and noisy.

Since her arrest, Famara had been incarcerated in several different cells, each one more isolated and unpleasant than the last. She had hardly noticed the difference, however, and her only regret was that now she could only catch rare moments of the sparrows' raucous chatter. Her present dungeon was windowless and perfectly dark, except when the door was open. It was cold and damp too, but Famara had grown used to that and barely felt the complaints of her stiff old bones. She was more interested in her gaoler – and the interest was mutual.

She had never met anyone like Maghdim, whom she saw in terms of a void, a substanceless shadow that reflected neither light, emotion nor magic. He in turn clearly found her fascinating, as someone who was not afraid of anything he could inflict upon her. A strange, antagonistic form of mutual respect had grown up between them, so that Famara almost looked forward to his daily visits – which she regarded as successive rounds in their duel. He would try to dull her mind, to strip the magic from her. She would merely sidestep his mental assault, using her memories of the quicksilver voices of Tek and her clan to escape and return unharmed. Maghdim would try to follow her, learning all the time, but never enough. At times he even laughed, and then his dark face cracked and glittered. It was like seeing a creature of stone awakening.

The door opened and Famara shielded her eyes from the dim light, which to her was a bright glare, but she knew instantly that it was not her usual visitor.

'Gods, this is a vile place.'

She recognized the voice and with it the stooped figure.

'It's good practice for when I'm in my grave,' she replied. 'What brings you visiting, Marco?'

'Need you ask?' the President replied. 'No one wants you to be in here.'

'Then give the order. Set me free.'

'It's not as simple as that, Famara, and you know it.'

'It seems remarkably simple to me,' she retorted. 'You're the President, are you not? You're the ultimate figure of authority in the land. You have only to decide.'

'Nothing would please me more, but you have to meet us halfway. Cooperate, Famara, please. Then we can put this unpleasantness behind us.'

'And salve your conscience?' she laughed. 'I've done nothing wrong. Why should I accept conditions for my release?'

'Because that foreign bastard will break you in the end,' he hissed. 'How much pain and suffering can you endure? And is it worth it?'

'He can't touch my mind,' she replied. 'And I've pretty much used up this old body, so it doesn't matter what he does to that. And *I* think truth and justice are worth a great deal.'

'This may be your last chance,' he said, sounding genuinely distressed. 'Please reconsider.'

'No. I'm right, and that's why you're here. It's eating you up inside, isn't it?'

'You're wrong and, as always, you're so stubborn you can't see it,' he replied angrily.

'Go away, Marco,' she said wearily. 'You're beginning to annoy me.'

Darkness returned as the President slammed the door behind him.

CHAPTER THIRTY-FOUR

The camels – nearly a hundred of them – had all knelt down in lines, nose to tail as they had arrived. Now they were placidly chewing the cud, sighing and belching occasionally. They seemed to take no notice of their surroundings and their handlers were equally relaxed, eating their lunch at the edge of the dusty field. Several children had ventured to the outskirts of the village to look at the unusually large caravan, but they did not come too close, knowing that camels could be bad tempered and occasionally vindictive. No one paid much attention to a tall young man with a dirty face who strode past on his way to the local tavern.

It had taken Andrin almost seven hours to reach the village, but he had chosen that location rather than anywhere closer to the Firebrands' base because he wanted to minimize any chance of betraying their hiding place – and because he still harboured a few doubts about the man he had come to meet. The journey, which he'd begun at first light, had been easy enough, for the most part using old prospectors' trails that were so faint in places that they had clearly not been used for many years. Even so, once the sun had climbed into the sky and the day grown warm, his progress had become laboured. The thought of a long cool drink was very appealing, especially as his now well-used disguise was making him uncomfortable and hot.

The small wine house was a single-storey, whitewashed building, with a canvas awning hung from poles on the flat roof. Alegranze Maciot sat alone at a table beneath this, in full view of everyone in the area. Perched above him was the small black bird who had played an important part in setting up the meeting. After looking about warily, Andrin climbed the steps that ran up the outside wall and went to join them.

'Glad you could make it,' Maciot remarked affably. 'Please, sit down. Will you join me in some celona?'

'Is this your idea of a secret meeting?' Andrin hissed, ignoring the invitation.

'The best place to hide something is in the open,' the senator replied. 'We are business associates discussing trade over a pleasant social drink. What could be more natural?'

Andrin's irritation subsided and, as he sat down on the second chair, Maciot picked up a jug and filled two tumblers with an aromatic liquid. Andrin waited until his companion had drunk before first sipping his own. The mixture of wine, water and fruit juices tasted wonderful, and he drank thirstily.

'At least we're not likely to be overheard here,' he conceded when he had finished.

'And no one will disturb us,' Maciot said. 'Being a senior member of the Travellers' Guild has its privileges, after all. Help yourself,' he added, waving a hand at the jug. 'How are you all coping?'

'Well enough,' Andrin replied cautiously.

'And our mutual friend?'

'She's recovered. Almost.'

'That's good to hear.'

'She's grateful to you for returning her belongings.'

'I thought she might need them,' Maciot said, nodding. 'Is there anything else you need?'

'Reliable news,' Andrin answered promptly.

'I was thinking of more practical help. My camels can transport anything, within reason, and—'

'Right now information is the most valuable thing you could give us.'

The senator nodded again. 'Then I'll gladly tell you all I can. I was planning on doing so anyway.'

'Are they still looking for us?'

'Of course, but it seems a half-hearted effort to me, not really serious. Other matters appear to be taking precedence.'

Andrin was openly puzzled. 'Tell me,' he said.

Maciot told him about the agreement with the pirates and the subsequent movement of troops.

'Not much of this makes sense,' he concluded. 'I'm sure Kantrowe's keeping something back and I'd wager he's up to something devious, but it's hard to see what at the moment.'

'If the treaty with the pirates is genuine, it could do a lot of good,' Andrin admitted reluctantly.

'Much as I dislike the idea of dealing with them, you're right.'

'Could the Senate be massing troops to attack us?' Andrin wondered aloud.

'Maybe. I don't know where you're based – and I won't ask – but even if they were to find out, this seems a little drastic. You hardly command a vast army.'

'We'll be a match for one,' Andrin claimed loyally. 'We've not been idle since we left the city.'

'That's one of the reasons I wanted to see you,' Maciot said. 'I take it you're referring to the development of your unusual abilities?'

'Yes.'

'Good.' He leaned forward and began talking rapidly, his

voice low now. 'You must know you have some friends in Teguise. Not enough to be able to make a move yet, but we're not without some influence. Kantrowe's actions have annoyed many people. Even if they approve of what he's doing, they don't like the way he's going about it. It'll take more than indignation to stir them into action, though. But the problems with the fireworms are getting worse, especially in the west for some reason, and although Kantrowe and his lackeys don't seem bothered by the plight of a few peasants, there are others – those with family or business connections in remote areas – who aren't so cynical. The main hope seems to be that the cooler weather is due soon, and should slow the worms down, but that's clutching at straws. More and more people are saying privately that we ought to at least consider your ideas.'

'Really?' Andrin said, his hopes rising.

Maciot nodded. 'But if we're to form any real opposition to Kantrowe, we'll need proof, a demonstration of some kind.'

'That shouldn't be so hard to arrange.' Andrin told his companion about the Firebrands' latest results, not just killing the fireworms but diverting them as well.

'Even better,' the senator said. 'That gives us an option for those who are still afraid of annoying the dragons.'

'That's nonsense—' Andrin began.

'I'm sure you're right,' Maciot cut in, 'but some people will need a lot of convincing.'

'We've killed more worms, and there haven't been any more eruptions,' Andrin pointed out.

'Yes, but nobody knows that. And whenever there's another tremor, you're going to get the blame.'

Andrin sighed, accepting the truth, unfair though it was. They spent some time discussing future contacts via the birds, and then Maciot called for the landlord and ordered food. Watching his guest eat hungrily, he smiled.

'Are you sure I can't get you anything in the way of provisions?'

'We can make our own arrangements,' Andrin said with obstinate pride. 'But I appreciate the offer.'

'It remains open,' Maciot said.

As soon as he'd finished eating Andrin left, going on through the village as if he were continuing his journey, before doubling back and starting on the long cross-country trek to the caves.

Ico found Vargo by a waterfall deep within the caves, where a tall, echoing funnel in the rock above allowed a little light into the darkness. He was sitting quite still, staring at the dark, glinting curves of the water.

'What are you doing?' she asked softly.

'Listening to the music.'

They were both silent for a while, the chiming and rippling of the rushing stream sounding gently in their ears, creating a strange, almost hypnotic melody.

'It sounds the same, but it never repeats itself exactly,' Vargo said reverently. 'Endless variations. I'd give anything to be able to write music like that.'

'It's lovely,' Ico said, glad to find that her friend was at least lucid, even if his train of thought was a little too esoteric for her.

Vargo was still often deranged, and on those occasions no one could make sense of anything he said or did – least of all Vargo himself. In between times he seemed like the Vargo of old, the melancholy joker, but he had not been whole since facing Maghdim; there was no telling when he would descend into madness again, and no way of judging how it would affect him.

Contributing to his divided self was the fact that both Ero and Lao were still with him, even though the hoopoe should have been on his way south some ten or fifteen days earlier.

Curiously, neither Vargo nor Ero himself seemed concerned about this; in fact both appeared certain that the bird would be staying longer, and even Lao had accepted the situation. For reasons that were not entirely selfless, Ico was glad too. She and Andrin pitied Vargo, but had realized that power lay in his madness. From the musician's own ramblings, plus the evidence of his team, they had deduced that his demented state had actually helped him to defeat Maghdim. And there was more than a distant possibility that the Firebrands would have to face this enemy again one day.

'It's the only music I have here,' Vargo said, still mesmerized by the liquid harmonies, 'unless you count what's inside my head.'

'You can sing.'

'It's not the same. I miss my lute and viol. If I know Pirolo,' he added, naming his former landlord, 'he'll have sold them by now to make up the lost rent.'

'We could try to replace them for you,' Ico suggested, but Vargo shook his head.

'I'm not sure I can play any more,' he said. 'My hands don't always obey me nowadays.'

'It'll come back,' said a voice from one of the dark recesses of the cavern. 'Skill like that doesn't just fade away.'

Ico was startled by the interruption, and her surprise soon turned to annoyance that someone should have been eavesdropping.

'What are you doing here?' she asked sharply.

'Cat watches out for me,' Vargo said fondly. 'In case . . .' He shrugged.

'I don't like him to be alone, but I'll leave him with you if you like,' Allegra said amenably.

'Thank you.' Ico realized that she was annoyed by the slightly possessive tone in the other girl's voice, and that she was actually jealous of Vargo's self-appointed nurse.

'Are you sure you'll know what to do if—?' Allegra went on.

'If I go loopy,' Vargo completed for her. 'It's all right, Cat. Ico's known me a long time. She can handle it, and anyway, you should get some rest.'

Allegra emerged from the shadows, nodded respectfully to Ico and went, soft footed, along the tunnel that led back to the central area. Vargo turned to stare at the water again.

'Do you remember our conversation in the old concert hall?' he asked.

'Which one?'

'When we talked about demonstrating magic in the very heart of Teguise.'

'It was a joke then.'

'Not any more. We each succeeded, didn't we? But all it achieved was to confirm the prejudices against magic – and against us!'

'That was forced upon us,' she protested. 'We'd have done things differently if—'

'Would we?' he cut in. 'Didn't you actually *enjoy* it, just a little bit? Being out of control, I mean.'

'No. It just happened.'

'I dream about Famara sometimes,' he said, as if this were a logical continuation of their discussion. 'She told me never to stop dreaming, and now I dream about her. Ironic, isn't it. "Dreamers are the only true realists,"' he quoted. 'I dream about dragons too, like you did.'

'Me?'

'In the market place, when the serpents came. They were from your dreams.'

Ico wanted to tell him to stop it, that he was frightening her, but then she asked herself where the dragons *had* come from – and could find no answer. And Vargo had sounded quite certain.

'The one thing I still can't understand is the mist,' he went on, oblivious to her confusion. 'It was real, not an illusion, so who or what was responsible? It was hardly a natural phenomenon.'

'No one has the answer to that,' Ico said. 'It's a mystery.'

'The magic of a true realist,' Vargo whispered enigmatically.

Ico glanced around, trying to be sure they were truly alone, and took a deep breath.

'How's the research on the nets going?' It was not what she had meant to say.

'I leave that to my team most of the time now,' he replied. 'I'm usually more of a hindrance than a help. Cat . . . Allegra can give you an up-to-date report.'

Ico nodded, though she had not heard a word he had said. Then, without any preamble and without using any of the words she had planned, she blurted out her secret. It had been weighing on her mind for some days now, as her own certainty grew, until finally she had to confide in someone. But now she wondered if it had been a huge mistake, if Vargo was in fact the last person she should have told. He had grown very still, like some irregular stalagmite.

'Vargo?' she whispered.

He began to sing then, but it was like no music she had ever heard before. It was unearthly, inhuman, spiralling up and down chaotically in a hurricane of wordless noise. It was the essence of madness turned into sound.

And then it stopped, and Vargo was no longer still. He was shaking, his face contorted with emotion. He was sobbing helplessly, and neither of them knew whether they were tears of joy or sorrow.

Andrin was more than a mile from the nearest cave entrance when he saw a familiar white speck in the sky above. He called silently, and watched with pride and even a little awe as the speck grew larger and took shape. Ayo in flight was a sight to stir the heart.

Is anyone near?

No humans for many swoops.

That meant that it was safe for the eagle to fly near his link without the risk of drawing attention to him or his destination.

Dusk was falling. It had been a long day and Andrin was anxious to get home, so he kept picking his way across the lava field, but he was determined to follow Ico's advice and talk to Ayo. As the great bird circled lazily, he felt again the tug of destiny. Whatever else he failed to achieve, his partnership with the white eagle was something no one could take away from him.

What do you know of magic, Ayo?

The sky voices have told me what I need, no more.

You mean the voices that call to migrating birds?

That is but their simplest function, the eagle replied a little pompously. *They guide us all in life.*

Do they speak to you often?

As often as necessary.

Can they talk to you anywhere? Andrin persisted, somewhat frustrated by the vagueness of Ayo's answers.

They fly everywhere, but there are some places that have greater significance.

Such as? he asked hopefully.

The greatest of them is Pajarito.

The mountain?

It is more than a mountain. It is a voice, the past and future, memories and prophecies.

An oracle? Andrin wondered, intrigued.

Yes.

Do you go there often?

Only when there is need, or when I am called.

Could I go there?

Our voices speak from the sky, yours come from the earth and fire. Pajarito will not speak to you.

Andrin was disappointed. *That's a pity. I could do with some discussion about the future,* he remarked, half joking. *And something to help me understand magic.*

Then why do you not go to your own place? the eagle asked. *Has it not called to you?*

What place?

There is an oracle for humans too.

Tell me more.

As Andrin drew nearer to the caves, a slim dark figure emerged to greet him. Ico was easily recognizable even in near darkness, but it seemed to Andrin that there was a lightness in her step, an exuberance that had been missing for a long time. When she flung her arms about him and then kissed him passionately, he was so surprised that he did not react at first. Then delight overrode any doubts and he responded in kind. When they drew apart he was breathless.

'I'm already exhausted,' he said, smiling. 'Are you trying to finish me off?'

'I'm just so glad to see you back safe,' she replied, her eyes shining.

'I wasn't in any real danger, but you . . .' He was lost for words.

'I'm finally over him.'

'That's wonderful,' Andrin said, and kissed her again as if to reassure himself that it was true. 'I have good news too.'

'Tell me!'

He related the details of his meeting with Maciot and of the possibilities it had raised. Both of them knew that this was the first step towards the long-term plan they had been searching for.

'But Maciot isn't the only one I've been talking to,' Andrin went on.

'Who else?'

'Ayo. I did as you told me.'

'About time too,' she said, grinning. 'Did it help?'

He told her briefly about Pajarito and its significance to all the birds.

'But the really interesting thing is that there's an oracle for us humans too,' he added.

'Really? Where is it?'

'It's not an it,' Andrin said. 'It's a she.'

'What do you mean?'

'That's what I asked Ayo, but he was a bit vague about the whole thing. He knows where she is, but he refuses to go there and won't tell me why.'

'Is she a person or a place?' Ico asked, thoroughly confused now.

'I don't know,' he replied, 'but I do know her name.'

'What?'

'Elva,' he said, and saw her eyes light up in recognition.

CHAPTER THIRTY-FIVE

'Elva, Mistress of Wings, is a part of the land and apart from the land; wait and speak softly beyond the earth's breathing, and you will be answered.'

Ico stopped reading and looked up at Soo, who was perched near one of the cave entrances. Like almost all the birds, Soo had an instinctive dislike of going underground, so Ico always came to the surface when she wanted to talk. The early morning air was unusually still, with not a breath of wind to ruffle the bird's feathers.

I've been meaning to ask you about this ever since I found it, Ico explained, *but so much has been happening it slipped my mind. It was only when Andrin told me what Ayo had said that it came back to me.*

The night before, when Andrin had returned from his meeting, Ico decided instantly that she must go to Elva. Her lover had first tried to dissuade her, and then, having found her conviction to be unshakable, he insisted on going with her. That had led to an argument in which Ico had again been victorious, by pointing out that if they both went, then the Firebrands would be effectively leaderless and they would also lose contact with Maciot. Andrin had reluctantly agreed to let her go, but only if she were accompanied by someone he could trust. Nino had been an obvious choice, and he had agreed readily. He was a man of the open spaces and the enclosed realm of the caverns had begun to oppress him, so the prospect of a long journey was more than welcome. Ico had been excited and had slept little that night but now, in the face of Soo's unreadable silence, she was beginning to feel a few tremors of doubt.

Do you know where it is? she asked tentatively. *Will you show us the way?*

I know where it's supposed to be, Soo replied. *Don't you?*

Not really. Andrin said Ayo was very vague.

You should know. You would if you'd been called.

Called?

Pajarito summons us when there is need. Elva would do the same for you. It is dangerous to abuse the trust of oracles.

I don't intend to abuse anything, Ico protested defensively. *Is it wrong to want answers to some questions?*

But you have not been called?

Not yet. Unless you think finding the quote in this book was a call. It was certainly a hint.

That book is very old, Soo pointed out. *Many people must have read it.*

But it came to me now. *Couldn't that be the message?* Ico did not want to tell her link that for reasons of her own it was essential that she go soon, if she were to go at all.

Soo cocked her head to one side and regarded Ico with characteristic intensity.

You do not sing our songs, she replied, *and we do not hear yours.*

Which, Ico thought, is her way of saying she doesn't know. At least it had not been a flat denial.

How does Pajarito call to you? she asked curiously.

Through the sky voices.

You hear them . . . as you hear me? Inside your head?
It's not hearing, it's knowing.
As I know I must go to Elva.

The sparrowhawk gave her a sharp, quizzical look but made no comment, and Ico found herself questioning her own motives. *Do I really know? Or do I just want to go? And why?*

Will you tell me what you know of Elva? she asked, hoping for enlightenment.

I know of the legend. Don't you pass such tales on to your fledglings?

Humankind has become lazy, Ico confessed. *We often forget or ignore what was important in the past. That's why we need your help.*

Soo relented then, and told the story. Several elements of the tale were familiar, and fitted in neatly with what the wizard had written, but other parts were new to Ico. She listened, spellbound, and did not interrupt.

Before time began, when all winged creatures were just shapes waiting to hatch, there were spirits who served the great Sky herself. One of these was Elva. When the dragons were born she fell in love with them and, in defiance of the laws, she became their mistress. She bore them many fledglings, and each clutch of eggs was the beginning of a new clan of birds. But Elva's wanton disobedience had angered Sky, the ancestress of all living things. She cast Elva down into the world and turned her to stone so that she could no longer fly – or mate. Elva became a floating island, between the land, sea and air, but in none of them. All birds are forbidden to visit her, but the dragons have never forgotten her. The sacred isle lies beyond a jewelled lake in a place where a whisper can shake mountains and, for those with the courage to travel beyond the world, she is the voice of the dragons.

***

Four days later, Ico and Nino completed their arduous journey. It had taken them from one lava field to another, via a fertile plain and several villages, and now they stood atop the huge semicircular cliffs that curved round the green lake. The birds had guided them there, partly by their own instincts, partly from the little Ayo had told them, but mostly by faith. And now that they had reached their destination, their recent toil and the hardships of travel seemed insignificant.

'The jewelled lake,' Ico breathed.

'It's beautiful,' Nino agreed. 'I've never seen anything like it.'

Even in shade the water shone with an almost luminous emerald sheen.

'And there,' Ico whispered, looking out to sea a little way, 'is Elva.'

The tiny island was little more than a single outcrop of amber-coloured rock, yet its wind-scoured surfaces and rugged, irregular outline had a singular quality to them. It wasn't just the contrast with the black shingle of the beach and the dark ridges of the cliff, but something more fundamental. There was a stillness about Elva, a quiet waiting that was at odds with the restless motion of the sea and the whirling cries of the gulls all around the cove. Ico sensed it, and knew she had come to the right place. At the same time she felt a featherlike touch of fear.

'Just looks like an ordinary lump of rock to me,' Nino remarked prosaically. 'Are you sure this is the right place?'

Ico glanced at him in surprise. She had taken him to be a sensitive and even poetic soul, but he had obviously not been affected in the way she had. Perhaps, she thought hopefully, it's because I've been called and he hasn't.

'I'm sure,' she said. 'The birds know it too. Ask Eya.'

The peregrine falcon was riding the updraft from the cliff, with Soo nearby. Initially wary, the two birds had learnt to work well as a team, respecting each other's skills.

'We can camp on the beach,' Nino said practically, 'but if we're going to get down before nightfall we'd better get a move on. This cliff should be easy enough, but I wouldn't fancy it in darkness.'

The sun would be setting behind them within the next hour.

'Me neither,' Ico said. 'Let's go.'

Erosion had turned the cliff face into an elaborate sculpture of horizontal ledges and twisted funnels. It didn't look easy at all to Ico, but she trusted Nino implicitly in such matters and followed him as they began the long descent. The surface of the rock was smooth and hard in places, sharp and brittle in others, and there were many small overhangs to negotiate, but they made steady progress. Both birds helped with advice about which route to take, but they seemed jittery and eventually became so distracted that Ico paused to see what was the matter.

Are you all right?

There are ghosts here, Soo replied, but would not explain further.

'Eya's nervous too,' Nino commented, noting Ico's preoccupied expression. 'There's something odd about this place.'

Ico nodded. 'Have you noticed that even though the cliffs are inhabited by thousands of birds, not one of them has so much as flown near the island, let alone landed on it . . . her?'

'Forbidden territory,' Nino observed.

They were about halfway down now and the shadows were lengthening. The cove was like a vast echoing bowl, with the cries of the seabirds and the crash of the surf magnified by the surrounding rock. Only to the southeast, where the waves rolled in to either side of Elva, was there space and the promise of silence.

'Is the tide coming in or out?' Ico asked.

'It's going out,' Nino told her. 'At a guess, low tide should be in about two hours. By the look of it we might be able to walk out to the island then.'

'Beyond the earth's breathing,' Ico whispered to herself.

'What?'

'Nothing. We'd better get on.'

When they finally reached the bottom Nino set about finding a sheltered spot at the base of the cliff where they could stow their gear and set up camp. Ico left him to these domestic chores and skirted round the lake. Close to, the water still seemed bright but its depths were murky, the fish within merely dark smudges below the surface. Crossing the humpbacked shingle beach, Ico came to the edge of the restless ocean and looked across the narrow channel to Elva. 'A part of the land and apart from the land' described the island well. At low tide it would be joined to the mainland – Ico could see the natural causeway below the waves now – but for the rest of the time it was separate, aloof. Floating. In that moment, she knew what she had to do.

It's a test, she thought. Of courage, of determination, of worthiness.

She went back to Nino, who had already set up a shelter and unpacked their bedrolls.

'Where do you want to sleep?' he asked.

'I won't be sleeping,' she told him simply. 'I'm going to spend the night on the island.'

'Oh no!' he exclaimed. 'I promised Andrin I'd look after you – and that's crazy. Once the tide comes in again you'll be cut off.'

'I know. That's the point. If I pass her test, then perhaps she'll speak to me. That's why we came here, after all.'

'But why all night? What's wrong with talking to her at low tide?'

'I have to show her I'm serious, that I deserve to talk to the oracle.'

Nino still looked doubtful, but Ico was in no mood to argue.

'I'm doing this, Nino. I appreciate your concern, but there's no way you can stop me.'

'No, I don't suppose there is,' he conceded eventually. 'So I'd better come with you.'

'No. This is something I must do alone.'

Nino looked into her eyes and knew that further discussion was pointless. 'Will you at least take some provisions? And some means of shelter in case the weather turns bad?'

'If I've been called, I'll be made welcome,' Ico said calmly. 'If not, none of that will help.'

Nino spread his arms in exasperation.

'Will you eat something before you go? Please. It's been a long day, and you'll need your strength.'

She agreed to his final request, even though she didn't have much of an appetite, and they ate in anticipatory silence.

An hour later they stood side by side, watching the swirling waters in the channel. The jagged rocks and unpredictable currents made it obvious that this was not a place to risk swimming, whatever the state of the tide.

'It's on the turn,' Nino said. 'If you're going, you'd better go now.'

Ico kissed his cheek lightly. 'Don't worry. I'll be all right.'

'You'd better be. Andrin will kill me if anything happens to you.' His voice was light-hearted, but she caught the tension beneath his words. 'Stay where I can see you,' he added. 'Good luck.'

'I'll see you in the morning,' Ico said and set off, carefully stepping over the slippery rocks.

Halfway across, a most curious sensation swept over her. At first she thought she had gone partially deaf, but then realized that all the seagulls had grown silent. In fact every single bird in the entire cove was now mute, and Ico had the insane notion that they were watching her. The sea still rumbled and hissed all around her, but even that seemed muffled now. As she reached the end of the causeway and stepped on to Elva for the first time, a larger wave swept round the island in a double curve, sending an explosive fountain of spray into the air when it met itself. Ico's isolation was complete.

She climbed steadily, carefully testing each foot- and handhold, intent on reaching the jagged summit before the last of the evening's light faded. During the ascent, without even realizing it, Ico was silently explaining her intrusion and asking Elva for guidance. When she reached the top she turned and looked back down to where Nino stood watching her. He waved and shouted something, but Ico only caught fragments of sound. She waved back, noting as she did so that the waves were now regularly surging all around the island, making it impossible for her to return to the beach even if she had wanted to. She sat down to wait.

True night came. The moon rose, then disappeared behind a thick layer of cloud which had moved in from the west, obliterating all the stars as well. The darkness would have been complete had it not been for the faint luminescence of the lake, a pale emerald glimmering that painted the cove in ghostly hues. The wind blew gently, the air grew cold and the rustle of the unseen ocean below became more powerful as the tide returned to claim its portion of the land. Ico was frightened by the thought that Elva might be completely enveloped by the waves, that she would drown on this floating island, but the rock beneath her remained solid and dry – and she told herself not to be stupid. Instead she prayed, in thoughts, in whispers – but nothing happened. She shivered and yawned, fought to stay alert and listened for any unusual sound. But nothing happened.

During the journey there Ico had spent much time wondering just how the oracle would make herself known. Would she be an invisible presence, a voice in the air? Or would she actually appear? And if so, what would she look like? A dragon or some other fabulous creature, or a human figure? What should Ico ask of her? Would she answer in riddles or in straightforward terms? The one question Ico had not been able to bring herself even to contemplate was: what was she to do if Elva ignored her altogether? Failure of that kind did not bear thinking about, but now, as midnight approached, it began to seem a distinct possibility.

'Ico? Are you all right?'

The voice floated out of the darkness, barely audible but clearly anxious, and Ico realized that even though he had not come to the island, Nino was matching her vigil. She felt a wave of affection and gratitude for the man who, though he was more than ten years her senior – and thus one of the oldest of the Firebrands – had always treated her as an equal.

'I'm fine, Nino!' she called back. 'Get some sleep.' She did not really think he would obey her but wanted to sound confident.

Some time later she saw his slim figure silhouetted against the green of the lake as he paced up and down the beach, and was comforted by his watchful presence. However, by then she was preoccupied by her own progress – or lack of it. She remembered Soo's doubts, and wished suddenly that the sparrowhawk had been able to come with her on this last leg of the journey. And then her own uncertainties began to assume even more ominous proportions. If I'd really been called, she thought hopelessly, I'd know what to do, what to ask – but I don't have a clue.

Then her ears caught a faint rhythm, a distant thrumming in the air. It seemed to be coming from out to sea and she turned eagerly to look that way, but could see nothing. The noise grew louder, drew closer until it was right overhead. A down-draught ruffled Ico's hair, cooled her upturned face, but still she could see nothing and the giant wingbeats flew on.

'Elva!' she cried. 'Help me. I need your help!'

There was no answer, not even any hint that her plea had been heard. Ico felt insignificant and desolate – and then felt the beginnings of anger.

'Why—?' she began, then was forced into silence as the air seemed to be sucked from her lungs. All sound ceased and her eyes became quite blind. The lake vanished, even the sea was motionless and she was alone in a grey featureless void.

Ico had no idea how long she remained suspended like that, but when she could breathe again, when her heart started beating, the eastern sky was showing the first signs of the dawn's brightness. The night was over and she had achieved nothing. Not only that, but she felt weak and sore, and her breath was coming in agonized gasps.

As she began to make her way down from the rock she heard again Soo's words of warning. *It is dangerous to abuse the trust of oracles.*

CHAPTER THIRTY-SIX

Vargo had found the lake of his dreams. He had followed the ancient corridors of stone deep into the uncharted maze, his way lit only by the flickering glow of Allegra's torch as she trod carefully behind him. He had not stopped to think what this tortuous journey must have cost his companion, had not sensed her fear or the bravery that had overcome it. He took her persistent loyalty for granted now. The labyrinth drew him on, until he reached the vast cavern and looked into the mirror lake.

It was just as he remembered it. He almost expected to be dragged unwittingly into the perfect illusion, and had to remind himself that this was real and not a dream.

'Be careful,' Allegra said, coming to stand beside him. 'It's a long way down.'

'No it isn't,' he replied, and explained about the stillness of the lake.

At first she did not believe him. 'Are you sure?'

'Yes. I've seen this place before.'

'When?' Allegra knelt down and stretched out her free hand.

'Don't touch it yet,' he said, more sharply than he had intended, and she froze, glancing up at him.

'We've never been here before. No one's been this far. How—?'

As she spoke, the surface of the water began to dance. It rippled and shivered, producing a million tiny spikes that glittered for a moment and then vanished, to be replaced by a million more. The reflection of the roof of the cavern had shattered, revealing the false nature of the canyon, but the patterns that replaced it would have been equally mesmerizing had it not been for the one terrifying fact that drove every other thought from their minds.

It was not only the water that was moving. The entire cavern was shaking too.

Nino knew the tremor was coming before the shock wave reached them. He glanced around hurriedly, assessed the potential hazards and decided that they were already in the safest place available.

'Brace yourself,' he told Ico, and prepared to protect her as best he could.

Although the earthquake was comparatively gentle, the noise and sudden uncertainty were unnerving. Without Nino to support her Ico would have fallen, and as it was her legs were shaky for some time afterwards. The area their path was crossing was relatively stable, but they heard the crash of rock slides from other parts of the lava fields. When it was over they had only one thought in their minds, and set off to complete their journey back to the caves as quickly as possible.

'Send Eya ahead,' Ico suggested. 'Maybe he'll be able to find out if they're all right.'

Nino did as she suggested, and the peregrine was soon out of sight.

'Do you think—?' Ico began.

'The caves will have survived,' Nino said, as confidently as he could. 'They're very old and they've withstood much more violent tremors than that.'

'I hope you're right.'

They hurried on, knowing that they were only an hour or two away. Returning from Elva had proved easier than the journey out, and they had almost made it back in three days. They had been only a few miles short when night fell, but Nino would not allow them to continue over such difficult terrain in the dark. Ico had been disappointed, but deferred to her more experienced guide. Instead they had risen at first light, intent on reaching the caves by mid-morning.

Eya returned sooner than expected, and Ico's frustration mounted as Nino and his link engaged in a lengthy and obviously complicated exchange.

'Well?' she demanded, not liking the serious expression on her companion's face.

'As far as Eya can tell, the caves are intact. Certainly there've been no major rockfalls in the area.'

'Thank the gods,' Ico breathed.

'But we can't go back just yet,' Nino said.

'What! Why not?'

'Because the whole area is surrounded by soldiers.'

Ico was horrified. This was a disaster she had not envisaged.

'The curious thing is, they don't seem to be attacking,' he went on.

'Are they just waiting for us to come out and surrender?' Ico exclaimed. 'They'll wait a long time if they think that.'

'I don't think so,' Nino said. 'It looks as though some of them are withdrawing, heading back to Teguise. As if they've changed their minds altogether.'

'That doesn't make sense. Why come all this way to do nothing?'

'I don't know. Even so, I think we'd better stay out of their way. I'll send Eya ahead again as a lookout.'

'Soo can go too,' Ico decided. 'Between them they might be able to find out what's going on.'

After the birds had sped away Ico and Nino set off again, but more cautiously now. They had no wish to run into any detachments of guards, no matter what they were up to. Eya was the first to return, and Nino passed on his welcome news.

'The troops are all leaving, and in a hurry too. Whatever's happening must be pretty serious because they've just abandoned the assault on the caves, even though they were apparently in perfect position to cut us off entirely.'

'Unless they were just trying to scare us,' Ico said, still trying to make sense of it all.

'That's an awful lot of effort just for a show of strength,' Nino commented. 'If they know where we are, what's to stop them attacking?'

'Maybe it's me they want – and they found out I wasn't there?'

'How could they know that?'

'How did they find the caves in the first place?'

'It was never going to be possible to keep them a secret indefinitely,' Nino said. 'There's all sorts of ways—'

'But we've been so careful!' Ico protested.

Their discussion was ended by Soo's arrival.

It's safe for you to return now. The soldiers are on their way. Is everyone all right?

Yes. The rockfall caused a few minor accidents, but no one was seriously hurt. Ayo and some of the others are on their way to Teguise to see if they can find out why the soldiers left.

Good. Did you see Andrin?

He is well, Soo reported. *And glad that you are safe too.*

Ico passed the news on to Nino, and they resumed their earlier fast pace. They arrived at the caves to find the Firebrands extremely busy. Andrin was waiting for them, and held Ico so tightly that she was almost unable to breathe. His joy at seeing her again was matched only by his obvious bewilderment at the morning's events.

'The night sentries thought they heard some unusual noises,' he exclaimed, 'but it was too dark to see anything. When the sun rose, the soldiers were just there. They weren't even trying to hide – which would have been impossible with that big a force anyway – but they'd got us completely trapped. There were strong detachments outside every exit – every one! It's almost as if they knew exactly where we were and how the caves mapped out. Anyway, after we got over the shock, we made what preparations we could. With the defences we've got set up, and with our knowledge of the cave system it was never going to be easy for them to storm the place, but for some reason it didn't come to that. They just upped and left.'

'Because of the earthquake?' Ico suggested.

'No. They were on the move before it hit. Besides, it was too small to cause a real emergency.'

'Worms then?'

'We've not seen any.'

'But the soldiers are going back to Teguise?'

'It seems so. At least that's the way they're heading.'

'How long will it take Ayo to get there and back?'

'I doubt if he'll make it before nightfall.'

They looked at each other in silence for a while.

'We're going to have to move,' Ico said quietly.

Andrin nodded. 'We're already making preparations, but I've no idea where we're going to go. I was hoping Nino might have some ideas about that.'

'How do you think they found us?'

'If I didn't know better I'd think we'd been betrayed.'

Ico, who had been thinking along the same lines, said nothing.

'We can't do anything about it now,' Andrin went on logically. 'We just have to be thankful for whatever saved us – and be more careful next time.'

They both knew that the chances of finding another hide-out with even a fraction of the advantages of the one they were being forced to abandon were remote. It was a depressing prospect, but the day could have brought much worse.

'I have some other bad news,' Andrin said reluctantly. 'There were some of our former colleagues with the soldiers, the ones Kantrowe rearrested. One way or another he's got them to work for him now.'

'Doing what?'

'I don't know.'

'Was Maghdim there?' Ico asked, feeling a sudden chill at the thought.

'Not as far as any of us could see,' Andrin replied, 'but I'd be surprised if he wasn't part of this somehow.'

'Vargo would have been able to tell. Have you asked him?'

'I haven't seen him this morning. Everything's been so chaotic.' He stopped abruptly and looked at her apologetically. 'How did you get on?'

'Not very well,' she admitted.

'You look tired.'

'I am.' She went on to describe the abortive visit to Elva, and was grateful when he did not reproach her for running off on what had indeed proved to be a wild goose chase.

'Oh well,' he said. 'It was worth a try. I'm just glad you're back. I've been having nightmares about us being separated.'

'Me too.'

They kissed, but both knew there was no time for dalliance.

'Have you heard any more from Maciot?' Ico asked.

'We'd set up the demonstration he wanted, which was to be tomorrow – if the worms obliged – but that's impossible now. No doubt he'll find out what's happened before too long.'

'Let's hope he keeps faith with us. We need all the friends we can get in Teguise.'

'If he *is* a friend,' Andrin said.

'What do you mean? Surely—'

'Just my suspicious mind,' he cut in, smiling to reassure her. 'That bird of his is pretty bright.'

'If Maciot wanted to hurt us he's had many opportunities,' Ico argued. 'Even if he *did* manage to find our location, why wait until now to sell us out?'

Andrin shrugged. 'Forget it,' he said, 'I'm just imagining things.'

The next few hours were spent in hectic toil, organizing their second exodus as best they could. Nino was given the task of plotting various routes and suggesting possible destinations for the evacuation but, apart from him and those on lookout duty, everyone else was involved in packing up their equipment and stores. Andrin reckoned everything should be ready by dusk, but wasn't sure whether to travel by night or to risk sleeping in the caves one more time and then leaving in daylight. In the event the choice became academic because of two messages that arrived within a few minutes of each other towards the end of the day.

The first was from one of the Firebrands who had been assigned to exploration and guide duty within the cave system. He came to Andrin in a state of some distress, clearly unhappy to be the bearer of bad news.

'What's the matter, Jada?'

'We've accounted for almost everyone. But two people are missing.'

'Who?'

'Vargo and Allegra,' the guide answered. 'We've searched high and low, but they've just disappeared. Either they've left the caves or they're lost beyond the mapped-out tunnels.'

'Vargo wouldn't have left without telling someone. They must still be inside.'

'What if he's not himself?' Ico asked delicately.

'Allegra's got too much sense to go wandering off,' Andrin replied, and turned back to Jada. 'Organize search parties, and make sure they don't get lost too. You know the drill.'

The guide nodded, but stayed where he was. 'There's something else,' he said unhappily. 'Two of the tunnels leading deeper underground have been completely blocked by rock falls. If Vargo and Allegra are trapped behind either of them, chances are we'll never reach them.'

Andrin swore under his breath. 'Do what you can,' he said. 'I'll come and help as soon as possible.'

As Jada left Andrin turned to look at Ico, his face stricken. 'I didn't need this,' he muttered.

'He'll be all right,' she tried to reassure him. 'Even if they've been cut off, there's bound to be another exit somewhere.' But she was silently cursing Allegra for allowing Vargo to get into such a predicament.

'Let's hope so,' Andrin said. 'If there isn't, they may run out of air before we can find them.'

'We won't leave without them, will we?'

'Not if I can help it,' he replied, but they both knew that they might not have any choice.

Worse still, it was possible that their friends might not be beyond the rockfalls but under them.

'Andrin?'

One of their lookouts was calling urgently, his voice echoing in the corridors and chambers.

'What is it?'

'Ayo's back.'

'I'm on my way.'

Ico followed her lover up to the surface, and stood watching impatiently while he talked with the eagle. She tried to read his expressions, which registered both amazement and concern, as well as a surprising glint of amusement.

'The Barber and his entire fleet just sailed into Teguise harbour,' he said eventually. 'They're attacking the city head on!'

CHAPTER THIRTY-SEVEN

Allegra woke to absolute darkness and paralyzing terror. None of her muscles would obey her, and she lay rigid on the unforgiving stone floor. It was only when she recognized the warm presence of Vargo's sleeping body pressed against her side that she found the courage to move, and then it was only to sit up slowly and painfully. Beside her Vargo stirred, muttered something unintelligible, but did not wake. Their torch had long since burned out and in the lightless subterranean world they were blind, having to rely on other senses. The only sound she could hear was Vargo's soft breathing. She could smell the dampness of the nearby lake, and touch the edges of the unseen rock around her – but it was not enough. She wanted to scream.

After the tremor, they had immediately headed back the way they had come, following the carefully marked trail that Allegra had left, only to find the way completely blocked by a massive rock fall. Fighting panic, they had investigated the other tunnels, but they all proved impassable. Finally, when they had been forced to accept that they were cut off from their companions, they had retraced their steps to the mirror lake and had then fallen into a stupefied slumber, born of both mental and physical exhaustion. Awake now, with no way of telling how much time had passed, Allegra was prey to all the fears that came crowding back into her mind, and desperately needed to reassure herself that she was not alone.

'Vargo?' she breathed, not able to trust her voice at anything more than a whisper. 'Vargo?'

She shook him gently. He shifted, coughed, then sat up. He put an arm round her and she clung to him, wanting to tell him how frightened she was but not wanting to add this extra burden to his load. Her faith in him was born of friendship, admiration, love and - on this occasion - absolute need. If anyone could save them it was Vargo.

'Aren't the stars beautiful?' he said.

Allegra's carefully nurtured belief began to shrivel. Vargo's madness was an integral part of him, but on this occasion she needed him to be sane and strong. 'There aren't any stars,' she told him. 'We're in the caves, remember?'

'I can see them. Look.'

She glanced up automatically, but her eyes met only black emptiness. 'You're imagining them,' she insisted. 'We're underground - and I need your help.'

'I can make them shine. Look.'

There was a loud, sharp crack, then a single brilliant flash of blue-white light came from the roof of the cavern and froze the scene on Allegra's retinae - the jagged, multicoloured strata, the flat surface of the water and the shadows beyond . . . And then it was gone. In the renewed darkness she was blind once more but her own imagination had sprung into action now. In the after-glow of that impossible lightning strike she had seen a hairy, wild-faced creature, cowering on the far side of the lake - but an instant later the very idea seemed more absurd than frightening. She wanted to ask Vargo how he had created the light, but her tongue did not seem to be working.

'I am not possessed,' Vargo said clearly and then, in a matter-of-fact tone, he added, 'We'd better go.'

'Go where?' she asked, her hopes rising again as he seemed to return to sanity.

'Over the lake.'

'But we don't know how deep it is. Can you swim?'

'It's shallow.'

'That was in your dream,' she objected. The idea of wading into the unfathomable, unseen water appalled her.

'Dreams are sometimes the only reality,' he told her, and laughed. 'Besides, we've tried everywhere this side.'

Allegra could not deny the truth of that. 'I thought . . .' she said hesitantly. 'I thought I saw something on the far side, a wild animal.'

'How?' Vargo asked, sounding puzzled. 'We can't see anything in this dark.'

'In the flash . . . you made . . .' Had he forgotten?

'You're imagining things,' he said kindly. 'Come on.'

They stood up carefully, finding it difficult to keep their balance on stiff legs, then edged towards the rim of the lake, hand in hand.

'Are you sure about this?' Allegra persisted. 'Why don't you try calling the birds again first?'

'I told you,' he replied. 'We need to be in a more or less direct line of sight to be able to talk to Ero and Lao. With any luck they'll be able to sense that I'm still alive, and they'll be searching for us. But we have to try and find our own way out of this mess.' He sounded perfectly rational now.

They crept onwards, into the lake. The water was cold but not uncomfortably so. To Allegra's relief it only reached just above her ankles and, although both of them stumbled several times on the rough surface, neither of them hesitated for long. They still held each other's hand, with their free arms extended in front of them. They had to rely on their joint sense of direction to guide them across and, when they reached dry rock again, Allegra couldn't help wondering if perhaps they had simply gone round in a circle and returned to their starting point. Vargo evidently had no such doubts.

'It's different this side,' he observed quietly. 'Do you feel it?'

'Feel what?'

'The warmth,' he replied, then, less explicably, 'and the memories.'

Allegra realized that it did indeed feel a little warmer, and her hopes rose a fraction. If the creature she had seen had been real, then that must surely mean that there was a route to the surface somewhere.

'I had the strangest feeling as we were crossing the water,' Vargo said, dispelling her optimism. 'As if the dragons were watching us.' He began to sing softly and sweetly, a wordless lament that was touched by his genius as well as his lunacy. It was an ancient song, one which the rocks around them seemed to join in. Allegra listened, spellbound but still afraid, holding on to his hand as though it were her last contact with the world.

As the last note died away she held her breath, thinking she must be dreaming. In the earlier torchlight and more recently in Vargo's blinding flash, she had noted several shadowed openings on the far side of the lake, any one of which might have been the entrance to a tunnel. Now, unless she was hallucinating, one of these was illuminated from within by the faintest glimmer of white light.

'Do you see it?' she asked in wonderment.

'Yes.'

She glanced at him automatically and found, to her amazement, that she could see the ghostly outline of his face. He was smiling.

They went on, moving with more confidence now. The tunnel narrowed so that they had to walk in single file, but they were moving slightly uphill – which was encouraging –

and every so often a crystal embedded in a wall or the roof flickered with delicate white sparks. It was beautiful as well as enormously welcome.

'Are these the stars you saw?' she asked.

'What stars?' he replied. 'What are you talking about?'

'The crystals. Are you making them shine?'

'No. This is too delicate for me. I could probably make them explode, but that wouldn't do us much good.'

Allegra considered his answer, decided not to probe any further, and was content to follow him into the unknown. The dancing, firefly light led them past several turnings, and on more than one occasion Allegra thought she saw a shadowy figure well ahead of them – but it always vanished in an instant and Vargo never commented, so she said nothing.

Eventually she became aware that the crystals were no longer shining – but she could still see. With a joyful start she realized that daylight was filtering into the corridor from somewhere ahead. Soon after that they saw the opening and the longed-for glimpse of the sky.

They emerged at the edge of a lava field not far from an ancient crater that neither of them recognized. They had no idea where they were, but neither of them cared. Their relief and happiness were overwhelming and made words superfluous. They were in each other's arms, embracing tightly and performing a small, ecstatic dance. It was only when they drew apart, flushed and laughing, that they heard the soft chirruping from nearby, quickly followed by a mocking call of hoo-poo-hoo. Vargo looked around wildly, his merriment increasing when he saw the two birds perched side by side on a rock only a few paces away. Ordinarily so different, they could on this occasion have been taken for twins, such was their shared disdain for their link's recent exhibition.

How did you find us? Vargo asked as Allegra also noticed the birds and laughed, sharing his delight.

The dancer showed us the way, Lao replied.

I would have found you anyway, Ero added, puffing out his chest self-importantly, *but he helped.*

Who is the dancer? Where is he now?

He was never here, Lao said enigmatically.

We can all do the dancing now, Ero put in, posing hopefully. *Without her,* he added with a disparaging glance at Allegra.

Did he possess you too? Vargo asked.

Lao turned to look at Ero.

His mind's not possessed, he remarked scathingly. *Most of the time it's not even occupied.*

'We have to go!' Ico declared.

'This is madness,' Andrin replied with equal vehemence. 'What's got into you?'

Ico instinctively put her hand to her necklace, remembering the scenes from that night's dream.

'Do you remember our journey here?' she asked. 'The flashes in my head that guided us? Well, this is like that. Those images were glimpses of the future, my future – and I know I should be in Teguise.'

'Because of a dream?' he asked incredulously. 'Have you forgotten what nearly happened to you last time you were there?'

'Of course not, but things are different now, and this is meant to be. I saw magic being used in the city, and I was one of those responsible. They *need* us.'

'That's absurd. It'd be like passing our own death sentences.'

Ico knew that she ought to remain calm and reasonable, especially as she could see that Andrin was going to take some convincing, but she could feel time slipping away from her – and keeping her temper had never been one of her great strengths. When, the night before, it had become clear that the Firebrands were not in any immediate danger from the retreating soldiers, she had seen it as a reprieve but also as an opportunity. It had happened that way for a reason. They had all spent one last night in the caves but, between the still unsuccessful search for Vargo and Allegra and her own preoccupations, Ico had got little rest. While she *had* slept, her dreams had been enough to persuade her of what their next step ought to be. When she'd woken she had felt sick and apprehensive, but since then her conviction had not wavered. Taking a deep breath, she tried again.

'We have to leave here anyway, and you said yourself that we'd be going back to Teguise one day.'

'At the right time,' he shot back. 'Not now!'

'But this is our chance to prove that we're not Tiguafaya's enemies,' she persisted. 'If we can help defeat the pirates, everyone will see that – and if we prove at the same time that magic can work for good, then it'll be a double victory.'

'Don't be so naive!' he shouted. 'Even if we *did* help, what's to stop Kantrowe turning round afterwards, saying thank you very much but now I'm going to execute you all?'

'He'd never do that,' Ico retorted, growing heated herself now. 'Don't you see? His credibility is almost gone. First we managed to get away from him, then his precious treaty with the pirates is shown to be a joke. He's lost face, and will never be weaker. If we demonstrate our worth, then the people will be on our side. We already know from Maciot that many of them are sympathetic. Maybe they'll even throw Kantrowe out altogether.'

'Are you blind?' Andrin exclaimed. 'Kantrowe was about to capture us. Does that sound weak to you? We're no match for him and, in case you haven't noticed, the people don't control the army, *he* does. Who's going to stand against the White Guard if it comes to a fight? We should just sit back and let the Barber do our work for us. Anything that weakens Kantrowe's forces is to our benefit.'

'But it's not just soldiers that will die,' Ico stated angrily.

'These are *our* homes they're burning, our families that are in danger. Have you forgotten?'

'That all changed when we left,' he said coldly. 'And anyway, if the army can't deal with a pirate attack, what chance would we have?'

'I told you,' Ico replied exasperatedly. 'We'd use magic!'

'And are you prepared to face Maghdim again?' he asked. 'Given that we won't have Vargo with us this time?'

'We must. It just feels right.'

'Like it felt right for you to go to Elva?' he added caustically.

Ico almost exploded then. She was still smarting from her failure at the oracle, and a small part of her knew that she needed to take this action in order to recover her own self-esteem. However, she was not about to admit that to anyone.

'This is different,' she claimed. 'That was just hope. I'm *sure* this is right.'

'How can you be sure? When did you become a prophet?'

'You think I'm making it all up?'

'I don't know what you're doing. Gods! Not so long ago I was supposed to be the rash one. If I'd ever suggested anything as stupid as this you'd have slapped me down so fast—'

'This is not stupid!' she yelled, losing control.

'Yes it is. If you weren't so obsessed you'd see that. At least my mistakes were honest.'

Ico did not wait to ask what he meant by that. She did not even want to know. She slapped him hard across the face, her hand moving of its own volition. The crack of impact echoed round the cave as his head jerked to the side. It was a few moments before he turned back to look at her, and then his expression was set in stone, his eyes like ice crystals. It would have been hard to tell which one of them was the more shocked, and the silence stretched interminably.

'We'd be too late to do any good,' Andrin said eventually, keeping his voice steady only with the greatest difficulty. 'The pirates will hit and run. Speed has always been their greatest asset.'

'How can you be so sure?' Ico asked quietly. 'It may be different this time. They've never attacked Teguise before.'

'All the more reason for them to take what they can and get out fast,' he argued. 'They can't hope to hold the entire city.'

'I know that,' she conceded, 'but this is more than routine scavenging. They'll still be there when we arrive.' She was recalling another fragment of her dream.

Andrin laughed, though there was little humour in the sound. 'Gods, where are you getting this stuff? From the sky voices? It would take us four days to get to Teguise, three at least – and the march would exhaust us.'

'We can do it quicker than that,' she said eagerly. 'In fact, I know just how we *can* do it.'

'Fly?' he suggested sarcastically. 'Perhaps you should ask Soo for lessons.'

'In my dream I rode a camel,' she told him. 'There were others with me too.'

'I give up,' he muttered disgustedly. 'These camels just appeared out of thin air, I suppose. How many more delusions are you going to dredge up from one dream?'

'I just know that I've got to go,' she said in a level tone. 'Don't deny me this, please.'

She took a careful step towards him, narrowing the gap between them. He started to retreat, then his hands shot out and grabbed her wrists. Ico, who had been just about to tell him that she loved him, and to ask for his forgiveness as well as a hug, was stunned. She froze, realizing that he thought she was going to hit him again. The red mark was still visible on his left cheek and she suddenly felt like crying, which in turn made her angry again. How could he misjudge her so?

'Are you afraid of me too?' she asked, unable to keep the spite from her voice.

'You're the only one I *am* afraid of,' he replied sourly. 'But I'm damned if I'm going to let you rush off on another idiotic adventure.'

'So what are you going to do? Keep me here by brute force?' she taunted, looking down at his hands which still manacled hers. 'Tie me up?'

He let her go then, and she took a step back before speaking again.

'I'm going to Teguise. Are you coming with me?'

He shook his head. 'Don't do this, please.'

Ico did not answer, but simply bent to pick up her gear, turned and walked out of the cavern. The adjoining cave was much larger and most of the Firebrands were gathered there. The sight of so many frightened and confused faces all turned her way was daunting, but she was not about to back down now. They must have overheard most of what had been said. Now it was time for them to make their own decisions.

'I'm going to Teguise,' she repeated defiantly. 'Any of you who aren't too cowardly are welcome to come too. We leave now.'

Andrin had followed her, but did not respond to her deliberately unjust words. Ico began to stride towards the tunnel that led to the surface.

'You want us to fight alongside Kantrowe?' Jair called in disbelief.

'I want us to fight *for* Tiguafaya,' Ico retorted, without turning round. 'That's what we all want, isn't it?'

Whispers and muttering filled the cavern. Although a few of the Firebrands began to follow Ico, most stood where they were, looking to Andrin for guidance.

'Let them go,' he said wearily. 'They'll come to their senses soon enough.' He was so distressed that he felt physically sick, but he had no intention of demeaning himself further by chasing after the stupid bitch.

CHAPTER THIRTY-EIGHT

The harbour sentries had been surprised but not worried when they'd seen the first ships heading towards the city. In the month since the treaty with the pirates, the seas had been at peace, and the lookouts in Teguise had become even more lackadaisical about their seemingly pointless duties. Even the unusual weather of the last few days had not aroused much interest. A bank of sea mist had been more or less stationary about a mile offshore, in defiance of the gentle but steady breeze that blew from the southeast. The direction of the wind was directly opposite to what would normally be expected at this time of year, and so the fog was reckoned to be a consequence of these peculiar conditions and nothing more. Subsequent events were to disprove this theory.

The fleet had been headed by several massive vessels, with few sails set, moving slowly with the wind directly towards the city. Their formation as they emerged from the mist had been ragged and they showed no identifying flags, but their destination was clear. The sentries at the end of the piers on either side of the wide entrance to Teguise harbour were about to alert their duty officers about the unknown and unexpected arrivals when they spotted something else about the flotilla. Something that was not only very strange but also ominous. Almost all the ships were trailing smoke.

Although no one yet knew what was going on, the alarm was raised and the garrison mobilized. The fact that the vast majority of the White Guard and several other army units were absent on an important but unspecified mission did not cause too much concern at first. The forces that remained were more than enough to deal with the present threat – if threat it was.

As the eleven ships drew nearer, the mystery deepened. There did not seem to be any crews on board, and they were drifting on the wind at odd angles. One had twisted almost broadside while two others had collided gently and were now moving in tandem, as if they had been roped together. The volume of smoke from each vessel had increased. By the time one of the watching officers realized what was happening it was too late to do anything about it.

'Dear gods!' he breathed in a horrified whisper. 'They're fire ships.'

Moments later he was proved correct as one of the leading craft exploded. The others soon followed suit and the nature of the danger to Teguise became doubly clear when, in the distance, a vast fleet emerged from the fog and followed the now flaming hulks. There was no doubting the identity of the newcomers. The Barber's flagship, the *Revenge*, with its unique blood-red sails, was instantly recognizable – but there was still considerable disbelief about his intentions. The idea of a direct assault on Teguise itself had long been discounted as absurd, and it took a great deal of mental effort to accept what was actually happening.

The arrival of the blazing fire ships caused havoc. As several of the ships that had been moored in the harbour tried to get under way and out of their path, there were many collisions and other accidents that only made matters worse. A few of the braver captains tried to attach hooks and ropes to the burning craft, but their attempts to tow them away met with little success. Several more vessels were soon burning, their crews either engaged in desperate fire fighting or abandoning ship. And still the wind blew the deadly hulks on, driving them remorselessly towards the docks. Soldiers and stevedores prepared to defend the jetties and the buildings beyond as best they could, but it was not long before they had other enemies to face.

The Barber's fleet, which consisted of far more than the eighteen ships he was supposed to command, had arrived to add to the confusion. With the benefit of full sail and crews to guide them, they had moved much faster than the drifting hulks, and now went into battle against an enemy that was both disorganized and demoralized. The pirates set to with a bloodthirsty joyfulness, using their bow rams, catapults and crossbows to rain terror on to the beleaguered ships and, in some cases, to add an extra dose of fire with the use of burning, oil-soaked rags. Later, when it came to hand-to-hand combat, few defenders had much stomach for the fight, and so the pirates' progress seemed unstoppable. And once they reached the docks, it appeared that they had a specific objective in mind.

Leaving the fire to occupy most of the townsfolk, they landed a large force of men who immediately set about capturing two large warehouses near the centre of the harbour waterfront. These buildings were used by merchants of all kinds, and on any given day were likely to contain several fortunes in jewellery, metals, spices, silk, furs, wine and other merchandise. Although defended by a considerable number of private sentries as well as by some of the White Guard, the stores were soon overrun by the pirates, who then set about securing their positions in readiness for the next stage of the operation. The Barber himself took up residence in the larger of the two warehouses, and directed his men with the authority of a tyrant who is respected as well as feared.

Once their enclave was safely established, the Barber wasted no time gloating over what had already been achieved, but waited for his opportunity to bargain with those in authority. This arrived when a foolish captain of the White Guard, who had tried to lead a counter attack against the now more or less impregnable pirate stronghold, was cut off from his men and then – rather to his surprise – captured rather than killed. He was brought to the Barber and thrown down on his knees. The raiders' leader ignored him for a few minutes while he finished inscribing a message on a piece of parchment. The Barber was held in awe among the buccaneers because – among his many other accomplishments – he could both read and write.

'This is a letter to Senator Kantrowe.' His voice was light in tone, like a boy's, but carried the unmistakable weight of authority. 'You know of him?'

The captive nodded, while some of the onlookers laughed.

'Good.' The Barber's hand suddenly became a blur, drawing a dagger from his belt and wielding the blade in one swift downward movement. The captain screamed as half of his left ear fell to the floor and blood spurted over the shoulder of his uniform. Wordlessly, the Barber handed him a scrap of cloth which the trembling soldier used to stem the flow, his frightened eyes flicking between the bloody remnant on the ground and his impassive tormentor.

'Be thankful I let you keep your balls,' the pirate said, provoking more laughter from his followers. 'But I need you to run an errand. Think you can run, Captain?'

'Yes . . . sir.'

'Good. Then take this to Kantrowe. Tell him he has one hour in which to comply.' The parchment was handed over. 'If he does not, we will leave Teguise as bloody as your ear. Understand?'

The captain looked around, hardly daring to believe that they were going to let him go, then rose on shaky legs. The pirates' mocking laughter followed him as he ran from the building, his left hand still clamped to the side of his head, and began to make his way towards the Vestry.

Kantrowe finished reading the letter for the third time, and threw the parchment on his desk in disgust. His rage had been burning white hot for some hours now, but this was more than he could bear. To be held to ransom by these sea-rats in his own city was an outrage but, as yet, he could not see a way out of it. By limiting their ambition to specific, attainable targets the pirates had not only demonstrated an unusual discipline but had also been very shrewd. In a straight fight, sheer weight of numbers would eventually have brought the defenders victory but now that the Barber and his vile, ramshackle army were ensconced in what amounted to their own fortresses, it would take more than mere strength to evict them. They controlled virtually everything on the water as well as the section of the harbour between the captured warehouses and the nearest jetties. There were apparently no weaknesses in their position, and certainly none that could be exploited with the reduced forces available to Kantrowe. The senator swore violently again and vowed that vengeance would be his – sooner or later. How could this have happened? Where were the other pirates – Zarzuelo and Agnadi – who had sworn to defend their allies against just such an attack? Come to that, where was Zophres? He was supposed to be keeping an eye on them, making sure they kept their half of the bargain, but Kantrowe had not heard from his envoy for several days.

More to the point, why had this disaster happened *now*? It seemed too much of a coincidence that the pirates had attacked just as he had been preparing to strike the final blow against the Firebrands. Was there some unholy alliance between the young rebels and the Barber? Or was there treachery within the ranks of his own allies? Kantrowe's furious mind began to sift through the possibilities, reviewing all the ways in which he could have been betrayed. Although Maghdim featured heavily in his thoughts, he knew that this was, in part, just personal prejudice. It made no sense for the foreigner to be a traitor. In fact, he had done everything Kantrowe had asked of him. He had activated the linkage to his spy among the Firebrands, ascertaining not only their location but also a great deal about their magical progress, without any of them even being aware of it. He had overseen the administering of tiny dosages of the tincture to the soldiers, so that they would be able to recognize and block out magical illusions, and had prepared his acolytes to add further reinforcements should they be needed. All had been ready, but their careful plans had gone to waste because of the accursed Barber.

Mazo Gadette came in to the office, his pale face flushed for once.

'Well?' Kantrowe demanded.

'We're fighting a losing battle.'

'That's not what I want to hear!'

'It's difficult to get enough water when we can't get near most of the harbour,' the aide explained, 'and unless the wind changes soon the fire's going to spread inland.'

Kantrowe tossed him the parchment.

'Read that.'

A few moments later Gadette raised his death's head and stared at his employer. 'You think it's true?'

'What do *you* think?' the senator retorted. 'The wind's been in the southeast for far too long to be natural, and that damned fog bank is just sitting there. Why didn't anyone think to tell me about it?'

'Because it didn't seem important,' the aide replied defensively, 'and you were rather preoccupied with other matters.'

Kantrowe grunted. 'When will Chinero and the rest get back?' he asked.

'A few units tomorrow, most of them two days after that.'

'That's too long,' his employer exclaimed. 'Commandeer all the camels you need.'

'That won't help much,' Gadette said reasonably. 'Few of them will be close enough to be of much use.'

'Find out, then! Do what you can.'

'Yes, Senator.'

'What about Maghdim? He'll be here tomorrow, I assume?'

'I believe so.'

'Make sure he is,' Kantrowe snapped.

'Yes, Senator. Until then?' He indicated the parchment.

'Tell them we agree, but that we need time to assemble what they want. We must stall them, at least until Maghdim returns, but get the Barber to stop that wind now.'

'You think he can?'

'If what he says about creating the mist and making the wind turn to the southeast is true, then he can turn it round again. If not, we'll have called his bluff. Either way, we have to control that fire. Whatever we do we mustn't provoke him into making the wind even stronger.'

'There are already some demolition teams creating fire breaks,' Gadette reported, 'and we're getting all the water we can from other sources.'

'What are the chances of our attacking the warehouses?'

'With our present forces, not good at all. We'd lose a lot of men with no guarantee of saving anything inside, or even of driving the pirates out. If we *did* storm them, there's always the chance they'll set them ablaze too.'

'So we wait for reinforcements,' Kantrowe stated bitterly. 'I've a good mind to burn them out myself.'

'The Guilds wouldn't like that. We'd lose all the merchandise.'

'We're probably going to lose it all anyway. In their position, would you leave such treasure behind?'

'What should we do if they start ferrying goods out to their ships?' the aide asked.

'Try to stop them, but don't risk too much. We must be able to position archers to make the undertaking seem an unhealthy prospect.'

'I'll see what can be done.'

'Make sure my answer goes to the Barber first,' Kantrowe added. 'For the time being, we've got to play that bastard at his own game.'

CHAPTER THIRTY-NINE

They were not the companions Ico would have chosen but, as she reminded herself bitterly, that option had been denied her from the start. There were seven of them, all men, all hot-headed and eager for action. If it came to a fight their support would stand her in good stead; if quick thinking were needed, then she was on her own. However, the group did include at least three whose magical abilities were considerable – and it was in that that most of Ico's hopes lay.

They covered the three miles inland to the road in good time, but their heavy packs were beginning to take their toll and it was clearly not feasible to carry them all the way to Teguise. On Ico's instructions they found a well-concealed opening amongst the tumbled lava and stowed their gear away, keeping only a few essentials with them.

'We can come back and collect them later,' Ico told her companions. 'Make sure your birds remember the spot, just in case you don't.'

All seven were linked, and messages were passed to the strange assortment of birds that were flying above them under Soo's watchful eye.

'Are you sure you want to do this?' Ico asked. 'I *have* to go, but it's risky.'

They all nodded.

'We've been sitting around doing nothing for too long,' one of them said.

'That's right. We'll never get anywhere if we're not prepared to take risks.'

'Let's go.'

It was obvious that none of them wanted to take this chance to back out, and Ico was grateful for that at least.

'Good,' she said. 'If I'm right, we won't have to walk too far. Let's get going.'

She led them north at a brisk pace, hoping her dream had not misled her. They had not gone more than a few hundred paces when Soo's voice sounded in her head.

Camels behind you. Gaining fast.

Ico grinned, but still needed to reassure herself on a few points.

Soldiers?

No uniforms, the sparrowhawk reported.

How many camels?

Six.

Go and take a closer look. If they're traders, I need to know who they are and whether they're armed. She was already considering her options – whether to beg for a ride, offer some sort of payment or try to commandeer the animals by force.

As Soo flew back, Ico told her companions what was happening and ordered them all to find hiding places amid the nearby rocks. Ico stood her ground in the open, her determination fuelled by faith – and by anger. She was furious with Andrin, not only because he had disagreed with her and not trusted her, but also because he had actually let her go. Although she knew that was not logical, she was hurt – and all the more determined to prove that her hunch had been right.

It's Tao and his link, Soo reported, returning from her reconnaissance.

Maciot? Ico replied, hardly daring to believe her luck. *Are you sure?*

Of course, Soo answered with exaggerated patience. *He has three other men riding with him.*

Ico waved her companions out into the open, and they waited as the cloud of dust raised by the caravan drew closer. The animals were moving at great speed, unlike the normal plodding pace of a merchant's camel train. As they neared the Firebrands, Maciot – who held the reins of the leading animal himself – waved in recognition, a broad smile on his face.

'Well, madam, it seems we are destined to meet in unusual circumstances. This is a surprise.'

'And a very pleasant one,' Ico replied truthfully.

'Where are the rest of your comrades?'

'I'll tell you as we go. We need to get to Teguise as soon as possible.'

'As do I.'

If the senator was surprised by her choice of destination he kept his curiosity in check, and wasted no time in rearranging the caravan so that each camel carried two people. Ico was placed in the seat opposite Maciot, on the other side of the beast's hump. Minutes later they were underway once more and, although the bouncing and rocking of their steed's ungainly but surprisingly effective gallop made talking an effort, they exchanged news.

'You've heard about the Barber, then?' Maciot said. 'So much for Kantrowe's precious treaty!'

'We're going back because of the attack.' Ico explained about her dream, about the use of magic and her hopes for the future.

Maciot listened thoughtfully and made no comment. She was grateful to him for not pointing out that what she was doing was full of dangers.

'What are *you* doing out here?' she asked, having said her piece.

'Funnily enough, I was looking for you.'

'Really? Why?'

'I'd heard rumours that Kantrowe was about to capture the Firebrands, and as soon as we noticed all the troops coming this way, I put two and two together. As a trader I have every right to travel when and where I please, so my actions should not have aroused any suspicions. I was hoping that at least some of you would escape, and wanted to be here to help if I could. It was a simple enough matter to follow the army, but then they all turned back in a hurry. I only found out overnight about the attack on Teguise, and decided to head for home. You obviously weren't in any immediate danger, and I have my own interests to look after.'

'Thank you for thinking of us,' she responded.

'Don't mention it. Where are Andrin and all the rest?'

'We had a disagreement,' Ico admitted ruefully.

'About returning to Teguise?'

'Yes. Do you think I'm being stupid?'

'I hope not. If you are, I'm likely to be implicated now.' He laughed. 'And then where will I be?'

At long last everything was ready, but the reluctance to leave seemed to touch everybody. The caves had been their home for over a month, and had represented a rare element of stability in the turmoil of their lives. Leaving them for another unknown destination was disturbing, especially when their leader was clearly troubled and the aftermath of his argument with Ico still hung in the air like poisonous smoke. The split had created much uncertainty and tension, and several of the Firebrands were unhappy about abandoning Vargo and Allegra.

Nino was to be their guide on the journey. He and Ico had slept in another promising group of caves on their way to Elva and, although they had not had the chance to explore them properly, the caves had the advantage of being closer to the sea and even more removed from any habitation.

The group were all above ground and about to set off when Andrin called the uplander to him.

'Nino, I'm sorry. I can't do this.'

'I know. I'd've told you to follow her if you hadn't decided for yourself.'

Andrin looked relieved.

'You'll be in charge,' he said. 'With me and Ico gone and Vargo lost, you're the obvious choice. Are you happy with that?'

'It's an honour. We'll be fine. Who will you take with you?'

'To be honest I'd rather go alone. I can move faster and try to catch up with them if I don't have to worry about anyone else.'

Nino nodded. 'Don't do anything too stupid,' he advised.

'No more than usual,' Andrin replied with a wry grin.

Although Andrin's announcement came as no surprise to most of his followers, it added another layer of unease to the morning's events. And even though Nino commanded general respect, in many ways he was still an outsider and few of them knew him well. With no indication as to when Andrin and Ico would return – or even contact them – the Firebrands' future seemed even more uncertain. Several volunteered to accompany Andrin but he refused, while expressing gratitude for their support, and set out alone while the main group moved out in the opposite direction.

Andrin was travelling light and moved quickly, but when he reached the road there was no sign of Ico and her companions. He wished again that he had Ayo's eyes to see through, but the eagle had vanished in the night, on an errand of his own. The road was deserted as far as he could see, except for a faint plume of dust rising from some travellers far to the north. He pushed aside all the far-fetched notions that his imagination immediately produced, and began to run.

***

Maghdim smelled the magic on the wind even before he reached the city. It enraged him, and made him feel sick. It was an abomination, a tampering with the natural order of the world, and he longed to snuff it out of existence. But he was wary now. Weather mages made dangerous enemies. Whoever had created the fog in Manrique Square had escaped his vigilance, so he would move cautiously against the magician responsible for this ill wind.

He arrived to find Teguise in chaos. The fire had raged through the night and all that morning, and efforts to slow its progress had been only partly successful. There were refugees everywhere, and several important quarters of the city were now under threat. These included the central district, where the Presidential Palace, the Senate, the Vestry and the Paleton were all situated, as well as the well-to-do residential districts to the north of that. Many people had already fled inland, fearing the worst, but most remained to fight both the fire and the pirates, and to protect their property as best they could. All army units had been stretched to breaking point, and the reinforcements that arrived with Maghdim's party were welcomed thankfully. It would be some time before the rest returned.

After a concise briefing from Mazo Gadette, Maghdim and his acolytes were sent to the harbour district. His job was to see if he could locate the source of the magic and counteract the unnatural wind. Although the breeze had got no stronger since Kantrowe had replied to the Barber's ultimatum, neither had it died away.

'We're stalling them on their demands for silver and crystals,' Gadette had told him, 'but we don't know how long it'll be before their patience runs out. We've already passed several deadlines, but they seem in no hurry – and meanwhile the fire is threatening to get out of hand. Senator Kantrowe wants you to make that your first priority.'

The area around the two warehouses was almost free from smoke, in marked contrast to the rest of the docks and the surrounding streets, but to Maghdim the air was fouler there than anywhere else. He began to organize his followers, and set to work.

Unnoticed in the continuing confusion, another sleek vessel sailed into the port and anchored far enough away from the fighting to remain safe. A small boat was lowered over the side, and a man was rowed ashore by four of his crewmen. He ran lightly up the steps to the jetty and was escorted to the main warehouse by some of the pirates on watch there. The Barber greeted the newcomer warmly.

'My friend, it is good to see you again.'

'Am I too late for the fun?'

'The best is over, but I'm sure we can arrange a few amusements for you.'

'Is everything going according to plan?'

'Perfectly. They're using delaying tactics over the ransom, of course, but we expected that. They will capitulate in the end, and meanwhile we have all this to compensate us.' The Barber waved an arm at the expanse of the warehouse. 'Take your pick.'

'I shall,' the newcomer said, grinning. 'How much time do we have?'

'Most of the White Guard won't be back for another two days – and even when they get here there won't be a lot they can do. Our position is secure.' The pirate leader paused. 'I trust my erstwhile brothers of the islands will not be disturbing us.'

'No. I made sure that they're at least three or four days' sail to the south,' his visitor replied. 'They'll be inspecting their new domains, no doubt,' he added, and laughed. 'We've no need to rush things here on their account. How is your wizard holding up?'

'Come and see for yourself.'

The Barber led the way to a small room guarded by two burly pirates. Inside, securely bound to a chair, was an incredibly ugly, wild-haired man whose twisted face filled with panic at the sight of the pirate leader.

'It's all right, Angel,' the Barber told him soothingly. 'I won't hurt you unless you let me down. You're safe as long as the wind blows from the southeast. You'll do that for me, won't you?'

Angel nodded fervently.

'And here's a good friend come to join us,' the Barber went on. 'Angel, you remember Jon Zophres, don't you?'

CHAPTER FORTY

The journey from Teguise to the caves had taken Ico and her friends eight days, but they had been travelling slowly then, mostly at night, in constant fear of capture and avoiding all roads. With the help of Maciot's camels the return journey was achieved in little more than a day and a half. This was in spite of the fact that they were forced to make several slight detours to avoid contact with the foot soldiers, who were marching back to the city at a slower pace.

Even from a distance, it was clear that Teguise had suffered a calamity. A thick pall of smoke hung over the city, drifting first inland and then, as it rose higher, back out to sea again, as if the wind was somehow blowing in two directions at once. However, it was not until they were within sight of the city walls that Ico and her companions noticed a stranger, even more ominous phenomenon. Mixed in among the smoke was what appeared to be a small cloud, whirling around as though trapped by a tornado. It was an almost dazzling white, and was illuminated periodically from within by what appeared to be flashes of lightning. Finally, as if to add one last bizarre touch to the scene, a rainbow appeared beneath the cloud.

'What the hell is that?' Maciot exclaimed. 'How can it be raining?' Apart from the area directly over Teguise, the sky was a clear blue.

Ico did not reply, but she knew that magic was involved somehow. Even so, she could not imagine how it could have produced such spectacular results. This was no illusion; this was a real storm.

As they had agreed earlier, Ico and the Firebrands left Maciot and his men outside the city. The senator might already be compromised, but he wanted to limit the number of people who saw them together, just in case he still had a part to play in Teguise. On foot again, Ico and the others made their way towards the centre of the disturbance – against the run of the human tide flowing away from the docks. Although she had made no effort to disguise herself, no one paid Ico any attention, not even any of the White Guard. Not surprisingly, everyone was preoccupied with other matters.

As she walked, Ico experienced several disconcerting flashbacks to her dream. A particular face in the crowd, a view as they turned a corner, the shape of a cloud above a specific rooftop – it seemed that anything could bring her memories vividly to life, if only for a moment. In a way, this confirmation that she was following a preordained path was as reassuring as it was frightening. Her comrades had no such reassurance, and were beginning to lose their earlier bravado. The dramatic turmoil in and above the city seemed on too grand a scale for their intervention to mean anything. Even Dani, the most vocal of them, had been quiet for some time now.

The closer they got to the harbour, the harder it became to make any progress. Although the crowds had thinned, both fire fighters and soldiers were running to and fro, and the noise and smoke were disorientating. The cloud overhead was invisible in the unnatural darkness, but the streets here were wet underfoot. Sudden squalls of rain obscured their vision, and occasional loud bursts of thunder made everyone nervous.

'This is hopeless,' Ico muttered.

'What are we supposed to *do*?' Dani asked.

'I'm not sure. All I know is that it involves magic – and I think we need to be down there,' she replied, pointing. 'Right next to the docks.'

The Firebrands regarded the open area she had indicated with some suspicion.

'There are archers everywhere,' one of them noted.

'Even the birds will have a hard time getting that close,' Dani added.

'There must be a way,' Ico stated. 'Perhaps Soo will be able to see it.'

After she gave the sparrowhawk her instructions, the Firebrands retreated to a relatively safe spot in the doorway of an abandoned, stone-built mansion. The bird returned quickly, with the news that she had been unable to get very close to her target. The weather was wild, with an impossible storm centred above two warehouses. That struck a chord with Ico.

Does one of the buildings have a green roof?

Yes. The larger of the two.

That's where I have to go. I saw it in my dream, but . . .

But what? Soo asked sharply.

Never mind, Ico replied. *Can you lead the way?*

During the second night of the attack, Maghdim had marshalled the negative powers of his own mind, along with the captive abilities of his acolytes, to oppose his unknown enemy. He had sensed a vague, unfocused mind, and had been frustrated by his own inability to strike at it directly. *He's a simpleton,* the anti-mage thought. *He's not even aware of the consequences of his own actions.*

The efforts of Maghdim and his team had had a noticeably dampening effect on the wind for a time, but their foe had then evidently increased his own magical pressure, and the battle had produced some wildly erratic conditions. The first wind had died away, then sprung back to life with renewed vigour, and had finally been transmuted into a whirlwind that created a towering, thunderous rain cloud. The potency of the weather magic had astonished and disgusted Maghdim, but he had noticed a slight lessening of its strength as the hours passed – and knew that in this extended meteorological wrestling match there could be only one winner. However, even though the rain had helped subdue the fires a little, the wind was still causing havoc, and his victory would come too late to save much of the city unless he were able to speed the process up. The physical source of the magic still eluded him and, if the stalemate was to be broken, Maghdim needed a first-hand sighting of his opponent. However, he had no intention of putting himself in danger. Someone else would have to do it. With that decision came the beginnings of a plan.

'Bring Fayna to me,' he ordered, and one of the guards ran to obey.

One of the interesting side effects of Maghdim's tincture was that it made most people extremely easy to hypnotize. He had long since perfected his technique, and so it was only a matter of minutes before Fayna had been given her instructions. She left at his signal, and the anti-mage settled back to see what would happen.

'It seems to me,' the Barber said, 'that it would've been safer for you to remain loyal to Kantrowe, rather than join forces with a renegade like me.'

'I've never been one to take the safest option,' Zophres replied, matching his companion's grin.

'I can see that.'

The two men were comfortably settled inside one of the inner rooms of the warehouse, taking advantage of some wine they had found in storage to reinforce their instinctive liking for each other. The night had been interesting, but the situation had stabilized now and they were waiting for Kantrowe to make the next move.

'People say I am invincible,' Zophres added, with a disparaging shrug. 'Certainly I've been lucky, but the life of an adventurer only means something if there is danger, risk and uncertainty. Paid employment, no matter how lucrative, becomes tedious in the end, and then I look for a new challenge. You provided it.'

'The brethren of the islands have a similiar philosophy,' the pirate said. 'It is only by testing ourselves that we prove we are alive.'

'Exactly. What's the point of being invincible if you never put it to the test?' the former envoy agreed, laughing.

'And if we can become rich in the process, so much the better.'

They raised their glasses and drank to the thought, and then the Barber changed the subject. 'Angel has a remarkable talent,' he observed. 'Tell me how you came to possess him.'

'I knew of him when I was a small boy,' Zophres replied. 'He scared the hell out of me then. Still does at times, though for different reasons. He was a talented seaman himself once but, after Zarzuelo defeated Madri, Angel left the navy and disappeared. Over the year he's been seen every so often in various ports, staring at the ships. Of course, most people shun him because of the way he looks, but that's only his shell. The real Angel is inside his mind, quite mad but also very powerful. I once saw him call up a wind squall to blow a stricken vessel away from rocks, and it was obvious then that he'd be a useful ally. I've discussed it with him, but he has no idea how he does it. He's completely open about it, though. He didn't even ask my name. I reckon magic like that is only possible in a mind that's at least partly destroyed. When I met you, I saw a perfect opportunity to use his talents. Then it was just a question of getting my colleagues to be on the lookout for him, invite him on board, and deliver him to you.'

'He didn't object when you set sail?'

'Yes, he did – very much. He kept saying that he couldn't go to sea without his master, whatever that means. He even threatened to capsize the ship, but he's too gentle a soul to actually do it. He abhors violence – which is one of the reasons he's so easy to control.'

'But he'd be unhappy if he knew what was happening here because of the wind he's been producing?'

'He'd stop it,' Zophres replied with certainty. 'Even threats wouldn't be much use then. Which is why we're better keeping him in the dark.'

'He's tiring, though, isn't he?'

'Looks like it. All magic exacts a cost, or so I'm told, so sooner or later he's bound to become exhausted.'

'We underestimated the enemy's strength,' the Barber noted, a slight undercurrent of criticism in his tone. 'What's the name of Kantrowe's pet sorcerer?'

'Maghdim. I've never met him. Until recently he was away in the west, doing the gods know what.'

'Let's hope Angel can hold out long enough.'

'How long until noon?'

'About an hour.' That was the time they had specified with their latest set of demands.

'If there's no response by then, we'll force Angel to become more aggressive,' Zophres decided. 'See if we can raise the stakes.'

'Agreed. In the meantime we'll start clearing out these warehouses,' the Barber decreed. 'If that's all we get, we'll still have done well.'

'And we can always come back once Angel has rested.'

They grinned at each other, tossed back the last of the wine and went to begin choosing their plunder.

***

Fayna walked unsteadily down the centre of the beleaguered street, heading erratically towards the warehouse. She was singing verses from an uncharacteristically vulgar song in between taking swigs from a bottle of rum. One side of her long skirt was in tatters, so that each step revealed the full length of her leg, and her blouse gaped open immodestly. None of the nearby soldiers made more than a token effort to stop her, and the pirate archers held their fire because she made an attractive and amusing spectacle. One of them called to the Barber's second in command.

'Cuero! Come and look at this.'

The pirate's eyes narrowed as he glanced out of the top-floor window. Cuero was young and ruthless, proud of his physical prowess and vain about his sharp-featured good looks. The only man he answered to was the Barber, and sometimes even that was grudging.

Below them Fayna was shouting now, looking up and waving the bottle.

'What's she saying?'

'She wants us to let her in. Says she wants to go with us.'

'Looks like she's ready for a little fun,' another buccaneer commented.

The pirates all glanced at Cuero, knowing of his liking for 'fun'. This whole adventure had been a novel experience to begin with, but the drawn-out negotiations and recent lack of fighting were beginning to pall. The girl offered a little entertainment at least.

'Rat, get down to the door and let her in,' Cuero told one of his men. 'Then bring her up here and we'll have some fun, whether she's ready or not.' He grinned as the others laughed approvingly. 'It's about time we saw some action.'

He then sent word to alert the archers, so that the chances of anyone else getting inside with the girl could be ruled out.

'On her own that little tart's no danger,' he explained, 'but we don't want to invite any of her friends in, do we?'

'You think it could be a trap?'

'If it is, it's a bloody stupid one,' Cuero replied, his eyes still fixed on the girl below.

'That's Fayna, isn't it?'

Ico nodded. Even from a distance she could see – or perhaps sense – the blank expression beneath the supposedly drunken bluster. Fayna had obviously been forced to swallow some of the tincture, and Ico shuddered at the memory of her own experience with the drug.

'She's never like that normally.'

'Her mind's not her own,' Ico said. 'She's being forced to act that way.'

'Why? What's going on?'

'I don't know, but I think it's time I found out.'

Her companions nodded, though she could see the uncertainty in their eyes. This was not the sort of fight they had envisaged, but she needed them to be strong now.

'I can't do this without you,' she told them. 'Is everyone ready?'

In the distance, a door opened briefly and Fayna was dragged roughly into the warehouse. As the door was slammed shut again, the Firebrands glanced at each other.

'We're ready,' Dani said.

Somewhere deep inside, a small, powerless part of Fayna was horrified by what she was doing and the things she was saying, but Maghdim's words dominated all her actions. This is what you will do.

Although the rum had burned her throat, it had had no discernible effect on her brain – but even in her hypnotic trance she retained enough sense to know that she ought to be terrified. As the pirates grabbed her and pulled her inside, another switch was thrown in her mind and thoughts implanted there rose to the surface. She tossed the bottle to one of the men, who caught it, his grin changing to an expression of surprise.

'Can I see the weather mage?' she asked.

'What?' one of her captors asked. 'Why'd you want to see him?'

'Magic makes me go all shivery inside.'

'We can make you feel like that without magic,' another pirate told her, and his companions laughed.

'Just let me see him, and I'll do anything you want,' she insisted.

'No chance,' Rat said. 'You're coming upstairs with us.'

'Oh, please!' she cried. 'Just for a moment.'

'What's the harm? Let her see. She looks worth it.'

'Yeah, why should that bastard Cuero have all the fun. We're the ones who got her in here.'

Rat hesitated, caught between the attractions of their arguments and his fear of Cuero.

'All right,' he decided eventually. 'Just for a moment.' He took Fayna's arm and marched her off, the others following.

The guards outside Angel's cell looked doubtful, but Rat shoved them aside and opened the door. Fayna stared into the gloom and saw two frightened, exhausted eyes gazing back at her. Another shadow thought enveloped her mind, and she froze. In that moment the pirates felt a sudden chill and stepped back instinctively. Outside the wind died away to nothing.

Maghdim felt the connection instantly, and saw his enemy clearly for the first time. Fayna's eyes were his eyes now. She had done her job and would soon be expendable. He prepared to strike the final crippling blow, to end this battle of wills once and for all, but just at that moment he was distracted by another surge of vile magic. What was more, he recognized its signature, the mental imprint contained in all sorcery, and he forgot all about the weather mage. He had another target now.

***

The black dragon walked upright, down a path of fire that sprang up from the cobbles beneath her taloned feet. Everyone who saw her was mesmerized, wondering where the creature could have sprung from – but if anyone chanced to meet the gaze of her dazzling yellow eyes they looked away quickly.

Inside the illusion that had been inspired by her dream and executed by her companions, Ico sensed the potency of her appearance. Wreathed in flames that did not burn, she walked slowly, adding all she could to the nobility of the dragon, and felt a tiny hint of the reverence they had once inspired. There was power here.

Her thoughts as she approached the warehouse were a mixture of doubt and confidence. She was sure she would get inside – after all, who was going to argue with a dragon? – but she had no idea what she was going to do then. The dream had not reached that far. Rescuing Fayna and defeating the magic being used to destroy the city had become her goals, but achieving them was another matter.

An eerie quiet descended on the scene as she reached the door that remained closed and bolted. It was as if the whole city was waiting and watching, holding its breath. Even the thunder was silenced.

'Open the door!' she roared in a deep, booming voice that was not her own.

There was no response, and she repeated her demand to no avail. Anger rose up within her, and she set her mind to magic of her own. Until then most of the imagery had been created by others, but she had grown into it now, and was involving her own talents. She stretched out a hand, saw a scaly clawed fist extend in front of her. It seemed so real, so much a part of her, and yet she knew it was only an illusion. Even so, she invested every grain of her own belief in the mirage, willing it into being. She had meant only to hammer on the door, to demand entrance, but when her alien fist slammed into the wood the impact was far greater than she had anticipated.

The door exploded, splinters of wood and iron flying in all directions as what was left crumpled on its hinges and fell inwards. Screams of pain and alarm came from within as Ico stepped over the threshold. Although she was reeling in astonishment, a small part of her was glorying in her sudden power – a power that was beyond her control now. She strode on, ignoring the pirates who were cowering from her or running for their lives, and went in search of her next challenge.

Fayna knew that she was being used. She felt a momentary pity for the deformed man who sat before her, bound to a chair. He was the object of her master's enmity – and he would soon be crushed. She winced as the air around her grew cold, sucking the life from everything. And then, abruptly, she was alone, abandoned, without purpose.

Angel looked up at her, and a faint hope sparked in his eyes. Fayna no longer knew where she was, nor why she had come there. She had been a link, a conduit for power, no more – and now that was lost. She did not know what to do.

'No!' Angel cried suddenly.

Something hit Fayna hard in the centre of her back, but she did not fall. She was distantly aware of a dull pain, but it hardly seemed to matter. There was something wrong with her breathing. No matter how hard she tried, she could not get any air into her lungs. She swallowed convulsively, hoping to clear the obstruction, then choked and felt the first touch of real fear. Looking down, she saw what looked like the blade of a long knife protruding inexplicably from her chest. The last thing she heard, before she fell forward into darkness, sounded like the harsh cry of a wounded crow.

Cuero pulled his sword from her body, wiped the blood from the blade, then turned away from the dead girl without a second glance and fixed his murderous glare upon Rat.

'I should skewer you next, you crackwit,' he grated. 'Couldn't you see what was happening?'

'I didn't—'

His reply was cut off by a blow to the side of his head from the flat of Cuero's sword which sent Rat sprawling.

'You didn't think!' Cuero began. 'You—'

'What's going on here?' the Barber demanded, arriving with Zophres at his side.

'I've taken care of it,' his lieutenant replied. 'She was trying to interfere with the mage.'

The Barber glanced at the ragged corpse on the floor, regarding it with contempt.

'You'd better see that Angel returns to his duties then,' he said evenly. 'The wind seems to have dropped.'

Cuero turned to do as he was told when an explosion from the far side of the now nearly empty warehouse made them all swing round.

Surrounded by a halo of flame, the dragon flew towards them.

There is some greater force at work here, Maghdim thought. Something he could not touch. It was a worrying idea, but he did not panic. All would become clear in due course. In the meantime he set his sights on the weather mage again – only to find that he was no longer there. Maghdim's conduit had vanished from his mental scope. What was more, the wind had suddenly risen to a howling shriek that fanned the flames of existing fires and brought embers back to life. Thunder boomed overhead as the tug of war was renewed in desperate earnest.

Ico was transported now. She *was* the dragon, in tooth and claw and flame. She could fly.

Most of the pirates had fled from the apparition but the

Barber, Zophres and Cuero stood their ground, their swords drawn. Even as she drew near, Ico could not help feeling a certain admiration for their foolish bravery. Her scales were impervious to their feeble blades and she could have crushed them all with a single blow – and yet they were still prepared to fight.

It was the sight of Angel, trussed up in the room beyond them, that made her hesitate. In that instant she knew that he was responsible not only for the wind but also for the earlier fog that had helped her escape. She realized too that he was being used for purposes that were not his own – and that was a violation, an abuse of magic she could not tolerate.

'Angel!' she cried in the dragon's deathly voice. 'You must stop this. Your wind is destroying Teguise.'

The weather mage stared at her in horrified amazement, and Ico could not be sure that he had heard or understood. In another moment she would be upon the three men who were guarding him and, once they were disposed of, she would help him escape.

The crooked bowl of Pajarito was full of the whispers of the sky. Ayo had been called there again but, as usual, he did not know why. On his arrival at the vast red crater, he had sought out the same boulder for his perch and waited. He had heard nothing but the unintelligible murmurings of the rock, and in the end he had called out himself. His question was the same as before.

Are the dragons still living?

On his earlier visit the answer he had received had been typically vague and enigmatic.

They have no wings, no eyes, no fire – but they dream still. And we do not forget our dreams.

This time, however, the oracle's reply was more direct, and the crater shook from the echoes of the voice of the sky.

The spirits of the dragons still live, Pajarito answered. *And they are angry.*

Ico fell to earth, alone, afraid and unprotected. The fire, the magic, the dragon were all gone – and she was left clutching at air as she crashed to the ground. As she sprawled there, helpless, she found the Barber's sword at her throat.

'You must teach me how to do that sometime,' he said with a smile.

Ico's breath had been knocked out of her, but even if it hadn't she still would not have known what to say. She couldn't understand what had happened, what had gone wrong. *This* had certainly not been a part of her dream.

'Angel's unconscious,' Cuero reported. 'He's out cold.'

'So you succeeded,' the Barber observed. 'Remarkable.'

Ico tried to reach inside herself for the magic, but there was nothing there. She knew she had not been responsible for Angel's collapse but she was too confused to say anything. Then she saw Fayna, and knew the extent of her failure.

'Let's go,' Zophres advised. 'We got most of what we came for. If the wind drops again, it won't be long before Kantrowe decides to risk an all-out attack.'

'Agreed,' the Barber said, and Zophres strode off, shouting orders.

'What about him?' Cuero asked, indicating the unconscious Angel.

'Leave him. We've enough to carry,' the Barber said, then turned back to look at Ico. 'We'll take her instead.'

CHAPTER FORTY-ONE

The eruptions that night were the most widespread and violent for thirty years, and Tiguafaya's entire volcanic range shook with the sound of the earth's protest. The rumbling was more of a vibration than a noise, so low pitched that it was almost beyond the boundaries of human hearing. A fire-born message was passed from mountain to mountain, as even long dormant craters awoke from their sleep and added their hoarse voices to the general outcry. The stars disappeared, replaced by a mottled patchwork of flame, smoke, steam and wind-blown ash, as the sky itself mirrored the havoc below.

Even from the relative safety of Teguise, people watched the pyrotechnic display in awe and fear, wondering what greater afflictions could possibly befall their country. In the firelands many fled for their lives as new lava flows threatened their homes. It would be several days before the last ash returned to earth, and some days more before a curious fact emerged from the chaos. No village, not even a single isolated farmhouse, had been totally destroyed, and no one had died as a direct result of the eruptions. The devastation of the land was extensive, but it seemed to the people of Tiguafaya that

358

the volcanoes' anger had been expressed as a warning, and not yet as retribution.

Long before that realization was made, however, the citizens of Teguise found themselves with more than enough to deal with. By the time morning came – with a spectacularly colourful sunrise – a degree of calm had been restored. The pirates had withdrawn, taking the last of their booty with them. Their retreat had been hampered by no more than a token effort by the White Guards. The soldiers, like everyone else, were just glad to see them go. The fire had been brought under control, now that the wind had turned back to the northwest and the fire fighters had access to water from the harbour, and the rest of the city was no longer in danger. All that was left was to count the cost of the damage and what had been stolen. Several facts were already clear. Some people had lost their lives, many were ruined, while others were homeless. However, the crisis seemed to bring out the natural resilience of the Tiguafayans, and that same morning saw the beginning of the city's recovery. Without much aid from their supposed leaders, the inhabitants of the capital set up shelters, arranged improvised hospitals and consoled the bereaved. Some belongings were retrieved from the smouldering ruins, and plans were drawn up for the start of the rebuilding. Even the army, whose failure to defend the city was neither forgotten nor forgiven, redeemed themselves, with the soldiers adding their considerable resources to the general effort.

The influence of the Senate, who should by rights have co-ordinated all these efforts, was conspicuous by its absence. Many senators were only concerned with their own losses – which in some cases were considerable – and almost all preferred to concentrate on their individual troubles before turning their minds to the overall picture. For Kantrowe the two were inseparable, and he knew he must move swiftly. Many of his most consistent supporters had suffered badly in the attack, and popular opinion was hardly likely to be sympathetic now that his treaty with the pirates had proved to be an abject failure. He could still rely on the loyalty of the White Guard and could fall back on the use of force if necessary, but that would be an admission of guilt – which was not Kantrowe's style. He needed first to understand what had gone wrong, and second to present the facts in such a way as to prevent outright rebellion. He had to reassert his authority both within the Senate and with the population as a whole. And to do that he needed some scapegoats.

Of those he had summoned, Maghdim was the first to present himself at the Vestry. The anti-mage was smiling slightly as he came in – which for him was a sign of celebration. Kantrowe found himself resenting the foreigner's high spirits and questioned him harshly about what had happened. Maghdim responded with a bold recitation of the facts that left the senator with several unanswered questions.

'So the dragon was an illusion?'

Maghdim nodded. He was sullen now, resenting the inquisition.

'Projected by whom?'

'I'm not sure,' the foreigner admitted, 'but it must have been someone outside our ring. However, what I can tell you is—'

'If it was just an image,' Kantrowe cut in, 'how was it able to smash the warehouse door?'

'Because there was a new surge of magic,' Maghdim replied, seething inwardly at the memory, 'but the so-called dragon was not the source. That creature wasn't real.'

'The source was this other power?' the senator went on. 'As such an *expert*, were you able to tell where it came from?'

'It was beyond human control, a freak of nature. Such phenomena occur at random,' Maghdim answered, hoping his master would not see through this screen of vague words to the ignorance beyond.

'So it wasn't controlled by the magicians who created the dragon?'

'No. It abandoned them as abruptly as it had come. It was then that I was able to strike, to make the last decisive attack. My cordon negated all magic in the area.'

'The cordon formed by your acolytes?'

'Yes.'

'I understand you lost one of them in the process?'

'She wasn't important. There are many more like her.'

'You should not be so careless of our resources,' Kantrowe warned. 'Don't forget, we have plans for them once these matters are resolved.'

'I'm aware of that,' the anti-mage replied coldly. 'If you had been able to subdue the Firebrands, such considerations would be of little consequence. We would have all the resources we need.' His expression remained neutral, but he saw his barb hit home and felt the glow of satisfaction return.

Kantrowe said nothing for a while, longing for the day when he no longer needed this impertinent foreigner. When he did speak, it was his turn to disconcert the other. 'What happened to the weather mage? Is he dead?'

'I don't think so.'

'Then where is he?' the senator asked sharply.

'Gone with the other pirates, I expect,' Maghdim replied awkwardly. In reality he had no idea. Then, speaking quickly to head off the obvious question, he added, 'But after the blow I dealt him he won't be in any hurry to come back. I may even have destroyed his abilities for ever.'

'Let's hope so,' Kantrowe remarked. 'You seemed to find him a difficult opponent.'

'You would have found him even more difficult without my help,' Maghdim pointed out with deliberate calm. Then, with a certain sadistic pleasure, he chose to pass on his last piece of information – which his master's earlier interruption had prevented him from revealing. 'The signature of the magic at the dragon's heart might interest you.'

'Signature? What do you mean?'

'All sorcery carries the mark of its originator's mind. It's as unique as the patterns of skin on a man's fingertips.'

'I thought you said you weren't sure who was projecting the image.'

'I'm not. But I know who was inside.'

'Who?' Kantrowe demanded.

'Ico Maravedis.'

'What!' the senator exploded, rising involuntarily from his chair on hearing the name of his nemesis. 'You're sure?'

Maghdim nodded, secretly enjoying the spectacle of his employer's fury.

'Where is she now?'

'Unless your White Guards found her body in the warehouse, I presume she was captured by the pirates. Either way, she's unlikely to bother you again.'

Kantrowe strode to the door and wrenched it open. 'Get Chinero here!' he yelled. 'Now!'

One of his secretaries replied that the captain had just arrived and was on his way up. The senator turned back to Maghdim. 'Anything else I should know?' he said angrily.

'Not that I can think of,' the anti-mage replied mildly.

'Then get out.'

Maghdim went and was soon replaced by Chinero, whose face was drawn and whose usually immaculate uniform was crumpled and smeared with soot.

'Was anyone left behind in the warehouses or on the docks?' Kantrowe asked as soon as the door was shut.

This was not the point at which the captain had been expecting to begin his report, and it took his weary brain a few moments to recall the necessary information.

'About twenty bodies,' he said. 'Mostly our own men, but

there were a few pirates our archers had managed to pick off.'

'Any women?' Kantrowe cut in impatiently.

'Only one. The acolyte Maghdim sent in. She'd been—'

'No others?'

'No.' The soldier looked puzzled. 'Should there have been?'

Kantrowe swore, ignored the question and began pacing the room. 'Was anyone left alive in there?' he asked.

'A couple of the dockers were badly wounded, but they might still make it. And there was one warehouseman tied to a chair. He was a real mess. He'd been tortured and was deeply unconscious.'

'Where are they now?'

'In one of the hospitals.'

'Find them,' Kantrowe ordered. 'I need to talk to them.'

'Why?'

'Just do it!' the senator shouted furiously, then relented and called the captain back to explain. Chinero was almost as astonished as his commander had been by Maghdim's intelligence, but it tied in with some other information he had gained.

'She wasn't the only Firebrand back in Teguise,' he said. 'We arrested six of them during the night. They could have been the ones who—'

'See if they confirm Maghdim's story,' Kantrowe snapped. 'But find the men from the warehouse first. And see whether anyone saw the pirates taking a woman away. The rest of your report can wait.'

As Chinero hurried away Mazo Gadette came in, as if on cue, and recognized his master's agitation at a glance. Even so, Kantrowe's first question caught him by surprise.

'Do we know where the Firebrands are now?'

'The last thing Maghdim told me was that they were moving south again, but now I hear that some of them were here last night, so they must have split up.'

'You don't know the half of it.' Kantrowe explained about Ico's part in recent events, with a small part of his brain taking some pleasure in the fact that – for once – he was able to tell his aide something he didn't already know.

'There are several contradictory rumours circulating about that dragon,' Gadette commented after he had absorbed the unexpected news. 'Some seem to think that it saved us by defeating the pirates and driving them away. Others are saying that it was a sign that our enemies are in league with supernatural forces. Either way, it doesn't make us look very good.'

'Well, we'll have to change that,' Kantrowe stated, regaining his habitual decisiveness. 'It shouldn't be too difficult.' He paused. 'Is there any news of Zophres?'

'None,' the aide replied gravely. 'Do you think . . .?'

'With him, who can tell? One way or another that maniac is going to have some questions to answer next time we come face to face. What about Zarzuelo and the Lawyer?'

'They're on their way north. Too late, of course, but it should make any repetition of this attack impossible.'

'Unless they double-cross us too,' Kantrowe said bitterly. 'Did Verier manage to save any of the ships he was building?'

'Two berths were completely burnt out, but the rest are salvageable. We'll have our own warships before too long.'

'Not before time,' the senator remarked. 'Any news from the west?'

'It's too early,' the aide said. 'But messengers have been sent to all the mines. We'll know soon enough.'

Kantrowe nodded. Having gathered as much intelligence as he could, it was now time to decide on his next step. 'It could have been worse,' he sighed. 'At least we didn't cave in and pay any ransom to those sea-scum.'

'Compensating the merchant community should be simple enough in the long run.'

'And the fire was kept within reasonable boundaries,'

Kantrowe added. 'If it had gone on . . .'

'We'll claim Maghdim's victory as our own, of course,' Gadette said.

'Of course,' the senator agreed. 'Explaining how the pirates came to attack us in the first place will be the hard part. We're supposed to have a treaty with them.'

'We can claim it was just the last desperate throw by some rogue element, with massive reinforcements from some foreign power,' Gadette suggested. 'There were far more ships in the Barber's fleet than we can account for – and the extra vessels must have come from somewhere.'

'I like that,' Kantrowe said, admiring his aide's ingenuity.

They both knew that the people of Tiguafaya needed little encouragement to succumb to xenophobia. Most foreigners were regarded with a suspicion that had its roots in their earliest history. 'Any chance that it's true?'

'I doubt it. Even the empire has some standards when it comes to choosing its allies.'

'So where *did* they come from?'

'I don't know,' Gadette admitted frankly. 'But we'll find out eventually.'

'On top of that, we can blame a lot of this fiasco on the Firebrands,' Kantrowe went on. 'Half the army was away because of them. The pirates would never even have got ashore if it hadn't been for that.'

'And by creating another dragon they played into our hands again,' Gadette added. 'No one will have any trouble linking that to last night's eruptions.'

'And we can use the six Chinero captured as witnesses.' The senator paused thoughtfully. 'Is it enough?'

'I'm sure you'll be very convincing.'

'I'm sure you're right.' Kantrowe smiled at the impassive expression on his aide's emaciated face. 'Call an emergency meeting of the Senate for this afternoon. And make sure there's a full turn-out. I want everyone there, even if they have to be brought in at sword point.'

Two hours later, amid the stream of messages that came to his office, a despatch arrived from Chinero. It contained both good and bad news. The bad news was that the two wounded dockers had died of their injuries, and that the guards had been unable to locate the warehouseman. The physicians who had dealt with him had said that he'd recovered consciousness and then just wandered off in the general confusion. Soldiers had now been detailed to search for him, but had had no success so far.

Kantrowe growled in annoyance at this, but read on grimly.

There were no confirmed reports of any woman having left with the pirates, but that was hardly conclusive. The one thing Chinero could say with absolute certainty was that Ico Maravedis had entered the warehouse – the captured Firebrands had confirmed Maghdim's information – but she had not been there when the soldiers finally reoccupied the docks. The captain was also prepared to swear that she had not escaped by land. The good news was that this left only two possibilities; either she was dead and her body was now floating with the other debris in the waters of the harbour or, more likely, she had been carried off by the pirates.

Kantrowe allowed himself a slight grin of satisfaction. Pirates were not generally known for their kind treatment of female prisoners. Ico Maravedis might soon be wishing that she had died in the sacrificial fire after all.

CHAPTER FORTY-TWO

Long before he had reached his destination, Andrin's journey had taken on a nightmare quality. He had driven himself to the limit of his physical capabilities and, when the walls of Teguise finally came into view, he was exhausted. Darkness was closing in as he entered the city, but at least the sky was peaceful now. The night before, the western horizon had been etched in fire and the ground had trembled beneath his feet. Sleep – even if he had wished for it – had been impossible. He had tried not to think about what these latest eruptions might mean, concentrating instead on his absolute need to see Ico again.

He found the city in the aftermath of a massive upheaval, and learnt a little of what had happened from the rumours and gossip that filled the streets. There was no doubt in his mind that Ico had been in the middle of such events, and he wondered if she had had anything to do with the dragon everyone was talking about.

He headed towards the harbour, which took him close to his old home, and when he saw the devastation caused by the fire he felt obliged to make a small detour to see whether it was still standing. It was not. The entire street had vanished;

all that was left were a few blackened timbers and piles of still-smoking rubble. Identifying the remains of his own house was difficult but, when he succeeded, Andrin realized that his parents must be dead. His father would not have been able to escape, and – in spite of their enmity – his mother would never have left him. He felt more alone than ever, and his longing to find Ico became even more agonizing. If he lost her too, there would be no point to anything. He turned his back on the dismal scene and walked away.

Surprisingly, the area immediately surrounding the epicentre of the pirate attack had been left relatively unscathed by the fire. There were many other telltale signs of conflict, however – smashed doors and windows, discarded broken arrows, bloodstains and, most dramatic of all, black scorch marks on the cobbles in the shape of taloned feet. Andrin tried to remain inconspicuous and to eavesdrop as much as he could, but he soon lost patience with such careful behaviour and began to ask questions of anyone who would listen. He was unconcerned by the fact that he might be recognized, and even approached some of the soldiers – but no one could give him any information that might relate to Ico. Hopelessly, he searched as much of the area as he could, with a similar lack of results, then paused to consider his options.

It was possible that Ico had already left the city again, but Andrin did not think that very likely. So, if she *was* still in Teguise, where would she have gone? Three possibilities came to mind; her father's house, Maciot's home, or one of the Firebrands' old hide-outs. Following a hunch, Andrin plumped for the first of these and made his way to the merchants' district. Damage here had been minimal, and many of the streets were eerily deserted. A lamp burned in an upstairs room of the Maravedis house, giving him a little hope. He knocked at the door and, when there was no response, threw stones at the shutters above. Eventually they opened a crack, throwing a thin arc of light across the street below.

'Who is it?' Atchen asked in a querulous voice. 'What do you want?'

'Is Ico there?' Andrin called back.

'No, she isn't! She's been gone for months, and she wouldn't be welcome here anyway.' The housekeeper's venomous tone was disconcerting. 'That young lady's brought nothing but grief on her poor father.'

'You've not heard from her at all?' Andrin persisted.

'Not once, the inconsiderate little minx. What is it you want with her?' Atchen peered suspiciously into the darkness.

'I just need to see her, to make sure she's all right.'

'Then you'd better ask her Firebrand friends, hadn't you. That's who she ran off with, to the shame of us all.' The shutters were closed again with a decisive bang.

Andrin left. It was obvious that Atchen had been telling the truth, and there was no point in continuing the conversation. He could have asked her to wake Diano, or even broken in to see for himself, but he knew Ico was not there.

He was rather more circumspect in his approach to Senator Maciot's house, watching it from the shadows for some time before creeping up to a side door. For a while no one answered his cautious knocking, but then he heard the sound of fluttering wings in the air above him and, looking up, Andrin caught a flash of Tao's iridescent plumage. A few moments later, the door was opened by Maciot himself and Andrin was ushered inside.

The subsequent conversation, over some much needed food and drink, filled in many of the gaps in Andrin's knowledge – how and when Ico had arrived in Teguise, details of the pirate attack and their eventual retreat – but, to his near despair, left him none the wiser as to where she was now.

'You didn't make any arrangements to contact her again?' he asked helplessly.

'She knows where I am,' Maciot replied. 'It was up to her.'

'I'd better keep looking then.' Andrin stood up, even though his legs felt like lead.

'Wait a bit. There's more. I don't know where Ico is, but I *can* tell you what happened to her companions.'

Andrin sat down again with a bump.

'What?'

'They were captured by the White Guard. Kantrowe paraded them in front of the Senate this afternoon, to back up his story. A pretty bedraggled bunch they were, too.'

Andrin swore wearily and put his head in his hands. Maciot gave him details of the meeting, not bothering to hide his disbelief at some parts of Kantrowe's tale.

'So we get blamed again,' Andrin grumbled miserably.

'Looks like it. Most of the Senate swallowed it whole, and there'll be more proclamations issued by morning to make sure everyone gets the message.'

They sat in silence for a while.

'How many of them were there, the prisoners I mean?' Andrin asked abruptly, trying to remember how many Firebrands had gone with Ico.

Maciot thought back.

'Six,' he said eventually. 'Which means that one of them is dead or missing.' He could have added, 'Like Ico,' but did not.

'What'll happen to them?'

'They're under sentence of death, but I doubt it'll come to that. If they really did create that dragon, then they're far too valuable to waste.'

'And Kantrowe didn't mention Ico?' Andrin asked.

'No,' Maciot confirmed. 'But he may have his own reasons for that.'

'Do you think . . .?'

'If she'd been captured, he wouldn't have been able to resist showing her off,' the senator reassured him. 'She's out there somewhere.'

Andrin glanced at his host, grateful for his optimism.

'You should be careful yourself,' Maciot added. 'Whatever's happened to Ico, you'd be quite a prize now.'

'I don't care,' Andrin whispered, 'unless I find her.'

'Then be careful, for her sake. That young lady is pretty resourceful and if she's escaped she won't thank you for getting yourself killed.'

Even in his depressed state Andrin could see the sense of that. 'I'll be careful,' he promised.

'Why don't you sleep here for what's left of the night? You look as if you need the rest.'

Andrin shook his head. 'I'll rest when I've found her,' he said. 'Besides, I can move more easily at night.'

'Fair enough. I don't know how long this house will remain safe, but you're welcome here any time.'

'Thank you. I . . .' Andrin shrugged, having run out of words.

'At least there's one good thing to have come out of this,' Maciot remarked, as they both stood up.

'What?'

'Your claim that the Firebrands can deliver effective magic won't be disputed now. Anyone who saw what that dragon did to the warehouse door can't help but be convinced.'

'But then the volcanoes erupted. That will have messed things up.'

The senator nodded ruefully. 'I'll do what I can,' he said. 'Good luck.'

Two hours later, after an increasingly desperate search, Andrin found the sign he was looking for. It was a simple chalk mark on a particular kerb stone and although it did not include Ico's sign, it directed him to one of the cellars where the Firebrands used to gather. When he got there and crept down the steps into darkness, it was so silent and still that he thought he must have been mistaken.

'Ico?' he called softly. 'Are you there?'

His heart leapt when there was a small movement from the far corner of the room, and he hurried over.

'It's me. Andrin. Are you all right?'

Groping in the darkness, his hands encountered cloth and cool flesh beneath but he knew, in that one heartbreaking instant, that this was not his love.

'Andrin?' said a hoarse voice. 'What're you doing here?'

'Dani? Is that you? Are you hurt?' Andrin's fingers felt the encrusted stains on his friend's clothes.

'A few cuts. Think I've broken a couple of ribs, too. Do you have any water?'

'Do you know where Ico is?' Andrin asked, unable to wait any longer.

'At sea,' Dani replied dejectedly. 'The pirates took her.'

In that instant, Andrin felt as if all the breath had been kicked out of him. A lump of iron the size of an orange had lodged in his throat, and his whole body was numb. His brain simply refused point blank to accept what he had heard, merely repeating a litany of impotent denials. It can't be true. Please, don't let it be true. Please, no.

'I'm sorry,' Dani whispered. 'We tried—' He began coughing weakly, wincing in pain at every movement of his chest.

For the next few minutes Andrin moved blindly, without thought, shutting out all feeling. He lit a taper, found some water for Dani and helped him drink it. He rewound some of the improvised bandages and warmed his companion's cold hands between his own – even though his blood seemed to have turned to ice.

'Tell me what happened,' he said quietly through gritted teeth.

Dani did as he was told, his voice faltering. He became animated only when he described their actions after seeing Fayna taken into the warehouse.

'The dragon was amazing!' he croaked. 'And we won. The storm stopped right after that. Ico beat them.'

Andrin chose not to tell him that others had placed a different interpretation on events. The Firebrands would get no credit, whatever the truth was.

'And afterwards?' he prompted.

'It was a mess. *All* the magic vanished. There was nothing we could do. I've no idea what happened.' Dani paused, catching his breath painfully. 'The pirates ran back to their ships, and the soldiers chased them. We went too, but it was too late to help Ico.'

'You saw her being taken?'

'Yes. At least I think it was her.'

'You're not sure?' Andrin asked, clutching at straws.

'Who else could it have been? Fayna was dead. But it was all so confused. We'd been recognized by then, and the White Guard grabbed hold of us. I think I was the only one who got away.'

'So you could have been mistaken?'

'It looked like Ico, and Sta – my crow – said that Soo flew out to sea after their ships. She wouldn't have done that unless . . .'

Andrin slumped, his last hope gone. In a frozen black trance he helped Dani to his feet and began the slow, painful journey to Maciot's house, where the Firebrand might find the care he so obviously needed.

Another part of Andrin's consciousness was far away, impotently raging against fate and thrashing around in a sea of regret. The one thought he could not escape – but dared not confront – was the idea that he might never see Ico again. The manner of their parting had been so cruel, with such bitterness and so many unkind and unjust words, that it made their separation even more painful. The thought that they might never have a chance to heal the rift was unbearable.

He wanted to howl, to scream, to tear his clothes and punch the stone walls with his bare fist – but he did none of those things. His body went on regardless, unaware that his heart had already died.

CHAPTER FORTY-THREE

'Well, what do we do now?' Allegra asked.

The euphoria of their escape had worn off, and they were beginning to recognize their predicament.

'If Ico and Andrin have gone to Teguise,' Vargo replied, 'then that's where I should be.'

During the course of a long and convoluted conversation with Ero and Lao he had learnt about the White Guard surrounding the caves, their inexplicable withdrawal and the subsequent departure of the Firebrands in two different directions. The reasons for the split were still not clear to Vargo, in spite of his persistent questioning of the increasingly perplexed birds, but it seemed obvious to him where his primary loyalties lay. However, Allegra had other ideas.

'And how do you propose to get there?' she asked. 'We've no transport, no provisions, nothing! We don't even know where we are!'

'The birds can guide us,' he said defensively.

'Forgive me for saying this, but those two may not be the world's most reliable navigators just now.' She bit back her opinion that the birds were almost as crazy as he was. 'And whatever's going on in Teguise must be dangerous, or they'd *all* be going. You're in no fit state to walk into the middle of a battle.'

'But Andrin and Ico—'

'Won't be in any position to help you. They won't even know you're there – assuming we get that far. There'll be soldiers everywhere on the road north.'

'They're my friends,' he protested.

'And so am I,' she retorted passionately. 'Andrin and Ico can look after themselves. They'd want you to do the same.'

Vargo looked at her, realizing that he had underestimated her. Although he had grown to take Allegra's care and attention for granted, he had to admit that he knew very little about her. Sudden shame made him feel awkward. 'I'm sorry, Cat,' he said softly. 'What do you think we should do?'

'Go back to the caves,' she answered promptly. 'The birds said the main party were planning to leave. For all we know, Nino might have delayed their departure for some reason. We should check whether they've really gone, see if they've left any supplies we can use – and that way we'd at least have somewhere safe to sleep tonight. We can decide what to do next in the morning, once we've got our bearings.'

Vargo thought that this seemed to be choosing to do nothing, but Allegra sounded so definite and so sure of herself that he merely nodded his acquiescence.

Privately, Allegra had already decided that they would set out to follow Nino and the main group the next day, but she kept that to herself for the moment. She knew that Vargo's memory was unreliable at the best of times, especially so now, and she had no wish to have to argue with him twice over the same subject. Persuading him once was going to be hard enough.

Allegra's doubts over the birds' navigational skills proved to be well founded. They tried to work as a team, one flying ahead while the other relayed information to their link, and then swapping roles. Unsurprisingly, Lao proved to be the more practical of the two – Ero could not grasp the concept that humans had to travel *on* the ground, rather than above it – but even the sandpiper was hesitant and sometimes ambiguous in his instructions.

Don't you remember the way you came? Vargo asked in exasperation when they were led into yet another patch of sharp and unstable lava.

No, Lao answered. *The dancer led us, but not with our eyes.*

Ero's answer to the same question proved even more enigmatic.

Hopping, he replied breezily. *One shiny thing to another.*

Crystals? Vargo guessed.

No. Inside.

Inside what?

Me, the hoopoe answered. *Can we sing now?*

Vargo laughed, despite his confusion. It was impossible to remain downcast in the presence of Ero's irrepressible high spirits, especially when the bird went into one of his airborne displays, all flashing feathers and absurd swerves and loops.

'You love him, don't you?' Allegra said, watching the deliberately erratic flight.

'I suppose I do. I've never really thought about it.'

'Is it far now? We seem to have been walking for ages.'

'I've no idea. We could be lost for all I know.'

'Who do you think this "dancer" is?' she asked, hoping to divert them for a few moments from their depressing lack of progress.

'I haven't a clue,' Vargo replied. 'I don't think they do either. But whoever it is, we owe him a debt of gratitude for leading the birds to us. I know they're not ideal, but without them . . .'

'Do you think it's the same person who lit our way out of the caves?' she asked.

'The delicate stars,' he whispered. 'Maybe.'

'You're not telling me everything, are you?'

'What do you mean?' he said, and his surprise seemed genuine.

'Never mind,' she replied, and would not be drawn.

Eventually, much to their relief, they reached some terrain

that they recognized and were able to guide themselves towards one of the entrances to the cave system. It took only a brief exploration to convince them that it had indeed been abandoned and, although there were some supplies left behind, there were only a few stale scraps of food. By the time they had gathered what little there was dusk had fallen, and they settled down to sleep as best they could, intending to make an early start the next morning.

In the dead of the night, a faint glow suffused the cavern and a dark shape emerged silently from the shadows. He gazed at the still sleeping couple with sad brown eyes, then set something down on the stone floor and left as stealthily as he had arrived. The crystal light faded.

In the morning, when she awoke, Allegra found a small pile of ripe figs on the ground next to where she lay. After she had overcome her shock and fear, she gratefully accepted the bounty – but could not help glancing at every shadow, wondering if they were being watched. Vargo did not comment on the unexplained arrival of the fruit, but ate his share placidly. When Allegra told him that they ought to follow Nino, he accepted the decision with an equal serenity, and they set out as the sun rose.

Allegra surprised herself by proving to be adept at tracking. No matter how careful they were, a large group could not trek across a lava field without leaving some signs, and the trail was easy enough to follow once she knew what she was looking for; scrape marks on the rock, crushed patches of lichen, an occasional footprint in the black gravel – all these things were signposts in the wilderness, and common sense did the rest.

Ero and Lao acted as scouts and lookouts, although both made detours on their own behalf whenever they spotted a possible source of food. Ero even brought back a particularly plump grub and ceremoniously offered it to Allegra. She was charmed, in spite of the fact that her half-empty stomach churned at the thought of eating such an unappetising morsel. Vargo watched the exchange with amusement.

'Don't you want it?' he asked.

'I'll have to be a lot hungrier than I am to eat that,' she replied, pulling a face.

What's she saying? Ero sounded affronted.

She thanks you for the thought, but we'll find our own food, Vargo replied, and then Allegra turned his silent words into the truth by speaking herself.

'But tell Ero I appreciate the offer.'

The hoopoe swallowed the grub whole. He had never understood why humans cut up and burnt their food when it tasted so much better fresh.

Yummy, he remarked in parting. *Wriggly.*

That night, their shelter was a less than comfortable hollow in the middle of nowhere. They were both tired and hungry, but all that was forgotten when the eruptions began. They clung to each other, then moved to higher ground for safety as the lava field shook and rattled all around them. Streaks of fire coloured the night sky, and Vargo watched as if mesmerized. Allegra wondered whether he was looking for omens, but said nothing. No new lava threatened their position, but they could not even consider sleeping. They merely sat side by side and waited until the multicoloured dawn gave them enough light to move on.

Over the next two days, Vargo occasionally lapsed into incoherence, babbling about music, dragons, and the ocean. He sometimes had long, animated but incomprehensible conversions with voices Allegra could not hear, but which clearly came from neither of his links. At these times she humoured him, keeping her friend from absentmindedly coming to harm as their journey continued. And then, at last, Lao brought the news Allegra had been praying for.

'Lao says he's met one of the other birds,' Vargo reported. 'The new camp is only a few hour's walk away.'

Nino and several others came out to meet them, and the reunion was joyful. Everyone had felt bad about having to abandon

Vargo and Allegra while there was still a chance of their being alive, and because many had convinced themselves that the missing pair must be dead, their reappearance was welcome indeed.

Their immediate physical needs were seen to at once, and they were brought up to date on recent events. The news of the Barber's attack on Teguise came as a shock to Vargo, although it did explain much that he had not understood before. The report of Andrin and Ico's dreadful row disturbed him, and he wished again that he had been able to follow them to the city. But he knew it would be pointless now. He would have to wait, like everyone else.

'You've done well here,' he observed, glancing round the cavern in which they were sitting.

'Considering we've been here less than a day, it's not too bad,' Nino replied. 'There's enough water, and we're near the sea. Some of the birds have already been fishing. There was one problem, but we've hopefully sorted that out.'

'What was that?' Allegra asked, thinking of the hairy beast she thought she had seen in the other caves.

'We found a nest of dormant fireworms in one of the inner chambers,' Nino told her. 'But we froze them out. It's clear now, at least as far as we've explored, and the crystals are set up. Still, it makes me shudder when I think that Ico and I slept here on our way to Elva.'

Vargo went cold at the idea, and could find nothing to say.

'Of course we don't have the space or the conveniences of the old place,' Nino went on, 'but it will do.'

'Nor are we surrounded by White Guards,' someone else pointed out.

'True enough,' Nino said. 'They'll be back in Teguise by now and, with luck, they won't have time to bother about us for a while.'

'I wonder what's going on there,' Allegra said, voicing the thoughts of them all.

CHAPTER FORTY-FOUR

The soldiers came to Maciot's house at dawn. Although Tao warned him of their approach, the White Guard had the doors covered by the time he was able to rouse his guests.

'Go down to the cellar,' he instructed them in an urgent whisper. 'There's a seat in an alcove at the end of the third aisle. Both of you get on it, then pull the iron wall bracket down sharply. Got that?'

Andrin nodded blearily, still half cocooned in sleep, and shook his friend awake. Dani opened his eyes reluctantly – they had only managed a few hours rest. The whole house seemed to shake as someone began hammering on the front door, demanding entrance.

'I'll stall them as long as I can,' Maciot hissed. 'Hurry!'

Dani groaned, but managed to get up and shuffle to the stairs. He moved stiffly, bent double like an old man, wincing with every step. Maciot waited until they were on their way down to the cellar, ignoring the increasingly strident calls from outside. When he finally opened the door it was to find a burly guard hefting an axe, about to start smashing the wooden panels. The senator glanced up at the now stationary blade, then down at the startled eyes of the soldier.

'Don't tell me,' he remarked pleasantly. 'You're auditioning for the role of statue, right?'

The axe was lowered slowly, and the embarrassed guard stepped aside as Chinero came forward.

'Is this really necessary, Captain?' Maciot enquired, his smile fading.

'I have orders to search your premises,' Chinero replied shortly. 'Step aside.'

'On what grounds?' the senator asked, not moving.

'You have been seen with suspected traitors.'

'And naturally I invited them to sleep here. You must think me very stupid.'

'Step aside,' the captain repeated, and pushed past.

Several of his men followed, and he organized their search. Two soldiers ran down the steps to the cellar.

'There's no one here except me,' Maciot said. 'My servants only come in during the daytime.'

'This is a big house for just one man,' Chinero observed.

'I prefer my privacy.' He winced as a crash sounded from one of the upstairs rooms. 'What exactly are you looking for?'

Chinero ignored the question, merely walking from one ground-floor room to another and listening to his men's progress. Maciot followed, dreading a sudden cry from below. It never came.

'There's no one here, sir,' the last of the soldiers reported.

To his credit, Chinero did not query the statement. His men were the best of an elite troop, and they knew their jobs.

'I trust I'll be reimbursed for any of these quite unnecessary damages,' Maciot said.

The captain gave him a malevolent, contemptuous glare, spat on the floor beside the senator's feet and led his men away. Maciot breathed a sigh of relief, knowing that it was not a lack of evidence that had prevented his own arrest, but his influence among other powerful citizens. Even that would be no protection soon if Kantrowe was allowed to continue as he was doing.

He closed the door carefully and then, when he was certain that the soldiers had gone, went down to the cellar to make sure no trace had been left by the Firebrands' hurried exit. The hidden tunnel had not been used in decades, but he had never been more grateful for the foresight of one of his ancestors in having it dug.

Andrin had shoved Dani on to the stone seat, knowing that any discomfort was outweighed by the prospect of capture. Sitting himself, he had reached up and yanked at the old bracket, which had originally been designed to hold a torch. He had not known what to expect, and the smooth, silent operation of the mechanism took them both by surprise. The lever and their weight on the seat combined to set pulleys and counterweights in motion and, as they sank, the stone wall behind them rose, revealing a dark space beyond. They half fell, half scrambled through, then crouched down as the ingenious apparatus went into reverse and lowered the stone slab again, leaving them in total darkness.

'Keep still,' Andrin whispered.

Dani's breathing was harsh and ragged but he did not complain, settling himself to wait as best he could. They heard movement on the other side of the wall as the guards searched the cellar, and Andrin braced himself to fight in case the secret door was discovered. It was only when the noise of the soldiers receded that he relaxed a little and began to wonder what they should do next.

'Is this just a cell, or is there another way out?' Dani asked quietly, echoing Andrin's thoughts.

'I'll find out.'

After a short investigation, feeling his way around with hands and feet, Andrin returned to Dani's side.

'It's a tunnel. Let's go.' Even if they could get back into the cellar, there was no guarantee that some guards had not been left on duty – and, leaving aside considerations of their own safety, they owed Maciot too much to risk betraying him.

Their progress was painfully slow – in Dani's case literally so – but the narrow tunnel was at least free from obstructions, running more or less straight for a hundred paces or so.

'This is worse than the caves,' Dani muttered, wiping cobwebs away from his face. 'Where d'you think it goes?'

'I think we're about to find out,' Andrin told him.

The tunnel had ended abruptly in what, at first touch, seemed to be a blank wall. Further exploration revealed iron hand rails embedded in the stone to form a ladder. Looking up, Andrin could still see nothing.

'I'll go up and check it out,' he said. 'Then come back for you.'

After a short climb, his raised hand found a heavy wooden trap-door. After pushing at it unsuccessfully for a while, he found the bolts that secured it and then discovered that it opened easily. Although it was quite dark overhead, there were a few welcome cracks of light. As he pushed the door back further, several objects slid on the floor and fell into the shaft.

'Hey!' Dani called softly. 'What's going on?'

'Sorry,' Andrin whispered.

Dani stooped to pick up one of the things that had fallen on him and couldn't help grinning. It was a lady's shoe.

As Andrin pulled himself up, he found himself enmeshed in cloth. He tried to push it aside, wondering at the soft and silky textures, but it was a few moments before he realized that he had emerged inside a wardrobe. Eventually he found the catch, opened the doors a crack and peered out. It was a room unlike any other he had ever seen before, but it did not take too much imagination to recognize its purpose. Escape might not have been the reason for the tunnel's construction after all.

The decorations were gaudy, a musky scent filled the air, and the paintings on the wall spoke for themselves. The space was dominated by a huge bed but, thankfully, there was no one in it. Andrin was about the climb down again when Dani's head appeared in the trap door.

'Where are we?'

'Unless I'm very much mistaken,' Andrin replied, 'we're in a whorehouse.'

'Oh good. I'd like two blondes please.'

'In your state, even one would be enough to kill you.'

The Firebrands' leader was smiling as he helped his companion into the room and closed the trap-door again. Dani looked around as Andrin set the wardrobe to rights and shut the doors.

'Let's hope she doesn't count her shoes,' he remarked. 'Now what do we do?'

They both froze as the bedroom door opened, but there was no time to react before a woman came in. She did not see them at first, because she was looking over her shoulder and laughing at something her companion had said, but then she turned back and let out a piercing scream. The man behind her pushed past, a thunderous expression on his handsome face.

'What the—' His gaze held on Andrin. 'You!'

'Deion!' shrieked the woman. 'Save me!'

Verier ignored her, concentrating instead on the two Firebrands and the knives they now held in their hands. Then he turned suddenly and ran from the room. The woman screamed again but the intruders paid her no attention, moving as fast as they could in pursuit. Verier was already yelling for help when Andrin dived and caught one of the senator's ankles. They both crashed to the floor in the plush corridor, and their brief struggle was ended by Dani's knife.

'Should have stayed at home with the wife, old man,' he said as he pulled the blade from Verier's chest and wiped it on the dead man's sleeve. 'Besides, it's much too early in the morning for this sort of thing.'

However, their troubles were far from over. The alarm had been raised and, although no one emerged from any of the other rooms to challenge them, when they finally reached the entrance and a door to the outside world, they could see a platoon of soldiers converging on the house.

'Go up to the roof,' Dani wheezed. 'You can get away that way.'

'What about you?'

'I can't run any more, but the others need you – you've *got* to go,' Dani replied, holding his side. 'I'll create a diversion.'

'No.'

'Don't be stupid. If you don't go, we'll *both* be captured or killed. At least this way I get to do something useful for once.' There was blood running down his arm now, where one of his cuts had reopened.

Andrin hesitated still.

'Go and find Ico,' Dani urged. 'The pirates don't deserve to keep her.'

The soldiers had reached the locked door now, and were in the process of battering it down.

'If you don't go, you don't deserve her either.'

Andrin clasped his friend's hand briefly, then turned and ran up the first flight of stairs. Some window shutters crashed inwards as the guards sought an easier entrance and, summoning his remaining strength, Dani moved. He unlocked the door, flung it wide and charged out, startling the soldiers who were still there.

'The Firebrands for ever!' he yelled, brandishing his knife.

Even wounded as he was, Dani fought like a madman, occupying the attention of the entire platoon for a few vital moments. But his fervour was no match for their swords. He fell in a haze of blood, and the soldiers ran inside.

Andrin saw his crumpled body from the roof of an adjoining building, and his flight was hampered by the tears that blurred his eyesight.

Two days later, having left the stolen camel to wander into the nearest village, Andrin was staggering across the lava fields, half blind with fatigue and grief. He was so wrapped up in his own misery that he did not even see Ayo until the eagle was close by. The bird's arrival was welcome, a single strand of hope in the vile tangle that Andrin's life had become, but the interesting news he brought seemed irrelevant. What use were dragons to him now?

By evening, with Ayo's guidance, Andrin arrived at the Firebrands' new home. He was welcomed joyously, and was deeply relieved to see Vargo and Allegra again, but the news he carried soon quelled any thoughts of celebration. A sombre atmosphere pervaded the caves, and Andrin made it clear that he needed to be alone for a time. He had eaten mechanically, without tasting anything, and was in desperate need of sleep – but that seemed an impossibility. If wine or rum had been available he would have been tempted to drink himself into insensibility, but there was only water.

He was still awake late in the night when Vargo came to join him in his solitary cavern. In the soft lamplight the musician's face looked supernaturally pale, and his eyes were so huge and so round that Andrin wondered if he was in one of his insane phases. When he spoke, however, his voice was pitched normally and his words were coherent, even if they were shot through with fear.

'There's something I have to tell you.'

'Not now, Vargo.'

'I have to,' he repeated, even though his reluctance was obvious. 'I've only just remembered.' He faltered, swallowing hard. 'You know what my memory's like these days.'

'What is it?' Andrin asked resignedly.

'It's about Ico. Something she told me when I was crazy.'

Andrin's heart lurched. He had thought things couldn't possibly get any worse, but now he wasn't so sure.

'She's pregnant,' Vargo said.

CHAPTER FORTY-FIVE

For the first time in almost two months, Senator Tias Kantrowe allowed himself the luxury of contentment. In the seven days since the end of the pirate raid, he had made remarkable progress and had resolved several issues. There were still some minor irritations to be dealt with, of course, but compared to the important matters of state they were insignificant. Tiguafaya would soon be immeasurably stronger and richer, able to take its proper place in the world without fear. History will revere my name, he thought arrogantly.

It would be months, possibly even years, before all the repercussions of the attack were erased, but a great deal had already been achieved. Teguise had been restored to as near normality as was possible; trade had started up again – with renewed confidence now that ships under the command of Zarzuelo and the Lawyer were on patrol and ready to escort merchant craft; reconstruction had begun and reparations made where appropriate. The dead, wounded and homeless had been attended to, or removed from public sight so that the distress they caused was minimized. Kantrowe's explanations were now widely accepted, with blame being laid firmly at the doors of the Firebrands, unknown foreigners and a few renegade pirates. It was a tribute to the effectiveness of his propaganda that Kantrowe was now regarded as a saviour, the only man who had been able to harness the suspect forces of magic for the good of the country – as well as the leader who would eventually solve all of Tiguafaya's problems to the benefit of almost all its people. He was determined to do just that and decided that he would now take the next important step down the road to victory.

He had been looking forward to this particular meeting for some time, and had chosen to hold it in his own luxurious home; the venue would demonstrate his relaxed state of mind, and perhaps disconcert his guest. Maghdim arrived punctually, glancing round at the rich furnishings of the unfamiliar setting. His expression was as noncommittal as ever, but Kantrowe could tell from a slight hesitancy in the way the foreigner moved that he was impressed. Probably never seen anything like this in his barbaric homeland, the senator mused idly, as he invited his visitor to sit and offered him refreshments. As always Maghdim refused wine but accepted a fragrant infusion of herbs and honey, sipping the hot liquid gingerly. Kantrowe attended to his own drink and let the silence stretch, wondering whether Maghdim's placid exterior masked more violent emotions.

'I presume you did not summon me here just to drink tea,' the anti-mage said eventually.

Kantrowe smiled and, having achieved his objective of forcing Maghdim to speak first, approached the real substance of the meeting.

'Where are the Firebrands now?'

'In the new cave system. They have no plans to move.'

'Good. Their mood?'

'Listless, irresolute, dispirited. Zonzomas has rejoined them, but apparently he's no longer much of a leader.'

'Too preoccupied with matters of the heart, no doubt,' Kantrowe remarked with a certain amount of amusement. 'What about magic?'

'They're gathering crystals, but other than that they don't seem to be doing much.'

'Perfect. Are you sure this information is accurate?'

Maghdim gave him a disdainful look, but could not puncture his host's good mood.

'It won't be long before we deal with them,' the senator said, 'but for the moment they represent no threat, so I want you to return to your original duties.'

'The mines?'

'Yes. I have certain specific objectives for you, apart from refining the techniques we've already developed.' He went on to describe the new tasks, watching Maghdim closely the whole time. 'Think you can handle that?'

'Of course. Do you have a particular location in mind for this test?'

'A village called Cumplina Orona.'

The foreigner nodded impassively.

'You are to report back to me personally once these objectives have been attained,' Kantrowe went on. 'In the meantime, you will leave one of your mind-links here to keep me informed. Any questions?'

Maghdim shook his head and made as if to stand.

'One last thing,' Kantrowe said. 'I want you to leave three of the least talented of the ex-Firebrands here in Teguise.'

'Why?'

'It's time to keep another promise. The dragons will have their sacrifices at last.'

'That's nonsense,' Maghdim said, his face revealing his distaste for the senator's plan.

'Of course it is,' Kantrowe agreed. 'But who am I to stand against popular opinion?'

'You told me yourself that my acolytes were a valuable resource. Why waste them?'

'Not waste. Utilize.' The senator might once have become annoyed at his employee's effrontery in questioning his decision, but now he felt too confident to care. 'You can leave such considerations to me.' He paused. 'I would also like the Firebrands in the south to know of the deaths of their friends. Can that be arranged?'

'Of course,' Maghdim said after a moment's thought. 'But it is dangerous. You risk exposing our spy.'

'I think it will be worth it even so, don't you?' Kantrowe said pleasantly. 'Be discreet if you can.'

'I'll see to it.'

'Good. You may go.'

Gadette entered the room from a side door a few minutes after Maghdim had left.

'Good morning, Mazo. You heard all that?'

'I did.' The aide had been in one of the small chambers of the house designed specifically for the purpose of eavesdropping.

'I confess, I rather enjoyed sending him out of Teguise,' the senator remarked. 'It will be even more pleasant when his absence becomes permanent. How soon will we be able to replace him with our own people?'

'A month,' Gadette hazarded. 'He's a good tutor, but he's had the sense to keep a certain amount to himself.'

'That's soon enough. Now, let me have your report.'

'The Shipbuilders' Guild have settled their differences,' the aide told him, 'so there shouldn't be much delay. With Verier gone they're forming a cartel to divide out the work.'

The death of their former colleague had been accepted calmly from the first. It presented some inconvenience, of course, but Kantrowe decided that in the long run it would actually prove beneficial. The place where Verier had met his end had not been unexpected, but the manner of it had. The establishment had been searched, its employees and customers interrogated, but the investigation had revealed little of any use. How the two Firebrands had got into the brothel remained a mystery; the only really annoying detail had been the escape of the second assailant who, from the available descriptions, had almost certainly been Andrin Zonzomas. However, it would not be long before he paid the full price for his crimes. Verier had died without a legal heir, so the disposal of his estates had presented some problems – but also some opportunities. Kantrowe had already made sure that important inheritances went to those he could rely on.

'And what about our whisperers?' This was the name they had coined for those in the Senate who were not wholly supportive of their measures.

'They're still whispering,' Gadette replied, 'but I don't think it'll amount to much yet. Too many people have vested interests to protect. I'll keep watching, but they're mostly amateurs.'

'What about Maciot?'

'He's the ringleader. If there's any plotting being done then he'll be at the centre of it, but he's having a hard time getting anything more than vague promises from most people. Do you want him arrested?'

'Not yet. We should preserve the semblance of democracy, at least for a while. But watch him constantly.'

Gadette shrugged. 'It wouldn't be hard to bring a perfectly legal, believable case against him,' he said. 'He's always been a thorn in our side.'

'No. We don't want to risk creating a martyr, and he'll lead us to others we may not know about.' Kantrowe paused. 'What about the army?'

'The White Guard are as secure as ever. Some regular units might be a little more susceptible to rumours, but they'll follow orders unless something really drastic happens.'

'Such as?'

'Such as Guadarfia deciding to oppose us.'

'You think that's likely?' Kantrowe scoffed, unable to take the suggestion seriously.

'No, but it's possible. The President is feeling his age, and doesn't want history to remember his term of office as the one when freedom was curtailed.'

'He's developing a conscience? How absurd!'

'Something or someone's got to him,' the aide said. 'He might be senile, but his word would still carry a lot of weight in some quarters – and the army's one of them.'

'What do you suggest?' Kantrowe asked, becoming grave at last.

'I think that the sad demise from illness of our beloved President is long overdue,' Gadette replied.

His master nodded, then smiled suddenly. 'Perhaps he should be assassinated, though,' he suggested.

For a few moments his aide looked puzzled, but then Kantrowe explained, and Gadette grinned. The senator thought that it was like seeing lights glow in the eyes of a skull.

Even though he was trying to maintain the appearance of studied calm, Senator Alegranze Maciot had never been busier in his life. Like most men of good sense, he was aware that Kantrowe was not revealing all his plans and, unlike most, was not prepared to take them on trust. He was doing his best to find out what they were, but infiltrating Kantrowe's organization was never going to be easy. It would involve a great number of secret conversations, messages and bribes, but he had to start somewhere, and he had a feeling that time was probably running out.

At the same time, Maciot was trying to remain in touch with as many as possible of those who opposed – or might be persuaded to oppose – Kantrowe. These included senators, merchants, officials and, importantly, some senior army officers.

All such contacts were necessarily clandestine. If he gained the reputation of being too dangerous an associate, such dealings would become even more difficult to arrange. As it was, he could not hope to keep everything secret from Kantrowe's spies, and so he endeavoured to include as much legitimate business into all his meetings as he could. His primary network of informers and messengers was built around those he could trust within the Transporters' Guild and they, together with several linked birds, fed him information constantly.

Andrin's escape had pleased him, but he wished that there was some way to contact the Firebrands. Even without Ico they represented a strand of hope for Tiguafaya, and if it were ever to come to open confrontation with Kantrowe and his cronies, Maciot wanted all the allies he could get. The very idea of civil war appalled him, but then so did the way the country was currently being run – and it might soon come to a choice between two evils. A bloodless coup was a much more attractive option, but that was going to be next to impossible to arrange, not least because the White Guard were ferociously loyal to Kantrowe.

There were times when Maciot wondered why he had not yet been arrested. Each knock at his door was an alarm signal. He had no intention of running, however, even though it did not take much imagination to see how trumped-up charges could be levelled against him. Indeed, in the narrow sense imposed by martial law, they need not even involve much trumping; he was guilty of sedition – and proud of it. He had taken the precaution of preparing various escape routes in case the worst happened, but he relied heavily on Tao for advance warning of any danger.

This evening the mirador chaffinch flew in his window and whistled softly.

What is it, Tao?

Someone's coming to the door.

Alone?

Yes. He's dressed in the uniform of a palace attendant.

That gave Maciot pause for thought, but as soon as the knock sounded at the door he decided that speculation was useless and went to see what the visitor wanted. The messenger passed over a letter that bore the Presidential seal, and waited while he broke it open and read it.

'Tell the President I'll be with him shortly.'

As the servant retreated, Maciot went inside to change his clothes, wondering what this unexpected summons could mean.

Maciot was used to seeing Guadarfia in the Senate and at the few ceremonial functions he still attended, so the President's frail physical appearance came as no surprise. However, meeting him in his own surroundings propped by cushions and half asleep, was like entering the lair of a hibernating animal. The old man's gaze rested on his visitor for a few moments before recognition showed in his eyes.

'Thank you for coming, Alegranze. Sit down. Pour us both some wine.'

Maciot did as he was told, passed a goblet to the President and looked at him expectantly.

'You're wondering what the old fool wants, aren't you?' Guadarfia said.

'Wondering, yes. Old fool, no.'

'I am undeniably old and I think I've been acting like a fool for some time.'

'What makes you think so?'

'I trusted Kantrowe,' Guadarfia replied simply. 'Was that the act of a sensible man?'

Maciot said nothing, wondering whether this was a trap or whether there could really be some hope of the President adding his voice to the opposition's as yet stifled argument. To give himself a little time to think, he sipped his wine.

'The senator and I have had our differences,' he said carefully. 'Why do you no longer trust him?'

Guadarfia laughed briefly, but without humour. The room's only window was a skylight, and both men looked up at it as there was a sudden fluttering of movement outside and a rapid tapping on the glass.

'Pigeons,' the old man muttered. 'Damn nuisance.'

Maciot's sharper senses had caught sight of a cluster of sparrows and heard a faint echo of their raucous song, but he did not contradict his host.

'You were saying?' he prompted.

'Have I really outlived my usefulness?' Guadarfia muttered softly, and took a gulp of wine.

Maciot did not get a chance to answer because, almost immediately, the President's face contorted with pain and he groaned. Moments later his eyes bulged, his face turned a hideous purple and he doubled over. It all happened so fast that Maciot could hardly believe his eyes, but he came to his senses a moment later and ran to the door, pulled it open and yelled.

'A physician here! Quickly! The President is ill.'

He returned to the old man and tried to help him, but it was already clear that it was hopeless. Guadarfia's pulse was racing and his breath rattled in his throat. By the time others arrived, he was dead. Maciot looked up for the first time, saw Mazo Gadette among the onlookers and felt an icy pre-monition. The wine he had drunk had come from the same bottle as the President's.

CHAPTER FORTY-SIX

An air of pervasive gloom filled the caves as the Firebrands found themselves without direction or purpose for the first time. Andrin had become silent and withdrawn and, although everyone understood the reasons for his grief, the absence of his leadership was acutely felt. He was still with them physically but his spirit was elsewhere. Nino and Vargo – when he was coherent – tried to keep the mood positive, but Andrin's solitary misery infected them all.

For his own part, Andrin spent his waking hours in bitter self-recrimination and tortured imaginings. He slept little but even then found no peace, sinking into terrifying nightmares in which Ico drowned or burned, was tortured or raped, while he could only look on helplessly, unable to intervene. Awake, he refused to give up hope that she was alive; asleep, he witnessed the horrors that such hope brought with it. By day he dared not even think of his unborn child; by night he saw her face. She had Ico's eyes, and they were always full of tears.

Adding to his woes, but almost insignificant compared to the loss of his love, was the rift between himself and Vargo. A lifelong friendship had been shattered in one fateful moment, by one unforgiveable failure. Vargo had tried to explain several times, but Andrin had screamed at him, threatened him with violence and denied him a chance to try and justify his actions. Andrin knew that this was unfair, that his friend was also suffering dreadfully and that Vargo's own misfortunes had contributed to the disaster, but he still could not forgive him. And at the heart of his anger was an unacknowledged core of jealousy. Why had Ico chosen to confide in Vargo rather than in the father of her child? How could she trust a madman but not her own lover? The hurt went deeper than any pain he could ever have imagined, and turned to black rage inside him. He was like a walking volcano, and everyone learnt to avoid him.

He did manage to achieve a few moments of brooding calm, however, and these came when he was alone with Ayo. The eagle's massive self-assurance and simple acceptance of his link's dejection made him the one solid rock in the shifting sands of Andrin's life, and they took to making the short journey to the ocean together. At the coast, Ayo would fish while Andrin sat and gazed out over the sea, his eyes unfocused and his mind blank.

On one such occasion, he heard hesitant footsteps behind him and turned to see Vargo a short distance away. He found that he had neither the strength nor the will to shout, and simply turned away again without a word. Left to make up his own mind, Vargo struggled for the courage to go on. He had wanted many times to tell Andrin that he had also loved – still loved – Ico, and that his sorrow at her absence almost matched his friend's. The fact that Vargo's love had never been openly admitted, had never found the means of expression that Andrin's had, only made the reality of its loss all the more agonizing – but he could not tell Andrin that. He felt the collapse of their friendship like a knife in his heart, and knew it would never be the same again. Even so, he was driven to try to repair the damage as best he could, and had noted

Andrin's relative tranquillity on his return from these trips to the sea. Vargo walked forward and sat down on the opposite side of the fish basket. The two men did not look at each other, but stared out at the eastern horizon. For a long time the only sounds were the rhythmic pulsing of the waves and the distant calling of some birds, and when Andrin finally broke the silence it was with a single word.

'Why?'

Vargo was not sure what Andrin meant, but he chose to assume it was the question he most needed to answer.

'She said she had to confide in someone, that you already had too much on your mind, and I . . .' He faltered, wanting Andrin to react, to make his task easier, but his friend did not move or speak. 'I was there,' he ended lamely, knowing that this was not the whole truth.

Another few moments passed in nervous silence.

'She made me promise not to tell anyone,' he stumbled on. 'For days I couldn't anyway, because my memory had vanished. But when you told me what had happened, it came back.' His voice was thick with guilt. 'I'm sorry.'

Andrin still did not say anything. He was thinking about Ico's action dispassionately for the first time. It had been a misguided and, in the end, tragic mistake, but it did make a certain amount of sense. And if she really felt that she could not burden him, who else would she turn to but Vargo? No one could have foreseen the events that were to follow. Regrets and recriminations were ultimately useless, even if they were a necessary stage in the process of acceptance. Nothing could remove the pain he felt – except the longed-for reunion that now seemed so horribly improbable – but somehow he had to find the strength to go on with his life. Otherwise he might as well throw himself from the nearest cliff right now, and that was something he could not do while the smallest glimmer of hope remained.

'There have been so many times,' Vargo tried again, 'when I wanted—'

'It's not your fault,' Andrin stated flatly.

In that moment Vargo felt the air change, and found that he could breathe again. At the same time, the admission shattered what was left of Andrin's composure. Somewhere deep inside him he felt the dam break, and he began to weep helplessly.

When Ayo returned with another fish vainly struggling in his talons, he found the two men sitting close together, their arms around each other's shoulders. The eagle saw their tears and was glad. The healing process had begun. Soon he would be able to help his link take the next step by telling him his own story. The time was coming when Ayo would be ready to break his self-imposed silence and unburden his heart. In all their years together he had never told Andrin about Iva.

When Andrin, Vargo and Allegra – who had come most of the way to the coast but stayed a discreet distance from the meeting – arrived back at the cave system, they found the place buzzing with excitement. Nino came to meet them with the news.

'We have a visitor.'

'Who?'

'Good question,' Nino replied. 'He claims to be Jurado Madri.'

The newcomers regarded this statement with disbelief. Madri was a figure from history. Even if he *had* come back to life, why would he make himself known to the Firebrands?

'*Admiral* Madri?' Andrin asked.

'That's what he says. I've got him under guard in one of the inner caverns. I don't think he represents much of a security risk, but I didn't want to take any chances.'

'How did he find us?'

'Says he's been living in the caves in this part of the country for the last thirty years.'

'So we're trespassing on his territory,' Vargo remarked, laughing. 'This should be interesting.'

In the lamplit cave, the man who claimed to be Jurado Madri sat so still that he seemed to be part of the rock formation. His clothes were patched and tattered, and his hair and beard were long and unruly . There was a feral glint to his eyes, and as Andrin looked at him he found it easy to believe that he had indeed lived as a hermit for the last three decades. He was more wild animal than human. Andrin was about to speak when they were all distracted by Allegra, who let out a yelp of astonishment.

'It's him!' she exclaimed, glancing at Vargo, then back to the unmoving figure.

'You know him?' Andrin asked.

'No, but I saw him when Vargo and I were trapped. He was by the lake in the other caves.'

'The delicate stars,' the musician said softly.

'You led us out,' Allegra said, speaking directly to the prisoner. 'You're the dancer!'

'Would you like to tell me what you're talking about?' Andrin asked plaintively.

Between them, Vargo and Allegra explained what had happened, and described the birds' references to someone called 'the dancer'. As they spoke, the man's uncanny eyes moved from one to the other as if measuring their worth.

'Was it you who helped us?' Allegra asked eventually.

The man nodded slowly.

'Can you prove it?' Andrin asked.

For answer the prisoner glanced upwards. Deep in the shadows small crystals – which had been invisible before – began to glow softly.

'Why did you help them?'

'Do I need a reason other than common humanity?' His voice was low and rasping, as though it had not been used for a long time.

'Did you follow us here?'

Another nod.

'Why?'

'I was curious. It's been a long time since anyone sought to share my exile of their own free will.'

'Hardly free will,' Andrin said. 'We were driven from our homes.'

'As I was thirty years ago,' the man answered, and the resentment was clear in his voice.

'You really are Jurado Madri?'

'Yes,' he said, with a touch of impatience. 'I've already told your colleague that. And yes, I'm *that* Jurado Madri, the one who was once an admiral, whose incompetence destroyed Tiguafaya, and who was forced to retire in disgrace. That's what you've all been told, isn't it? You're too young to know any different.'

Such was the embittered ferocity of his words that no one spoke for a while.

'It's not true?' Nino asked eventually.

'Which part?' Madri said. 'Never mind. You're not interested in ancient history.'

'What have you been doing since then?' Andrin asked.

'Surviving.'

'On your own?' Allegra said, horrified by the idea.

'Not quite. One of my men knew the truth and wasn't prepared to lie to save his reputation. He came into exile with me.'

'Where is he now?'

'I don't know. He goes where the whim takes him, keeps me in touch with a little of what's happening in the world. In spite of his illness, Tre is not one to hide. He has a sixth sense which allows him to find me whenever he wants to. I've no idea how he does it, but I think your birds could probably tell you,' he added, looking at Vargo.

'His name's Tre?' the musician asked.

'Tre Fiorindo,' Madri confirmed. 'But you know him better as Angel.'

For a second time his audience was struck dumb.

'He seems to have taken quite an interest in you,' the old man went on. 'You call yourselves the Firebrands, don't you?'

In the discussion that followed, Andrin and the others talked openly, instinctively trusting the newcomer. Without any conscious decision, they had each come to the conclusion that he was who he said he was. They discovered that he was reasonably well informed about the political situation, although somewhat hazy on recent developments, and that he shared many of their opinions on the current state of affairs. He was also personally aware of the fireworms, and was fascinated by their efforts to combat the menace.

'There was a time when we never even knew they existed,' he commented. 'Something must have changed.'

When Kantrowe's treaty with the pirates was mentioned, Madri became fiercely animated. With a sudden burst of manic energy that alarmed his companions, he strode about the cavern, gesticulating wildly and mouthing foul oaths.

'And they called my actions treachery!' he half shouted. 'This is beyond belief.'

It was soon apparent to everyone that Jurado was on their side when it came to the future of Tiguafaya. What was less clear was just what benefit would come from having a half-mad old hermit as an ally.

Later that evening, Andrin and Madri continued their conversation alone. Although the old man's voice was hoarse from all the unaccustomed talking, he was still keen to learn all he could. In fact he seemed to have lost the aura of a wary, wild animal and was now displaying a lively intellect, quizzing Andrin on future plans, strategy and communications. Somewhat bemused by this turn of events, Andrin did his best to paint the entire picture, but the Firebrands' efforts to date sounded feeble, even to him.

Eventually the talk moved on to more personal matters. For some reason, Andrin found himself telling Madri about Ico – about their dreadful row, her kidnap, and his belated discovery that she was pregnant. The former admiral looked at the younger man with new understanding in his eyes.

'I don't know which is worse,' he said. 'Knowing or not.'

'What do you mean?'

'My wife was killed in the aftermath of the battle thirty years ago. No one noticed – they were too busy blaming me for the country's ruin.'

'I'm sorry.'

'So was I. I loved her beyond anything. And she was pregnant.'

The two men, one old and one young, looked at each other in mutual sympathy.

'Did you . . . did you ever get over it?' Andrin asked.

'No,' Madri replied with brutal honesty. 'And I'd hate myself if I did. Even if she had not been carrying our child, Mallina was irreplaceable. Everything else that's happened to me is incidental by comparison. But, from what you've told me of Ico, there's every chance you'll see her again,' he added with a tentative smile. 'She sounds like a very enterprising young woman. Don't give up hope. History doesn't always repeat itself.'

The next morning, by a curious process of osmosis, it had been assumed by everyone that Jurado Madri was now one of them. His arrival, far from being a distraction, seemed to have given them a new sense of purpose – although exactly what they were supposed to do was as yet undecided. His continued presence was taken for granted, and the Firebrands' leaders included him in their discussions. One thing they all agreed upon was the need for better information about what was happening in Teguise. Various options were discussed, most of them involving the birds, but nothing had been decided when news came from a most unexpected source.

Jair's face was pale as he entered the cavern, and everyone there turned to look at him.

'It's started,' he said breathlessly.

'What has?' Andrin asked, alarmed by the horror on the boy's face.

'Two of the Firebrands who were captured with me have been sacrificed,' Jair blurted out. 'Kantrowe had them burnt at the stake.'

CHAPTER FORTY-SEVEN

At the end of the debate which ratified his inauguration, President Tias Kantrowe looked grave as he accepted the congratulations of his peers. The vote had been a formality, of course; the official transfer of power had taken place the previous day, under the provisions of martial law, but a display of strength had been pleasing as well as advisable. Not even his enemies could claim that he had reached his exalted position by anything other than legitimate means. The new president had declared the traditional three days of general mourning, and was himself dressed all in white to signify his own sorrow and respect. Inwardly, though, he was congratulating himself on the achievement of a long-held ambition. His hands had been on the reins of power for some time, but public recognition was a reward he intended to enjoy.

Looking back, Kantrowe felt that the last three days had been quite momentous. First he had managed to get rid of Maghdim temporarily, dispatching him to the west. Then Guadarfia had done him the favour of dying at last – albeit with a little help. And yesterday, after being installed as ruler of Tiguafaya in name as well as fact, his first duty had been to oversee the sacrifices. The executions had provided less of a spectacle than he would have liked, because Maghdim had drugged the victims heavily before he left the city, but the fires had been an appropriately gruesome reminder of recent events, and had satisfied a deep-seated need for revenge. The pirates were beyond the reach of the people's righteous anger, so a couple of Firebrands were the next best thing. The demonstration had also served to reassure the citizens that something was being done to appease the volcanoes and the dragons that controlled them. A third prisoner was still waiting in his cell, should another attempt at propitiation become necessary. And today he had gazed benevolently over the Senate from his chair and heard his praises sung by the great and the good of the land. All that remained to complete his satisfaction was to get a progress report from Maghdim.

Kantrowe returned to his office to begin planning his move to the presidential palace.

Famara's life, such as it was, seemed to be ebbing away. Her gaolers had not fed her yesterday and, while she did not miss the tasteless food, she could feel herself growing weaker. Curiously, parts of her mind seemed to be becoming more perceptive as her outward senses were deprived of any stimuli. She had known of Marco's impending death, had sent her sparrows in an attempt to warn him about the poison, but to no avail. Although he had become a foolish old man, she regretted his passing and was saddened by the memory of their final parting. Had she been wrong to prick his conscience? Had her efforts made any difference at the last? She would never know now.

Maghdim was gone too. He had not been to see her for three days, and this unexpected absence left her feeling surprisingly bereft. Even her enemies seemed to hold her of no account now; in a strange way, she missed their mental contests.

The unrelenting darkness of her cell began to seem like an invitation. She slept for much of the time, not really caring whether she ever woke up again.

Maciot could not understand why he was still alive. The last two days had been a nightmare of waiting and wondering. At first he had been convinced that Guadarfia had died because the wine had been poisoned, and had been sure that he was about to die as well. Then, as the hours passed and he showed no adverse symptoms, he began to look for possible explanations. Could he have drunk so much less than Guadarfia that it had had no effect? That seemed highly unlikely, given the President's violent and instantaneous reaction. Could the old man have had some existing medical condition that made him susceptible to the poison when Maciot was not? That too seemed improbable. Perhaps the poison had been in the goblet before the wine was poured. If that was the case, then why had it been only in one? Maciot had been left to choose which cup the President drank from, and if the old man had indeed been murdered, then that seemed a very haphazard way of going about it. He could just as easily have been killed himself.

The immediate investigation had been conducted by Gadette and a captain of the palace guard. The physicians had been noncommittal about the cause of death, and although they had examined Maciot as well, they found nothing untoward. Seeing no reason to hide the truth, he had told them that he had drunk wine from the same bottle – which had been taken away for testing, together with the goblets – but no results had yet been made public. The announcement of Guadarfia's death had referred only to the President's great age and long history of illness, but that would probably have been the case no matter what the real story had been. However, Maciot was now beginning to wonder if the old man had genuinely succumbed to natural causes.

Maciot was sure about one thing; if it *was* murder, then Kantrowe was responsible. Given Guadarfia's final remarks, it was clear that he had the potential to stand in the Senator's way. Subsequent events had reinforced the motive, and Maciot began to wonder about some of the more bizarre aspects of the tragedy. The timing of his own visit had been an astonishing coincidence, unless it had been engineered by someone – probably Gadette – at Kantrowe's behest. Had they needed a witness who would be believed even by their enemies? Or was there a more sinister motive involved? It had even crossed his mind that he was being set up as the assassin, a convenient scapegoat to catch two fish on one hook. But if that was the case, then why was he still at large? Surely they would have arrested him immediately and 'found' the necessary evidence to convict him. As it was, he had been questioned and then released – and that had been the last he had heard of it. It didn't make sense! If Kantrowe was involved, the story released to the public could not possibly be as innocent as it seemed. But what other explanation was there?

The next day had brought further horror and death. This time it had been two Firebrands who had died, in the most appalling manner possible. Maciot had watched in utter revulsion, wishing he could do something to prevent this obscene mockery of justice, but knowing that his hands were tied. He also knew that he was not alone in his feelings of disgust – but the objectors were apparently in the minority, a fact that made him angry as well as despondent. There were no last-minute rescues this time, no magic, and he wished again that he could have found some way of keeping in touch with Andrin and his followers.

However, the sacrifices did prompt him into more action and less introspection. He must do as much as he could while there was still time. He redoubled the efforts of his network, using recent events to press his possible allies for a commitment. Soon, rumours reached him that various purges were in the offing. With Kantrowe as President, administrators and army officers would be obliged to swear a new oath of allegiance, and those who hesitated or refused would be in trouble.

Kantrowe's complacent and hypocritical performance in the Senate the next morning drove Maciot to distraction, although he was at pains not to show his feelings, and he knew without doubt that if he were ever to challenge the status quo, then he would have to do it soon. Later that day he gained some information that gave him a chance to do just that.

The fireworms descended on Cumplina Orona in unprecedented numbers. No one escaped, no house remained intact. In an astonishingly short time the screams died and the village became a place of fire and ghosts. Nothing was left except ash, smoke and the pitiful, shrunken remains of the people who had once lived there.

Watching from afar, through his own eyes and through those of his acolytes, Maghdim permitted himself a smile. The operation had worked perfectly. They had come a long way from the first crude manipulations of the fireworms using simple sources of heat and cold. Now, with the help of his trained telepaths and the energy of the crystals, they could use the creatures not only to improve the yields of any given mining operation, but could also steer the swarms in open flight. Clearing any part of the land of unwanted settlers was now a simple matter – as he had just demonstrated – and, with their fast improving methods of capturing and corralling the swarms, anything was possible.

Maghdim prepared and sent a jubilant message to his master.

The Senate met again the next morning, at the command of the new president. Still dressed in funereal white, Kantrowe told them of the distressing events to the west. The fate of Cumplina Orona cast a pall of silence over the assembly, but there were more surprises to come. He announced that research was being carried out in an effort to try to control the movements of the fireworms, and thus protect the population. When someone objected that this was just what the Firebrands had been trying to do, the President begged to differ.

'They were intent only on killing the worms,' he replied. 'And that was what led to the present crisis. We simply want to defend our people.'

'How can we do that? The dragon spawn don't respect our boundaries.'

'We can use the natural forces of the land to divert them to remote, uninhabited regions,' Kantrowe answered. 'We can place protective cordons around all our settlements. This will take time, of course, and we must act according to agreed priorities, but there is hope that at some time in the future fireworms will no longer be a danger to us. Tragedies like the one I described today will become a thing of the past – as long as we can prevent the Firebrands from doing any more damage by the malicious misuse of sorcery, and avoid provoking either the worms or the dragons.'

'And how do we do that?'

'The appropriate measures are being taken.'

'What measures?'

'I am not prepared to reveal that yet, in the interests of security,' Kantrowe replied smoothly. 'You'll just have to trust me.'

'Why *should* we trust you?'

Maciot had chosen his moment well, and everyone turned to look at him as he stood up.

'I think my record speaks for itself, Senator,' Kantrowe said coldly.

'I agree,' Maciot said. 'Which is why I ask whether we should trust a man willing to give away a large part of Tiguafaya to the pirates.'

In the uproar that followed this statement, Kantrowe also rose to his feet.

'What is this nonsense?' he shouted.

'I have here a letter, signed by Senator Kantrowe, which was sent via Envoy Zophres to Galan Zarzuelo and Vicent Agnadi,' Maciot shouted back, waving a piece of paper. 'In it they are offered unrestricted ownership of all lands south of a line from Hervideros to Tinosa!'

'It's a forgery!' the President cried. 'This is preposterous.'

'In other words, the entire southern province,' his accuser went on remorselessly. 'This is the true price we have paid for the treaty.'

'This ploy will not save your skin!' Kantrowe roared. 'I have a warrant here for your arrest – for the murder of President Marco Guadarfia. Guards!'

'The letter was given to me by Zophres himself,' Maciot shouted, as pandemonium broke out anew. 'It's no forgery.'

'He hopes to escape justice by falsely discrediting me,' Kantrowe countered. '*He's* the traitor.'

And then the chaos in the Senate Chamber made further exchanges impossible. The senators, spectators and attendants were all on their feet, some intent on confrontation, others on flight. Soldiers were entering from the corridors outside, and a hundred heated arguments were taking place. Fights broke out and furniture crashed to the ground. Maciot vanished from sight in the mêlée but, from his elevated position, Kantrowe looked down on them all with murder in his eyes.

CHAPTER FORTY-EIGHT

'How do you know?' Nino asked, after Jair's dreadful news had begun to sink in.

The young man looked confused. 'What do you mean?'

'How did you find out about the sacrifices?'

'I was told . . .' It was clear that Jair wasn't sure *how* he'd found out.

'Who by?' Andrin asked.

'One of the birds . . . I think. Does it matter?' There was a small spark of defiance in his voice.

'We need to know if it's true,' Andrin told him. 'Was it your link?'

'Yes . . . no . . . *I don't know*. Why would they tell me if it's not true?'

'Tell us exactly what was said,' Madri advised calmly.

Jair glanced at the ex-admiral, his doubts obvious in his frightened eyes, then thought hard.

'It was a mixture of words and pictures,' he replied eventually. 'Just something I was supposed to know.'

'Can you repeat the words?' Andrin asked.

'No . . . I . . . No.' He was having to fight to stop himself from crying now.

Allegra went to his side and put her arms about him. 'It's all right,' she said soothingly. 'It's all right.'

He glanced at her gratefully, swallowing hard.

'Let me talk to him,' she said to Andrin. 'You're all making him nervous.'

Andrin nodded, and the pair turned to go. But before they left the cave, Jair spun round again. 'I saw them burn,' he whispered.

'Come on,' Allegra said gently, aware of his distress.

'Wait. There's more.' Jair put his hands to his head, screwing his eyes shut as if he were in pain. 'It says there'll be more sacrifices unless the Firebrands all give themselves up.'

'*It* says?' Nino queried.

'The proclamation,' Jair explained, opening his eyes again. 'President Kantrowe issued a proclamation.'

'*President* Kantrowe?' Andrin exclaimed.

'Let me . . .' Allegra took Jair's hand and led him away. 'I'll see if I can calm him down, make some sense of this,' she said over her shoulder.

'You think it could be true?' Vargo asked when they had gone.

'How the hell am I supposed to know?' Andrin snapped, then sighed and gestured in apology.

'And where's it coming from?' Nino wondered.

'That's what worries me,' Andrin said. 'Do you think it might be Maghdim? Planting false information in Jair's mind, or the mind of his link?'

'He *was* a prisoner for a while,' Vargo pointed out. 'Who knows what happened then?'

'So this could all be lies, designed to lead us into a trap.'

'Or it could be the truth,' Nino said. ' The effect would be the same.'

'Alternatively, it could be some delusion Jair's dreamt up all on his own,' Vargo said.

'But if it *is* true, what's to stop Kantrowe from killing all the hostages, unless we give ourselves up?' Andrin said. 'And our families too. It might never end.'

'There's nothing to stop him doing that even if we *did* surrender,' Vargo argued.

'I don't see too many people standing in his way,' Nino agreed, 'especially if he really is President now.'

'Let's hope Allegra can get some sense out of Jair,' Andrin said. 'Then at least we might know whether we should be taking all this seriously.'

Madri stirred slightly, as though he had just woken from a light sleep. 'I think this . . . episode . . . tells us two things,' he said. 'First of all, it reinforces our need for a reliable system of communication with Teguise. That shouldn't be beyond us. At the very least we can send some of your birds to check on the story. And secondly, have you considered that if Jair *is* getting reliable news from someone in Teguise, then it might be a two-way exchange?'

There was silence as the implications of this sank in.

'You mean he might be telling someone there what we're doing?' Nino said.

'And where we are!' Andrin exclaimed. 'That could be how the White Guard found us at the old caves.'

'And how they could find us here if they want to,' Nino added.

'Gods!' Vargo breathed. 'A spy in our midst. Do you think he's aware of it?'

'From his confusion just now, I'd guess not,' Madri answered. 'If he's consciously working for your enemies, he wouldn't have risked betraying himself. In any case, this is all speculation. We need to test a few theories.'

'How?'

'That,' Madri said, 'is what we need to discuss now. If we can figure out how this works, we might even be able to turn it to our advantage.'

While Allegra tried, unsuccessfully, to coax more information from Jair, the others made several decisions. Now, at noon on the following day, they had already acted on most of them. Several birds, including Nino's peregrine falcon Eya, had been dispatched towards Teguise. Their mission was to find Tao and thus communicate with Senator Maciot; failing that, they were to observe as much as they could, and contact any other linked birds who were willing to talk. More birds were spreading out to villages to the south and west of the capital, with a similar if rather more vague brief to gather intelligence on anything of interest. The idea was to keep them all in almost constant motion, so that the flow of information was continuous.

In addition, Ayo had been sent out over the sea in the hope of spotting some sign of the Barber's fleet, or of finding birds who might have seen it. It was a pretty hopeless task, but one that the eagle had been glad to undertake when Madri suggested it. Andrin had silently cursed himself for not having done this earlier. The Barber had probably retreated to some distant island by now, and the ocean was too vast for a whole flock of birds to be able to search more than a tiny fraction of its surface. But it was worth trying, even though the chances of success were minimal. Andrin had been in a state of numbed mental turmoil for too long, and Madri's arrival had brought back a semblance of common sense. Sooner or later, the Barber's ships were bound to be seen by someone. By then, of course, it might well be too late for Ico, but that . . . He cut off the thought savagely and returned to other practicalities.

The mass separations between the Firebrands and their links entailed by these measures were unnatural, and led to a great deal of uneasiness on both sides of the partnership. However, everyone saw the sense of such plans. They had also begun to think about what might happen if their present location was indeed known to their enemies. In this Madri proved to be a mine of useful information. Half of his life had been spent in the caves of the firelands, and he knew them better than any man alive. He suggested several alternative escape routes, both above and below ground, and many possible hide-outs. He was also able to advise them about sources of water and food, and give them various survival tips. The Firebrands had discovered some of these for themselves but others, like the sweet and nutritious juices that could be squeezed from the flesh of certain cacti, were new to them.

Lastly, it was agreed that, as far as humanly possible, their specific plans would be kept secret from Jair. Instead, they would feed him carefully chosen pieces of information and try to monitor any reaction from their enemies. In the meantime, he was to be kept under constant observation, so that if he received any more news – from whatever source – they would be able to question him immediately.

The Firebrands' enthusiasm for their own magical endeavours was renewed as a result of this flurry of activity. Prospecting for crystals continued, and various techniques were practised – both for creating illusions and for using the energy of the dragon's tears. Vargo played a leading role in this and Madri, while simply watching in fascination most of the time, also lent his expertise when he could. The old man's abilities were limited to a few useful 'tricks' as he called them – such as making the underground crystals glow – which he said he had learnt either from Angel or from the necessities of his life in the wilderness. Even Allegra helped, relaying results from one group to another and making sure that everyone was aware of the latest developments. In fact only one person found himself excluded from the process. Andrin was becoming more and more convinced that he had no magical talent at all, a fact that depressed and confused him. It was not for the want of trying; his efforts were considerable, but came to nothing. In the end, at Madri's suggestion, he concentrated on other matters.

'Goatherd's delight!' Vargo exclaimed gleefully.

Allegra was at his side in an instant. Always alert, she recognized the signs.

'What do you mean?'

'Red sky at night. That's what they say, isn't it?' His laugh was a high-pitched cackle. 'There must've been a lot of happy goatherds recently, what with the eruptions and all.'

He seemed to find this idea outrageously funny, and Allegra could not help smiling too. They were in the open, some distance from the caves, overseeing a trial involving three Firebrands and their combined flock of starlings. Although the experiment was almost over, it would obviously have to wait until Vargo returned to his senses.

'Do goats lay eggs?' he asked, his voice more subdued now, his eyes looking at something only he could see.

'I don't think so,' Allegra replied, humouring him. 'Why?'

'There are lots of them. Lots and lots.' His voice changed as he began to hold a conversation with himself, alternating between a bass growl and a squeaky whine.

'You can't make an omelette without breaking eggs.'

'But I don't even want an omelette.'

'That's not the point.'

'Yes it is.'

'There's no use crying over spilt eggs.'

'That's milk.'

'Do goats lay milk?'

His expression changed with each nonsensical statement. Allegra became aware that Ero and Lao were close by, watching their link's performance with interest, but when she glanced at them they did not seem unduly worried. Ero was bobbing up and down, occasionally hopping from one leg to the other, and flirting his long tail while he called softly in time. Lao held his head high, his neck stretched and his long bill pointed skyward. He too was chirruping quietly.

'They danced once, but there's no music any more.'

Vargo began to whistle and then to dance himself. Mindful of the rough ground on which they stood, Allegra tried first to restrain him, then held on to him and became his partner in the dance, hoping to curb his wilder excesses. The birds grew excited, their calls louder. Ero fanned his crest as he joined in with the rhythm of the dance. Hoo-poo-hoo-poo-hoo-poo-hoo-poo . . .

As Allegra was whirled around, she was afraid that they might stumble and fall at any moment, but Vargo's feet were nimble and he kept them safe. Ero exploded noisily into the air, unable to contain his exuberance, and even the usually restrained Lao seemed infected by the general mood of abandonment as his normally mournful song became positively ecstatic.

By now the other Firebrands were watching the performance and, although they were used to Vargo's periodically eccentric behaviour, they obviously found this exhibition somewhat unnerving. At last the dance ended, with Vargo flushed and wild-eyed and Allegra breathless. She knew she ought to be relieved, but instead found that she was a little sad that it was over. The birds settled down again, and silence returned.

'Are you all right?' she asked.

'Absolutely,' he replied brightly.

'Well, in that case,' she told him, 'I think you'd better not talk about omelettes while there are birds about. They tend to be a bit touchy on the subject.'

For a few moments Vargo's expression was blank, but then he smiled.

'Ero hears voices too,' he remarked casually, then his face twitched as he seemed to be listening to something Allegra could not hear.

'The dancer's coming,' he said.

'Madri?'

Vargo shook his head, and howled.

Angel's arrival caused some consternation at first. He came running, his misshapen limbs moving erratically over the lava field as he wailed unhappily. Heading by instinct straight to the place where Madri was sitting with Andrin, he fell to his knees before the ex-admiral. It was some time before they were able to coax him to talk, and even then he made little sense. In between ramblings about apples, fog and dead crows, Madri caught a reference to a village that he knew Angel visited often.

'Calm down, Tre,' he said gently. 'What happened at Cumplina?'

'Eaten, all eaten by the spawn. All gone, burning inside.'

There was no need for anyone to translate this particular utterance or the feeling that came with it. Angel was clearly distraught, and the Firebrands shared some of his horror. The fireworms were obviously on the move again.

'Cumplina's a big place,' Nino said quietly. 'If it's been wiped out, then nowhere in the interior is safe.'

The others knew that Nino's home was only a few miles from the village that had apparently been devastated. They returned to their work in a sombre but determined mood, and the waiting for the birds to bring back news took on an added sense of urgency.

'I'm going to Guatiza tomorrow,' Andrin said. 'There's a prospector there who's supposed to have a large stock of crystals. He might be willing to give us some.'

'Be careful,' Allegra said. 'There's an army garrison at the port only a few miles from there.'

'Don't worry,' he replied. 'They'll never even know I've been there.'

They walked on, away from the entrance to the cavern where Jair had been installed.

'Do you think he heard?' Allegra whispered.

'I'm sure he did,' Andrin said. 'And tomorrow we'll find out what he does about it.'

They emerged into the late afternoon sunlight and, looking

up, he saw Ayo flying towards them. Instantly all thoughts of Jair vanished.

Any news?

Nothing yet, the eagle replied. *But I will fly again tomorrow.*

It had been no more than he had expected, but Andrin could not suppress a surge of disappointment, and he wondered for the thousandth time whether he would ever see Ico again.

CHAPTER FORTY-NINE

The ship's movement exacerbated Ico's morning sickness. After each bout she felt weak and wretched, but because there was nothing she could do about it she endured it as best she could. And she knew that this was the least of her worries. The *Revenge* had been out of sight of land for several days now, and she had needed to keep all her wits about her ever since she had been dragged aboard. She could hardly have remained unaware of the crew's mixed feelings about her presence. All sailors were superstitious, pirates especially so, and having a woman on board had caused considerable agitation. The resentment had been intensified by the fact that the Barber had taken personal charge of his captive. Ico had not been imprisoned in the hold, as would have been usual, but installed in a tiny cabin next to the captain's own quarters. This had led to angry speculation that the pirate leader was keeping her for his own private pleasure when, by rights, a percentage of all booty belonged to every man aboard. The rumours were given extra spice by the fact that the Barber was a well-known woman hater, often expressing his utter contempt for their weakness and stupidity. He had not even lowered himself to use them on land raids when rape was a common form of entertainment. So why, the pirates wondered, was he so protective of this girl?

It was true that she was unusually good-looking, and they had all heard the stories of her brief display of sorcery, but that surely did not justify such unprecedented possessiveness. Even the nominal reason – that they should keep her unharmed in order to exchange her for a large ransom – did not bear close examination. Their recent exploits had netted them a vast haul of valuable cargo, so money was not an immediate issue. And none of the pirates had ever heard of the Maravedis family, whose fabulous wealth was supposed to pay this ransom. In any case, the Barber had as yet made no plans to ask for payment – and what was the point of taking hostages if no one knew about it? Because they received no answers to their questions, feelings among the pirates had been running high, but no one – not even Cuero – had yet been bold enough to confront their leader on the issue.

Ico stepped back from the gunwale, as the vile heavings of her stomach finally eased, and walked back to her cabin with what little dignity she could muster. She was acutely aware that she was being watched by many members of the crew. Some were amused by her discomfort, which they took to be mere seasickness, but others followed her movements with more dangerous emotions in their eyes. Anger and suspicion mingled with undisguised lust was a potentially explosive mixture, and Ico found herself feeling unexpectedly grateful to the Barber. He had at least treated her with some degree of respect, and his authority had kept the jackals at bay. Even so, she knew the situation could change at any moment. No one on board knew that she was pregnant. That was something she wanted to keep in reserve, a last trick to play on their superstitious minds if all else failed. It would have to be a last resort because, for all she knew, admitting to the fact that she was carrying a child might be the last straw, and could get her thrown overboard. That she had survived unharmed so far had been a matter of using her own wits and, on occasion, her fighting spirit. During the general celebrations that had accompanied their departure from Teguise, many pirates had become inebriated on a mixture that they called grog, and Ico had had to repulse the unwanted attentions of several drunkards. That she had done so by a mixture of natural agility and a sharp tongue had made her some enemies but gained her the grudging admiration of others, including – crucially – the Barber. The unspoken pact between them had been sealed later the same day when they had been alone in his cabin, the only place in the overcrowded ship where any privacy was possible.

Ico had showed him her still soft hands as evidence of her worth, but he had not seemed particularly interested in a ransom. An early return to Tiguafaya was clearly not on the cards.

'You show some spirit at least, for a woman,' the Barber remarked. 'There are those among my crew who would take pleasure in breaking it.'

'If you let them.'

'Any reason why I shouldn't?'

'My father's not likely to pay for my release if I'm . . . damaged.' It was a weak argument and she knew it, but she couldn't think what else to say.

'Tell me about magic,' he said unexpectedly. 'How did you make the dragon?'

'I don't know,' she replied truthfully. 'It started out as an illusion, but . . .'

'It became more than that?'

Ico nodded, wishing she had not been so honest.

'Could you do it again?'

'If I needed to,' she claimed, knowing that he would see through her bluff.

'Then why did you stop?'

'I was distracted by Angel.'

'You don't strike me as someone who would be so easily distracted.'

'Think what you like,' she told him defiantly.

He sat quietly for a while in contemplation, and Ico could not help recalling the disastrous events in Teguise. That had been *real* magic. The door had actually shattered – and you couldn't do that with an illusion. And she had flown! The memory of the power, her sense of purpose, the certainty of her invincibility – all these things had been real. And then everything had been wrenched from her. The residual anger left over from that untimely withdrawal still had the power to disturb her. She had done something wrong, but she had no idea what.

'Show me an illusion then,' the Barber challenged, breaking her train of thought.

'Why?' she asked stupidly.

'Because I'm curious.'

'I'll need my talisman back.' The necklace had been taken from her as soon as she had come aboard.

The Barber gave her a measuring glance, then went to fetch the jewellery.

'Remember where you are,' he advised, before handing it over. 'If you seek to take advantage of me with your sorcery, it could leave you at the mercy of Cuero. He might not be as understanding as I am.'

Ico was coming to the same conclusion. To survive, she needed the Barber as her ally. In any case, she had no idea how powerful her magic might be. Her recent exploits had left her feeling weak.

'You have lovely hair,' he added. 'I'd hate to see it up there.' He waved an arm at the grisly collection of trophies tied to a net strung along one wall of the cabin.

'What do you want to see?'

'Anything you like.' He sat down again and folded his arms.

Ico held the necklace in both hands and let her thoughts die away. She sank into the depths of the blood-coloured stones, and let her imagination stir the embers of their fire. The image came without conscious effort, forming itself in exquisite detail on the surface of the cabin table. It was a perfect miniature representation of a little girl, perhaps four years old, who looked about with wide-eyed innocence. Ico stared at her, wondering what part of her mind the image had come from. Was this an unconscious memory of someone she had once known, or a vision of the future, of her own daughter? Or was it a pure fantasy, a creation of her imagination? Then she glanced at the Barber, who was staring at the image with a mixture of horror and disbelief. Was it someone he knew? *His* daughter perhaps?

The illusion faded, leaving Ico feeling intrigued but very tired. She yawned. The Barber stood up, his face a mask, and pulled aside a sliding panel to reveal a secondary cabin just big enough to contain a narrow bed.

'You sleep in here,' he said shortly, then left Ico alone.

She fell asleep with her mind still full of questions.

Now, several days later, she was no nearer the truth. Although the Barber had not asked for any more demonstrations, the sleeping arrangements had remained the same and Ico had even begun to feel safe in his company. He was certainly different from Cuero and his ilk. Indeed, it was the lieutenant's brooding malevolence that now concerned her the most. If she was ever to persuade the Barber to return her to Tiguafaya, the opposition of his second in command would have to be overcome first.

She knew that tensions were running high amongst the crew, and this had been intensified by the arrival of another unwelcome passenger. Soo rode on the topmost perches of the rigging, keeping out of reach of even the most nimble sailors, and her presence was a great comfort to Ico. They were able to talk only intermittently, but the sparrowhawk was her only true friend on board. It meant a great deal to Ico that her link was willing to undergo considerable hardships, in what to her was an alien realm, in order to stay close. On one occasion,

Soo had even protected her from an overaggressive pirate who had tried to take advantage of Ico's early morning distress. His face still bore the scratches from the bird's talons, and he often glanced nervously up at the sky. Others had tried to scare the bird away, or even kill her, but soon gave up their efforts as a waste of arrows and contented themselves with grumbling about having women *and* birds on board.

The Barber's fleet of seventeen vessels – one had been sunk in Teguise harbour – eventually made landfall at their island base. The other ships, those commanded by Snake and Zophres and their respective followers, had gone their separate ways soon after leaving the coastal waters, and no other craft had been seen since. There followed a period of intense activity, after the relative ease of the time at sea, as plunder was unloaded, trading began, repairs were undertaken and reunions were celebrated. The Barber and Ico did not go ashore, but she was grateful for the stillness of the water within the lagoon, and found that she was no longer so nauseous when she awoke.

'Don't you have a home here, on the island?' she asked. 'Family?'

'This is my home,' he answered, spreading a chart on the table and studying it intently.

'What are you going to do with me?' she said, finding the courage to ask a direct question for the first time.

'I haven't decided,' he said, without looking up.

'I'm not exactly much use to you, am I?' she persisted. 'Why not—'

'Shut up!'

'I'm just as much of an outlaw as you are, you know.'

The Barber laughed, raising his gaze at last. 'And how have you reached that conclusion?'

'Have you heard of the Firebrands?' Ico began, then told him all about the dissident group.

The fact that she was under sentence of death appeared to amuse him, and when she had finished her story he even seemed to be impressed. For Ico's own part, talking about her recent history had brought back painful memories of her parting with Andrin, and she realized, guiltily, that she had been so preoccupied with her own predicament that she had hardly given him a thought. She wondered what he was doing now, whether anyone had been able to tell him of her fate. His child was growing inside her, but there was no way he could possibly help her now. Grief threatened to overwhelm her, but she suppressed it as best she could. If she was ever to see him again, it was up to her. She was on her own.

'You tell a good story,' the Barber conceded. 'You really think the fireworms will destroy all Tiguafaya?'

'Unless we stop them, yes. That's what makes the Senate's stubbornness so infuriating. We're cutting our own throats. And if Tiguafaya is decimated, where will that leave you?'

'The brethren of the islands will survive,' he replied complacently. 'There will always be plenty of opportunities for a man with a strong arm and a good ship.'

'But not so many targets as easy as us,' Ico argued. 'And who's to say the worms won't travel further – even to this island?'

'I doubt they'd be able to fly so far over water.'

'I wouldn't be so sure, if I were you. Not so long ago they never came near the coastal plain, but several villages there have been wiped out in recent months.'

The Barber smiled. 'You'll have to do better than that,' he remarked.

'What do you mean?' she asked, feigning innocence.

'Do you want a drink?' he offered, ignoring her question.

'No, thank you.'

'Pity. You might not be so straight-laced after a few shots of rum.'

Ico was not used to being described in such terms, but tried not to let her surprise show. The Barber produced a large flagon and poured himself a cup. A pungent aroma filled the room as he drank and then poured again.

'Sure you won't join me?'

Ico shook her head.

'You've had your say,' he went on. 'Now it's my turn to tell *you* a story. When I'm done, you tell me if you still think the Firebrands and pirates are the same. Fair enough?'

'All right.' Ico had already overheard several tall tales being swapped by various members of the crew, but their captain had not taken part.

'Many years ago, one of the brethren contrived to steal a treasure map from its previous owner. This pirate was not too bright, and he was so afraid that someone else might steal it from him before he was able to recover the supposedly priceless loot that he decided to have the entire chart tattooed on his own body. This he duly did. Unfortunately, the only space large enough to copy the whole map in the necessary detail was his back, but he went ahead anyway. When it was finished, our hero destroyed the original parchment and inevitably, as an extra precaution, killed the tattooist. Then he realized that, without the aid of two mirrors – which were even rarer and more valuable then than they are now – he was unable to read the map himself. Even then he was only able to see a small, distorted portion at a time, and the process involved incredibly awkward contortions.'

Ico could not help smiling at the ridiculous images conjured up by the Barber's words, even though she was already convinced that the story was not true.

'Neither could the pirate find anyone he trusted to read the map for him,' he went on, 'so the treasure languished while he zealously guarded his secret. He kept his shirt on at all times, even when he was sleeping, or when it was unbearably hot, but eventually the inevitable happened. The tattoo was discovered and he in turn was murdered for it. This time the map was recovered by the simple expedient of flaying the skin from his corpse.'

He smiled at Ico's expression of disgust. 'The new owner tried to find the place on the map, but he was unable to do so, and assumed that either the tattooist must have missed out some vital detail or that there never was any treasure in the first place.'

'And?' Ico prompted, when he did not continue.

'Nothing. That's the end of the story.'

'That's it?' she exclaimed. 'What was the point of telling me that?'

'To demonstrate that we're not the same. For the Fire-brands, life is serious. For us it's a game.'

'And all those deaths were pointless,' she said, catching on.

'As are all games,' he agreed. 'You understand now.'

'You made it up,' she accused. 'Tall tales don't prove anything.'

For answer the Barber opened a drawer underneath his table and took out a roll of what looked like vellum. Ico felt her gorge rise as he untied the string that bound it and unfurled the tattoo. The skin was distorted and creased but still recognizably human, complete with some scars and two moles which had been cunningly worked into the design of the map.

Ico stared at it, so revolted that she hardly saw the lines of the map at first, but then a familiar shape caught her eye and she gasped involuntarily.

'Is that where the treasure is supposed to be?' she asked, pointing without touching.

'For what it's worth, yes.' He was intrigued by her un-expected reaction. 'Do you know where it is?'

Ico was thinking fast, considering her options, her new hope. Eventually she decided on the direct approach.

'I do know where it is,' she said. 'I've been there before.'

CHAPTER FIFTY

'If I show you where it is,' Ico went on, 'will you take the treasure as my ransom and set me free there?'

'So it *is* in Tiguafaya,' the Barber remarked.

'Of course. How could I have been there otherwise?' Ico was determined to keep the location secret as long as she could, to add strength to her bargaining power, but she knew she had to give her captor some information.

'I've sailed round the entire coastline of your country,' he added, 'but I've never found this place.'

'The map is not strictly accurate,' she told him. 'Some of it is symbolic rather than factual.'

'I see.' He was obviously amused by her earnest expression. 'So what makes you think your interpretation is the right one?'

'I'm not going to tell you any more until we're under way. But I *can* take you to where the treasure is.' Privately, Ico thought it quite possible that the treasure might not be of much interest to the pirates. Indeed, in their terms it might not exist at all – but she was not about to tell him that. Sometimes, she told herself, you have to tell the truth as it should be, instead of the way it is. 'Do you want to go or not?'

'Perhaps.'

She could tell that he was intrigued, but if he decided she was bluffing, just trying to find a way to get home, then she was in trouble. She had no proof that what she said was true.

'But there's no hurry, is there?' the Barber remarked casually. 'My men have been looking forward to a little recreation, to spending some of their ill-gotten gains. They won't thank me for dragging them off on a wild goose chase.'

'It won't be,' Ico promised.

'I only have your word for that. Why should I take the risk?'

'So much for your eagerness for the game,' she said scornfully. 'I thought you *liked* taking risks! Would the brethren of the islands rather sleep soft and waste their time with whores than enlist for an adventure?'

The Barber laughed. 'Do not think to goad me, Ico. Women are not the only ones capable of guile – or of recognizing it.'

'If I don't lead you to the place marked on this map,' she stated passionately, 'you can cut off my hair – and my head with it! Are you as timid as the man whose skin this was? Why own the map if you're just going to hide it in a drawer and do nothing with it?' Although she knew she was pushing him close to the limit of his patience, this was too important for her to be held back by caution. 'Think of it as a gamble, if you like,' she went on. 'My life and freedom in exchange for unknown wealth. Is that such a bad wager? It'll be a lot more fun and a lot less trouble than getting my ransom any other way. And as you seem to have no other use for me, it would be the best use of all your assets.'

She stopped abruptly. All humour had drained from his face, and his eyes regarded her malevolently. 'You think I would not make use of you if I wanted to?'

'That's your choice,' she whispered. 'I—'

'I could devour you and spit out your bones for the dogs to chew on.' He waved a hand to indicate the other sailors beyond the cabin walls. 'Is that what you want?'

'No,' she breathed, realising she had gone too far. 'You've been good to me, and I'm grateful.'

'That I have,' he agreed. 'Don't you forget it. Now get out of my sight.'

Ico withdrew to her cell-like cabin and closed the door. Lying on the bed, she was overwhelmed by a sudden loneliness, an anguish that cut through her like a knife. She closed her eyes and saw Andrin's face.

Much later, she awoke from a fevered dream in which he had been searching for her, calling her name and pleading. Although his gaze had rested upon her several times, he had looked straight through her as though she were invisible and, no matter how hard she tried, she could not attract his attention. He had faded away at the last, disappearing in a haze of smoke.

Ico wept, unable to detach herself from the emotions of the dream, then started violently as her door was thrown back with a crash. She could not see the Barber's face properly through her tears, but even in the pale lamplight it was obvious that he was angry. Ico cowered, pulling the bedclothes up to her neck, as she smelt the rum on his breath.

'What's the matter with you?' he demanded harshly.

He was still fully clothed, even though it was the middle of the night, and Ico wondered why he chose to drink alone.

'Well?' he barked. 'Birds got your tongue?'

'I miss him,' she managed to whisper.

'Who? Your lover?' He sounded contemptuous.

'Yes.'

'Poor little fool,' he muttered.

'I'm carrying his child,' she said before she could stop herself.

The Barber sat down on the edge of the bed with a bump. Ico shrank back, but all the aggression, all the tension, seemed to have left him.

'I did wonder,' he said wearily.

'I . . . I didn't want anyone to know,' she mumbled, feeling a queasy sense of relief.

He nodded, understanding. 'What will you call her?' he asked. 'If it's a girl, that is.'

'I've no idea,' she replied, surprised by the question. 'Why?'

He did not respond. In fact, he was so still and silent that Ico began to wonder if he had fallen asleep, but eventually he stood up and put a hand on the sliding door.

'I'm going to accept your wager,' he said, and shut her in again.

Ico woke the next morning with a sudden ray of hope brightening an otherwise dull and cloudy day. The Barber was not there and the outer cabin was locked, so she had no alternative but to wait impatiently. It was almost noon before she heard the key turn.

'The crew voted to sail,' he told her as he came in. 'We'll leave tomorrow.'

Ico was too delighted to say anything, and merely grinned happily.

'You'd better not be deceiving me,' he warned her. 'Some of the others think you are, and they'll have my permission to do whatever they like with you if you prove them right.'

'They're wrong,' she replied confidently.

'I hope so. The other ships are voting this afternoon. Then we'll know what sort of fleet we'll be taking with us.'

'I had no idea this was a democracy,' Ico remarked.

'It's not,' he told her. 'At sea they obey me, but for decisions like this they wouldn't tolerate a dictator. They're all free men.'

In the event, all but three crews voted for the expedition, so it was a party of fourteen vessels that raised their sails and headed out of the lagoon the next day. With the help of the captain's charts, Ico had told the Barber to set a course that would not take them directly to their destination, but which would not take them too far out of their way. The weather had taken a turn for the worse, with a good deal of cloud cover and the occasional stinging shower of rain. The ocean was rougher than on the outward journey but Ico was acquiring her sea legs now, and hardly felt sick at all. She spent more time on deck, in spite of the cold wind, and neither the weather nor the glowering looks she received from some of the crew could dampen her mood. One way or another, against all the odds, she was convinced that she would be back in Tiguafaya before too long.

You're looking better.

The sparrowhawk alighted on a spar near Ico, and kept a wary eye on the nearby sailors. Her plumage, which had become ragged, was sleek again and her eyes were bright.

You too, Ico replied. *Island life must've suited you.*

I could hunt, at least. Where are we going?

Home.

How did you manage that? Soo asked admiringly.

Oh, I just used my natural charm. Ico grinned – then told her link the rest of the story.

Let me know if there's anything I can do.

We'll think about it when we're in sight of land, Ico replied. The possibility of getting a message to Andrin via their links had already occurred to her, but she had not wanted to risk Soo's being killed on a foolhardy venture. Besides, the bird's presence was a source of comfort she was reluctant to lose.

When will that be? Soo asked, her antipathy for life at sea clear in her tone.

A few days. It depends on the wind.

You might have chosen a faster ship, the bird commented wryly, then took to the air as two pirates passed below her perch.

The trouble began two days into the journey. The weather had seemed to be improving steadily, with large breaks in the

cloud and gentler, warmer winds, but a sudden squall caught
them unawares. In its wake, as the *Revenge* slewed sideways, a
cry went up from one of the lookouts.

'Water spout!'

The twisting column of water hit the ship almost before anyone had time to react, creating a miniature hurricane on deck.
Sails flapped wildly, rigging stretched and snapped, and the whole
vessel lurched and groaned beneath the shrieking wind and
spray. It was all over in a few moments, and damage was minimal,
but as conditions returned to normal another cry went up.

'Man overboard!'

In fact, two pirates had been swept into the sea, but they
were lucky and were picked up by one of the following vessels.
Ico had been in the cabin when the water spout struck and
had known only an instant's panic, but she soon became aware
of mutterings among the crew, of venomous sidelong glances
directed at her, and a growing mood of unrest. It came to a
head with terrifying speed that same afternoon.

The confrontation seemed to spring up out of nowhere. One
minute the crew were going about their normal business, the
next they had divided into two opposing armies, facing each
other across the middle deck. Ico was outside now, close to the
helmsman in the stern, and she watched fearfully, knowing
that her future was in the balance. To no one's surprise the
leader of the malcontents was Cuero, and it was to him that
the Barber addressed himself.

'What's this? Have you decided you're tired of living?'

'Not me,' his second in command replied. 'Neither am I
besotted with some piece of skirt.'

Their respective supporters murmured warily when they
heard the accusation but, as yet, they were content to leave
the talking to their leaders.

'Do you have a point?' the Barber enquired coldly.

'The point is, we're on our way to god knows where because

of a *woman*,' Cuero said derisively. 'Even a crackwit can see that's asking for trouble. She shouldn't even be on board. And if you want proof that she's bad luck, then why did that spout hit us and none of the other ships?'

'How do we know the witch didn't use her sorcery to create the spout?' one of Cuero's followers shouted.

'Of course! She used magic to try and sink the very ship she's on,' the Barber exclaimed sarcastically. 'That makes perfect sense.'

'She was below decks.'

'And it wasn't her that was swept overboard,' Cuero pointed out.

'Ah, so she's going to pick us off one by one,' the captain declared. 'What's next, do you think? The crow's nest struck by lightning? Being squashed by a giant squid? If you believe that, you might as well call *yourselves* women. *Old* women!'

'She shouldn't be on board,' Cuero repeated flatly.

'You knew the situation when the vote was taken,' the Barber stated. 'You should have thought of it then.'

'Things have changed. Some of us weren't sure about this trip.' His face took on a sly expression. 'It was a close call and with Spear and Rabel gone over the side, I doubt you have the numbers any more.'

'You're demanding a re-count?' the Barber said, laughing. 'After the event? Well think again, Cuero. I'm captain of this ship, and the answer's no.'

Until then it had been just talk. No weapons had been drawn, even though several hands had searched out the hilts of their blades. But at the Barber's emphatic denial, there was a rustle of movement, and knives and cutlasses suddenly glinted in the newborn sunlight.

'Mutiny?' the Barber said incredulously.

'You leave us no choice,' his adversary answered. 'Throw the bitch overboard and we'll all be happy. If not . . .' He let the words hang in the air.

While the two principal opponents glared at each other, their supporters shifted nervously. The opposing forces were evenly balanced, and they all knew that the consequences of a fight would be serious, but no one wavered in their allegiance. Although the Barber's sword had remained in its sheath, he took a step forward into no-man's-land. Cuero tensed but did nothing more.

'Let's settle this between the two of us, Cuero. To the death. The winner does what he wants with the girl.'

The challenger hesitated. He was confident that his men would prevail in a mass brawl. In solo combat, however, he knew the Barber would be a formidable opponent – even though Cuero had boasted many times that he was the better swordsman.

'Not got the courage of your convictions?' the Barber needled. 'If we all fight, there won't be enough crew left to sail anywhere. This way at least it's clean and simple.'

'Take him, Cuero!' someone shouted, and suddenly the air was full of advice for both men.

When the noise died away, Cuero spat on the deck and raised his sword.

'Agreed.'

The Barber drew his own weapon as the spectators fell back to give them space. From her vantage point, Ico watched the two men begin to circle warily. She held her breath as the first skirmishes took place.

From the start it was clear that they were evenly matched. The Barber was faster and more agile, but Cuero had the edge in strength. They were both expert swordsmen, their blades weaving and clashing as they evaded or parried the other's thrusts. At first they fought in an eerie silence, their faces grimly determined, but the onlookers soon began urging them on, cheering each attack and counter. Both men took advantage of the arena, trying to manoeuvre his opponent to where he might trip over a coiled rope or slip on wet boards, while keeping their own feet clear of any obstructions. Both moved easily, adjusting instinctively to the gentle swaying of the deck and using the base of the mainmast to mark their position and, occasionally, as a shield.

To Ico the fight seemed endless, a prolonged torture, but she had the presence of mind to know that she ought to prepare for the worst. If Cuero was victorious, she would not go without a fight of her own. She looked around for a weapon, but her eyes were drawn back to the duel.

Soo! she called. *I may need your help.*

The sparrowhawk flew down from the rigging.

Do you want me to help him?

No, that'll only make things worse. Can you find a knife for me? Her eyes were still glued to the contest.

We'll give them a good fight, Soo stated fiercely, flexing her talons as she took off again.

Stay close, Ico warned anxiously.

A shout went up then, as one of the men drew blood. Ico began to feel sick as she saw a red stain spreading on the Barber's left arm, but his mobility did not seem to be affected. They were tiring now, their efforts becoming more desperate. Cuero pressed home his new advantage by chasing his opponent around the mast, raining a succession of vicious blows at his head and shoulders. The Barber parried them all, but then he stumbled and almost went down. Cuero lunged forward triumphantly but, instead of retreating further, the Barber sprang up from his half-kneeling stance, jumping into and under his enemy's attack with his own sword thrust upward in a deadly arc. The blade plunged into Cuero's stomach, then up behind his rib cage. Cheers and groans resounded as the Barber twisted it savagely and threw his victim to the floor. Cuero's body shuddered for a few moments, then lay still, a look of surprise frozen on his face.

'Throw that carrion overboard,' the victor commanded, then turned to face those who had supported the dead man. 'It's over. We go on. And she stays.'

No one argued.

That evening, as the *Revenge* cut through the waves, Ico stood near the prow, gazing ahead. She felt the pull of fate. This time she needed no premonitions, no dream images, to sense the hand of destiny. She had known as soon as she saw that one particular feature on the map – among all the fanciful and misleading details – that she was on her way to Elva. And this time she really *had* been called.

CHAPTER FIFTY-ONE

'You're not fooling anyone, you know,' the Barber said as the helmsman turned the wheel and other sailors adjusted the rigging. 'This is our third unnecessary course change.'

'I know,' Ico replied, 'but I like to keep you busy.'

'Sooner or later you'll have to tell me the real direction, and then I'll know where the treasure is,' he pointed out. 'Aren't you afraid I'll go back on my word, take it *and* keep you?'

'And renege on a bet?'

'You actually think I'm honourable?' Her captor was doing his best to look offended.

'For a pirate,' she replied, smiling. 'Besides, you'll still need me once we get there.'

'Really? Why?'

'You'll see.'

They were sailing parallel to the coast now, although the land was still out of sight, and it would soon be time to turn and head towards the shore. That would be the crucial moment, when the destiny Ico had imagined so fondly for herself was either fulfilled or dashed on the rocks of treachery. Studying the skin map and comparing it to real charts, Ico had reached the conclusion that the coastline must have altered through the encroachment of lava flows or massive erosion. Either that, or the fertile imagination that included whirlpools, serpents and what looked like fountains in the tattoo had also taken liberties with the shape of the land. The only part that appeared accurate was the cove itself, complete with the lake, the tidal island and the cliffs. Even here, the seaward approaches were not as Ico remembered them. When she had been to Elva the cove had faced open sea; on the treasure map it was set at the end of a long, narrow inlet, which was itself marked with several curious signs. She had located their destination on the Barber's chart, and there it looked exactly as she remembered it – although again there were some curious markings that she did not understand and dared not ask about yet, in case he guessed the reason for her interest.

'How long before we get there?' he asked innocently.

'Do I *look* stupid?' she answered and then, looking at his grin, she knew he had not been expecting an answer. By her own calculations they were perhaps a day and a half's sail away. They would be in sight of land before that, and then she would have to decide whether to send Soo ashore.

'Sail ahoy!' The cry came from the crow's nest. 'Dead ahead.'

'Well now. Who could this be? Endo!' he called to the man who was his newly promoted second in command. 'Send signals to the rest of the fleet. We may be in for a fight.' Turning back to Ico, he said, 'If we are, I want you in the cabin. Understand?'

'Ashamed to have the other pirates see you with a woman?'

He was about to reply when the lookout's next shout demanded his attention.

'It's the Lawyer!'

'How many ships?'

'Twenty. Maybe more.'

'Get below,' he told Ico shortly, then turned away and began yelling orders.

As Ico obeyed, she could not help thinking that a note of unholy joy had crept into his voice at the prospect of battle. The gash in his left arm, which he had insisted on bandaging himself, had not seemed to hamper him at all and she wondered whether, in a perverse way, he actually enjoyed the pain. The fact that they were badly outnumbered frightened her – for her hopes to be dashed by an apparently chance encounter at this late stage was almost too dreadful to contemplate – but the Barber seemed to relish the challenge.

The only view from the cabin was from a small porthole that faced astern, so she could get no clear picture of what was going on. She was aware of various manoeuvrings and could see part of the formation of the other vessels behind the *Revenge*, but she had no idea what their enemy was doing or when the actual fighting would begin. She realized too late that she could have asked Soo to let her know what was happening and tried, without success, to call her. She had just decided to risk a quick visit to the deck when she heard a flurry of running footsteps and urgent shouted orders, and thought better of it.

Then the ship lurched so violently that Ico was thrown to the ground. From somewhere came the sound of splintering wood, accompanied by a great deal of yelling. The *Revenge* had lost way abruptly, and Ico realized that they must have rammed another vessel, using the solid point that protruded from her bows at water level. The battle had obviously begun in earnest.

She could hear faint sounds of cheering and the clash of metal, and then the *Revenge* seemed to buck in the waves and pull free to ride the wind again. As the ship went forward, Ico saw the crippled remains of the other vessel, now sinking fast. There was debris floating on the water, smoke in the air, and here and there men were thrashing about as they tried to stay afloat. It was a terrible scene, but Ico could not help but feel glad. It meant there was one less of the Lawyer's fleet to worry about now.

She saw several separate engagements from her porthole, but couldn't be certain which side was winning. Several ships had been set ablaze, others apparently crippled and many boarded so that the conflict became a matter of hand-to-hand combat, with men swarming over the gunwales and chasing each other over decks and in the rigging. As far as the *Revenge* herself was concerned, there were several brief skirmishes but nothing more than that. The ship was steering an erratic and – to Ico – incomprehensible course amid the carnage, as though the helmsman had gone mad. She soon realised that this was because the Barber was intent on attacking one particular ship – presumably that of the Lawyer himself.

A sudden fluttering in front of the porthole made Ico jump.

If you're ever going to help, Soo advised her, *now would be a good time.*

Me, help? How?

Magic, you idiot. Had you forgotten?

But what . . . ?

How should I know? the sparrowhawk said impatiently. *You're the expert.*

Are we in trouble?

Not yet, but we're going to be. This madman is trying to board a ship that has twice as many men as he has.

Ico needed no more convincing. She tried to fetch her talisman but, naturally enough, the chest in which it was kept was locked. It doesn't matter, she told herself. You can use anything as a talisman. It's just a matter of making the connection. On impulse she snatched up the tattoo map. The skin felt like soft leather and she shuddered at the touch, but hesitated no longer. She wrenched at the cabin door and found to her horror that it too was locked. He had locked her in! Indignation made her exclaim out loud, her face burning with rage. How dare he? Without thinking she funnelled all her pent-up anger into a single kick, throwing the weight of her entire body into that violent motion. To her amazement the wood surrounding the lock shattered and the door slammed back on its hinges. She wasted no time admiring her handiwork but ran out and scrambled up the steps to the deck.

The scene that greeted her was chaotic. Men were running everywhere, while others lay dead or wounded. There were small fires burning in several places, and arrows fizzed through the air. There were several ships nearby, all apparently heading in different directions, but the one that held everyone's attention was running alongside the *Revenge*, only about fifty paces away and closing fast. Soon they would meet broadside, and swords and axes would take the place of crossbows as the main weapons in the contest.

No one paid Ico the slightest attention and she stood there feeling rather foolish, not knowing what to do. It was all very well Soo telling her to use magic, but what exactly was she supposed to *do*? She still didn't even know the limits of her abilities. A fire-arrow thudded into the deck beside her and as she stamped on it instinctively, putting out the flames, an idea came to her. If nothing else, she thought, an illusion might cause the enemy to panic. She clutched her new talisman tightly and summoned her imagination, her will and her need. She had done it before, after all . . .

A most curious sensation overtook Ico then, and she felt as though another pair of eyes were looking out from her head. The feeling only lasted a moment, and was forgotten as the results of her efforts exploded into illusory life. Bright orange flames enveloped the entire side of the enemy vessel, licking around the gunwales and roaring up among the sails. She heard screams and yells of surprise, watched with satisfaction as the bemused sailors scurried to and fro in fear, and heard her own crew raise a ragged cheer. The Lawyer's flagship veered away from the *Revenge*. Ico was delighted – until she saw the Barber staring at her, his eyes blazing.

'Did you do that?' he shouted across the deck as the false flames died away.

She nodded. He swore, yelled new orders to his helmsman, then turned back to Ico.

'Stay out of this, you stupid bitch. We almost had them there—'

A cry of fear went up then, soon echoed in many voices. It was a few moments before Ico realized what they were saying and looked over the bows to the west. To her horror she saw them immediately, a sinuous grey line squirming above the water. They were too far away yet to be able to be seen as individual fireworms, but they were moving fast and it was clearly a large swarm. And they were heading straight for the *Revenge*.

Without giving herself time to think, Ico ran towards the front of the ship, yelling as she went.

'Douse all the fires! Douse them now! They're attracted by heat.'

The confused pirates hesitated, several of them glancing at their captain.

'Do it!' he ordered after the briefest pause, then ran after Ico. He caught up with her and grabbed her arm.

'What are you doing?'

'We need cold, to turn them away,' she told him, her eyes still fixed on the swarm. 'Do you have any dragon's tears on board?'

'A few. In my chest.'

'Get them now! Quickly!'

He ran, moving with an athletic grace that belied the urgency of the situation, while Ico tried to summon up her strength. A few heartbeats later he was back.

'Here,' he said breathlessly.

'Let me have them.'

There were only three crystals, but it was better than nothing. Ico quickly took the measure of each in turn, then selected the largest and handed it back.

'When I tell you, throw it into the path of the swarm.'

He did not object or question her, but waited at her side, as all around them the crew's dread grew palpable. Fearless against human foes, they were justifiably terrified by this unnatural enemy – known only by its gruesome reputation. The fireworms were close now, each swimming shape discernible against the blue of sea and sky.

'Now!'

The Barber hurled the crystal as far as he could, and Ico watched the arc of its flight carefully, praying she had got the timing right. Just before the stone hit the water, she sent the telepathic impulse. A thin screaming filled the air as a miniature iceberg began to form in the ocean and the swarm veered away from the spreading cold.

'Turn the ship to starboard,' she urged, and the Barber turned to yell the order.

The *Revenge* began to turn as the fireworms went the other way, passing by the port bow.

'Be ready with the next crystal,' Ico said, handing it to him, but then found she did not need it. She discovered that she could shape the cold radiating from the disintegrating crystal so that it formed a windblown barrier in the air, guiding the swarm away from the ship. With a deliberate and calculating ruthlessness she set them on a new course – heading directly for the Lawyer's flagship.

Everyone on the *Revenge* watched in a mixture of relief and horror as the swarm fell upon their new prey. The screams were appalling to hear, and soon flames – real flames this time – were engulfing the entire craft.

'Gods,' the Barber breathed in awe.

Ico was perspiring heavily, and shaking now as he put a hand on her shoulder. She was grateful for the gesture of support, but knew there was still work to do.

'Get as many of your ships as possible over to our starboard side,' she gasped. 'I might be able to keep the swarm away from them.'

The Barber gave the instructions, and the signals were sent. The battle was over for everyone except Ico. After seeing the fate of their leader, the Lawyer's men had no stomach for the fight and fled in haphazard fashion. At least two more ships were caught by the remaining swarm and sank in flames, but most appeared to get away. None of the Barber's fleet was trapped by the lethal creatures, but two had been sunk earlier in the fighting and almost all the rest had suffered casualties and some damage. When it was clear that no more fireworms were abroad, the Barber ordered everyone to head for the coast of Tiguafaya, where a wide bay would give them a safe anchorage in which to lick their wounds and make repairs. Once they were under way he knelt down before Ico, who was sitting slumped against the main mast, utterly exhausted.

'We owe you our lives,' he said, loud enough for most of the crew to hear. 'And we repay our debts.'

There were murmurs of agreement from all the pirates, who now regarded Ico with a respect that bordered on reverence, but she did not hear them. She was fast asleep, the map still clutched tightly in her hand.

CHAPTER FIFTY-TWO

For Andrin, time had seemed to stand still after Ico's abduction. Now it was flying past with frightening speed. Days had passed in an angry haze, unnoticed; now there was so much to occupy him that he hardly had time to draw breath. He had become coldly fanatical, grimly determined to continue the fight against both Kantrowe and the fireworms until both had been obliterated. In rare quiet moments his thoughts strayed to memories of Ico, but he told himself that she was dead – and was almost convinced. Sometimes he even thought it would be better if she *had* been killed, rather than suffer the all too easily imaginable torments of her captors.

In the days that followed Jair's mysterious outburst and Angel's distressed arrival, the Firebrands had learnt a great deal about what was happening elsewhere in Tiguafaya. However, the news brought by Eya and the other messenger birds was almost universally bad. Marco Guadarfia was dead and Kantrowe had usurped the rank of President; two captured Firebrands had indeed been sacrificed; and the city was now in the iron grip of the White Guard. Anyone opposed to Kantrowe had either been imprisoned or had fled, and the purges had extended to all sections of public life. Elsewhere the fireworms were becoming increasingly active, moving in swarms of unprecedented size and destroying at least two more villages. They also discovered that a large part of the pirate fleet that had been guarding Teguise was now sailing south on an unspecified mission.

The only good news was that Senator Alegranze Maciot, after apparently accusing Kantrowe of treason and in turn being labelled a murderer, had avoided arrest and escaped from the capital, along with others sympathetic to his views. Maciot and the rebels, who included several detachments of the regular army, were now based in the interior, at the remote villages of Corazoncillo and Quemada. The combined resources of Maciot's allies in the Transporters' Guild and the Firebrands' birds had enabled the two renegade groups to make contact, and they were now working together, determined to end Kantrowe's tyranny. In truth, their efforts owed more to optimism than organization. The withdrawal from Teguise had been a chaotic, piecemeal affair motivated by several different factors, and the consequent amalgam of humanity that was gathering in the firelands was hardly a cohesive military force. It was held together by a mixture of idealism, fear and stubborn practicality which made it hard to control. Maciot did his best, knowing that his dream of a bloodless coup was now impossible, and that their refuge could not remain undiscovered for long. If they were ever to have the chance of returning the country to a more democratic form of government, then it would have to be soon. As civil war now seemed inevitable, he was determined to see that the right side won – and with the minimum loss of life.

Strangely enough, the White Guard and the other troops loyal to Kantrowe had so far made no attempt to search for or attack the rebels. It was as though they were trying to lull them into a false sense of security – something that had given Maciot many sleepless nights. On the other hand, he appreciated the respite. He had been delighted to hear from the Firebrands, astonished to learn of the contribution of Jurado Madri, and encouraged by their devoting their magical resources to his cause. Although the Firebrands were few in number, Maciot knew that their influence might be considerable. If all went well, the new group of allies would present a combined threat to Kantrowe that the usurper President would be unable to destroy at will. They could not hope to defeat the White Guard and the rest of Kantrowe's forces in a pitched battle, but if they chose their targets carefully they could win a war of attrition. The freedom fighters, as they now thought of themselves, believed they could also win the war of words. If they could convert enough of the population to their way of thinking, Kantrowe would be forced to relinquish power, and the rebels would eventually reclaim Teguise and the whole of the land. Although this was a distant prospect at best, at least it was something they could aspire to.

Maciot knew that some of those who had chosen to remain in Teguise, and who were paying lip service to the new regime, secretly believed the accusations he had made in the Senate. The letter he had produced had been a fake, of course – Kantrowe would never have been stupid enough to commit such damning evidence to paper – but the facts he had claimed as its contents were true. Zophres had convinced him of that before he vanished again, presumably to sea. That was why Kantrowe had been so enraged, and had immediately counterattacked with the murder charge that many people had found to be less than credible. If the rebels' efforts proved effective, public opinion would become a dangerous weapon against which Kantrowe would have little defence, other than even more draconian oppression. And that, Maciot hoped, would finally prove to be self-defeating.

Zophres' reasons for telling Maciot about the clandestine details of the treaty were a mystery, and one that he did not waste much time analyzing. The envoy's personality was in many ways like that of a mischievous child, always doing the last thing anyone expected, always seeing how much he could get away with. Maciot was under no illusion that he could rely on Zophres for any more help. If the envoy saw any advantage or amusement in betraying the rebels to his old master, then he was more than likely to do it. The gods knew where he would turn up next.

All this information had been relayed to Andrin and the Firebrands by an increasingly sophisticated communication network involving the tireless efforts of the birds. In fact, the only link who had been unable to achieve the results he wanted was Ayo. The eagle had been unable to get any word of Ico or the Barber, even though he had covered hundreds of square miles of the endless, unchanging ocean, in several days of constant flight. This, as much as his own realism, had been responsible for Andrin's fatalistic attitude, and he had thrown himself into his work as an antidote to pain.

Under Andrin's zealous leadership, and with the knowledge of their alliance with Maciot and the increasingly valuable advice of Jurado Madri, the Firebrands had at last begun to look to the future. Their plans had been assisted by two important breakthroughs. The first had come when Andrin watched from a nearby hillside and saw the soldiers move into Guatiza on the day he was supposed to be there. It had been all the proof he had needed that Jair, unwittingly or not, was supplying information to their enemies. This presented the Firebrands with an obvious problem, but also an opportunity. As Madri had pointed out, it could be very useful to feed misleading information to Kantrowe at some point in the future. To date they had been keeping this card up their sleeve, not wanting to tip off their adversaries too soon, but a variety of options had already been discussed. The problem was the fact that because Jair was aware of their location, so too, it was assumed, was Kantrowe. They did not know what his reasons were for not acting on this knowledge, but it was clear that he was biding his time. The Firebrands began to prepare several different bases for future use, making sure that Jair only knew of a few of them. At the same time, they began a systematic exploration of several other underground labyrinths. This had been prompted by a bizarre and, for the most part, unintelligible conversation between Angel and Vargo – which the musician could not later remember, and which Angel refused to discuss, even with Madri. Those who had overheard it had caught references that might possibly have been to certain fireworm breeding grounds. It was thought that if the Firebrands could find these and destroy them with the freezing crystals, then the future threat from the creatures would, at the very least, be drastically reduced. It was from this initiative, orchestrated by Madri and led by Andrin, that the second breakthrough came, several days after the first.

Andrin had come to admire Madri's calm grasp of strategy, displayed in all aspects of their efforts. The old man's knowledge and opinions were always worth listening to, and informed most of the decisions made by the Firebrands. Andrin was now firmly convinced that, whatever misfortune had befallen the Tiguafayan navy thirty years earlier, the responsibility for its failure could not have been Madri's. The ex-admiral's obvious reluctance to discuss the past made further enquiry impossible, however, so Andrin's natural curiosity went unsatisfied. For his part, Madri now regarded Andrin almost as the son he had never had, recognizing the personal doubts and fears beneath the dedicated and tireless exterior. He also recognized the young man's courage, especially in the way that he dealt with his own pain.

'There's Tisaloya, of course,' the old man said, naming one of the volcanoes that had been among the most active over the previous two decades.

'There are caves there?' Andrin sounded surprised.

'The whole mountain is riddled with them,' Madri confirmed, 'but I didn't explore very far. The air's probably poisonous, and it was very hot.'

'Sounds like the perfect place for fireworms to breed.'

'Maybe.'

'Let's ask Angel,' Nino suggested.

'He won't talk about it,' Andrin said.

'Perhaps he will, if we ask a direct question,' Madri said. 'He doesn't lie well.'

'I'll fetch him,' Nino volunteered.

'Bring Vargo too,' Andrin called after him.

The two men were laughing when Nino led them to the meeting.

'What's so funny?' Andrin asked.

Nino pulled a face and shrugged.

'I've no idea,' he said. 'These two speak a language of their own.'

'We sing the ripples in the water,' Vargo announced, rolling his eyes.

'And hear the echoes of the stone,' Angel added, capering like a jester, and they both dissolved into laughter again.

Andrin glanced at Nino, then Madri, his eyebrows raised in mute question. Vargo's madness appeared to feed off the strangeness that Angel took with him everywhere, and it seemed unlikely that they would get any sense out of either of them while they were in this mood. However, Madri was determined to try.

'Tre?' he said. 'Do you remember talking about the place where the fireworms hatched?'

The sound of the ex-admiral's voice sobered Angel quickly, and he stared at his old companion intently.

'You want to hurt them,' he muttered. 'That's bad.'

'They're our enemies, Tre. They kill people. We need to stop them. Are their breeding grounds at Tisaloya?'

'The place of eggs,' Vargo said unexpectedly. 'I saw them.'

Angel cast a worried glance at his friend.

'Is that where we can find them, Tre?' Madri persisted. 'It's important.'

Angel's reluctance to answer told its own story.

'Have you seen them?'

'Yes, yes. Bad place, can't breathe. No apples.'

'Will you show us *where* you saw them?' Andrin asked.

'Tre?' Madri prompted when he did not answer.

'Too much hurting already,' Angel said, sullen now.

'Omelettes,' Vargo commented sagely.

'I will take you there if *he* comes,' Angel decided, pointing a crooked finger at the musician.

'All right,' Andrin agreed readily. 'Vargo will come too.'

The deformed man seemed to relax then, and he soon wandered off as the others discussed the make-up of the party that would go into the firelands of the interior. Vargo stayed, but paid no attention until his own name was mentioned.

'Vargo, we're going to Tisaloya,' Andrin told him, speaking slowly and clearly. 'Do you want Allegra to come with us?'

'What? Oh, yes. She'd better.' He sounded quite lucid now. 'I need to go somewhere on the way, though.'

'Where?'

'Back to the lake in the old caves.'

'Why?'

'I just have to.'

'All right,' Andrin said. 'It's not far out of our way.' He knew that Vargo could be incredibly obstinate when he wanted to, and a short diversion would not cost them much time. 'Will you remember the way in?'

Vargo did not answer. Indeed he gave no sign of even hearing the question. There was a sudden lost look in his pale grey eyes.

'Ero's gone,' he said quietly.

'You mean he's finally flown south?' Andrin said, wondering what that would mean for his friend's mental state.

'No,' Vargo replied. 'He's been called to Pajarito.'

CHAPTER FIFTY-THREE

'I can put you ashore here if you want,' the Barber said. 'You've earned your freedom.'

The fleet rode at anchor, apart from two ships that were patrolling the approaches to the bay. Ico had slept for an afternoon and a night before waking to find the *Revenge* no longer in motion. Now, as she sat quietly on the aft deck, she was sorely tempted by the pirate's offer. She did not know exactly where they were, but it couldn't be too far from where the Firebrands had been heading when she had left them what seemed like a lifetime ago. Soo had vanished during the night, and Ico was hoping that her link would soon return with news of Andrin and her friends. But she knew she still had unfinished business at sea. Elva had called her.

'No,' she replied, hardly believing that she was turning down the chance to go home. 'I said I'd take you to the treasure, and I will.'

'Fair enough. I don't think you'll find too many of the crew have any objections to having a woman on board now. They all saw what happened.'

'Still think the fireworms won't reach your island?' she asked.

The Barber shrugged. 'We can't fight them,' he said.

'We can teach you how,' she told him. 'Why don't you join us, join the Firebrands? We share the same enemies, and we'd make quite a team.'

'Pirates have their own teams,' he replied. 'You fight your wars, we'll fight ours.'

'Even if they're the same one?'

'Perhaps we can help each other sometimes,' was all he would say.

Some time later, he returned to her side with his charts. 'We'll be ready to sail in an hour or two,' he told her, pointing to their position on the map. 'Which way do we go?'

'South,' she replied, seeing no further reason for subterfuge. She no longer had any doubt that the Barber would be true to his word. 'It's not far from here.'

'Why are we heading out to sea again?' Ico asked. 'I told you to stay close to the shore.'

'There are shoals under the water along this part of the coast. Shifting bars of sand,' he explained. 'We could run aground if we get too close.'

'But we need to go in there,' she protested, pointing. 'That's the cove on the map.'

'Hell's teeth!' the Barber exclaimed. 'You want me to sail in there?'

'Yes, of course. That's where the treasure is.'

'You're sure?'

'Yes. Look—'

'Never mind. If I'd known you hated me this much, I'd have insisted we put you ashore earlier.'

'What are you talking about?'

'That, young lady, is known as the Dragon's Throat. Apart from the fact that there's only a narrow channel between the shoals, there are currents that make no sense and, to top it all, there are rock pinnacles that grow under the water.'

'Rocks don't grow!'

'These do,' he replied seriously. 'I've seen them. One year part of the channel will be clear, the next it's full of teeth. It'd be suicide to go in there.'

Ico looked out over the apparently innocent stretch of ocean.

'You'll be telling me next the place is haunted.'

Although she had meant it as a joke, he took the comment at face value.

'All I know is that I've seen things here that I can't explain, things I've never seen anywhere else.'

Ico wanted to laugh, to mock his superstition, but she remembered Soo's words – *There are ghosts here* – and felt a flicker of doubt. At the same time, she was even more certain that she *had* to reach Elva.

'So you can't take me in?' she said.

'Not can't. Won't. It's not worth it.'

'Not even for the treasure?'

'Whoever hid it there knew what they were doing,' he stated.

'Then you *are* reneging.'

'As I recall, the wager was your life and freedom for the treasure,' he replied calmly. 'I'm giving you your price, and I don't need the treasure. So there is no bet.'

The ships had been moving out to sea while they had been arguing, and the *Revenge* was now directly opposite the cove, at the end of the channel between the shoals. According to the treasure map, the ship should have been at the entrance to the inlet – which made a kind of sense. Elva was clearly visible in the distance.

'You're a coward,' Ico accused the Barber angrily. To be in sight of her goal and not be able to reach it was immensely frustrating.

'I'm just not a fool,' he responded, his voice tight with carefully controlled anger.

'Then give me a rowing boat,' she demanded. 'I'll get myself to the cove.'

'Don't be an idiot. The currents in there could rip a boat to pieces.'

'Have you got an answer for *everything*?' she cried.

'Look. I'll put you ashore in the next bay. You can come back to the cove overland.'

Ico took a deep breath. 'If you say one more reasonable thing, I'll kill you,' she hissed. 'I swear it!'

For a moment the Barber looked taken aback by her vehemence, and then he threw back his head and roared with laughter. She was about to berate him again when he preempted her words.

'Nobody accuses me of being reasonable,' he said, and looked round for his second in command. 'Endo!' he yelled. 'We're going into the Dragon's Throat. Signal the others. They're to decide for themselves whether they want to follow, but make sure at least four of them stay on watch out here.' He turned back to Ico. 'Happy now?'

'Thank you,' she said, feeling jubilant and ashamed at the same time.

As they were now sailing directly into the wind, the first part of the channel proved slow going, with lookouts on all sides watching for underwater hazards as the *Revenge* crept forward. All went well, however, and half the remaining fleet followed them in.

'It seems I'm not the only fool here,' the Barber remarked with a touch of pride in his voice.

When they were about two thirds of the way to the cove, Ico spotted several white shapes circling in the sky above the cliffs. They were bigger than seagulls, but she couldn't identify the species. She hoped that one of them might be Ayo, but she had never seen him keep company with other eagles before, and as the birds came no closer she dismissed them and concentrated on the convoluted shape of Elva. The water around the ship seemed clear and calm, and the channel was wider than she'd imagined. Ico began to wonder why the Barber had made such a fuss. This was easy! The small nagging thought that perhaps it was *too* easy would not go away, but their painfully slow progress continued.

Then Soo came diving out of the sky like a small brown thunderbolt. She screamed and chattered aloud in a manner quite unlike her usual calm self, and when she spoke inside Ico's head her voice was full of a desperate anxiety.

Go back! Go back! You can't come here. They will punish you.

What are you talking about? Ico asked, thoroughly alarmed now.

Tell him to turn the ship round before it's too late.

'What's going on?' the Barber asked.

'Nothing. Wait a minute.'

Soo was circling in tight curves in and out of the ship's rigging.

Please explain, Ico begged silently.

Too late, Soo replied, and soared away into the blue.

Ico followed her flight, then lowered her gaze as she heard expressions of astonishment all around her. The reason for her companions' amazement soon became clear. The sea immediately surrounding the ship had begun to boil.

Within moments, their surroundings had become a scene from a lurid nightmare. The water belched forth great fountains of gas, steam and smoke. There was an occasional brief flash of blue or green flame, and the air grew fetid. A succession of small eddies raced on the water's surface, joining and spinning around each other until the currents began to pull the ship in all directions. The *Revenge*'s timbers groaned, and the few sails that were still set slapped and shifted in the suddenly turbulent air.

The Barber was at the helm now, trying first to control, then to turn the ship around, but he was having little success. Behind them the other vessels were in similar difficulties, although these appeared less severe the further out to sea they were. Caught by a sudden rush of seething water, the *Revenge* swung round, and there was a hideous tearing sound as the keel scraped across some sharp-toothed rocks. Sailors were running to adjust ropes and help secure loose canvas, but Ico kept her eyes on Elva. The island was now shrouded in a thickening bank of smoke and mist, which burned and bulged and whirled as if the air itself was in torment. What have I done? she thought, horrified. What have I done? The answer came to her in a dream-like flash as huge yellow eyes glared at her and black scales glittered in the shuddering light of a storm. She had dared to use the dragons' power, to steal their shape and terror. She had flown on their wings without permission. And they were angry.

'But I didn't mean it!' she cried aloud. 'I didn't know. I was only—'

Her words came to an abrupt halt as the entire sea growled and thundered. *They will punish you.*

By this time, several of the following ships had managed to turn themselves around, and were now running before the gentle wind in an attempt to escape the Dragon's Throat before it swallowed them whole. It was only then that the full extent of the disaster became apparent. The ships that had been left to guard the entrance to the channel were under attack from a much bigger fleet. Two were already ablaze, and another had run aground while trying to flee. The others were being forced back into the channel as the enemy pressed on. Ico stared at the scene in horrified disbelief, knowing that she had been the one to lead them into this trap.

By now the Barber had managed to turn the *Revenge* around, but the ship was sinking lower in the water, and it was clear that she was badly damaged. Compressed into an ever-shortening stretch of the narrow channel, the Barber's fleet had almost no room to navigate, and the underwater eruptions continued to cause havoc. The air was acrid and the noise deafening.

Punish me, Ico thought, but not them. Please. They don't deserve this.

The fleet was all now virtually within hailing distance. Unable to flee, they could only turn and fight while trying to survive the assaults of nature. A few of the enemy vessels were closing fast, heedless of their own safety as they pressed home their advantage. The first few arrows thudded into the wood of the *Revenge*'s superstructure. The Barber was still struggling at the helm and Ico went to his side, trying to think of something she could do, or say. As she reached him, a crossbow bolt flew past her shoulder and hit him in the chest. Ico screamed as he fell and, as another pirate grasped the wheel, she threw herself down beside him. His face was pale and vulnerable with pain, but he was still alive and he recognized her.

'Get me . . . to . . . my cabin,' he gasped.

Ico found the strength from somewhere, taking most of his weight as they half fell down the steps and stumbled into the room. The Barber collapsed on to his bed and she made to strip away his shirt and tend to his wound, but his hand caught her wrist with surprising strength.

'Leave it. It's too late.'

'No,' she protested. 'You'll be all right. Let me—'

He struggled, but the life was draining out of him fast and he could not prevent her from doing as she wished. Ico tore away the thick material – and froze, her eyes clouding with tears. She began to say something, but the Barber silenced her with a pleading look. Ico understood and gently covered the pirate up again. He would die as he had wanted to, even though Ico now knew the truth. She would protect the secret.

The Barber smiled, and drew her last breath.

Ico sat beside her, realizing that the tattooed man had not been the only one who had needed to keep his flesh covered until the moment of his end. She knew now why the Barber had been so unexpectedly sympathetic about her pregnancy.

Even though she had tried to conceal it, the Barber had retained some vestiges of womanhood. Ico felt a surge of sorrow and regret that she would never discover the whole story of the pirate's strange life. She also realized where the image of the little girl had come from when she had demonstrated an illusion. The memory had been there in the room – the memory of the Barber herself as a child, a child who had been denied for so long and who was now at peace.

'Goodbye, my friend,' Ico whispered. 'I'm sorry.'

In her mind she heard him say, 'How else is a pirate supposed to meet his end?' and she smiled through her tears.

Ico left the cabin, locked the newly repaired door behind her and went up on deck. The *Revenge* was burning and riding very low in the water. Most of the crew had already abandoned ship, and Ico knew she had no choice but to do the same. She ran to the stern, climbed the gunwale and dived into the churning sea.

Much later, after a gruelling swim that left her exhausted, cold, nauseous and filthy, she crawled out on to the lower edge of the island of Elva. Night was falling, and the tide was rising. With her last ounce of strength, Ico dragged herself to the top of the rock. Even from there she could see nothing of the battle through the enveloping fog. She was where she was supposed to be, but the knowledge gave her no pleasure. Any 'treasure' she might find could hardly be worth the price that had been paid for it – and she expected nothing but more pain, which she would accept as her due.

Ico made herself as comfortable as was possible, and began her second vigil at the seat of the oracle. She asked nothing, but simply waited for the dragons to decide her fate.

CHAPTER FIFTY-FOUR

The party chosen to go to Tisaloya assembled at first light the next morning. It consisted of Andrin, Vargo, Allegra, Angel and three other Firebrands, all of whom had proved themselves adept at underground exploration and at using crystals. Of these Jada was the last to arrive. He came running, his face flushed and anxious.

'It's Tisaloya!' he gasped as he reached them.

'Not so loud,' Andrin hissed. As it had been impossible to keep their departure a secret from Jair, the rest of the Firebrands had simply been told that Andrin was leading an expedition up the coast. The only people who knew their real destination were Nino and Madri, both of whom were there to see them off.

'What about it?'

'It's going to erupt,' Jada told them breathlessly. 'Two birds just returned from the area, and they both tell the same story.'

The group were silenced by this unexpected news but Nino, who was the most familiar with the telltale signs that preceded an eruption, soon wanted to know more.

'What have they seen?'

'Smoke. Earth tremors. The wells nearby have dried up suddenly, and the spring at Ola's turned red. The local people are all packing up and leaving.'

'When did this start?'

'The day before yesterday.'

'How long do we have?' Andrin asked.

'I don't know the area very well,' Nino replied, 'so it's difficult to be exact. But I'd guess three or four days, at the most.'

Jada nodded his agreement.

'It's enough,' Andrin decreed.

'Do we really need to go at all now?' Allegra asked. 'I mean if Tis— if the volcano explodes, won't that kill the fireworms?'

'Maybe not,' Nino replied. 'They could just be forced out by the explosion, spread far and wide.'

'A plague,' Vargo said solemnly.

'We can't risk it,' Andrin decided after a pause. 'We'll just have to get there as fast as we can. Are you all still prepared to go?'

Everyone nodded.

'Then let's go.'

Just before dawn two days later, as the group roused themselves from the few hour's rest Andrin had allowed them, Vargo joined his friend as he was packing his equipment.

'I must go to the lake.'

'We haven't got time.'

'I don't have any choice.'

'Of course you do,' Andrin told him, irritated by the musician's vague insistence.

Ever since Ero's departure Vargo had been in a quiet, sombre mood, but there was often a faraway look in his eyes that was a reminder of his madness.

'You don't understand.'

'Then explain it to me.'

'I can't,' Vargo confessed. 'It's as if I've been called, like the birds are with Pajarito. I *need* to be there.'

'We haven't got time,' Andrin repeated firmly, unimpressed by the explanation. 'We're not making any diversions.'

'Then I'll go alone.'

'Don't be stupid. I haven't got the time or the energy for this.'

'You go on,' Vargo persisted. 'Allegra and I can catch you up later.'

That was nonsense, and they both knew it. Once they dropped behind, there would be no chance of closing the gap.

'No. You come with us. Angel won't help us unless you're here.'

'I'll talk to him,' Vargo said, and strode away before Andrin had a chance to argue.

A few minutes later he returned. 'Angel understands. Lao will stay with him.' The curlew had been flying with the party, together with the links of the other three Firebrands. The only birds absent were Ero and Ayo, who was still at sea. 'He'll help you,' Vargo promised.

Andrin stared at his friend, wondering what was going on behind those sad grey eyes.

'Do what you must,' he said eventually, though he still felt uneasy.

Shortly after that, as the early morning light crept into the sky, the group divided. Allegra had accepted Vargo's decision without comment, and the two of them set out on a course that diverged slowly from the others and then turned into a gully. As the two parties lost sight of each other, Lao called softly in farewell.

'I hope he knows what he's doing,' Andrin muttered to himself, but Jada, who was close behind, overheard.

'Those two make a pretty good team,' he said, his respect obvious. 'It must be something important to send them off like that.'

'I hope so,' Andrin replied. 'It seems to me he's risking a lot for something he can't even explain.'

'We're all having to deal with things we can't explain,' Jada commented wryly.

That's certainly true, Andrin thought. He pressed on doggedly, thinking uncharitably that – given Vargo's mental state – he and Allegra might eventually have slowed them down. Dealing with one madman was quite enough. For all his lack of grace, Angel moved with surprising speed and had no difficulty in sustaining Andrin's rapid pace over the rough terrain. Nevertheless, his presence was always a little un-nerving and Andrin could only hope that, with Vargo gone, Angel would indeed remain cooperative.

Although Tisaloya was not yet in sight, it would be before the end of the day, and Andrin took comfort from the fact that they couldn't see any smoke rising into the sky. He had never before walked deliberately towards the site of an eruption, and the possibility that this was one expedition from which he might not return had already occurred to him. He found he did not really care. All that mattered was that they should succeed in their task.

For the first time in his life, Ero was overawed. It had taken him several days to reach Pajarito – not because it was any great distance, but because he had fought the impulse that drew him there every wing beat of the way. When the sky voices first spoke to him, his initial reaction had been one of disbelief. Who, me? Then he had tried to ignore them, as he had ignored the call to fly south, but that proved to be a mistake. The voices had become so loud, so insistent, so *big*, that they had frightened him – and so, reluctantly, he went. This was the sort of thing that was supposed to happen to birds like Ayo, not to him. And besides, he had the feeling it wouldn't be much fun when he got there. He made many stops along the way, constantly making excuses to himself about hunting for food or talking to other birds, but he knew the voices weren't fooled. From time to time he even tried singing and performing little dances to cheer himself up, but the calling had been relentless. Now, in the harsh light of midday, he had finally reached the most hallowed place in the avian world.

Here, Ero knew instinctively, his beauty counted for nothing. His music and dances were unregarded extravagances. His whole existence was meaningless apart from his ability to listen and learn. A weaker ego might have been shattered by such thoughts, but Ero made a valiant effort to shrug off his fear and play the part expected of him. Learning had never been one of his strong points – the only things he could usually remember were songs – but even his limited reasoning could work out that if the voices had chosen him, then it must be because he had some talent that was necessary, perhaps even something he was unaware of. It occurred to him suddenly that the voices had picked him rather than Lao, recognizing his evident superiority. That idea instantly revived his flagging self-esteem. Perhaps I'm a prince of birds, he thought grandly, or a great warrior. Or a famous soothsayer. After all, he had predicted that the sun would rise that morning.

The great red crater whispered and sighed all around him, apparently content to let the hoopoe indulge his grandiose imaginings. Gradually Ero grew bored. Why wasn't anything happening? He kept thinking that he heard something in the secret murmurings of the wind, but it was forever out of reach. Then he began to notice other things about the place, like the fact that there was no life there at all – no other birds, no insects or lizards, not even any plants or lichen. He was absolutely alone. And the colour of the rock was interesting too. At first glance it was a uniformly dull red, but on closer inspection it proved to consist of a multitude of small patches and streaks of different textures and shades – ochre, crimson, russet and coral – that all merged into one gigantic pattern. From his perch Ero began to play games with the shapes he saw, picking out several types of fruit, a fan that could have been his own crest, and even a lopsided camel. But that entertainment palled after a while and, belatedly, it occurred to him that perhaps he was supposed to *do* something.

He flapped his wings, raised and lowered his crest a few times and called as loudly as he dared. His attempt to attract attention produced only a few fading echoes, so he subsided, feeling perplexed and aggrieved. He began to think hard, a process he usually avoided because it gave him a headache. In a dusty corner of his mind was the memory of other birds referring to Pajarito as an oracle. Ero didn't really know what an oracle was, but thought it might have something to do with asking questions.

Hello? He paused, but there was no response. *If there's something I'm supposed to know, could you just tell me, please, because I don't know what questions to ask.*

Pajarito did not answer him, but the silence seemed to grow more profound and expectant. Ero tried to think what he might be expected to ask. He was sure it must have something to do with his link's recent preoccupations. There was much the hoopoe did not understand about what was happening, but there was one thing he *could* be certain about. Vargo missed Ico, and was worried and sad about what had happened to her.

Is Ico all right? he asked hopefully.

There was still no response.

Only it would be a pity if anything happened to her, he went on. *She's really quite pretty, for a human.*

He waited, but even the wind seemed quiet now, and Ero decided that it couldn't have been the right question.

Are you angry with me for not flying south? he asked fretfully, the thought having just occurred to him.

Again there was no answer.

Is it something to do with the fireworms? he tried.

Do you want me to sing you a song?

Is it about me carrying crystals?

Shall I come back another time? Only I'm getting hungry and there's nothing to eat here.

In the continuing silence, Ero began to study his feet, lifting one toe at a time in sequence to make sure they were all there. He had run out of ideas.

What am I supposed to do then?

WAIT.

The single word was so vast, so terrifying, that it threatened to crush him. He sank down, hunching his head into his shoulders, and flattened himself against the rock. And then, when he had made himself as small and as inconspicuous as possible, he waited.

As soon as they entered the tunnel, Vargo began to sing softly. It was a quiet, wordless crooning that Allegra found oddly soothing, like a lullaby. Although they had a lamp with them this time, Vargo did not seem to need it, treading confidently down the corridor of stone into the darkness. Occasionally, Allegra saw a faint glimmer of reflected light in crystalline deposits and recalled the earlier journey when, as she now knew, Madri had led them to the surface. Retracing their steps, the distance did not seem nearly as great. Before she knew it they were standing on the ledge where, from the other side of the lake, she had seen what she had taken to be a hairy animal. She smiled at the memory.

The water in the lake was so utterly still that it was invisible, its surface a perfect mirror, creating the illusion of a vast cavern rising both up and down from where they stood. Even knowing that in reality it was only a handspan deep did not prevent Allegra's feelings of vertigo as she looked down into the illusory chasm.

'Wait here,' Vargo told her.

'What are you going to do?'

He ignored her question, and stepped into the water. As soon as his boot touched the surface the illusion was literally shattered as ripples spread out over the lake. He walked on slowly but steadily, then stopped near the centre and began to sing again. Echoes of his voice built up a pattern of sound that was at once beautiful and complex, like the most exquisite multi-layered music, and Allegra found herself unaccountably moved. As Vargo stopped singing, the other phantom voices continued faintly for a while, and she waited to see what would happen next.

'I don't know where I'm going,' Vargo said clearly.

In the next instant, Allegra's world changed from wonder to horror and disbelief. In the blinking of an eye, Vargo was simply not there any more. Only a few ripples in the middle of the lake marked where he had stood.

'Vargo!' she screamed, and paused only to set down the lamp before running into the lake, her boots sending splashes of water in all directions. 'Vargo!'

Frantically, she searched around the spot where he had been standing, kneeling down in the shallow water and testing the lake bed for hitherto unseen crevices. But there was only solid rock for several paces in all directions. And yet she could have sworn he had not moved before he disappeared. It was impossible! She was near to tears now, with frustration as much as distress, but she would not allow herself to give up. She went on searching, calling out his name every so often in case he was trapped somewhere, out of sight. But in her heart, Allegra knew that was not the case. She did not understand how it had happened, but Vargo was lost to her. If he was indeed under the water in some hidden cavern, then he must surely have drowned by now. She didn't want to believe that he was dead, but what other explanation could there be? He would surely not have just abandoned her.

The only thing that forced her to give up was when the light from the lamp began to fail. Without that she would be lost herself, and that would do no one any good. Reluctantly Allegra left the cave and returned to the surface, emerging at dusk. In the open air once more, distraught and despairing, she finally broke down and wept.

Far below, the waters of the lake gradually regained their perfect stillness. In the faint residual light from the crystals in the ceiling, the reflection on the surface was unchanged – except for one detail. At the bottom of the mirrored hollow lay a man. His eyes were closed and he appeared to be sleeping peacefully, but beneath his lids his eyes were moving constantly. Vargo was dreaming.

CHAPTER FIFTY-FIVE

Belda Zonzomas had been living at the Maravedis house for a month now. In that time, under Atchen's cosseting, she had grown less thin and pale, and her movements had lost their frenetic, birdlike quality. This physical transformation had been matched by a mental rejuvenation. Diano had spent a lot of time with her, talking about himself and his work and, in turn, trying to coax her story from her. Although she was reluctant at first, he persisted, and the dismal picture that emerged emphasized not only the differences between their lives but also the similarities. The loss of their respective spouses – albeit in quite different circumstances – and the continued absence of their children forged a common bond between them that grew stronger as the days passed. Outside events shocked and worried them, but nothing really counted for much beside the unknown fate of Ico and Andrin. Belda never wavered in her belief that her son would eventually return and, after a time, Diano began to share a little of her irrational optimism. He also began to think seriously about the stand Ico had taken, seeing it now not so much as rebellious obstinacy but as justifiable anger at the way the country was being run. He wished he could have shared some of her passion, her bravery, but he knew that – like all her admirable qualities – it must have come from his wife. As there was nothing he could do for Ico, he concentrated his efforts on Andrin's mother.

Belda's dependency on alcohol had not been beaten by a month's abstinence – which Diano had chosen to share – but it was at least under control now. Her craving was still desperate at times, and he held her while she shook and cried, realizing that she was the first woman he had held so close in many years. It was even possible to see that she had been pretty once, and Diano occasionally caught in her eyes a glimpse of trust and gratitude that awoke in him feelings of protectiveness he had not experienced for a very long time. She became the one small part of the world that he could redeem. All the rest would have to take care of itself. There was nothing he could do about it – or so he thought. That a dream would change his mind was something that would never have occurred to him.

To an outsider, Kantrowe mused wryly, it might seem that Tiguafaya was tearing itself apart. Only he knew that the present upheaval was just the next step along the path he had chosen for his country. Teguise was already his – recent events together with a few summary executions for treason had seen to that – and by the end of the following day everything else would fall into place. The army detachments, together with Maghdim's acolytes, had left three days ago and would soon be in position. The anti-mage himself was also ready, just waiting for the presidential command. That too would come tomorrow – and then, within hours, the entire country would be under Kantrowe's full and permanent control. He could hardly contain his excitement.

The last few days had seen several unexpected developments, but each seemed, in retrospect, to have been fated to work to the new president's advantage. At the time, Maciot's outburst had been infuriating, but now it could be seen as a gift from the gods. Kantrowe had not believed that anyone would be so stupid as to accuse him openly, and it had meant that the 'proof' concerning Maciot's murder of Guadarfia – which he had intended to keep for a more suitable time – had had to be used immediately. The truth of the matter, which was known only to Gadette and himself, was that Guadarfia had earlier been fed the first part of the poison. The second had been in the wine. Either part was harmless on its own, but deadly when combined. This set-up had been designed to leave Maciot as the only plausible suspect, and thus give them a hold over him. Even though the timing of their accusation had been preempted, it had nonetheless served its purpose.

When Maciot had escaped, and had left the city – something else that had initially enraged Kantrowe – it had become apparent that he was now the focus for all opposition. When his temper had cooled down, Kantrowe had made a conscious decision to allow other opponents to escape, knowing that they would gravitate to the renegade senator. This saved him the expensive and time-consuming chore of hunting down all his adversaries. He simply waited for them to betray their allegiance, and then deliberately drove some into exile rather than imprisoning or executing them. By now they would all be together – just waiting to be crushed. Teguise had been purged with little effort and Kantrowe's enemies could be dealt with ruthlessly, away from the gaze of the general populace. Once that was achieved, and the remaining Firebrands captured, he would be able to turn his attentions to more pleasurable matters. The land clearance, which had had to be postponed because the fire-worms were needed elsewhere, could resume. It would have to look like a natural process, of course, in case the pirates realized what was happening, but eventually the land that had been promised to them would be useless – fit only for the mining of the minerals and precious stones that lay beneath the surface.

Untold riches would become available – to Kantrowe and his associates.

By then, of course, he would effectively control a magical monopoly, and would thus no longer need the services of Maghdim. The foreigner's position had always been absurd. His distinction between magic, which he reviled, and his own 'natural' suppression of it, was mere semantics as far as Kantrowe was concerned. Both could be used as a tool to control certain aspects of the world and, now that the acolytes were capable of the necessary tasks, their mentor would no longer be required. Final proof of that would come with the success of the expedition to the south. Gadette had convinced Kantrowe that their own adepts were more than capable of doing the job without Maghdim – which was just as well, because he was needed elsewhere. Experimentation had defined the optimum dosages of tincture for the soldiers, and their knowledge of the Firebrands' whereabouts made the success of the operation an almost foregone conclusion. The telepath monitoring this was under Gadette's personal supervision, and the aide was confident that the linkage was still reliable, in spite of a few apparent miscommunications. The most puzzling of these had occurred when they had learnt that Andrin Zonzomas intended to go to the village of Guatiza to collect some dragon's tears. Although Kantrowe had no great desire to capture him alone, he had been concerned about the Firebrands getting their hands on any more crystals than was necessary, so he ordered the nearby garrison to investigate. It may have been that the soldiers had blundered in and frightened Zonzomas away but, whatever the reason, he had not shown up and no cache had been found. Since that episode, Kantrowe had harboured a few doubts about their spy in the Firebrands' camp. Other intelligence had proved accurate, however, and soon it would not matter any more. That thought made the President smile. He had called a full meeting of the Senate for the following morning, and would then announce his final successes.

Night came, and with it the most unexpected visitors.

It was Famara who sensed their presence first. Even though she was blinded by the darkness of her cell, and so weak that she hardly ever moved, she could see further than she had ever done before. The sparrows – who were still tormenting the Paleton guards – were her primary source, but as her body failed her mind became ever more attuned to stimuli that went beyond the mere senses. Even her dreams had taken on a new air of reality.

Famara saw them more clearly than almost anyone in the whole of Teguise, but no one remained ignorant of their arrival for very long.

The dragons flew in one massive flock. Their shiny black scales were almost invisible against the night sky, but their burning eyes and fiery breath left red trails across the heavens. There were hundreds of them, too many to count. They were huge, and moved with incredible speed in eerie silence. Their presence struck a dark fear into the hearts of all who looked up and witnessed their flight.

Everyone had their own interpretation of the visit, a theory to explain why the dragons had come now and what the consequences would be. Their appearance was claimed to be an omen of great events, both good and bad, each self-appointed oracle turning the night to their own purpose.

And then they were gone, as swiftly and as silently as they had come. They had done nothing except inspire awe and fear. Most people were grateful for that while others, more sensitive than the rest, knew that the encounter was not over. They had sensed the dragons' emotions – and knew that the one overriding sensation to come from the sky had been implacable and enduring hatred.

CHAPTER FIFTY-SIX

They had gone on through the night, carefully picking their way across the lava field. Although the terrain was made passable by moonlight, and by the ominous red glow from the mountain ahead of them, it was still a treacherous landscape in which one false step could lead to broken bones. Their progress was necessarily slow, but as Andrin urged them on they had no thoughts of turning back. As dawn broke they reached the foot of Tisaloya.

'Where's the entrance?'

Angel pointed upwards, but before he could speak there was a subterranean rumbling that shook the ground beneath their feet. It needed no special awareness to know that the volcano was about to erupt. Andrin looked at the openly terrified faces of the three Firebrands.

'I need one of you to come with me, as well as Angel,' he said calmly. He did not need to explain why. They all knew that their leader was unable to detonate the crystals.

'We'll all come,' Jada said.

'No. We need someone to report back if this goes wrong, to let the others know what happened. And there's no reason to risk all our lives.'

There was a long pause.

'I'll do it,' Jada said.

Andrin nodded, and the other two could not help looking a little relieved. They handed their crystals to the others and then retreated, on Andrin's instructions, to what they hoped would be a safe distance. Their birds, and Jada's, went with them. At the same time, acting on his own initiative, Lao turned and flew away.

'Let's go, Angel,' Andrin said.

The earth growled as the three men began to climb. Flares and jets of smoke rose from the upper reaches of the mountain, though there were no signs of any disturbances lower down.

'If necessary we'll use some of the crystals to cool the tunnels down before we go in,' Andrin told Jada. 'As soon as we get to the breeding grounds it'll be up to you. All right?'

'I'll do my best.'

The air was growing warm and sulphurous now, and Andrin wondered if they would be able to breathe underground. However, when they reached the entrance to the caves, he was relieved to find that the air in the passage was relatively clear.

'How far to the worms?' he asked as he lit the lamps.

'Too far,' Angel replied.

'Take us anyway.'

Angel limped obediently into the tunnel and the others followed, clambering over the rough surface. After they had gone about fifty paces, another tremor sent them all crashing to the ground, and the air filled with dust. They went on, holding cloths over their faces. Although the rock all around them was hot, it was not unbearably so, and Jada did not need to use any of their precious crystals. Angel was shaking with nerves now, but he led them on, remaining true to his promise. Eventually it grew so hot that Jada tossed a dragon's tear forward and released its power. The wave of cold that swept over them was welcome, and made the next part of the journey considerably easier. They repeated the process and crept on until the tunnel opened out into a vast cavern.

'Here,' Angel stated.

'What do you mean, here?' Andrin replied, peering into the smoky gloom. 'I don't see any worms.'

And then he looked again and suddenly felt sick. He could see nothing *but* worms. There were millions of them, covering every surface, so that he had at first taken them to be part of the rock itself. They were tiny compared to the worms he was familiar with, and they did not move, but their shape and malevolence were unmistakable once he realized what he was looking at.

'This is just the first cavern,' Angel told him.

Andrin was aghast. There were more worms in this one cave than they could possibly hope to destroy.

'How many more caves *are* there?'

'Five, maybe six.'

Andrin turned to Jada, knowing their task to be hopeless, but not wanting to give up without at least some token effort.

'Do what you can. When you run out of crystals we'll get out of here.'

To his credit, Jada – who had been gazing at the horrifying spectacle in awe – went into action immediately and the cavern was soon echoing with the dying screams of fireworms. As each crystal detonated, the three men moved forward, their boots crunching over frozen corpses. Andrin stamped vindictively on a few at the edges of the cold, who were still struggling, but he knew his efforts to be a mere drop in the ocean. The further they went, the more creatures they saw.

Jada looked at the three crystals in his hand.

'These are the last,' he whispered in dismay.

They had covered only half of one cave of the breeding grounds. If the worms that were left ever hatched, they would be more than enough to devastate the entire country. But there was nothing the Firebrands could do about it.

'It's coming,' Angel said.

The cave was filled with a roaring that deafened them all instantly. The mountain trembled and cracked, and prepared to unleash its fire. The eruption had begun.

The same dawn that saw Andrin arrive at Tisaloya was marked for Ico only by a gradual change from black to grey in the mist that surrounded her on Elva. During the night she had occasionally heard the sound of wings overhead, and had cowered each time, expecting pain or punishment. But her presence had been ignored, and her fear gradually turned to frustration. She remembered Soo telling her that Elva was a place where whispers could shake mountains, that it was the voice of the dragons – but *nothing* was happening.

Ico no longer doubted that the dragons still lived, but their indifference was almost as hard to accept as their anger. She had tried calling out, with both her voice and her mind, but there had been no response. 'Wait and speak softly beyond the earth's breathing, and you will be answered.' The words written by the wizard long ago mocked her, and she felt her anger stir. What else was she supposed to do? She had been called and she had come, in spite of the difficulties placed in her way. Many people, including some she had come to think of as friends, had made huge sacrifices to help her, and she was quite prepared to accept whatever penance her crimes had earned. Wasn't that enough? What more could they want?

Blinded by the mist, she did not even know what had happened to the rest of the Barber's fleet, and the fact that she had been responsible for their fate was a heavy burden. She longed to leave, to clamber down to the beach, climb the cliff and head inland, but – in the fog, with no more than a rough idea of the state of the tide – she knew that such a journey was madness. In any case, she dared not move until

Elva gave her permission to go. Ico glanced around, rubbing her cramped and aching limbs, hoping the mist might be thinning a little.

A slight movement caught her eye then, and she jumped up, a mixture of fear and sudden hope making the blood rush in her veins. When she saw who was climbing towards her she was overjoyed.

'Vargo!'

He stopped and looked up at her, smiling.

'What are you doing here?' she asked incredulously.

'Dreaming.'

'Is the tide out already?' She began to move towards him, but stopped when she saw the puzzled expression on his face. Her own unease increased when she saw that he was carrying his lute.

'How did you get here?' she asked.

'I came from the mirror,' he replied. 'The lakes are all the same, whether they shine like stars or emeralds. It's another sort of link.'

Ico's heart sank. He sounded rational enough, but his words made no sense. She needed him to be sane, to help her understand her predicament, but it was obvious that he was in one of his lunatic phases. Vargo started climbing again, and Ico felt another twinge of alarm. It was a moment or two before she realized what was making her so nervous. Vargo's boots were making no sound on the rock; in fact she thought they seemed not to be touching the damp surface at all. She blinked, wondering if she was hallucinating, and took a step back as he drew near.

'It's all right. You know I'd never hurt you,' he said, looking at her fondly, then glancing down at his feet. 'It's just so good to know you're alive,' he added shyly.

This was the Vargo Ico knew and loved, and she relaxed a little.

'Where did you find your lute?'

'Everywhere's the same in the mirror,' he replied.

It occurred to Ico then that she might be looking at a ghost – with all that implied – and she shivered, not wanting to believe it.

'Then what are you doing here?' she asked.

'I always knew I'd be here one day,' he replied happily. 'Although I didn't know where here was. I've dreamt about it often, but it's more than dreams now.' He sat down and settled the lute in his lap. 'I'm going to play for the dragons.'

His fingers began to move over the strings, picking out a slow, precise melody that was both stately and melancholy. Ico listened, not understanding his purpose but spellbound by his artistry. Vargo was lost, his eyes unseeing, his whole being centred on the glorious music he was producing. He was a creature of air, of alchemy, of thought translated into sound, of pure emotion.

Ico found herself moved beyond words. In all the years she had known him, she had never heard him play like this. As the wordless song ended, Vargo looked up and smiled, but the joy in his eyes was not for her. He was in another world, one of his own making, and she could not follow him there. In the new pristine silence, something had changed. There was a sense of expectancy in the air, a reluctant fascination that emanated from the mist above them, and for the first time, Ico caught an inkling of what he was trying to achieve.

'They danced once,' Vargo stated clearly, and launched into an intricate and sprightly tune that seemed to strike sparks from invisible heels. Within moments he was transported, his fingers a blur as he set his instincts free, improvising over the flying rhythms. It was ecstatic, sensual music, conjuring up movement and swirls of colour. Vargo rocked back and forth, his eyes closed now – not in concentration, for he needed none, but in pleasure. Here was the culmination of his young life, the essence of his consciousness, his soul laid bare in music.

Ico was mesmerized, in delight and wonder. She could not move, but her heart was dancing. He's playing as if it were the last time he'll ever make music, she thought, as if he's pouring every last drop of his skill into this one performance.

The dance grew louder, the bass notes thrumming through the rock while the higher ones glittered in the air like fireflies.

'Ero?' Vargo called suddenly.

Ico glanced round in alarm. The hoopoe could not come here. Elva was forbidden to all birds. But there was nothing to be seen.

'Ero!' Vargo repeated. 'Help me!'

In the distant crater of Pajarito, Ero heard the music like an echo from afar. He was still huddled against the rock, after a long and lonely night, but now the waiting was over. He knew what to do.

He shrugged off his self-induced stupor, rose to his feet and stretched stiff muscles. Then, as the faraway music grew more insistent, he began to sing. He sang as he had never sung before, matching the lively sweep of the tune with his calling. He sang in an ancient language that he had not even realized he knew, remembering words from other lives, from every bird who had ever raised his voice in joy, sorrow or alarm, or simply because that was what he had been born to do. And then, when he ran out of memories, he began to improvise, adding his own mark to the ledgers of avian history. This, he knew, was his talent, the reason he had been chosen, and he was determined to prove worthy of the trust. He tried to remain solemn and serious, but it was impossible. The music possessed him. He danced.

He was inspired now, his movements becoming wilder and more flamboyant, propelling him into the air as he hopped and then burst into rapturous, noisy flight, dancing on the wind. He had never been happier in his life.

Ico heard the rumbling over the passion of the music, but it was some time before she recognized its source. The guardians of Elva had come at last, and they were no longer indifferent. Vargo had got his wish. He was playing for the dragons. And they were laughing.

'Thank you, Ero,' he said quietly.

It was not the cruel, mocking laughter that Ico might have expected, but simple amusement. Whatever Vargo and Ero had done, the dragons had responded to it with natural enjoyment.

The last notes died away slowly, and Ico was left feeling drained but elated. Vargo looked up and smiled briefly – and then his eyes went blank.

'I have to go,' he said. 'It's up to you now.'

'What is?' she asked in sudden panic.

But there was no answer. Vargo simply faded from her sight, proving what she had always known – that he had never really been there. She was alone, but the sense of watching and waiting remained.

'Hello?' Ico tried.

What is it you want of us?

The voice came from all around, as well as from inside her head. It was so vast, so intimidating, that for a few moments Ico was unable to answer.

We need your help, she said eventually.

You aspire to magic?

Yes.

And yet you abuse it?

No! Not intentionally. I didn't realize . . . I'm sorry . . .

Why do you think yourself worthy now?

Ico did not answer immediately, knowing that this was her one and only chance to enlist the aid of the most powerful

creatures in all Tiguafaya. Vargo had gained their attention; it
was up to her to keep it.

Our country faces many perils, she began. *There is evil in the
hearts of some, and we—*

*This is no concern of ours. Your race has proved itself unfit to
protect this world. What happens to you does not matter. We
will return when the land is cleansed.*

Return? she exclaimed, caught off guard. *Surely you're still
here?*

*Our spirits live on, but you do not see us. The apparitions are
mere phantasms. They are your warped creations.*

Mine? She had no idea what they were talking about.

*All mankind's. You have distorted our memory and corrupted
our servants, and now you try to kill them. Soon you will
destroy each other and we can begin the world anew.*

Ico recalled the words of the old wizard. 'The grey
amphistomes consume fire, but do not corrupt the land unless
they are themselves corrupted.'

The fireworms are your servants? she guessed.

They were once.

Ico felt completely out of her depth.

If we all die, our music dies with us. Do you want that? She
was clutching at straws now, hoping for understanding. *What
do you want from me?* she cried. *I'm telling you the truth.*

*Truth? What would you, or any of your kind, know of truth?
The damage is done.*

The bitterness was unmistakable now, though it was tinged
with regret.

We can try to repair it, she declared desperately. *Surely it's
possible, with your help.*

You are not worthy of our help.

*How can you know unless you try? Unless you give us the
chance?*

There was no answer but, as Ico gazed hopefully up into

the blank grey sky, she saw a flash of movement and another voice entered the debate.

She is worthy, Soo stated firmly. *All the birds know this. Why else would we risk our lives for her cause?*

The dragon spirits did not respond, but the sense of listening intensified.

We share with you the common ancestry of all winged creatures, Soo went on. *Surely that must count for something. In the name of all our species, I ask you to help her.*

You are forbidden to come here, the spirit voices warned.

Ico is needed, the sparrowhawk continued heedlessly. *Lend her your strength and she will restore her people's belief, heal their sickness. Is such a prize not worth a little risk?*

Silence greeted her question.

Take my life as a token of faith, Soo added. *If she fails, then it is forfeit.*

The sparrowhawk stopped hovering, and swooped down towards Elva.

'No!' Ico cried. 'No!'

She tried to lunge forward, but was too late. As Soo alighted on a pinnacle of rock, a crackle of blue fire swept through her plumage and she fell. Ico rushed to her side, and stared in horror at the bird, who lay quite still, her usually bright eyes glazing over. The wrenching sense of loss threatened to unhinge Ico's already disordered mind. She howled in agony, then gently picked up the lifeless body of her link and held it against a cheek now wet with angry tears.

'You bastards!' she screamed at the sky. 'Is this how you reward such bravery?'

There was only silence now. No voices, no sense of waiting. Nothing had changed. Soo's sacrifice had been in vain.

CHAPTER FIFTY-SEVEN

The mood in the Senate that morning was subdued. Recent events had made everyone cautious, and the appearance of the dragons was an omen that no one could interpret and many feared. Even Kantrowe, on the day that should have marked his ultimate triumph, looked grave. He had no more idea than anyone else what the massed flight had meant, but he took some comfort from the fact that the dragons had done no more than make their presence felt. By morning the creatures had gone, and he did his best to dismiss them from his mind. The news from elsewhere was as good as he had hoped, and he intended to make the most of it.

The murmur of conversation in the chamber died away as Kantrowe entered and took his place in the President's chair. Once the formalities were over he rose to his feet.

'I called for this session because—' he began, but was interrupted when a commotion outside one of the doors spilled into the room. He was astonished, and mildly amused, to see that Diano Maravedis was its cause.

'You've no right to come in here!' one of the guards shouted as the struggle continued.

'Are you so afraid of what I've got to say?' Diano yelled back. 'Let me speak.'

'Let him go,' Kantrowe commanded.

The soldiers retreated and Diano, mindful of his dignity, straightened his disordered clothes.

'Well, Diano. This is an unexpected pleasure,' Kantrowe remarked agreeably. 'Do you have business with the Senate?'

This was not the reaction the intruder had foreseen and he hesitated, beginning to doubt his own determination.

'It's usual for citizens to petition the authorities before being allowed to speak in the chamber,' Kantrowe went on, 'but as President I can grant you permission. If you have something to say, please say it.'

'That's very magnanimous of you,' Diano replied sarcastically, 'given that anyone who's tried to oppose you has been silenced one way or another.'

'Unpleasant measures are sometimes necessary when state security is at risk,' Kantrowe answered mildly. He was enjoying this exchange, knowing that he could break and humiliate his opponent whenever he wished.

'That is the argument of a tyrant,' Diano said. He turned away from the President and swept the other senators with his gaze. 'Look around you!' he cried. 'Don't you see all the empty seats? The men who aren't here? Do you really believe they're all traitors?'

'Do innocent men flee?' Kantrowe countered. 'Their absence proclaims their guilt. The innocent have nothing to fear.'

'Are you all men of no sense?' Diano pointed an accusing finger at his adversary. '*He* is the one who has poisoned Tiguafaya with his lies and deceit.'

'I hope you have proof of this slander.'

'You betrayed the people of the south by selling them to pirates.'

'Oh, not that old nonsense,' Kantrowe said wearily.

'Why would Maciot lie about such a thing?'

'To further his own political ambitions. Having murdered one president, he sought to discredit the next. His failure is self-evident.'

Diano was obviously disconcerted by Kantrowe's absolute confidence.

'The dragons flew last night as a warning,' he declared. 'They too have been angered by your desecration of the land.'

Kantrowe raised his eyebrows and spread his hands in a theatrical gesture of mock surprise.

'Really?' he said. 'Exactly how do you know this?'

'I was told by the one person in all the world I trust the most.'

'And who is that?'

'My wife.'

Kantrowe's amazement was genuine this time, but he recovered immediately.

'Forgive me, Diano, but hasn't your wife been dead for more than a decade? Did a ghost speak to you?'

'It was in a dream,' the jeweller replied, remembering her voice, her eyes and the very real presence of the night. He had been devastated when he awoke to find her gone.

'I see,' Kantrowe said, unable to suppress a smile. 'And you felt you had to speak out.'

A ripple of laughter ran round the chamber, and Diano realized for the first time just how foolish he might appear. His conviction did not waver, however. He had to do *something*. What she had told him had been real, even if the dream had been interrupted by confusing images – of Ico, the dragons, several birds and an unknown musician.

'Anything else?' Kantrowe enquired with exaggerated patience.

'The Firebrands are only trying to save the country,' Diano said doggedly, 'to help us the best way they know how. They may have made some mistakes, but at least they were honest. They do not deserve to be branded as traitors.'

'That's patently absurd. We all know of your unfortunate connection to the Firebrands, but everyone is aware of the damage wrought by their pernicious efforts.' Kantrowe smiled again. 'I am glad to be able to report that these will soon be a thing of the past. I received word this morning that the White Guard have surrounded their hide-out. Before long they will all be arrested and brought back to Teguise to face trial, and their threat will be stamped out for good.'

Diano regarded him in horrified disbelief. 'No. You can't do that!' he exclaimed. 'My daughter—'

'Your daughter is dead,' Kantrowe stated harshly, and watched with satisfaction as his adversary crumpled.

'No.' It was no more than a whisper.

'She was killed by pirates soon after the attack on Teguise,' the President went on, knowing he had won. 'And all her equally wrong-headed comrades will soon be in our hands.'

'Don't let him do this!' Diano cried helplessly. 'He's evil, he's—'

'I think we've had enough of these ravings,' Kantrowe decided. 'Guards! Get rid of this madman.'

The soldiers hurried forward and led the now unresisting Diano away.

'Well, that was entertaining,' Kantrowe remarked lightly. 'Now perhaps we can return to more serious business. As I have already mentioned, the remaining Firebrands will shortly be captured. It is my hope that once they have seen the error of their ways, most of them can be trained to put their undoubted talents to use for the good of Tiguafaya – as indeed some of their former comrades already have.' He paused, savouring the moment. 'In addition, I can reveal that the Barber's fleet is now being pursued by the superior forces of our maritime allies. The last major threat to our coastline will soon be eliminated. Finally, we have pinpointed the location of Alegranze Maciot and the rebels who were misguided enough to join him. They are based in and around the villages of Corazoncillo and Quemada. My commander in the area informs me that the entire valley is now surrounded by our special forces and, within a few hours, the enemy will be utterly destroyed.'

In fact, Kantrowe thought contentedly, there will be nothing left of either the rebels or the villages. Once Maghdim's fire-worms had swept the valley, nothing would be left but a desert of flame and death.

'To sum up, gentlemen,' he concluded. 'We will shortly be rid of *all* Tiguafaya's enemies.'

He sat down to a spontaneous round of cheering and applause.

Captain Chinero regarded the disposition of his troops with satisfaction. The acolytes formed a complete ring around the cave system, and his soldiers were protected from magic by the tincture. Everything was ready.

'Send the signal for all detachments to advance,' he ordered. 'Let's finish this.'

'They've taken the bait,' Nino said.

He and Madri were watching from a concealed position some distance away.

'This time,' the ex-admiral agreed. 'But we won't be able to keep this up for long.'

They had been told about the army's movements by the birds, and had arranged for Jair to believe that the Firebrands would be staying where they were. Some time later, the unwitting spy had been given a sleeping potion, and the entire party had moved to one of their alternative bases, some two miles distant. They had travelled partly underground and mostly at night, relying on their better knowledge of the terrain to avoid detection by the advancing guards.

This morning Nino and Madri had gone to see whether their plans had been successful. As they walked out into the dawn they had seen smoke and steam rising from somewhere to the southeast, which Nino reckoned must be close to Elva. He had pointed this out to his companion, but as neither of them could see any special significance to what appeared to be a small underwater eruption, they had returned to their own concerns.

'We'd better get back to the others,' Nino said.

'The White Guard are going to be pretty mad when they realize they've been duped,' Madri commented. 'If they're prepared to leave this many men in the field, we're not going to be able to run for ever.'

'Sooner or later we have to fight?'

'It's either that or give ourselves up.'

'All right,' Nino said. 'What do you suggest?'

CHAPTER FIFTY-EIGHT

'This way,' Andrin urged. 'Make for that crevice.'

'It's too late,' Jada replied, coughing. 'We'll never get out in time.'

Huge boulders were falling from the roof of the cavern, together with choking, blinding dust. The air was sweltering now, in spite of the lingering effect of the crystals. There was no way back to their tunnel, and Andrin had looked around desperately, seeking another exit in the failing light. He too believed they were about to die, but he would not accept his fate without one last attempt at escape. The dark crevice was the only chance he could see.

They clambered over the trembling worm-covered rock and began to climb towards their goal. Surprisingly, for all his awkwardness, Angel proved the most agile now, moving like a huge, ungainly insect. Another distant explosion rocked the mountain and, at the far end of the cavern, Andrin saw the first flames as molten lava burst from its constriction and gushed forth in a blazing fountain.

'Come on!' he yelled, taking Jada's arm and shoving him on. 'We're nearly there.'

'What's the point?' Jada gasped.

Following Angel, they fell into a small rock chamber. He was already on his feet, looking about with a stupefied expression on his face. Crystals glowed green in the ceiling and it was a little cooler – but it was immediately obvious that there was no other exit. They were trapped.

Jada slumped to the ground in a dead faint and Angel turned to stare at Andrin, his mad eyes wide, his mouth working noiselessly.

'It's over,' Andrin said resignedly. 'At least we tried.'

'We can't let this happen,' Angel blurted out.

'There's not much we can do now.'

'We have to save them!' the wanderer cried over the renewed roaring of the volcano.

Andrin shook his head, not sure whether he had heard correctly, then noticed that Angel was pointing at several curious boulders arranged in a group next to the far wall of the cave. They were smooth, black and shiny, each one about as large as Andrin's torso, each shaped like a giant egg.

'Save them,' Angel repeated. 'Save them!'

Andrin ignored the increasingly hysterical outburst, but he was intrigued. They looked too uniform to be natural rock formations. Could they really be eggs? He climbed across and laid a hand on the surface of one of the boulders. It was cold and hard and . . .

Andrin pulled his hand away with a jerk, thinking that he must be going mad too. Angel began wailing, tearing at his hair and flailing his arms.

'There's nothing I can do,' Andrin told him, fighting to remain calm.

'Maybe there is.'

Andrin swung round to see Vargo standing at the centre of the cave. He was so astonished that he fell back, and his arm brushed against one of the black stones. His brain felt as if it were about to explode.

'There's power enough here,' Vargo stated urgently. 'All you have to do is harness it.'

'Vargo? How did you get here?'

The musician ignored the question. 'If you don't act quickly you'll all be killed very soon,' he said, and the volcano growled and shook as if to emphasize the point. 'Use the magic.'

'But I don't *have* any magic!'

'Everyone does. You just have to find it. It's up to you, Andrin. There's no one else.'

Andrin glanced around. Jada was unconscious on the floor, Angel was jibbering and rolling his eyes, and only Vargo seemed unaffected by the inferno that surrounded them.

'Why can't *you* do it?'

'Because I'm not here!' Vargo replied in exasperation.

Andrin stared incredulously.

'Hurry!' the musician urged.

'What do I have to do?'

'Get the crystals, then ask them for help.'

'Who?' Andrin asked, utterly bewildered.

'The dragons, of course.'

Ignoring the clamour in his brain for some sort of explanation, Andrin scrambled over to Jada, retrieved the three crystals and then, knowing it was his only option, returned to the black eggs. He forced himself to put a hand against one of them again. Behind him, unseen, Vargo vanished into thin air.

Andrin's eyes burned, his lungs were full of cinders, and his mouth was full of smoke. He choked and felt hot tears stream down his cheeks, but the fire inside did not release him. The small cavern was invisible now, and he was lost in a world of flame and liquid sparks. It was oppressive, it made no sense, and it was too huge to comprehend. He was flying – but with no direction, no height or speed. He was ancient, so old that he had seen mountains born and die, had watched the insignificant scratchings of mankind's emergence from ignorance, and had seen the fires of the sky return to their underground furnaces while his thoughts flew among the stars. Andrin's own personality, his sense of self, were overwhelmed, swept away by a deluge of experience and emotion until only a minute thread remained, like a single human hair cast adrift in an ocean.

He clung to this for dear life, knowing that if he let go of that tiny strand then he would be lost for ever.

Help me!

A sudden rush of heat and light flooded through him, shredding his humanity with superhuman indifference. The hand that still rested on the dragon's egg arched in pain, while in the other the three crystals jumped and cracked as though they were alive.

Ice, Andrin thought. Ice as hard as diamond.

The air around him glittered and chimed, like a multifaceted jewel . . . and then Andrin, his two companions and the eggs were *inside* the transparent gemstone. It surrounded them like a crystalline cocoon.

Tisaloya exploded around them in a torrent of fire and molten rock, hurling itself towards the sky in its last act of self-annihilation.

Vargo's strength was gone. He had done all he could. It was up to the others now. He tried to move, to struggle back to the world, but he was held fast. The mirror had claimed him in return for the gifts it had bestowed on him, and he was entombed within a place that was not a place, under water that was not wet, in rock that was not solid. He was lost in silence, neither in the world nor out of it.

Idly, he wondered how long it would be before madness claimed him permanently. Death would have been preferable; at least that was an end. He had served his purpose, was glad he had done all he could to help the two people he loved more than anything in the world. They might never know his fate now, of course, but that was not really important. If the gods were willing, Andrin and Ico would find each other again – and that would be enough.

Looking up through the depths of the nonexistent lake to the cavern above, he saw the faint green stars in the crystals of its roof and knew that this constellation would never change. He closed his eyes and tried to find acceptance, but it was impossible. He thought of Ero and his impossibly heroic performance; he thought of Lao and his beautiful sadness; he remembered Andrin's bewilderment turning to courage; he saw Ico's warm brown eyes as she smiled. Vargo wished them all goodbye, and hoped that his heart would finally break.

Ico had conceived the hopelessly optimistic notion that if she took Soo away from the forbidden island, then her link might miraculously revive. Although in her heart she did not really believe this, it was better than doing nothing. Something was needed to fill the gaping void inside her created by Soo's death. Ico was about to risk climbing down from Elva, in spite of fog and tide, when a sudden looming presence made her hesitate. Indistinct shapes filled the mist with shadows, and she knew that they were watching her again.

You have many allies.

The dragon spirits were back and for the first time they sounded sympathetic.

There are many of us that respect our land and its past – and honour you, she replied.

So it seems.

Ico did not know what had caused their change of heart, but new hope sprang up inside her.

Then you'll help us?

If you keep your promises.

Of course! Ico exclaimed joyfully.

And you continue to protect our children.

Protect . . . ? She had no idea what they meant.

Leave the sparrowhawk when you fly.

Can't you—?

She has made her bargain, the spirit voices told her. *Now you must honour yours.*

But—

You are found worthy.

With this pronouncement the shadows disappeared and, moments later, so did the fog. As the sudden wind whipped away the last shreds of vapour, Ico looked out to sea. Several ships had foundered, some wrecks were still smoking, but the majority were now far out on the ocean, spreading out in all directions. They were too far away to tell whether the fighting was still going on, but Ico took heart from the possibility that some of her former allies might have escaped.

Glancing down again at Soo, she felt a sadness tinged with a new determination.

'Leave the sparrowhawk when you fly,' she said aloud.

She laid Soo's body down gently, and turned to stare inland just as the ground beneath her feet began to shake and a distant rumbling reached her ears. Far away, a huge column of fire and smoke climbed into the sky like a giant red flower.

'Fly!' Ico told herself.

She tried to recall the sensations from her time in Teguise, when she had *become* the illusion, when the image of the dragon had been made real by her belief. This time she did not have others to help her, nor did she have her talisman – that was on the sea bed with the *Revenge* – but she had obtained something of far greater value; permission.

Memory and imagination became faith as Ico grew a second skin, a second shape. Black scales glittered, talons scraped the sacred rock, and burning yellow eyes saw the world with searing clarity. Ico raised her head and howled her promise to the sky in words of flame. She spread her wings and flew.

CHAPTER FIFTY-NINE

Ico had only been flying for a few minutes, and was still glorying in the ease with which she had taken to the air – soaring above the emerald lake, the cliffs and the lava fields beyond – when she sensed another pair of wings nearby. Beside her Ayo was tiny but majestic still, and his speed matched hers.

You fly well for a novice, the eagle remarked.

Ico's heart leapt at the chance of talking to Andrin's link.

Where's Andrin? Is he safe?

I haven't seen him for several days. He sent me to search for you and you proved elusive.

Although Ico wished he had more definite news, she was still thankful for Ayo's company.

Were you one of the white birds I saw over Elva? she asked.

I was with them but not one of them, he replied. *They are not part of our world.*

Ghosts? Ico hazarded, remembering Soo's words.

Ayo did not answer. She sensed his reluctance and did not pursue the subject.

Do you know what happened to the rest of the Barber's ships? she asked instead.

We helped them make their escape, the eagle replied proudly. *Once I knew which were your friends and which your enemies, it was easy enough. Sailors are very superstitious about birds, especially large white ones.* He sounded amused. *We made their attackers break off and flee.*

Ico wanted to ask who 'we' were, but decided against it. She was grateful to them, whoever they were. Some of the Barber's crew might survive and, if so, might still be her allies in the future.

Thank you.

Not all of them got away, Ayo admitted gravely.

Without you I doubt any of them would have done, Ico said.

They flew on, side by side, heading back towards the firelands.

Nino led his small band into another tunnel at a full run. They had led the White Guards a merry dance, always keeping one step ahead of the soldiers but luring them on with the promise of capture. All the chosen runners were swift and nimble, but it was a dangerous game nonetheless. One of their number had already been killed by a crossbow bolt and there had been several other near misses, but now the crucial moment was approaching.

The Firebrands' first efforts at resistance had been largely unsuccessful. For some reason their magic had been ineffective, and the illusions were ignored by the soldiers as if they could not even see them. A few well-placed crystals had generated considerable mayhem, but the effect was localized and only lasted a short time. Something more was needed – which was why Nino and Madri had devised their current tactics.

Nino splashed through the shallow lake that covered the entire floor of the large cavern, with the others close on his heels. As they emerged on the other side of the water they dived into several different tunnels and chambers, all of which were lit by the glow of concealed lights. Madri and most of the rest of the Firebrands were waiting there. Some carried weapons but they would be used only as a last resort. The noise of shouting and the clash of steel drew nearer as Captain Chinero led his men into the cavern. Seeing the lights, they yelled in triumph, thinking they had finally cornered their prey, and rushed on into the water.

'Wait!' Madri hissed. 'Not yet.' Then he glanced at his breathless companion. 'Did they all follow you?'

'Not all,' Nino gasped. 'Most.'

The ex-admiral looked back at the advancing soldiers. Those furthest forward were almost across the lake now, while those at the rear were just wading into the shallows.

'Now!' Madri called.

Simultaneously, twenty Firebrands detonated twenty crystals beneath the surface of the water. Moments later the entire lake was one solid frozen mass. Several guards fell, breaking bones as they did so; others found themselves trapped, their feet encased in unbreakable ice. Although a few escaped the frozen clutches, they went headlong, skidding in all directions, losing their weapons as they went and knocking themselves senseless. The scene came to an almost complete standstill. In the vanguard Chinero looked down at his boots, invisible now beneath the opaque white, and screamed in rage and disbelief. He at least was still upright. Others were less fortunate and were crying out in pain.

Nino stood up and faced their immobilized enemy.

'I hope you don't suffer from chilblains,' he remarked cheerfully. 'Otherwise the next few hours could be quite painful.'

Chinero made a strangled noise deep in his throat, his face red with anger and embarrassment.

'It'll thaw out eventually,' Nino added, 'but by then we'll be several miles away. If I were you I'd think twice about trying to follow us.'

'I'll kill you, you little shit!' Chinero snarled. 'You'd all be dead now if we weren't under orders to take you alive.'

'We could cut you all down now if we wanted to,' Nino pointed out. 'Think about that while you're waiting. You're serving the wrong master, Chinero, and sooner or later you'll realize it.'

The Firebrands went on their way, following other routes to the surface and leaving Chinero swearing and hacking ineffectually at the ice with his sword. As they emerged into the daylight, lookouts informed them that a second group of soldiers, together with several civilians, was still at large and coming towards them. Jair, who was still groggy and who had to be helped to walk, suddenly cried out and clutched his head.

'What is it?' Nino asked.

'They're trying to read my mind. I can't stop them.' He looked terrified.

'Kill him,' Madri said flatly.

'No!' Nino exclaimed as the others gasped.

'He's too much of a liability now,' the ex-admiral argued. 'If we don't get rid of him he'll lead the enemy to us and we could all be killed. Is one life worth more than many?'

'I won't murder one of our own.'

'Then drug him again and leave him behind.'

'They were my friends once,' Jair said unexpectedly. He had been paying no attention to the discussion of his future.

'What do you mean?' Nino demanded.

'We were captured together. But I got away.'

'They're Firebrands?'

Jair nodded.

'Maghdim made them ill,' he said bitterly. 'They curse magic.'

'Tell them they don't have to be ill any more,' Nino said urgently. 'We can make them better.'

'So that's why the illusions weren't effective,' Madri commented. 'This Maghdim must have trained them to block them.'

'It can't be that simple,' Nino argued – and then their attention was drawn elsewhere.

'What's going on over there?' one of the lookouts cried.

The soldiers and acolytes were milling around in apparent confusion. The reason soon became apparent.

The dragon swooped low over the guards, scattering them in all directions, then flew on towards the Firebrands. Most of them ran for cover, but Nino and Madri had seen Ayo flying alongside and stood their ground in spite of their fear. The dragon alighted on a nearby rock, fixed them with an intimidating yellow glare and spoke in a hollow booming voice.

'I don't think you'll have any more trouble with them. Where's Andrin?'

'He went to Tisaloya to find the fireworms' nests, but the mountain erupted a little while ago. I've no idea where he is now.' Curiously, Nino found himself not in the least overawed by the fearsome creature. There was something oddly familiar about it.

Without another word the dragon rose into the air again, climbing steeply and then cutting through the air with incredible speed.

Ayo followed, doing his best to keep up, while the Firebrands watched in awe.

Andrin had seen several eruptions, but nothing as spectacular as this – and none of them *from the inside*. Although everything was distorted by the prisms of ice that enclosed them, and it was hard to make sense of what he was witnessing, it was still possible to pick out some details. Floods of molten rock gushed past in orange streams, boulders the size of houses turned ponderously in the air while smaller pieces of stone flew past at astonishing speeds, ricocheting or shattering in thousands of impacts every moment. Smoke and glowing dust billowed in expanding clouds, blotting out the sky. And through it all the shield of ice rode serenely on the storm, defying all logic, impervious to any assault and protecting those inside.

I should be dead, Andrin thought as their impossible flight continued. Maybe I am dead and just don't know it yet.

He glanced at his free hand. The three dragon's tears had turned to powder, and yet he did not even feel cold. The temperature inside the crystal was like that of a pleasant summer's day.

Jada still lay unconscious. Angel also lay on the floor now but he was fully alert, gazing about him in childlike wonder. And the clutch of eggs were as cold and seemingly lifeless as ever. Andrin knew better now, of course. There was life here, and power. There was history and the future. They were the ones who were keeping them all safe; he was only the conduit, the shaper of their power, the ice mage. It had taken the imminence of death to reveal it, but Andrin had at last found his magic.

He was aware that they had been rising for some time, moving with the general flow though untouched by its extraordinary violence, but now the crystal sphere had begun to fall again. Andrin only knew this from watching the change in the pattern of events outside, because the laws of gravity seemed to have been suspended for him and his companions. He wondered briefly how far they would fall, what would happen when they hit something solid, but the questions – indeed all rational thought – had long since ceased to have any meaning. He could only keep his faith in the connection with the dragons and wait to see what would come next.

A sea of lava engulfed them. Different currents slid past in sinuous orange and red curves. Bubbles of fiery gas kissed the ice as it passed, and showers of darker solid flotsam swirled away. The sphere continued to sink, but more slowly with every moment until – like a heavy piece of wood thrown into water – it began to rise back towards the surface. Then, at last, Andrin was able to take a tenuous grasp on reality. The upper half of their shield was now in open air. The rest was riding the current of a lava flow as it rolled away from the mountain that had once been Tisaloya, but which was now being rebuilt by the inner forces of the earth. They were sailing on the stream like a boat, rising and falling with the red waves, swerving round obstacles, always going forward. Behind them a vast tower of smoke and ash obliterated the sky, and to either side Andrin could see other tributaries of lava fanning out like rivers of blood. With every minute they were carried further from the centre of the devastation, but they took the fire with them, and even now Andrin could not see how they could possibly complete their escape. That he had come this far was already beyond belief.

Angel began to whimper then, as a grey mist seemed to descend on the land about them, obscuring the view. There was a pattering sound at the top of the sphere, which lost some of its brilliance as the darkness grew. It was some time before Andrin realized what was happening. When he did, he felt a revulsion so great that all the amazing events, all the strange beauty and terror that had gone before paled into insignificance. All their efforts had been for nought.

On the plateau of Tisaloya and for miles around, it was raining fireworms.

CHAPTER SIXTY

The closer Ico got to Tisaloya, the more worried she became. It was clear that there had been a catastrophic eruption, and if Andrin had been anywhere near the volcano the chances of his having survived were very slim indeed.

Is he still alive?

I can't feel the link, Ayo replied gravely, *but I don't think it's been severed.*

What does that mean?

I don't know, the eagle admitted.

From a distance the grey fallout from the explosion looked like dust, but as they grew closer, the sight filled Ico with an inexplicable dread. And then she saw the sphere, bobbing on the surface of the lava liked a jewelled buoy. Its outer shell was faceted, like a perfectly cut gemstone, but it was covered partly by grey debris and partly by a sparkling white power which – if it had not been such an absurd idea – Ico would have taken for hoarfrost. It was some way from the volcano itself and still moving, albeit sluggishly now that the lava was beginning to cool down a little.

What is that? Ico asked. She was starting to feel strangely confused, as though someone was trying to whisper to her, just out of hearing.

Ayo did not answer, obviously as baffled as she was.

Do you feel Andrin yet? she asked a little later, unable to contain her anxiety.

No. I would have told you if I had, Ayo replied patiently. *But we should not go any closer.*

Why?

The sky is full of fireworms.

Ico realized then why the grey clouds had disturbed her so. *Are they alive?* she whispered, already knowing the answer.

They're alive, the eagle confirmed.

How did this happen? Ico was horrified, feeling utterly helpless in the face of such evil.

They flew on, angling away from the deadly rain, each contemplating the scale of the disaster that had befallen the country. If even half of these fledgling worms survived and grew active, Tiguafaya would be utterly devastated.

For some time Ico's mind had been a jumble, with random words and ideas interrupting her train of thought for no apparent reason. She tried to concentrate, but it was no use. The random interventions went on, frustrating her every attempt until, in exasperation, she began to listen to them rather than try to push them aside.

The weather mage is there.

Ico looked round to see which bird was talking to her, but there was no one near except Ayo, and it was definitely not his voice. This was too light, too small, innocent and unafraid.

The weather mage? Ico responded tentatively, wondering if she was going mad. *You mean Angel?*

Yes, but he's upset.

Where is he?

In the bubble.

How do you know this? Ico asked, amazed.

The babies told me.

Babies? Are they in the bubble too?

Yes, but they're sleeping, like me. They have hard shells though.

For a moment Ico almost lost her sense of the dragon she had become. She was human again, with human fears – and falling. She caught herself in time, remembered how to fly.

We can dream, though, the voice added, and Ico knew, with an absolute and overwhelmingly emotional certainty, who was speaking to her.

Are the dragon babies helping us? she asked. *Will they do something for us if we ask them?*

Oh, yes, her unborn daughter replied happily. *They like us.*

'Angel! Angel, come here!'

Andrin did not dare take his hand from the dragon egg. He was sure it was the only thing keeping the sphere from disintegrating into dust and plunging them into the lava, but he knew now what he had to do. He held out his free hand.

'Angel, please. This is important.'

The wild man edged closer reluctantly, his eyes darting from side to side as though looking for a way of escape. He trembled for a moment when Andrin took his gnarled hand and held it firmly.

'You're a weather mage, aren't you?' Andrin said, but Angel would not meet his imploring gaze. 'I know you are, Tre. They've told me.' He hoped that using his real name might bring Angel back to some kind of cooperative sanity. 'We need cold. Lots of it. More than you've ever known before. All around, for miles. You understand?'

'Too much,' Angel whispered.

'They'll help you,' Andrin said quickly. 'Put your other hand on the egg. The dragons will give you all the power you need, but *you're* the one who can change the weather.'

Angel shook his head and tried to pull away, but Andrin held him without difficulty. His renewed determination had given him strength.

'You've got to do this, Tre. You must. Otherwise everyone will die. Everyone.'

Angel glanced at him with frightened, tear-filled eyes.

'It'll hurt them!' he cried.

'Would you rather they destroyed our country?'

Angel gave him a despairing look, held up his free hand in front of his face as if measuring his crooked fingers, then placed it on the egg with a sudden, convulsive movement.

It began as a wind – a wind that blew *downwards* from the limits of the sky. It spread in waves, propelled by flashes of lightning, small whirlwinds and wild thermal currents. It drew from the chill of the distant oceans, from the winter that was still to come, exchanging it for the heat of now. Icy fingers stirred the clouds of dust and ash, creating a vast frigid layer in the still expanding column.

The cold intensified, an endless cycle that made the tortured air shriek and crackle and the ground shiver. Even the lava grew more sluggish as the heat was leached from its surface. The main fury of the volcano was spent now, and around it new clouds gathered, piling themselves up in mountains of frozen mist.

For the first time in the living memory of Tiguafaya the weather did not relent. It began to snow.

Ico watched in amazement as white replaced the grey. She had never envisaged her suggestion producing such spectacular results. Although she knew what snow was, having listened to ancient tales from distant corners of the world, she had never seen it herself. In fact, when the blizzard began, she had had no idea what was happening. It was only when a few icy crystals had fallen on to her scales that she realized her prayers had been answered.

Flying closer, she could see that the tiny fireworms falling from the sky were lifeless now. Similarly, those already on the ground were also dead, their skins cracking as they were covered in ice. A few – the ones that landed in active lava – would probably survive, but that was something the people of Tiguafaya could cope with as before. The important thing was that the threat of an overwhelming plague had been averted.

The snowstorm had only lasted a few minutes, but in that time a huge area had been covered by a thick white blanket. It created a landscape of extraordinary, eerie beauty. From the air Ico could see it all – a panorama of snow fields, pristine in their smooth, luminous curves, split only by red rivers of the volcano's molten outpourings. Steam rose from the edges of these rivers, but otherwise the air was clear. Only the tower of dust from Tisaloya remained to dim the sunlight, and the crystal sphere glittered even more brightly. A few dark shapes were visible within, but nothing was recognizable.

'And continue to protect our children,' Ico thought, wondering whether Angel's efforts in saving the eggs had been the reason for the dragons' change of heart at Elva. 'You have many allies.'

She felt a surge of gratitude and affection for the weather mage, the wanderer who was shunned by most people because of his grotesque appearance, but who had been her friend from the beginning.

Give Angel my thanks.

There was no response. The voice inside her was silent again, returned to her embryonic sleep and private dreams. Ico felt a sense of loss, but also pride. Her daughter had spirit.

Her thoughts returned to Andrin then, and her recent elation vanished. She asked Ayo for news, but his answer was as vague and unsatisfactory as it had been earlier.

Angel might know where he is, the eagle suggested, and Ico immediately cursed herself for not having thought of this earlier.

We have to get him out of there, she decided.

However, before she could set her wings to glide down to the sphere, Ayo spoke again.

Tao's coming.

Ico looked, and saw a tiny black speck in the sky grow larger and take form. The mirador was obviously close to exhaustion but relieved to have found Ayo. If he was amazed to see the dragon he hid it well, and delivered his message in urgent but concise terms.

You must come quickly. My link and all his followers are trapped, and Maghdim is about to unleash his fireworms upon them.

What do you mean, 'his' fireworms? Ico asked.

He's found a way to control their movements. We were willing and able to fight human foes, but we can't stand against the worms. It'll be a massacre.

Where? Ico demanded succinctly.

The Corazoncillo valley.

I'll gather as many birds as I can, Ayo said. *We may be able to find some crystals.*

Ride with me, Tao, Ico said.

As the chaffinch clung to her back, she dived towards the sphere. It was more urgent than ever now to release Angel. If they were to save Maciot, the weather mage would be needed. The fact that events had moved so fast during her absence did not surprise Ico. That rebel forces were encamped far from Teguise was actually encouraging – but would count for nought if they weren't protected from Maghdim.

What is that? Tao asked, as they approached the sphere.

I'll explain later, Ico told him, and flexed her talons.

Once he knew that the blizzard was taking effect, Andrin had relaxed a little. The power that the dragon eggs had released and the efficiency with which Angel had shaped it had been astonishing. Andrin knew that he too had played some part in the process, but he could not describe what he had done or how.

As the immature fireworms died, the air cleared and the upper part of the sphere became translucent again, revealing a fragmented view of ice and fire. Their journey went on, slower now but still relentless in its advance. Without the protection of the crystal barrier, the heat of the lava below them would have killed them all in an instant, and it might be days, even months, before it cooled enough for them to abandon their shield. Eventually their haven would become a prison.

Andrin glanced at Angel, whose hand he still grasped, and was surprised to see that he was crying silently, his misshapen face crumpled in misery. He seemed smaller, somehow, as if the ordeal had drained him of substance as well as energy. Before Andrin could ask him what the matter was, Angel went limp and fell to the floor, releasing himself both from Andrin's hand and from his contact with the egg. He lay so still that Andrin wondered if he was dead – but he did not dare relinquish his own hold on the black shell to find out.

It was then that he saw the dragon. It came like a thunderbolt from the sky, with such speed and grace that he held his breath until the giant wings opened wide to brake its descent, and two massive sets of claws extended to either side of the sphere. From the first it was obvious what the dragon's intention was – it had come to claim the eggs, to carry their young to safety – but at first even those mighty talons found it hard to get sufficient purchase on the faceted surface of diamond-hard ice. Instinctively, Andrin altered the shape of his thoughts so that the perfect symmetry of the sphere now contained a few minor flaws – which the dragon used instantly to grip it tightly.

Even then the struggle was not over. The great wings swept the air, scales flashed and muscles strained. Andrin held his breath, hoping it would succeed, but the lava was reluctant to release its captive, sucking it back into the glutinous stream. The dragon screamed, emitting flame as well as sound, and with one final effort lifted its prize from the molten river. Once free it rose swiftly, carrying the sphere and everything within it with arrogant ease, and sped away northwards.

Andrin looked down through the crystal beneath his feet at the ground, now far below, and wondered whether this day could possibly contain any more marvels.

For the first time in his life, Alegranze Maciot was at a complete loss. It had been the birds who had brought the news that they were surrounded, that the sentries in the hills had been slaughtered and, worst of all, that two huge swarms of dragon spawn were massed at either end of the valley. The fact that these swarms seemed to be controlled by men filled him with cold loathing. This was certainly Maghdim's work, at Kantrowe's behest, and the sickening truth about some of the earlier massacres became clear now. Maciot knew that he and his allies were trapped, and he could see no way out. Both routes out of the valley were blocked by their enemies, and it would take far too long to attempt to climb out any other way. With more warning he might have been able to organize something, but the speed, stealth and precision of their entrapment had been astonishing. He wondered why their foes had not completed the job immediately, instead of delaying and – apparently – gloating. He could only suppose that the eruption to the south earlier that morning had caused some concern. It had shaken the ground even in Corazoncillo, and might have disrupted Maghdim's plans – although it was hard to see why it should. Perhaps it was just a sadistic joke on the foreigner's part. It was a hopeless, sickening feeling to have to just sit and wait. They had already taken all the precautions they could, inadequate though they were. If there really were as many fireworms as had been reported – and he had no reason to doubt the birds – then they were doomed.

'They're coming!' someone yelled.

Maciot looked towards the western end of the valley, saw the wave of grey advancing, and then, in response to another shout, turned to see a similar sight to the east beyond Quemada. Knowing it was pointless, he drew his sword anyway, and went to take his place among those who had chosen to be the first to meet the onslaught.

Maghdim watched the departing swarm with satisfaction. It had taken much longer than he had intended to set them on course because – for some reason he did not understand – the fireworms had become restless at the time of the distant eruption and even more so during the storm that had followed. Although they had settled down eventually, Maghdim and his assistants had had to work hard to achieve their purpose. However, all had been set in motion now, with no harm done, and it was just a matter of sitting back and observing the results. Guiding the swarms to their targets was child's play. The next hard work for his acolytes would be when they came to gather up their charges again.

He was surprised by the arrival of the dragon, with its strange burden, but not unduly alarmed.

The dragon caused a great deal of alarm among the rebels. They assumed it was part of the attack on them, and its fearsome appearance, not to mention its enigmatic load, reduced the already panic-stricken men and women to abject terror. They fled from the open space in the centre of Corazoncillo when it became clear that this was the creature's destination, but the dragon merely set the shining sphere down and took off again.

***

As the journey ended Andrin looked about, saw Maciot among the onlookers and knew he was among friends. Then he noticed the approach of the swarms. It seemed that his ordeal was not yet over, but for the moment at least he had no need of the shield. He took his hand from the egg and the crystal instantly melted away to nothing, leaving only a few fading sparks in the air. Angel and Jada lay comatose and the clutch of eggs settled gently on the ground, unmarked by their travels. Feeling suddenly frail and vulnerable, Andrin looked up as the dragon's voice boomed out.

'Angel, we need more cold. Quickly!'

Andrin saw immediately what the intention was, but knew it would take more than snow to stop full-grown worms. He grabbed Angel and shook him, but he was deeply unconscious. As Maciot and several others approached cautiously, Andrin wasted no more time, telling himself that there was no one else, that he would have to do it. He had claimed to be an ice mage; now was his chance to prove it.

Steeling himself for the trial of contact, and ignoring Maciot's astonished cries of recognition, Andrin deliberately placed each hand on one of the eggs. This time the introduction to their world was less traumatic, but he still felt as though he were being consumed from the inside by liquid fire.

Help me.

The ice claimed him.

Ico did not glance back as she rose into the air again. Her whole attention was focused on the approach of the fireworms, and in trying to judge which group posed the more immediate threat. She was still climbing when the birds arrived. Every species was represented, all shapes, sizes and colours. They came from every direction, answering the summons of their wings.

We are here, Ayo reported, *but there are no crystals.*

Ico's heart sang.

We don't need them! she cried. *Follow me!*

The first tendrils of cold were snaking out from the centre of Corazoncillo. To Ico they were like solid rivers of malleable ice, invisible to all but avian eyes, but palpably real. She swooped to take one of the magic streams and shape it to her will. Ayo and the other birds soon realized what she was doing and joined in. Together they flew back and forth, weaving a pattern of frozen air into barriers between the villages and the swarms that threatened them. They met resistance, counter-magic from the acolytes at the ends of the valley, but it could not match their joyful resolution. Soon, various flocks of birds were taking the plan a stage further, not only halting the fireworms' progress but driving them back – and cutting off small groups, which could then be inundated with the unceasing flow of cold from the centre of the valley. The screams of dying worms echoed as the men below cheered, hardly believing what was happening.

Before long, nothing was left of the swarms except a few ragged groups, which were being harried by the jubilant birds and hunted down by human scavengers when they fell. One such group found themselves trapped in a net of invisible ice and driven back towards the man who had once controlled them. Most of the acolytes had long since given up and fled, knowing they were beaten, but Maghdim had stayed where he was. He could not believe that he had been defeated. As the remnants of the swarm were forced towards him he made a negligent, impatient gesture to ward them off – and found it had no effect. He tried again, feeling anger rather than fear, but his efforts foundered on the multiple nature of the magic he opposed. The worms came on, sighting their target now. As Maghdim threw every last particle of his power into one final effort, the fireworms hesitated, then came on, accompanied by a raucous twittering. Maghdim screamed as the first of the creatures latched on to his flesh, but his tongue was soon silenced, leaving only a scorched and shrivelled corpse. Tek and the rest of the sparrows watched in disgust and morbid satisfaction. Even though she was many miles away, Famara had had the last word in their contest.

Jada stretched and groaned, looking around in bewilderment.

'Where are we?' he asked. 'What's happened?'

No one knew how to answer him.

'It's over,' Maciot said, shaking Andrin gently by the shoulder. 'You won.'

Andrin glanced at him blindly, hardly aware of who was talking to him. He was too exhausted even to smile, drained of everything except the most basic elements of life, but he glanced up as the dragon flew down to land a few paces away.

For a stunned instant he could not catch his breath, could not believe his eyes. And then he was on his feet, his weariness forgotten, his eyes blurring with tears. The dragon was gone and Ico was running towards him with her arms outstretched and a look of joyful disbelief on her face. They fell into each other's arms in an embrace that burned brighter than any volcano.

CHAPTER SIXTY-ONE

Vargo?

The voice entered his dreamless void like a sudden burst of sunlight after endless grey hours of suffocating cloud. His mind, the only part of him that was not atrophied, was instantly alert. In his changeless world this was either the longed-for advance of insanity, or it was real.

This isn't good enough, Vargo, the voice added tetchily. *You can't just lie there.*

Famara? he whispered. *Is it you?*

Who else would it be?

He could see her now, a transparent shade standing above him. She looked more frail than ever before, but the well-remembered spark was still in her pale grey eyes.

You've done well, she remarked. *But you haven't finished yet.*

Praise from his mentor was rare and, as Vargo's hopes rose, he immediately wanted to know more.

Did Ico and Andrin—?

They succeeded, thanks in part to you. And they're together again.

Vargo felt a glow of contentment that almost made his confinement bearable.

You deserve to know what happened, Famara went on, *but I haven't much time, so listen carefully.* As she painted a brief yet evocative picture of everything Vargo's efforts had set in motion he listened, spellbound, wanting to ask so many questions but knowing he must not interrupt. Famara was fading before his eyes.

It's a victory, she concluded. *The best we can hope for at present.*

But? Vargo prompted.

It's not over yet, she told him. *Nothing is ever that simple, and you are the only one who will be able to understand it all.*

Can't you . . . ? he began.

I'm dying, Vargo.

He began to protest, then stopped. She would not lie to him, would take no consolation from false comfort. The evidence was before his eyes.

I'm stuck here, he said. *What can I do?*

You must follow the path, she replied. *Ico and Andrin both glimpsed it, but they are too wrapped up in their own affairs to see where it leads. You have clearer vision.*

But how—?

I'm not quite helpless yet, she told him with a return of her old spirit. *I can release you.*

No. You need your strength.

What for? A few more empty hours of darkness? Allow me to choose my own end, Vargo. For some time now my spirit has been itching to be gone, and there is so little else of me left. Even the sparrows are free now.

You released them? he asked, knowing that if she had, then Famara was truly at the end of her life.

They had a job to do, she said simply. *Come.* She stretched out a hand.

Vargo struggled, willing himself to respond, knowing that he owed her that at least. He felt some of her remaining vitality transfer to him, and made even greater efforts to reach out. His arm extended with agonizing slowness – and then he was able to begin to sit up, stretching. Their hands touched, then clasped – and as the mirror shattered, Vargo found himself sitting in the water of the lake.

Keep dreaming, Vargo! Famara called. She was invisible now, pure spirit at last. *Farewell.*

Marco was waiting for her, his hand stretched out in welcome, his eyes full of regret. Famara went to him with forgiveness in her heart and accepted his invitation. Together they danced, as they had so often when they were young.

The scene that greeted Vargo when he finally reached the surface took away what little breath he had left. In the distance, the column of ash and smoke from Tisaloya was still expanding like a giant tree, but beneath its spreading branches the air was clear – and the land was covered with snow. He had only ever seen it before in dreams when he flew with Lao and, even though Famara had told him what to expect, nothing could have prepared him for the shock of its pure beauty. The afternoon sun, slanting in under the dust cloud, illuminated the particles of ice so that the whole world seemed to be made of light. As Vargo stood, staring in wonder, there was a fluttering nearby as a bird alighted on a snow covered rock.

I came south to get away from this stuff, Lao complained.

Vargo laughed.

It'll be gone soon, he said.

Another arrival claimed his attention then as Ero crash-landed, skidding helplessly in the slippery crystals and sending a flurry of snowflakes into the air. He got to his feet gingerly, with an air of mortally offended dignity, and called in greeting before his own plight took precedence.

It's biting me! It's biting me! he cried, hopping from one foot to the other in a vain attempt to escape the snow's cold embrace.

It looked so like a manic version of one of the hoopoe's dances that Vargo could not help but smile, but then he felt a great emptiness inside him as he remembered that a part of his life was over.

It's time, Ero, he said sadly. *Fly south. Your work is done here.*

The shivering bird cocked his head to one side as if considering this novel idea, then evidently reached a decision. Perhaps the sky voices have spoken to him, Vargo thought. Ero exploded into flight, scattering another cloud of snow-flakes, and circled briefly.

It was a good dance, wasn't it?

Yes, Vargo replied. *The best.*

We'll dance again next year, the hoopoe added excitedly.

No, we won't, Vargo thought, but kept the knowledge to himself.

Farewell! Ero cried, and sped off towards the warmth of the south.

'Farewell,' Vargo said quietly. There was a lump in his throat.

Alone at last, Lao commented, watching the hoopoe as he flew on and out of sight.

Vargo bent down to touch the snow, picked up a handful and felt the cold seep into his fingers as it had already crept into his heart.

'Keep away from me!'

The shrill cry sounded from behind a nearby mound of rock. Recognizing the voice, Vargo reacted instantly and, even though he almost fell several times in the slippery terrain, he reached the scene of the confrontation in moments. Two White Guards, their normally perfect uniforms torn and bedraggled, were threatening

Allegra with their swords drawn. Their eyes were wild, and they were clearly intent on stealing her food and the warmth of her fire. She defied them, armed only with a knife and her own courageous spirit. Vargo had nothing but his own fury, but that was enough. He charged down at the soldiers, yelling wildly. Seeing Allegra in such danger had led to a revelatory surge of love and protectiveness. Nobody dares hurt my Cat! The thought roared in his mind as he crashed into one of the soldiers, sending him sprawling across the ground.

Taking advantage of this unexpected help, Allegra leapt forward at the other man, but he had already had enough. He turned and ran for his life. When Vargo picked up his lost sword the other guard followed suit, scrambling away, falling every few paces but jumping up again each time in his haste to get away from the madman.

'Vargo!' Allegra yelled, flinging her arms about him. 'I thought you were dead!'

'There were times when I wished I was,' he said, luxuriating in her touch. 'How long was I in there?'

'Less than a day.'

'Really?' It had seemed like half a lifetime.

'You're soaked,' she exclaimed, releasing him. 'Come and dry out by the fire.'

They talked as the day waned and the unnatural cold withdrew a little, allowing the thaw to begin. Allegra accepted his tale, did not question how he knew all that had taken place, and sensed his sadness in spite of what seemed to her to be a tremendous, improbable victory. She put his mood down to Famara's death and Ero's departure, which left Vargo with the melancholy of his link to Lao. She knew many people found him difficult when he was like this, preferring his happier, summer self, but she loved him in all his guises. The joy she had felt when her vigil had been rewarded was proof enough of that.

'So what do we do now?' she asked.

'I have a path to follow,' he replied. 'And it's not going to be easy. Will you come with me?'

'Of course.' She had wanted to say that she would follow him to the ends of the earth, but the words would not pass her lips. She had seen the look in his eyes, heard the hopelessness in his voice when he had talked about Ico and her reunion with Andrin, and knew it would take time. That did not bother her. His love, once won, would be worth the wait.

For his own part, Vargo felt a huge sense of relief at her unhesitating agreement. He would be lost without her now.

Much later, as they lay huddled together for warmth, Vargo looked up at the distant stars and knew there were still things he needed to say before he could sleep.

'Cat?' he whispered. 'Are you asleep?'

'That's a stupid question,' she answered contentedly.

'There's something you should know.'

'What is it?' After all his recent revelations she did not know what else to expect. She thought she was ready for anything, but he surprised her even so.

'There's no music left in me. It's all gone.'

'It'll come back,' she assured him, knowing what an integral part of him his music was.

'No, it won't. If you gave me a lute or a viol now I wouldn't even know how to hold it, let alone play.' He held up his hands, knowing they were useless on their own. Music came from inside, from the core of the soul, but his was silent now.

'You can't be serious,' Allegra said, knowing that he was.

'Playing for the dragons took all I had. There's nothing left.'

'You can learn again.'

'No. It's gone,' he stated. 'I just needed you to know, that's all.'

His confession had taken the last of his strength, and he slept. It was Allegra's turn to lie awake.

***

It took nearly a month of wandering, following Vargo's haphazard instincts, before they came to the end of the path. In that time they had begged food from strangers, scavenged what they could from the land, slept in caves or in the open, and ventured ever deeper into the remote mountains of the northern interior. Many times Vargo thought that, in his preoccupation, he would not have survived had it not been for Allegra's steadfast and practical friendship. That she put up with all the hardships for his sake was a cause of wonder, one that gave him hope for the future.

The path eventually led them to a small but deep crater, at the top of a circular mountain that did not even have a name in the language of humans. As they made their precipitous descent into the bowl, a sense of timeless awe enveloped Vargo, and he knew his quest was over. Near the bottom of the crater, the ground was covered with a soft grey dust that might have lain there for centuries. He signalled for Allegra to stay where she was while he went on, his boots kicking up small eddies in the powder. Here and there tiny flakes of a shiny black material were mixed in with the dust, but Vargo was headed for a pile of white rocks at the centre of the depression. When he reached them his eyes confirmed what his instinct had already told him; these were not boulders but ancient bones.

He reached out a hand to touch one of them, felt the rough surface with his fingertips – and began to dream. As he stood there, lost in another world, he was filled with a mixture of powerful emotions – serene majesty and lofty indifference, abandonment and loss, and finally a sense of watchful distance. And Vargo began to understand.

'The last of them actually died out many years ago,' he said later. 'The eggs Andrin found are all that's left of their race.'

He had returned from his dream full of energy and purpose, eager to talk.

'Then what has everyone been seeing?' Allegra asked. 'There have always been sightings, and you said they flew over Teguise only last month.'

'Those were illusions,' he replied, 'created by the minds of everyone in Tiguafaya. We've seen how magic becomes more powerful when more people witness it. Well, it's the same principle. We needed to believe in the dragons but they went away, and as time went on we became more and more afraid of the unknown. So our fears were expressed in communal delusions. Ignorance breeds hatred, and that hatred created the monsters. The dragons became our enemies.'

'So none of them were real?'

'They were once, but not recently.'

'Then how did they help Ico and Andrin? And why?'

'Their spirits are still alive,' Vargo said, 'and I think they just decided to give us a second chance. I don't suppose we'll ever know all their reasons, but they never really hated mankind. That was our invention. In fact they used to regard us as rather insignificant.'

'Charming,' Allegra commented.

'That's just their way,' he explained. 'They looked at us in the same way we regard ants.'

'But that changed?'

'Yes,' Vargo confirmed. 'Because of the fireworms.'

'I don't understand.'

'In the time when the dragons were still physically present here, the fireworms were their servants. They lived below ground then and did their masters' bidding, which was to control the underground pressures in the volcanic fields by absorbing and releasing heat, making the whole place more stable.'

'They were actually *helping* us?' Allegra said in disbelief.

'Exactly that,' Vargo replied. 'By preventing disastrous eruptions and diverting lava flows, they made life more convenient for the dragons – and safer for us.'

'What happened?'

'When the last of the dragons died the worms were left directionless,' he went on. 'They performed their duties by instinct for a time but eventually, as people began to think of the dragons as evil, the sickness spread to the worms.'

'*We* made them the way they are?' she exclaimed.

'Yes. Our madness was contagious. Everyone thought they were working for evil masters, and all that negative mental energy had to have an effect eventually. The worms changed, became spiteful and sought revenge. And that's why they learned to fly.'

'That's what the old wizards meant,' Allegra said quietly. 'In the book Ico found.'

Vargo nodded. '"The grey amphistomes consume fire,"' he quoted, '"but they do not corrupt the land—"'

'"Unless they are themselves corrupted,"' she completed for him. 'Can we cure them? Make them sane again?'

'I don't think so. All the ones alive now are irredeemable.'

'Then we were right to kill them.'

'We had no choice,' he agreed. 'Sooner or later we'll have to wipe them out or they'll do the same to us.'

'But that means . . .' She broke off as the full impact of what Vargo had been saying sank in.

'We just have to hope that there's a new generation of untainted fireworms still waiting somewhere,' he said. 'We need them. And we have to change people's attitudes towards them, or they'll just be driven mad like all the rest.'

'If we don't, the volcanoes will eventually destroy us all,' Allegra whispered.

They sat in silence for a while.

'Can't the dragons help us?' she said eventually.

'Maybe,' Vargo replied. 'Who knows when those eggs might hatch? But in the meantime, we have to do the best we can on our own.'

CHAPTER SIXTY-TWO

It was almost a month before Ico and Andrin felt sure enough of their welcome to return to Teguise, and a great deal changed during that time. After their joint victory against the fireworms – a triumph that made everyone except Angel very happy – they soon realized that while one struggle was over, another was about to begin.

Maciot had not achieved the bloodless coup he had wanted, in spite of his best efforts, and the last throes of Kantrowe's political life had been a dark time for the capital. The President had not given up without a fight. As the news of what had happened in the firelands gradually filtered back to Teguise, even Kantrowe's staunchest allies began to have their doubts, and his opponents took heart from the way in which popular feeling was swinging against him. His repressive measures became more and more extreme, alienating even some sections of the White Guard, and eventually a state of civil war existed within the city, with various army units – who had previously fought side by side – now facing each other as enemies. Treachery was commonplace, and among those to suffer was Captain Chinero. He was murdered – apparently by one of his own junior officers – and with his death the divisions within the military ranks grew even wider.

The turning point came when Mazo Gadette, realizing that Kantrowe was doomed, betrayed his former master and revealed the truth about his plans for Tiguafaya – confirming the claims made first by Maciot and then by Diano Maravedis. But Gadette went much further. He had been close to Kantrowe, and had known about the dreadful use of the fireworms as instruments of massacre and land clearance. The public outcry that followed meant the end of the President's career. All his remaining allies deserted him and, like many others before him, he was forced to flee for his life, abandoning both his family and his wealth as he did so. That he succeeded in escaping was a source of great bitterness to many, but most were content merely to know that he had gone.

A great deal of political manoeuvring followed, together with peace talks between the warring factions within the army. Maciot returned to the city and was greeted warmly. He played a leading role in negotiations involving the guilds, the military authorities and spokesmen for the rest of Tiguafayan society. These eventually led to an agreement whereby elections would be held to choose a new President and a new Senate.

While all this had been going on, Ico and Andrin, after a few days' rest, had set out to join the other Firebrands in the south. Although their reunion was a joyous occasion, the celebration had been marred by the fact that – in spite of a vigorous search of the caves and the surrounding area – no sign of Vargo or Allegra had been found. They had not been close enough to Tisaloya to be directly affected by the eruption, but the associated earth tremors had caused several rock falls in various cave systems, and it was feared that they had been trapped underground. The fact that both Ico and Andrin had seen Vargo as a ghostly apparition did nothing to allay their fears.

Soon after that Ico, accompanied by Andrin and Nino, made a pilgrimage back to Elva. She could not help hoping for a miracle, but when she climbed to the spot where she had left

Soo's body there was nothing to be seen, and Nino's falcon, Eya, could find no sign of the sparrowhawk in the surrounding area. Ico thought of asking the dragon spirits for their help, but decided against it. She had not been called, and did not think they would answer. Andrin consoled her as best he could, pointing out that they could interpret the fact that Soo was not there as a hopeful sign. Although Ico was grateful, she could see in his eyes that he meant only to comfort her.

They returned to the Firebrands' base, and learnt that more news had come from Maciot. He told them of Kantrowe's exile, and of the new political initiatives. One of these was an agreement to organize protection against the remaining fireworms. Several of Maghdim's former acolytes had volunteered to help in this. The anti-mage's death had rid them of his pernicious influence and the effects of the tincture were wearing off, allowing them to think for themselves once again. However, the Firebrands would be needed to lead the way. Their exploits were now common knowledge throughout the country, and most people had come to regard them as heroes. The fear that they had been antagonizing the dragons had been overcome by the fact that one of the giant creatures had actually helped the Firebrands defeat the worms. Maciot's message ended with the simple statement that it was time for them to come home.

This they did in style, riding camels that he had sent for them. However, when the walls of the city came into view, they could not help feeling nervous, even though they had been assured of a warm welcome. Too much had happened since they'd left Teguise – so much changed and so much lost. One of the unhappiest pieces of news to reach them had concerned Famara. When the prisoners had been released from the Paleton, several bodies had been found, and one of these was Famara. Her emaciated corpse had been found in a dark cell, one that Ico remembered all too well. The men who brought her out reported that she weighed little more than a bird but, curiously, in spite of the horrific manner of her death, there had been a contented smile on the old woman's sunken face.

Ico thought of this and of many other things as the camel she was sharing with Andrin plodded steadily along the trail. She became so lost in memories and speculation that at first she did not realize that Andrin was speaking to her.

'Sorry – what did you say?' she asked, looking round.

'What were you thinking about?'

'Oh, nothing,' she replied. 'Everything.'

'Are you feeling all right?'

Ico's pregnancy was beginning to show now, and since their reunion Andrin had been fiercely protective of her wellbeing. Although she sometimes found his attentiveness a little irritating, she was grateful for his tenderness and obvious concern.

'I'm fine.'

'You know,' he said, 'I can't help wondering whether we really protected the dragon eggs at all. I mean, I'm not sure it was really necessary. Those things looked indestructible and would probably have survived anyway. I think it was just a test of our good faith.'

'To see if we were really their friends?'

'Exactly. When you think about it *they* saved *us*, not the other way round.'

'So it was the thought that counted,' Ico said.

'And we passed the test,' Andrin agreed.

'I'm glad you did,' she added, patting her stomach. 'We'd have been lost without you.'

'Well, you're stuck with me now,' he told her.

Ico said nothing, but just stretched out her hand for Andrin to take in his own.

'I wish Vargo was here,' he said quietly.

'Me too.'

'I wouldn't want anyone else to play at our wedding, would you?'

Ico couldn't answer. Her eyes filled with tears as she fell prey to wildly conflicting emotions. She tightened her grip on Andrin's hand.

Riding on the camel behind, with Angel, Madri watched the lovers and cursed himself for a sentimental old fool. The fact that Ico – unlike his own wife – had returned gave him a huge amount of bittersweet pleasure. He knew the pair still had many trials to face, but he had no doubt that together they would be more than equal to them.

He was less optimistic about his own companion. Angel was clearly unhappy about his role in recent events, but either could not or would not explain why. His loyalty to Madri had never wavered, however, and when the decision had been made to return to Teguise, there was no question of his not going. The ex-admiral's re-emergence was known to everyone now, and there were even some who had suggested that he should be placed in command of building the new navy. This idea had been instantly quashed by Madri himself. If, after all his years in exile, his advice was suddenly found to be valuable, then he would give it freely. But he would do no more than that. In fact, he found the whole situation rather ironic. His years of service had been ignored after the débâcle at sea three decades ago, as had the treachery of some of his junior officers, but now, by his brief association with the Firebrands, he was back in favour. And to add to the irony, Tias Kantrowe now found himself in the same position that Madri had endured thirty years earlier – outcast, discredited and broken in spirit. Perhaps Madri thought, there is some justice after all.

'What do you think, Tre?' he said, hoping to alleviate his friend's gloom. 'When we reach Teguise, let's go to the docks and find a ship's captain willing to take two old sailors on board. One last voyage together. What do you say?'

He was rewarded by the first smile he had seen on Angel's face in a long time, but his companion had one condition.

'We can't be away too long,' Angel said. 'I must be back for the birth of Ico's daughter.'

'Agreed,' Madri said happily. He knew that Ico and Andrin had already asked Angel to be present, and he would not want to be too far away himself. He did not think to ask how his friend knew that the baby was a girl.

Once inside the city walls, the Firebrands split up. Madri and Angel had been invited to stay with Maciot. The rest of them – apart from Andrin – all had homes and families to go to. Naturally enough, Andrin went with Ico to the Maravedis home. When Diano saw his daughter, he did not say a word, but simply stepped forward and hugged her as if he would never let go. Andrin watched them, feeling a little of their silent joy, and wishing he had had someone to come home to.

When his mother appeared, he gasped in disbelief. Belda looked better than she had done in years, and the haunted look had finally gone from her eyes. She put out a tentative hand towards her son.

'I always knew you'd come back,' she said quietly, and he reached out and took her in his arms.

As the Firebrands began to settle back into their lives, Ayo was on his way to Pajarito. When he got there, much to his surprise, he found that he was not alone. Another white eagle was already perched on the rock where he had landed on earlier visits. He approached cautiously, not sure what this meant, but when the other bird rose into the air to meet him, Ayo realized that this time the oracle was not needed. The questions had all been answered.

She was not Iva, could never be Iva, and yet they both knew why they had been called to the sacred mountain. It was too early for mating, too soon to start building a nest but, here and now, high above the red crater, their courtship could begin.

And there, no longer alone, Ayo danced with the most beautiful white eagle in all the world.

Another month passed, and the reorganization of Tiguafayan life continued. After much persuasion and internal debate, Ico had agreed to stand as a candidate for the Presidency, and now it seemed almost certain that she would be elected. It was a measure of how drastic the changes had been that a woman – especially one who was now obviously pregnant and only betrothed rather than married – could even be considered for such a post. Her life was so full that she sometimes longed for a return to a simpler time, but it was typical of Ico that she could do nothing in a half-hearted manner, and her energy and resourcefulness impressed everyone.

Fortunately, she managed to find some free time to be with the ones she loved, and it was during one of these evenings that a strange message arrived from Nino. He, like the other Firebrands from outlying parts of Tiguafaya, had returned home before those from Teguise, and he had sent a report that his own village had not suffered badly during the recent unrest. Since then he had been to see the dragon eggs at Corazoncillo, and it was about this that he now wrote. The eggs had not been moved – no one dared touch them, and they would have been far too heavy anyway – and the site had become a place of wonder and veneration. Corazoncillo was now visited by many people curious to see this evidence of the elusive creatures who had once had godlike status, and several tales had already sprung up about the eggs. One of these was that of a bird – some said a sparrowhawk – who had spent many days hovering over the clutch as if it were waiting for some sort of sign. Eventually the bird had landed on one of the eggs, had turned black, and had then flown away and not been seen since.

Inevitably, the story reminded Ico of Soo and the pain of her loss.

'You don't suppose . . .'

'I don't know,' Andrin said, not wanting to raise her hopes, but not wishing to dash them either. The mystery of what had happened to Soo still troubled him too.

A few minutes later, Atchen's shrieks of alarm brought them running into the hall, where the flutter of wings was loud and frightening. The bird half fell to the floor and drooped in exhaustion.

Soo? Ico exclaimed, hardly daring to believe it was true. *Soo!*

The sparrowhawk raised her head and fixed her link with a tired but fervent stare.

I kept my part of the bargain.

Ico knelt before her, noting the bedraggled plumage and the streaks of black in some feathers.

And I mine, she said. *Where have you been?*

I've flown with the dragons, to the heavens and back, Soo replied. *But I'm home now.*

The contentment in the bird's voice made Ico's heart swell. She would hear the rest of Soo's story another time. For now, her mere presence was enough.

I am not the only one to return, Soo added. *Go to the western gate.*

Andrin and Ico hurried to the city wall, and climbed the guard tower next to the gate. Looking out over the land beyond, it was hard to see anything at first in the fading light, but gradually the shapes of two people appeared, trudging along the road. A bird flew alongside. They were moving slowly, the taller of the two stooped as though the weight of the world was on his shoulders, but he was familiar even so.

It was Vargo. And as the two lovers shouted and waved from the city wall, the distant figure looked up. Whatever burdens he was carrying, they were not enough to prevent a smile lighting up his face.

FIRE MUSIC

Julia Gray

In the Firelands, music is the ultimate magic.

The new government of Tiguafaya has finally brought peace to a people long suppressed by its tyrannical rulers. But it may not last, for now a much greater power threatens the Firelands – the mighty Empire to the north, whose Emperor will not tolerate the Tiguafayans' heretical belief in magic. Attempts to resolve the dispute by diplomacy will all count for nothing, however, if the fire and lava shaking the ground cannot be controlled.

Passion, politics and magic collide in FIRE MUSIC, the magnificent sequel to ICE MAGE.

'All the ingredients of great fantasy . . . If you enjoy moments of terror and moments of delight, with a handful of firecracker surprises along the way, this is the book for you'
Maggie Furey on ICE MAGE